T0040795

INTERNATIONAL GUY

Volume 4

ALSO BY AUDREY CARLAN

International Guy Series

Paris: International Guy Book 1

New York: International Guy Book 2

Copenhagen: International Guy Book 3

Milan: International Guy Book 4

San Francisco: International Guy Book 5

Montreal: International Guy Book 6

London: International Guy Book 7

Berlin: International Guy Book 8

Washington, DC: International Guy Book 9

Madrid: International Guy Book 10

Rio: International Guy Book 11

Los Angeles: International Guy Book 12

Calendar Girl Series

January

February

March

April

May

June

July

MADRID · RIO · LOS ANGELES

INTERNATIONAL GUY

Volume 4

#1 *NEW YORK TIMES* BESTSELLING AUTHOR

AUDREY CARLAN

Montlake
Romance

This is a work of fiction. Names, characters, organizations, places, events, and incidents are either products of the author's imagination or are used fictitiously.

Text copyright © 2018 by Audrey Carlan

All rights reserved.

No part of this book may be reproduced, or stored in a retrieval system, or transmitted in any form or by any means, electronic, mechanical, photocopying, recording, or otherwise, without express written permission of the publisher.

Published by Montlake Romance, Seattle

www.apub.com

Amazon, the Amazon logo, and Montlake Romance are trademarks of Amazon.com, Inc., or its affiliates.

ISBN-13: 9781503904668

ISBN-10: 1503904660

Cover design by Letitia Hasser

Cover photography by Wander Aguiar Photography

Printed in the United States of America

MADRID:

INTERNATIONAL GUY

BOOK 10

To Maria Guitart, my Spanish editor,
and the entire team at Grupo Planeta.

Madrid is for you.

I'll never forget the commitment,
support, and love you've shown my stories.

I'm so happy to be working with you on this passion project.

Besos.

1

SKYLER

I smile widely when I hear the elevator chime. "Daddy's home!" I squeal to my pooches, who are both hanging out near my feet while I make dinner. Parker doesn't admit it, but he *loves* that I can cook and shows me he does by gobbling up everything I make as though he hasn't had a meal in weeks. I usually make him a homemade breakfast too. Makes me wonder what kind of women he dated in the past, aside from that witch, Kayla, who cheated and betrayed him. I'm happy we've gotten past that hurdle; Kayla and Johan are both history. Bringing up former romantic relationships does nothing but stir the pot, and Parker and I are focused on nothing but the future.

At the sound of the elevator doors opening, Midnight jumps up, his little black body wiggling as he jets off to the living room and entryway. Such a daddy's boy.

"Parker, honey . . . ," I call out while wiping my hands on a dish towel and heading toward the living room. "Come on, Sunny, let's go greet Daddy." Sunny follows along, her body touching my legs, when I hear the now familiar sound of Midnight growling.

I turn the corner and find not Parker, but Tracey, standing there with her hands up in the air as if she's just been caught red-handed by the police.

"Trace, what the heck are you doing here?" I'm shocked to see my bestie in the flesh and unannounced for that matter. She's supposed to be in New York.

"Um, Birdie, care to call off your guard dog?" Her voice wobbles as she takes a step back. Midnight growls more, his little lips pulled back, teeth visible.

I start to laugh and scoop up my dog, who's getting almost too big to pick up. "Midnight, that's Tracey. She's my best friend, silly." I coo to the dog and nuzzle his neck with my face. "See, baby, she's fine. Trace, extend your hand slowly, palm down."

She does so, and I bring Midnight closer. I pet Tracey's hand. "See, baby, she's fine. She's Mommy's best friend and your auntie now. It's okay; we love Tracey."

"Is this really necessary?" Tracey replies sarcastically.

Midnight watches my movements intently as I bring him closer to her hand. He sniffs it but still growls low under his breath, as if he is not buying what his mommy is selling him. Weird.

"Baby boy," I say more firmly. "Tracey is fine. No need to protect me from her. She's family." I bounce my dog and walk over to the treat bin near the entryway, lift the ceramic lid, and pull out an organic doggy bacon bit and hold it out to Tracey. "Here, give him this. It will help win him over."

She rolls her eyes and sighs dramatically but takes the treat. "Here, here, boy." She dips her voice as if her desire is to sound sweet, but she really just sounds exasperated. "Take your treat." She holds out the bacon bit. Sunny jumps up against my leg, knowing full well what I gave to Tracey.

Finally Midnight eases his nose out and takes the treat, but he still makes a little growling sound. Odd. "It's strange that he doesn't seem to be fond of you."

Tracey huffs. "I'm not really fond of him either. Besides, I'm not a dog person. Cats are more my gig. They do what they want, leave you alone, and look beautiful doing it."

I shrug, get a treat for Sunny, and give it to her. She wags her little booty in pure glee. "Guess so. Anyway . . ." I set down Midnight, who promptly runs off, his sister chasing after him. I spin around and hold out my arms.

Tracey beams and pulls me into her embrace.

"Glad to see you, Flower, but I'm totally surprised. I didn't expect you in Boston. What brings you out?"

Tracey frowns. "You didn't expect me here? Sky, I'm going to come here to visit you all the time now that you live in Boston. Besides, Geneva James is planning to arrive in a couple of weeks, and we're meeting with the producers about the *A-Lister* shoots."

"In a couple of weeks? Uh . . ." I look down and notice not one or two, but *three* good-size suitcases standing in my entryway. "Then why are you here now?"

Tracey's head jolts back as if I've slapped her. "Did you not want me here?"

I open my mouth and shake my head. "No, no, not at all. Of course, you're always welcome; it's just . . . I mean, Parker and I are kind of living on and off at one another's houses, so it will be a bit of a . . . um . . . a plan changer to have an unannounced guest." I glance over to the patio, where I've set out a romantic dinner for two. "I was just making dinner, but you know"—I wave my hands—"I can just change it up, or we can go out. Help you get to your hotel."

Tracey's voice lowers, and she frowns so deeply it leaves two little lines in her forehead with her efforts. "Hotel? Sky, this is *me*. Trace. Your only friend. I didn't book a hotel." She scoffs. "I'm staying with you."

She laughs and enters the room more fully, moving around to the couch and plopping down with a groan. "It has been such a long damned day. Looking forward to soaking in your huge Jacuzzi tonight and chilling with my best girl."

I bite down on my bottom lip and try to figure out how to approach this situation. When I lived with Johan before, he didn't care when Tracey dropped in. He actually seemed eager to have her there as often as possible. Why, I didn't know. He always said he just loved having her around. Parker is not going to feel that way. He's a much more private man. He doesn't even like Rachel and Nate hanging out when he's home. When it's his time to settle in for the night, he likes it to be me, the pups, and whatever we've decided to do, whether it be watch a movie, a show, read our own books, hang out and talk, play with our fur babies, take a bath, or a mixture of the above. What that list does *not* include is an unexpected guest he would feel he had to entertain and share space with when he wants to just relax.

"Hmm, well, since my Jacuzzi is in the master bedroom, I'm thinking that's not going to happen. Parker should be here any minute . . ."

"So?"

"Well, Trace, as I told you, we're living together now. Going from his house to mine, but mostly mine. He thinks it's confusing to the pups to keep going back and forth, and since we're on the lookout for our own home, it shouldn't be too long before we find and buy the right place. It will make it easier on the dogs to not be moving around all the time."

"What does that have to do with me wanting to spend time with you and taking a bath?" Her jaw seems to tighten, and her lips come together in a reproaching little snarl.

"The bathtub is in our *bedroom*, Trace. As much as I want to spend time with you, this last case really did a number on my man. He's different lately. A bit more on edge. He's questioning everything. Not to mention the fact that they can't get a read on this stalker/fan/texter person. It's driving him mad."

"Why? You're not in any real danger. I mean, are you?" Her voice rises with her concern.

"I don't know. Maybe. It's freaky either way. Mostly, though, Parker has a lot on his plate, especially with us looking to buy a home together and move in with our pups."

Tracey leans an arm along the couch and rests her head in her hand. "Have you thought about the fact that maybe it's too soon to be moving in and adopting animals together?"

Her words hit me like sand that has just been power blasted into my face. It's gritty, raw, and it hurts. "Why would you say that?" I rub at my chest and sit down next to my dearest friend.

She grabs my hand and holds it in both of hers. "Sky, sweetie, you guys haven't even been together a year, and you're already moving in with one another, buying a house, not renting or leasing. You adopted two animals together. That's serious, life-changing stuff. And not long ago, he threw you away like yesterday's trash and was kissing another blonde in Montreal. Let's not forget about that debacle."

I suck in a harsh breath. "That's not fair; it was my fault, and for the most part, it was a misunderstanding."

"Yeah, one in which you didn't do anything wrong. He assumed you cheated. Any man who can believe you'd cheat on him isn't worth your time," she says frankly. "And, honey, that's the simple truth."

I squeeze my eyes shut and run my hand through my hair, a sense of hopelessness burning at my chest. "Trace, what are you saying? This is so out of left field."

"No, you moving in with your on-and-off-again boyfriend after only a minute of happiness is out of nowhere and crazy, if you ask me."

I want to lash out and remind her that I didn't, in fact, ask her, but what she's saying hurts too much. She brings her hand to rest over my thigh.

"Do you not like Parker?"

She purses her lips and remains silent for a long time. It feels like the earth has just crumbled under my feet at the cliff's edge I'm standing on, and now I'm free-falling into a pitch-black ocean of nothingness.

"I liked him for the job I *hired* him to do. He encouraged you. Helped you get your muse back. He's good at his job; there is no contesting that . . ."

"Except you . . . you don't think he's right for me?" I can barely mutter the words, not even believing the sentiment could be possible.

Tracey puts her arm around me and hugs me to her side. "It's not that I don't think he's right for you, it's just you're doing all the changing for him. What has he done to make his own commitment known?"

"Besides agreeing to move in together, buy a house, and adopt animals?" I say a little cynically, but still cuddle next to my bestie, wanting her warmth, compassion, and approval in this as I do in all areas of my life. It's the people pleaser in me coming out in a flourish.

She sighs. "I'm just worried about you. I'm your girl. I've always been your girl. Ever since your parents died, it's been me holding you up, making sure you're at the top of your game and the best in your field. It's my job to protect you and keep you safe from any and all threats. Whether it be a crazy fan, a producer trying to lowball your fee, or a man insinuating himself into your world so completely that, all of a sudden, you've picked up and moved out of New York and are planning to buy a home in Boston. *Boston* of all places." Her voice rises on the city name with an intense sense of disdain. "It's a city, but it's not *the city*. You've always called New York home base."

I frown. "Well, yeah, because a lot of business is done in New York and you're there."

"Exactly. Now you're all the way over here, and I have to get on a plane to see you. It's the pits, Birdie. I don't like being this far away from you, but I can't leave my business and staff to be closer to my best friend for too long."

"And your best client." I grin, puffing up my chest.

She smiles. "Yes, my best client. Still, is this you? Really? Domesticated. Next, you're going to tell me you want to get married to the man."

Marriage.

The thought has crossed my mind a lot more recently. I've always wanted to find my other half, create a home, and build a life together. And that life would include family and children of our own. "I'd marry Parker in a second if he asked me," I say dreamily, imagining just that. Parker in a tux, holding my hand, saying "I do" in front of his family and our friends.

Tracey gasps. "Did he ask you to marry him?" Her eyes are wide and horrified, studying my face as if I'm keeping a major secret from her.

I'd heard the elevator doors open, and Parker walks in, a beautiful smile on his face as he answers Tracey's question. "No. I didn't, actually. Though when we take that step, we'll make sure you're one of the first people to know."

My man chuckles, looking absolutely delicious in his navy suit and crisp white shirt, unbuttoned at the collar just enough to see a sexy swath of tanned skin. My mouth salivates as he approaches me, his eyes taking in my flirty dress and bare legs. I stand up as he reaches my side and wrap my arms around his neck. Parker dips his head down and kisses me hello.

Best part of my day.

The moment when my man comes home from work and kisses me with a desire and passion that resonates through me straight to my toes is *awesome*. Every time he lays those kisses on me, it's as if he's been gone a month, not ten hours. When he's taken his fill, he leans back and caresses my nose with his. "Hi, baby. How was your day?"

I smile and lift my head to the ceiling, letting my hair fall back, enjoying being in my man's arms. "Good. As you can see, Tracey has surprised us with a visit!" I try to sound chipper about it, but for the first time ever, I'm not. She should have called first, especially if she planned to stay in our guest room. It's just, in the past, she's never had to because I've always been alone. Things have changed, and I need to find a better way to make that clear to her without hurting her feelings.

"Oh, that's nice. Hello, Tracey. It's good to see you." He hooks his arm around my waist and keeps me at his side.

"Yeah, figured I'd come and hang out for a couple of weeks before Geneva James comes to town," she states flatly.

Parker's face lights up at the information, obviously missing the part that she plans on staying two weeks. He genuinely liked spending time with Geneva James in London. He runs his fingers across the leather band at my wrist that says "LIVE YOUR TRUTH" before maneuvering us both down to the couch, me tucked next to him. I run my thumb across his leather bracelet that says "FOLLOW YOUR HEART" so he knows I got his gesture and feel the same about our time in London.

"You're planning on staying two weeks, Trace? Isn't that hard with your company and the rest of your clients?" I ask, hoping she gets the hint that two weeks is a lot to drop on a newly shacked-up couple.

She smiles. "Oh, Birdie, I've got my laptop and my cell. Mobile office. I can work anywhere, and there's nowhere I'd rather be than with my best friend. It's been too long since we've spent some real time together, and with all of these changes happening in your life, I thought you might need me close."

Now how the heck am I gonna tell her I feel the exact opposite? That Parker and I need privacy during this stage in our relationship? I sigh against Parker's neck, and he comforts me with a squeeze.

I'll figure it out. With my man at my side, I can handle anything. Even nosy best friends who don't quite yet know their place.

2

PARKER

"I thought you might need me close," Tracey finishes.

"I'm sorry, baby, did I miss something?" I focus my gaze on Sky, trying to see through to what she's *not* saying.

She licks her lips and twiddles her fingers. Uh-oh. That's not a good sign. When Sky is nervous, or doesn't want to tell me something, she gets fidgety.

"Sky . . ." I tip my head.

"I'm staying here in the penthouse for a couple of weeks," Tracey says. "Spending time with Skyler and meeting with the producers and movie investors to get everything dialed in for the beginning of the shoot. We want things in place before Geneva moves here from London."

Tracey's tone and body language are almost smug, maybe even snide, but why? I shift my body on the couch so that I can look at both women. "A lot was just said. First, Geneva is moving here?"

Sky's pensive expression disappears, and one of pure happiness fills her face. God, she's pretty when she's happy. I mean, the woman is fuckin' drop-dead gorgeous all the time, but when she's smiling and happy? Move over Gisele Bündchen; Skyler Paige is in the house.

"According to her agent, Amy Tannenbaum, she's already leased an apartment in the city. Not far from here," Tracey elaborates.

"I wonder if it will be long term or just for the movie?" Skyler says, excitement in her tone.

I rub her bicep and lean back next to her, knowing having a friend close will give her joy. Most of her friends started out as my friends; it'll be good for her to have some of her own, present company included. "Now on to the part where you're here for a couple of weeks?" I gesture to Tracey with a wave of my hand.

Tracey tips her head and scans the room nonchalantly. "Yeah, thought it would be fun to slumber party with my bestie." Tracey smiles, and Skyler's body goes rigid against me.

I nod and continue to rub her arm, relaxing and soothing my girl as I go. "Which is a kind gesture, Tracey, though I wish you'd called. Unfortunately, we're leaving in a couple of days," I state flatly.

Tracey frowns as Skyler blurts out, "We are?"

"Yeah, I was going to discuss it with you over dinner. That client Royce booked while we were in DC really needs us to come immediately. They've got the girl signed on and will be recording her debut album, but they need us to get her ready for the media, stage, touring, TV time, and all that. And, babe, she's young. We thought she was in her twenties, but it turns out she's only nineteen. Probably scared out of her mind. I didn't want Bo and me to go in guns blazing and scare her off. Thought if I could bring you in, with your experience in showbiz, you might be able to give her, and us, a few pointers. Plus, we can spend some romantic time alone in Spain together." I waggle my eyebrows in an exaggerated manner.

"Really?" Sky's voice is breathy and fuckhot. If her friend weren't here, I'd slide my hands up those bare legs and divest her of her flirty little dress in two seconds flat, and then I'd fuck her until she was calling out my name in that lust-filled tone that makes my dick weep at the tip.

"Yeah, Peaches. I need you there." I run my hand down her thigh to her knee. "I'm not ready to go away on another trip, but I have to. Except it's too fuckin' soon, and I . . ." I swallow down the dryness in my throat, thinking about all we'd just been through with that pharmaceutical company, the animals, and the overall stink that case left on my soul. I don't want to sound like a wuss, but I just . . . I can't be away from her right now. It's like she's my security blanket, and I'm not letting the fucker go until I'm no longer afraid of the monsters hiding in the dark. Or in this situation, the monsters left over in my head, prodding at my mind and digging their claws into my heart. Sky's the only thing that takes away the nasty feeling trailing behind from that case.

She cups my cheek and runs her thumb over my lips. "Shh, shh, shh. I'm here." Her eyes glow a golden caramel brown in the low light of the room. She pets my lips and holds her thumb there, so I won't speak over her. "You need me; I'm yours. You know that, honey."

I smile and kiss the pad of her thumb.

She giggles, and Tracey clears her throat from behind her. Fuck, for a moment, I forgot she was even here.

"Sorry, Tracey. You're welcome to stay here, but I need my girl on this case with me." I tug Sky into my lap, her ass sitting sideways where I can wrap my arms around her waist and kiss up her jawline.

"I'm sure Tracey has a lot of work to do to prepare for the shoot and get all the stunt doubles, locations, wardrobe, and everything else in place before I come on set anyway. Rick and I have been reading over the script, meeting every few days. I'll just do our read-through by phone this next week or however long it takes for you and Bo to finish the case." She nudges my cheek and kisses my jaw. When she does so, I hear the click of little nails on hardwood, rushing through the room.

I look over my girl and note Sunny and Midnight have realized I'm home. I ease Skyler off my lap and pick up both pups when they reach my side, one in each hand, and set them on my lap. They both attack me with their brand of puppy love and kisses.

"Hey, guys, you miss me? Huh?" They both head-butt me and demand scratches.

Tracey stands up, her hands fisted at her sides as both Sky and I play with the pups. "I'm tired. I'm just going to go on to bed. Spare room ready for me?"

"Absolutely," Sky says, and stands up. "You sure? You were talking about a bath . . ."

Tracey looks over at me, and for some reason, her jaw goes tight, as though she's pissed at me for whatever reason. Frankly she's the one who showed up unannounced, so I don't really care if she feels like the third wheel.

"No, it's fine. I'll just take a shower in the spare room and head to bed. I'm beat, and I have some work to check on anyway. Breakfast tomorrow?" she says with a note of hope mixed in equal part with frustration.

"Definitely!" Skyler smiles and hugs her friend. Tracey holds her for a long moment, looks down at me, and something I can't define flashes across her gaze but is gone before I can get a read on what it might mean.

"You gonna make my favorite?" Tracey steps out of Sky's arms and walks toward the hall.

"French toast? Sure thing."

"You're the best friend a girl could ever have," Tracey says dotingly.

"Right back atcha!" Sky says, smiling like the sweet girl she is.

Tracey looks at me, then back to Sky. "Have a nice dinner."

"We will. Sleep well," I offer, and watch her walk to her suitcases and roll them down the hall. I'd help, but the rigidity in her body language warns me off. "What's her deal?" I whisper when she's out of earshot.

Skyler's shoulders sag, and she spins around, her dress fluttering with her movements, giving me a nice gander at her bare legs. "The beast" takes notice, going semihard against my now too-tight slacks.

Skyler pouts. "She's acting weird."

"Kinda noticed that, Peaches. What's going on? Did she talk about it before I got here? The scene seemed a little heavy, especially when talking about marriage—something that should be between you and me, not the two of you. You feel me?" I send a sharp look her way so she knows I'd rather keep our private stuff private.

Sky shrugs, then grabs my hand. "Yeah. Let's get the food I'm keeping warm in the oven and eat out on the patio where we can have some quiet time alone."

I follow my woman, fingers interlaced, pups at our heels. She pulls out our plates and puts them on a tray. I grab the tray, and she pours herself a glass of white wine and a beer for me. Together we head to the patio, where I find she's set up a romantic dinner for two.

"Guess you really didn't expect a guest this evening." I set down the tray on a side table and move each plate to our respective seats.

"No, I didn't," she says tiredly, sitting in her seat and putting down both glasses. "Honestly, it's weird."

"Her showing up out of nowhere? Agreed." I flap the napkin over my lap.

I get another shoulder lift as she sips her wine. "Yes and no. She used to show up unannounced all the time when I lived with Johan and, of course, back in New York, but I mean, she had to get on a plane and come here. You'd think she'd call first, make sure we were home and didn't already have plans."

I take a pull from my beer. Its hoppy taste flows over my tongue, and I groan appreciatively and lick my lips. My girl can pick some good beer, not to mention the spread looks amazing. Baked chicken breast in some type of sauce, couscous, and sautéed asparagus. "First off, baby, this looks amazing. Thank you for making dinner and going the extra distance to make it romantic."

Sky beams at me, her long blonde waves tumbling over her shoulders like a golden halo surrounding her face.

"Second, my guess is you'll have to have a heart-to-heart with your girl. She needs to know that you're not living alone anymore. Her visiting is cool, but she needs to run it past you so that you can double-check we don't already have plans. We're just barely getting settled with Midnight and Sunny, I've got another fuckin' case . . ."

Sky reaches out and rubs a hand along my arm closest to her. "I know, honey, I know. And I'm sorry. I'll talk to her. It's just . . ." She bites her lip and looks out over the balcony toward the setting sun.

"It's just what? Did she say something that upset you?"

She sighs and pokes at her chicken as I cut into mine and take a bite, moaning when the garlic and spice hit my tongue. There's an herb glaze that adds to the subtle seasoning, making the flavor burst on my taste buds. Sky looks up and smiles softly as I let the juiciest, most tender, flavor-filled chicken I've ever had take over my senses.

"Damn, my woman can cook," I murmur around another bite of delicious food.

"I'm glad you like it. Another of my mom's recipes." She smiles sadly. Every time she brings up her mom, she gets this melancholy expression. I hope one day she'll be able to speak about her mom with joy in her voice instead of sadness.

"Well, your mom must have been talented in the kitchen because, baby, you are an excellent cook." I cut off a hunk of asparagus and pop it into my mouth, the buttery goodness mingling with the chicken perfectly.

"Tracey told me she thinks we're moving too fast," Sky blurts out.

That stops me midchew as I assess her, realizing my girl is nervous and jittery as all get-out. I finish chewing my food and swallow. "Do you agree with her?" I wait patiently for her to speak, wanting to know her thoughts, while suppressing my instinct to overreact.

She shakes her head. "I've never been happier in my entire life. How can anything that feels this good be too fast?"

I reach over the table and grab one of her hands, bring it over our food and to my mouth, where I kiss each of her fingertips. "Because it's not. We're moving at the pace that feels right *to us*. I'm happy; you're happy. My mother is fuckin' ecstatic. The guys love you; Wendy thinks you're the shit. My brother, Paul, told me you're the hottest woman alive, and I better put that on lock before it slips away from me." I grin at her and give her a saucy wink.

Sky giggles and smiles so wide her cheeks pinken.

"Don't worry about what Tracey thinks. You and I are the only ones who matter. She may be your best friend and have known you for a long time, but she's not living your life, babe. We are. You and me. Only the two of us know what's best for us. Right now, that's shacking up and making a life for ourselves together with our pups. Is that what you still want?"

"God, yes," she says with awe in her voice. "It's all I've ever wanted. One day, Parker, all I want to be is a good wife and a mother. I love to act, but it's not like I need the money. I have enough money to last me a lifetime. You're doing well. Together, I know we'll have a great life, and I want that so much."

I squeeze her hands. "Then don't fret. Tracey probably means well. A good friend will definitely warn you, but she has nothing to worry about. You and me, we're solid, and I don't see anything on the horizon that could change that. Ever."

Sky grins, stands up, cups my cheeks, and kisses me hard. "Thank you. You always know the right thing to say."

I wrap an arm around her hips. "It's my job. Your happiness, it's all that's important to me."

She leans over and kisses me softly this time. "I love you."

"I love you too. Now, woman, can I please eat this fan-fucking-tastic dinner so I can get to the part of the evening where I fuck my woman into next Tuesday?"

She shivers in my hold. Hell yes, my woman loves the idea of me fucking her into next week.

I accept another soft kiss as she holds my jaw. "'K, honey."

"Okay. Tuck into your food. You're going to need the fuel. I'm feeling a long night of lovemaking is on the agenda. Wanna see my woman come while riding my cock, maybe while riding my face too."

Sky squirms in her seat. "What if I said I wasn't hungry?" She smirks.

I shake my head and cover my smile with my hand while holding my fork. "Then I'd say you're going to be *very* hungry later."

"Honey . . . ," she says breathily, not touching her dinner, her normally brown eyes now black pools of lust and desire.

"Eat your food . . . and hurry," I command, and she licks her lips, pokes an asparagus stalk, wraps her tongue around the tip, and works the length into her mouth before bringing it out again and cocking an eyebrow coyly.

I drop my silverware to my plate. "Fuck eating. Now I'm hungry for something a lot hotter and a whole helluva lot sweeter." I stand abruptly, move to her side, dip down, and put my shoulder to her stomach as I grab ahold of her hips to lift her up into a fireman's carry. Once I've got her settled over me, her upper body dangling over my back, I head toward our bedroom, Sky laughing and squealing the entire way.

***

"That's it . . . ride it," I grate through clenched teeth, and grip her hips, digging my fingers in. "Fuck yeah. Faster."

Skyler whimpers, her body undulating over me. One of her hands is up in her hair, her body on display in the sexiest light, her other hand on my shoulder.

I've got my back against our headboard, knees cocked up, and her gorgeous naked body in my lap, my dick buried in tight, wet heat.

"Jesus, woman, you ride me so good." My balls draw up, and heat builds at the base of my spine.

She tips her head back, letting her hair fall in cascading waves, tickling my fingers as I hold on. Her breath leaves her body in puffs of air through moistened, glistening lips. I run my hand over her bare midriff, dipping my thumb into her belly button until I hear her breath catch. With my fingers splayed I slide my hand between her perfect tits, but I don't stop there. No, I keep going until I've lightly encircled her throat, where I can feel her pulse going wild as she continues her ride.

I move my hand to cup her cheek, my thumb sweeping her lips. She opens her mouth and sucks my thumb, swirling her tongue around the digit, reminding me how good it feels when she does the same thing to the beast.

"Fuck me," I growl and slam her down on my hard cock, clenching my teeth with the effort not to blow my load in a second flat. I want this to last. Hell, I want this feeling to last a lifetime.

Sky sucks harder, her mouth worrying my thumb as her arousal coats the space between us. She sighs as her sex locks down around me in the tightest, filthiest kiss possible.

I remove my thumb from her mouth, tunnel my hand into her hair, and bring her face to mine, taking her mouth in a vicious plunder of tongue, lips, and teeth.

She cries out as her body spasms and convulses, her thighs locking next to mine as she grinds down, crushing her clit against my pelvic bone. "Honey," she whispers against my lips, tremors rippling through her body as her sex rhythmically squeezes my dick.

"Oh yeah, fuck yeah, you're *there*. Riding your man's cock like a champion and making me see stars." I lift her up and down as she climaxes beautifully, her eyes hazy, lost to the euphoria of this moment. "Now it's my turn," I murmur against her neck, running my teeth up the column, tasting the salt on her skin while her peaches-and-cream scent mixes with the musk in the air, filling my nose with our combined scent.

Heavenly.

Wrapping my arms around her, I shift her body, rolling her over onto her back, where I hook her behind both knees and press her legs up to her fucking ears. I glance down at her body split wide, the lips of her sex straining around my girth, glistening with her release.

My mind swims and my nostrils flare. I slow it down before I lose all control. Every piece of me is focused on the gentle glide and sway of entering my woman in the most carnal way. "Fuckin' beautiful, Sky. Every damned inch of you is perfect, and all mine, for a lifetime."

"Parker," she gasps, the feeling in her clearly building again. I can see it come over her face as a flash of heat burns through her gaze and her muscles clench around me. She repeats my earlier request of her. "Fuck me." Only she's got the upper hand. With some magical voodoo, she locks her internal muscles and squeezes the head of my dick as I ease it out, leaving just the tip inside.

I grind my teeth and work my way back inside. "You playing like that?"

She gifts me a sultry smile. "Oh yeah. Just like that."

"What'd I tell you before we started tonight?" I grind out each word, still holding back from losing my mind in her body.

"Hmm . . ." She stretches her body as much as she can, trying to put her legs down so she can get her arms around me.

"Nuh-uh. What I said was I was going to fuck you into next Tuesday. And I'm a man of my word." It's the only warning she gets before I push her legs back up and drill into her. I'm relentless in my pursuit of making her scream in pleasure. With each plunge I hit a little wall of flesh that I know drives her out of her mind with lust and will make her come like a freight train.

The heat between us builds, and sweat mists over my chest and runs between the boxed squares of my abs and down the side of my neck as

I pound long and hard into her slick center. Her eyes are closed tight while her head tosses from side to side with each deep plunge.

"Parker, honey, I can't. I can't . . ." Her head presses into the mattress, her chin coming up, and her mouth opens in a silent scream before she mewls, "Gaawwwd."

"Yes. You. Can." I grind my teeth and double my efforts by dipping a hand between our bodies. I use two fingers to rub fat circles around the little kernel of nerves peeking out of its hiding place, already swollen from her last orgasm.

"Par . . . ker!" she screams, and I cover her mouth with mine, wanting to drown in her taste and muffle her sounds at the same time. When I pull back, I focus all of my attention on finishing deep inside my woman.

I press into her until my thighs burn with the effort and my forearms can no longer hold out. I let go of her legs and let her wrap those sexy limbs around me. I slide my arms under her back until my hands reach her shoulders, where I cup them. My head goes right into her neck as my abdominals work to keep fucking her.

Just keep fucking her.

Just keep fucking her.

Until everything burns with lust, love, need, want, and all the spaces in between. "Love you. Love you. Love you." I grip her shoulders and snap my hips. She rides each thrust with me, her arms wrapped tight around my back, her heels digging into my ass.

"Yes, honey, let go. Just let it go." She holds me close as I heave into her, trying to merge every inch of my skin with hers. Trying to mold us into one being as my orgasm races up my spine, scores through my chest and down to my groin, powering out my dick in fiery jolts, coating her insides, marking her as mine in the most primitive way possible.

All mine.

I groan long and low, easing my cock in and out in slow, unhurried movements, working out the rest of the aftershocks. Skyler holds me through it, her grasp never lessening, staying with me to the very last second. When it's left me and there's nothing but the sweet euphoria of being spent left behind, I let all the air out of my lungs and roll us over so she's splayed on top of me.

Sky snuggles against my chest, most of her body a dead weight, except her lips moving over my skin at random, wherever she can reach. One of her hands is trailing up and down my rib cage in teasing, soothing strokes. I'm not sure if the act of petting me is soothing her or me, but I love it all the same.

"How you doing, Peaches?" I cup her ass cheek tenderly, my other hand around her neck.

She hums, lifts up her head, looks me dead in the face, and says, "Now, I'm *really* hungry."

I burst out laughing, and before long, we're a pile of naked limbs, giggling, kissing, and whispering promises to one another about a future we're both committed to having. Once we've settled, having slaked the lust that overtook us during our semiromantic dinner, I get up, put on a pair of pajama pants, and go into the kitchen to make my woman her favorite.

A peanut butter and jelly sandwich and a fat glass of cold milk.

3

SKYLER

"Morning, Birdie," I hear from a few feet behind me.

I grin and place the powdered sugar over the perfectly grilled bread in front of me that's loaded with heated maple syrup. The pretty sugar dust is the final touch on my self-proclaimed famous french toast.

"Voilà!" I spin around and present the plate loaded with three thick slices of my homemade specialty.

Tracey smiles and presses her hand to her chest. "For me? Aw, you shouldn't have." Her voice changes to a poor interpretation of a southern accent. "Nah, you absolutely should!"

I chuckle and set the plate in front of her as she settles on one of the stools. "Coffee?"

"Absolutely!"

"Coming right up." I smile, happy that Tracey seems to be in a good mood this morning. I still need to talk to her about my plans with Parker and our future, so she understands that nothing is changing. She may think we're moving too fast, but the two of us hashed it out last night and believe we're on the right path for us. In the end, that's all that matters, and as my best friend, she needs to support me in this decision or keep quiet and let me make my own mistakes, if that's what she thinks I'm doing.

I gear up to bring the topic up until my phone buzzes on the counter. I glance over and note Wendy's calling. Now that the wedding is only a couple of months away, things have really heated up in the planning phase. As her maid of honor, I want everything to be absolutely perfect for her big day.

I grab the phone and lift it to my ear. "Hi, girlie!"

"Guess what?" she screeches happily into the phone.

"What?"

"You're going to be *thrilled*. It's kismet, I tell you!" She continues yapping cheerfully in that way she does, which I find makes her more endearing.

"Well, if you'd tell me, I'd know and could possibly agree with you. Is this about the wedding?"

Tracey's eyebrows rise up, and I cover the phone with my hand and whisper, "Wendy and Mick."

"Thank God," she mumbles, and shoves another bite of french toast into her mouth.

I frown and turn around, not wanting to see her sour face.

"Wedding shmedding! This is about a certain someone looking to buy a house in a certain gated community that's only four acres down from me and my McMansion!" Her voice rises along with her excitement.

My heart patters out a chipper beat. "No way. There's a home available?"

"Just came up today. I was walking Lauren, and my girl likes to roam. Having been in a cage for two years of her life, she needs to be *free*. As in, the stretch of open road ahead of her needs to be *long*. And since I want my baby to have whatever she needs, Mick and I take turns doing her long morning walk—"

"Wen . . . the point? I'm dying here!" I cut her off, knowing that Wendy loves her beagle mix, Lauren, to distraction. The girl can go on for days on end about her baby, and she hasn't had her very long. I guess when it's right, they just make your world better. I know Midnight and Sunny have done that for Parker and me. They've made us a family, and that alone is priceless.

"Oh yeah, anyway, Lauren and I hit the end of the street to the left and saw the neighbor come out to walk their dog. We got to talking, and she told me they were going to put their home on the market by week's end. And girl, the house is *phat*. It's not as big as ours, because it's more like a house you'd find on a farm in Savannah, Georgia. It has a huge wraparound porch in the front, and it's all one story. Still, it's around twelve to fifteen thousand square feet, so it's not small; it's just not forty thousand like ours."

"My goodness . . ." I gasp, imagining my man sitting in a rocker on his porch, his dog at his feet with his children by his side.

"How much land?"

"Five acres. We have twelve, but it runs the line of our property. It even has a separate two-bedroom guesthouse, with a separate driveway and garage, that's about eighteen hundred square feet on its own, separate from the main home's square footage."

"No . . ."

"Yes! And get this . . ." Her voice rises in pitch.

"Stop. Wendy, I'm getting too excited." I can barely say the words since I'm losing my breath.

"Babe, it's yellow with white trim. I swear they pulled that house right out of a farm in the South and plopped that sucker down outside of the city limits of Boston."

Parker's dream house.

"When can I see it? Are they putting it on the market now? Parker and I are leaving tomorrow for Madrid." I bite into my lip and worry a lock of hair around my index finger.

"Well, then, it's a good thing I made an appointment for you to see it after work today. Told the owner I have a great couple who would be interested in buying it right away, if the house is right. She was totally down with that since she was hoping to get it on the market ASAP. Turns out her only son and his three children are moving to Florida because he's career military. She wants to be near the grands. Her husband already found them a new home."

"This sounds too good to be true!" I whisper, my heart now pounding against my chest, making it even harder to catch my breath.

"I know. We might be neighbors! Our dogs can play together and have doggy dates, and when we have the babies, since Mick is working *hard* to get me prego, our kids and dogs can have playdates!"

"That would rock!" I bite into my lip harder and imagine Sunday dinners with Mick and Wendy and our combined families, the Ellises coming over to spend holidays and birthdays. The guys and whatever women they settle down with popping over to play football in the yard, or basketball in the driveway. "I'll need to get a basketball hoop."

"For sure! You'll have so much space you can build a barn and have horses if you want!"

Horses.

"Wow. Wendy, I'm freaking out over here. I can't wait to tell Parker!"

"You think I'm putting a lid on this news when he gets into the office? Girl, you are *crazy*. I've already put the meeting on his calendar. Just be down at five, and we can head over. I'll introduce you to the owners, and we'll go from there."

"Thank you, Wendy. This is such great news and timing!"

"Word. Oh! Parker just stopped in my office. Gotta go talk to your man! Eeek!"

I hang up, laughing and grinning like a loon.

"What's going on?" Tracey asks, an odd expression on her face.

"Wendy just found out there's a farm-style house in the gated community they live in. It's top-notch, Fort Knox–type security but open

24

land between houses. Neighbor of hers is moving to Florida and going to put it on the market. Her finding out early means we'll get first dibs. Everything I ever wanted is working out perfectly." I hug myself and spin around. "And just so you know, when I'm done with the *A-Lister* movies, I'm going to take a serious step back from acting."

Tracey drops her fork onto her plate and wipes her mouth, and her gaze turns cold. "Excuse me?"

I nod, grinning. "I want to focus on building a life outside of acting. One with Parker. I was actually thinking of maybe even opening an acting academy in downtown Boston. Work with less fortunate kids and teens who show some talent for the craft. Help them get their foot in the door."

"What the fuck are you talking about? Less fortunate kids. Donate to a fucking charity for crying out loud." Tracey's voice is brimming with anger.

I tilt my head back and place my hand on the counter to brace myself for the sudden onslaught of fury I'm feeling coming off her in waves, directed right at me. "I told you years ago that, eventually, when the time was right, I'd slow down. Focus on other things I want to do."

"Skyler, now is not that time. You're at the peak of your career. Everyone wants you. Do you have any idea how many scripts come across my desk? I don't even look at them unless they're in the ten- to twenty-million-dollar range or higher."

"But what if the role is on my wish list? Especially in the theater?" I had given Tracey a wish list of directors I wanted to work with, parts I wanted to play, and even some theater I wanted to do if the right role came about.

"Sky, the theaters can't afford you," she says dryly. "It's a waste of your time."

"Not if it's a role I want. Tracey, you know I worked long and hard on that list. Come to think of it, you haven't put anything I've requested in front of me for a long time. I did several of the Angel movies, which were fun, but it's not like they were hard to play."

She scoffs. "Maybe not, but you made a mint off each one, and they helped keep you at the top. Big budget is the way to go. Keeps us both in penthouses and the upper echelon of the industry."

"Trace, I don't give a crap about being at the top. I care about the craft. Why do you think my muse was having such a hard time when you hired Parker?"

"A mistake I'll never forgive myself for," she says with a hint of malice in her tone.

"What? Are you insane? Tracey, Parker coming into my world was the best thing to ever happen to me. He's everything I could ever need or want, and *when* we get married, *not if*, I'm going to suggest we start on having our family right away. Something about my man and the way he loves his family tells me that he's likely not going to have a problem with this decision. Things are changing. I don't want the huge roles unless they're parts I want to play and do not take me away from my new family for months on end. I won't do it."

"You can't mean that. Sky, you're in puppy love. This will pass, the same way it did with Johan."

"No, Johan was a drug user and a cheat. Parker is neither of those things."

"Give it a few more months. All I'll have to do is offer him a pay-out and a line of coke the same way I did to Johan. He'll show his true colors just like the hunky, weak model did."

"The same way you did to Johan . . ." My throat dries up instantly as if powdered concrete has been poured down my esophagus.

Memories of Johan and Tracey sharing whispered conversations back in the day flit through my mind. Her stopping by randomly to drop off a package to Johan. The women he cheated with always were low-level actors or extras from one of my movies.

My neck prickles and heats as the dryness in my throat makes it hard to breathe. I swallow a few times and breathe through my nose, trying to calm the panic teasing the back of my neck. I rub at the sore spot on my chest. "Trace, did you—"

"Supply Johan with his taste for coke and women?" She smiles evilly. "Yeah, Birdie, I did."

A wall of flame couldn't have burned me any more than her words just did. "Wh-wh-why would you do something like that? He was all I had after my parents died."

She snorts. "He was all you had? Sweetheart, that man was weak as hell and proved it every time he fell in love with the white lines I made available to him instead of being with you. He wasn't good enough for you. Those women? He fell all over them when they were put in his presence. Like I said, *weak*. You needed to scrape him off. I just helped make it possible. I'm always looking out for you, and I always will."

Tears fill my eyes as I realize the magnitude of my best friend's betrayal. "Tracey . . . I can't . . . I can't believe you. H-how could you do that to me? I thought . . ." I shake my head as a tear falls. "I loved him."

Her gaze narrows. "And then you learned he wasn't worth that love. Don't you see I saved you from a lifetime of misery?"

I wave my hands between us. "This is not okay. I don't even . . . I don't know what to do with this information. You've crossed the line . . ." I choke on a half sob, needing to go somewhere else, just get away.

Tracey stands, her light eyes narrowing on me as I back up. "Birdie . . ."

"Don't call me that!" I screech. "You hurt me. You destroyed what I had with a good man."

She shakes her head emphatically and keeps moving toward me as I'm moving away.

"No. Sky, just think about it. If he was worthy of you and your commitment, he would have never cheated on you. He wouldn't have snorted crap into his brain. Just because I made it a little easier to get it doesn't mean I'm the one at fault."

"You contributed to his problem, his addiction!" I shriek, and run my hand through my hair, pulling at the strands, embracing the pinch of pain that helps bring me back to the here and now.

"When you're rational, you'll think this through." Her tone has moved into the mothering one she uses when I'm panicking. "It's my job to protect you. I always have your best interests at heart. Ever since I took over your management when your parents died in the freak boat explosion, I was there for you. Got you the best-paying jobs. Made your career something you could be proud of. That we can all be proud of. That was me. I've always put you first. *Always.* Even when you told your mom you wanted to stop showbiz. I was there, making sure you made the right decision. I took care of you, and I'll always do that because it's my job, Sky, as your manager and your best friend."

Everything she's saying is heartfelt and gut wrenching, but I'm confused, and it's twisting my head into a jumble of emotions. I'm unable to wrap my mind around the years of lies going back to what I feel is her betrayal. "You never told me about Johan. I had to find out on my own that he was using and cheating."

She nods, but her expression is one of sadness and concern. "Because if you hadn't, you would have never let him go. I'm so sorry you had to go through that awful time, but I was there for you, wasn't I? Held you while you cried. Gave you a place to live. Made sure you were busy as could be and focused on much healthier things, like building your career and empire."

Actually that's true. She did take care of me. Helped get me on my feet when my parents died, and then took me in when I caught Johan cheating and using.

Still, I can't fathom that she'd help him destroy himself and our relationship. It doesn't make sense, and I'm not sure what to think or believe right now.

"I think you need to go." I swallow and firm my chin. "You need to leave my house."

"You're kicking me out?" Her expression telegraphs her shock.

I narrow my gaze and inhale deeply. "You don't live here. You came unannounced. It will be no trouble at all for you to find a hotel or go back to New York. Frankly, Trace, I can't look at you right now. I need to think."

She approaches me and holds out her hand. "Sky, you don't mean that, and you don't need time to think. I only did what I did to protect you from a man I knew wasn't worth your time or energy. I knew he would hurt you terribly, and he did. At least you didn't marry him and have his children. Then where would you be?"

I clench my teeth and purse my lips, thinking over her words. I still can't wrap my head around the fact that she'd enable someone to hurt themselves and me in the process.

"You need to go." On that note, I dig into the drawer that has my dogs' leashes. "Come here, guys!" I holler out. Both Midnight and Sunny run into the kitchen and jump playfully around my legs as more tears threaten to fall. I clip on their leashes and head toward the elevator.

"Sky, *Birdie*, come on, let's talk about this."

I turn around and put my hand flat out in her direction as she is advancing toward me. Midnight growls and puts his little ten-week-old body in front of me like the guard dog he's becoming. Sunny whimpers behind me, and that pisses me off even more. Her scaring my baby like that. She's had enough shitty things to get past in her life at the puppy mill. The last thing she needs is to be scared by someone who's supposed to be my family.

"I don't want to hear it. You've said quite enough. Now I'm telling you: I need time to think, to be alone. You need to pack up your things and get a hotel or go back to New York." My voice is firm, and for a split second, I'm proud of myself for being direct and straightforward about my feelings instead of cowering and hiding out. Parker would be proud of me too.

Parker.

I need him like I need air and water to survive.

Tracey huffs dramatically. "Fine. I'll leave, but I'm not leaving Boston. I'm going to be here when you get back from your trip, ready to talk when you've had some time to realize that everything I've ever done, I've done for you. Because I love you. Because I care more about you than *anyone* else in this world. Once you've had time to think about that, you'll realize it's true."

She takes off down the hall, and I tug on the leashes, get in the elevator, and press the button for the IG offices.

***

"That's intense, baby," Parker says as we walk hand in hand around the park near his office. Each of us has a leash with a pup on the end of it; this time Sunny is being walked by her daddy, and I have Midnight. I've just finished telling him the explosion of information that happened earlier and how broken I feel over it.

"You're telling me." I pout and focus on the breeze through my hair and the sun glinting off my man's lush, sandy-brown hair, which brings out some slight coppery tones. The tortoiseshell Ray-Bans he's wearing fit his business-casual style to perfection.

"At least for now she's out of the house. Besides, we're heading to Spain tomorrow evening, taking the red-eye so we arrive first thing the next morning. You'll have plenty of time to work out how you want to handle Tracey before we get back."

"Uh, did you talk to Wendy?" I ask, switching gears.

He stops as Sunny sniffs a bush. Midnight gets in on the sniffing action, only he chooses to pee on it for good measure.

Parker grins. "About the house. Yes. What do you think about it?"

"It sounds perfect for us," I respond wistfully.

"I agree. Though, the comps in the area are putting it at a hefty ten to twelve mil, and that doesn't include the community fees or yearly taxes, which are going to be steep."

"Honey, if we love this house, I want to buy it. We're setting up our life together, and I have twenty times more money in my account than—"

He presses two fingers over my lips. "Shh. I'm trying to let go of this macho need to be the one to provide my woman with the world." He moves his hand to cup my cheek, and I nuzzle into his palm.

"But I want to provide you with the world too," I whisper, and pout.

"It's taken me a long time and a lot of talks with Royce and Bo to accept the fact that you are always going to make more and have more invested than me. The nature of your job makes it so. Still, I need to do my part. So, here's what I'm thinking . . ."

I smile so wide, thrilled with the fact that he's willing to put his machismo aside and compromise for our future.

"I'll pay the twenty percent down to get things going. I've got the cash. You can pay the remainder so we don't have a mortgage payment."

"Honey . . ." I gasp as tears prick at the backs of my eyes, knowing this is costing him but loving more than anything that he'd take these steps for me.

"Ah, ah, listen . . . ," he warns.

I nod and press my lips together.

He grins and continues. "I will pay the property taxes and community fees due each year. You can furnish it how you want as long as you keep in mind the fact that your man is not a girly man. I do not do pink in my bedroom. In a tie or a dress shirt, sure. In the bedroom or the primary living spaces . . . no dice. Seeing as you have an eye toward comfort over cost, I don't think we're going to have a problem.

However, I buy our bed. My woman will be made love to and fucked within an inch of her life in a bed *I* paid for. End of. That's my deal."

"Deal!" I squeal, and jump into his arms so completely he has to catch me by the ass, and I wrap my legs around his waist. I kiss him wild and for a long, long time until I hear the camera clicks going off in the background. I pull back, still smiling, knowing I'm making a spectacle and not caring one iota because Rachel and Nate will make sure the paps don't approach, though there's nothing we'll be able to do about the pictures.

"You realize this little move is going to be on the cover of every tabloid from here to Timbuktu?" His eyes sparkle with mirth, but he's gotten used to being the center of attention around me. He just ignores it or goes with it. Another reason he's my perfect other half.

"Did my man just agree to a compromise on a home purchase and buying a new bed that's *ours*, not his or mine?"

He nuzzles my neck and kisses me there while breathing me in. Parker is such a scent whore. "Yes, I did."

I slide down his body, but he keeps a firm hand on my ass, making no bones about the fact that he will grope and touch me any way he likes regardless of who's watching. Hell, he probably does it because the whole world is watching. Staking his claim, fulfilling that little bit of caveman I know hides inside of him and comes out with some of his overly alpha tendencies.

"I can't wait to go see this house! I'm hoping beyond anything that it's the right one for us. It's, honestly, ideal timing and near Mick and Wendy, which makes it even better. It's also close to your work and where we're doing most of the shooting over the next couple of years."

Parker kisses my forehead. "It sounds perfect, but don't get your hopes up. I don't want you sad our entire trip to Spain."

"Not possible. I'm going to be with you. No matter what, we'll have a blast."

"That's true. Come on, the pups are getting antsy the longer we don't move."

I look down at our dogs and realize they've twisted themselves up in one another's leashes. Once I've gotten them situated, Parker loops an arm around my shoulders and we continue our walk.

"You feel better?" he asks, referencing the mood I was in when I arrived with a broken heart and on the cusp of a panic attack.

"In your arms? It's pretty hard to feel bad, honey."

He snickers. "I mean about Tracey."

I shake my head. "I don't like knowing the lengths she went to in order to break Johan and I up. I mean, he wasn't the right man for me, but what's to say she wouldn't try to do that with you and me?"

Parker laughs out loud and squeezes the ball of my shoulder. "Oh, Peaches, let her try to get between us. She'll have the fight of a lifetime. Although, if you think about it, she's never been anything but cordial to me. She hasn't offered me drugs, women, or money of any kind."

"Maybe because she knows those aren't vices you'd succumb to . . . thank God." I frown and remember how much it hurt when I found out about Johan's cheating and drug use. It broke me into pieces that took a long time to heal.

"This is true. I'm not sure there's anything she can do or would want to do. She might think we're moving too fast, but she's never hinted before that she didn't like us together. She set up those media interviews, did press releases on our relationship. To be fair, I'm not getting the vibe that she's going to be my best friend because, in truth, I'm the one lessening her time with you. Except she also knows I'm not trying to get between the two of you either. I'm sure this will all blow over, and regardless of which way that wind does blow, whether it brings you two closer or farther apart, I'll be there for you, right by your side, keeping you standing."

"I kind of wish we weren't walking through the park with the paparazzi on our tail," I huff with a little drama.

He chuckles. "And why is that?"

"Because I'd really like to jump your bones right now."

His eyes flash with a heated desire I recognize intimately. He dips closer and presses his lips against my temple. "Good thing my office has extra-thick walls and a comfortable couch. Wouldn't mind tipping your tight ass over the arm, pounding you hard from behind, tickling your little hole with my thumb while I do it."

"Honey . . ." I shiver in his hold, my mind flashing with the seductive imagery he instigated with his filthy promise.

"I think my girl wants to get herself fucked over the couch in my office." He chuckles.

"Yeah . . ." The word comes out in a throaty, needy, single syllable.

"Time to go, kids." He takes my leash and his own into one hand and leads our dogs back toward his office.

"Seems I didn't do what I promised last night. It's only Thursday baby, not Tuesday."

I grin all the way back to our building, my mind on his leather couch, my panties soaked, and my heart so filled with love I can barely catch my breath.

4

PARKER

"It's perfect." I stare in awe at the yellow home with white trim. Around the entire house is a full-size wraparound porch reminding me so much of my grandparents' home I can hardly speak as the memories flood my brain.

Skyler nudges my bicep with her nose and wraps her arms around my waist, staring at the house. "What did you think of the inside?"

The sun is setting as I scan the house. There's an open field in front that seems to go on for days until it hits a huge wall of trees separating the edge of the property from the next.

"Hmm." I stare out at the landscape as the sun streaks color across the treetops and grass. I can easily imagine playing Frisbee with our dogs. Soccer and football with the guys and my future children. Skyler setting up a blanket and lazing in the sun in one of her flirty little sundresses.

"The inside?" She eases my chin toward the house.

I shrug. "It has a lot of antique furniture in it." I make a stink face, and Skyler giggles against my side.

"Yes, and it will all be removed in the next four to six weeks. It has seven bedrooms and four bathrooms. A huge den. A game room. A man cave that doubles as a fully finished basement. An open kitchen and dining room. Two good-size living rooms and an entryway. A beautiful pool, firepit, fountain, and garden already growing veggies. And I asked Rachel what she and Nate thought of the guest house. They love it. It's bigger than their apartment with room to have a child. Something they've been talking about."

I wrap her in my arms and lift her chin up with my thumbs so I can look into her eyes. "Do you want to live here with me, make a home, build a life, bring our babies home here?"

"Real or fur?" she teases.

The act of caressing her nose with mine is instinctual. "Both," I whisper against her lips, then kiss her softly.

She hums into my mouth and nods. "I feel at home here, and I can tell you're in love with the view."

I grin and kiss her again. "My woman knows me well."

"Yes, I do! And I'll make the inside something you'll never want to leave to go to work," she promises.

"So, we doing this? Buying the farm so to speak?"

She grins wide. "Yeah, honey. Let's do it."

"All right. We'll get things started. Come on, let's tell the current owners the good news and contact our Realtor."

"We have a Realtor?" she asks with surprise.

"Wendy set us up with Mick's. They've already drawn up the paperwork." I chuckle. "Wendy was that confident this was the house for us."

"Seriously?"

I nod. "We're going to have a ball of wild on our hands with her living just down the road."

Sky smiles wide. "I sure hope so. I've always wanted a nosy, well-meaning sister. Looks like I'll be getting one."

I rub her arm as we head up the stairs to meet with the owners, who'd given us some privacy by staying inside while we talked outside.

"Peaches, your world just exploded with friends and family," I remind her, knowing how much everyone in my life loves her.

"Best decision of my life," she murmurs, and bites at my bicep.

I stop and loop an arm around her waist, plastering her front to mine.

"What did you say?"

"Parker Ellis, taking you to bed was the best decision of my life."

I can't stop my laughter. "I'm pretty sure I took *you* to bed."

She shakes her head. "No way."

"Yes way."

"I jumped you the first day," she says with a determined pout as we continue walking.

"Yes, but I didn't take advantage. You were drunk. I was drunk. That would not have been chivalrous."

"So, waiting a few days later until I made it so by jumping in the shower with you, and you had no choice but to take advantage, was?"

"Totally."

She laughs as I hold the door open for her.

"I think we should put in our offer and take this discussion back to the penthouse. I'm feeling a wild case of naked wrestling is necessary to put this disagreement to rest." She smirks and steps through the door.

I grab her around the waist and slam her ass against my semi, dipping my lips close to her ear. "Deal." I hum against the skin of one of the places on her body that make her sigh. "Whoever wins gets to tie up the other and do *whatever* they want to the other's body."

She gasps in my arms and rubs her ass back against me with more intent. "Hmm. I'm feeling a little winded, I might not fight at my best," she teases, still rubbing her pert ass in dizzying circles against my much harder lower half.

I have to bite down on my cheek not to go fully erect against her sumptuous booty. "Figured you might want to throw this round."

She hums again, and the sound threads through my body like an arrow shooting straight for a bull's-eye. She one-ups the sensation by reaching back and strategically wrapping her hand around my cock through my slacks, giving it a playful squeeze. "Maybe I'm feeling generous."

I tilt her ass and hand away from my body, knowing that the owners could catch us in a precarious position at any time. "I'm thinking you're feeling greedy to be *worked over*."

She grins wide and cocks an eyebrow. "I guess you'll just have to find out."

"Looking forward to it, Peaches."

Interlacing her fingers with mine, I lead her into the kitchen area, where I can hear the owners laughing over a cup of coffee. One day, that will be us.

When we arrive in the room, two gray heads come up and look at us with smiles.

"We'll take it," I announce, and their smiles get wider, but neither is as brilliant as my woman's.

***

"I cannot believe you did this. Rented a freaking jet?" I growl and take one of the lush, camel-colored leather seats on the private plane.

"Do these seats go all the way back?" Bo asks Skyler, who's trailing behind him with our dogs.

She grins, and I frown, still pissed that she chartered a private jet to and from Madrid so that she can bring our dogs.

"Yes, they do, Bo, but there's also a couch that folds out bigger if you want."

Bo shakes his head and takes a captain's chair farther back in the belly of the plane. "Naw, I'll save that for the two of you if you need it." He waggles his brows suggestively.

"Bo, simmer down. We're not going to fuck out in the open on a plane."

He lifts his hands up in a gesture of surrender. "Whatever. It's cool, man. Just leaving your options open. I have total noise-canceling headphones I could put on. Do whatever you gotta do."

I can feel my nostrils flare as my irritation rises.

Skyler continues with fighting her side of our current disagreement. "Honey, I couldn't leave our babies behind for a week or more. I'd miss too much of their lives."

Rachel and Nate lumber onto the plane and pick a couple of chairs at the very front. "Baggage is loaded, and the captain is ready to initiate takeoff," Nate grumbles as he settles into one of the chairs, then sighs deeply.

"Plus, we needed to book three tickets extra for me, Rach, and Nate."

"We talked about having Wendy watch the pups for us," I remind her for what feels like the thousandth time.

She scrunches up her nose. "Honey . . ." She picks the seat next to me, and both dogs jump up on the small love seat across from us and get comfortable. She grabs the blanket hanging over the side of the loveseat and tucks in our dogs. They immediately close their eyes and yawn. They've had a lot of activity today and need the rest. Watching them get settled cools my ire a little but not much.

"It was too soon to leave them. They've already had a rough go at life. We can't let them feel abandoned, plus Mick and Wendy are just getting settled with their fur baby, Lauren. I just . . ." She sets her cool hand over my forearm. "I couldn't be without them. Not yet. I haven't had enough time with them, and when I get back, I'm going to start filming the first *A-Lister* movie. This really isn't a big deal. I mean, I'm technically part owner of this charter line anyway. We're not even paying for these, if you really think about it."

I frown. "You own part of this airline?"

She nods. "Yeah, forty percent. My financial planner said it was a good investment years ago, and look . . . I'm finally taking advantage of it, aside from the cashola I make quarterly on the sales of the flights."

"Jesus." Sometimes her wealth is staggering, and what I make with IG is nothing to sneeze at.

She shrugs. "Told you I had more money than I'd need in a lifetime. Now just sit back and enjoy a comfier ride to Spain than you would have on a stuffy domestic flight where you wouldn't be able to snuggle your pups or kiss the daylights out of your woman." She blinks at me prettily, knowing she has one over on me.

Her ribbing makes me smile, which cuts through the frustration. Really I don't have any reason to be upset. She booked us a private jet. It's her money to do with however she wants. I inhale long and slow, turn to her, cup her cheek, and smash her lips to mine. I delve my tongue in deep when she gasps and taste the cherry-flavored gum she was chewing in the car. Her hand comes up and tunnels through the hair above my ear. She tangles her tongue with mine, getting her own tantalizing licks in before we're both sucking in huge bouts of much-needed air.

"Am I forgiven?" Her lips are swollen from my kiss as one side of her mouth tips up into a smirk.

"There was nothing to forgive. It's your money. You spend it how you want," I admit, voicing the conclusion I just came to.

"Okay." She pecks me on my lips three times in quick succession.

That's it. Easy peasy. No more conflict.

I ease back into the *very* comfortable seat and reach for her hand. She holds mine and sighs, settling in, our fingers laced with one another's.

This is my life.

This is always going to be my life with Skyler.

Easy. Beautiful. Filled with love.

I lift her hand and kiss the back of it while I watch my dogs sleep and prepare for takeoff.

***

"*Bienvenidos*, Mr. Ellis, Ms. Paige. Come in, come in." Our client, Alejandro Rodriguez, gestures to a large swank office in a unique building in the heart of Madrid. It's one of the sleek, contemporary buildings fashioned with tons of glass and steel, reminding me very much of our building back in Boston. Flanking it are older, more historical-looking structures. It's as if the heart of the city decided to marry historical and contemporary together in one big jumble of old and new.

"Mr. Montgomery, *bienvenido*. Thank you for coming." His accent rolls around the English language, sounding exotic, and befits his handsome style, trim form, and metrosexual vibe. He has slicked-back hair, perfectly coiffed, which goes well with his tailored clothing. Everything about Alejandro Rodriguez oozes class and money.

I'm used to dealing with men like this. Driven. Focused solely on the almighty buck. I clench my jaw and fall in line behind Skyler to a black leather couch surrounded by glass tables. She sits, and I undo my jacket button and sit next to her, my arm around her shoulders, casual, with a hint of professionalism.

Bo saunters in, all dark jeans, black tee, and white leather blazer. It's his version of professional dress, although he's pushed the sleeves up his forearms and not removed the studded leather bracelets crawling up his wrist.

Alejandro claps his hands, goes over to his desk, and picks up the phone. "Call for Juliet and bring her here within fifteen minutes," he orders, before replacing the receiver.

"First of all, the work you did on my friend's modeling campaign . . ." He puts two fingers together and kisses them. "*¡Magnífico!*"

"Thank you. We've read over the file you sent, but there wasn't a lot to go on. As we understand it, you have new talent that you'd like to mold into a superstar. Is that correct?"

Alejandro grins, and combined with that face, he could probably grace the cover of the Spanish version of *GQ* magazine and sell a million copies. "*Sí.* Juliet is a dream with the voice of an angel."

Bo plucks at his goatee and sits back, ankle crossed over one knee as he shakes his foot in what most people would consider a nervous gesture. With Bo, it's just the annoyance of inaction. Bo likes to keep moving. Doesn't prefer to stay in one place for too long. If there's no food, brews, or game on a wide-screen in front of him, he gets a tad jittery. "What's the girl's deal, then? She lacking sex appeal?" He rotates his pelvis. "Maybe needs to learn a few moves?"

Alejandro crosses his arms over one another. "*Sí.* Those things for sure. Only it's more than that."

"Enlighten us," I state, not wanting to drag this conversation out. I'd prefer to get on with the case, get what we need done, and head back home.

Alejandro tips his head and purses his lips. He swivels his hand in the air in a circular movement. "She needs . . . how do you say? Work."

"Work?" Bo frowns. "As in a makeover?"

"*Sí.* More like plastic surgery. And a diet. A big one. She's too fat."

"Whoa, dude. That's harsh," Sky interjects, and I rub the ball of her shoulder, knowing that, once upon a time, she was told she needed to be the perfect size zero in order to act or she wouldn't be taken seriously or looked at as beautiful. I got her past that, and now she's a healthy weight and has never been prettier.

Alejandro shrugs. "Tis true. You will see."

Right after he says the words, there's a tiny knock on the door.

"Come in." He smirks as the door is opened and a petite woman and a tall, stately, modelesque brunette enter holding hands.

"Aw, *hermosa* Violeta." Alejandro greets the tall young woman with a kiss to each check. He then leans at least six inches down and does the same to the petite child standing next to her, because that is what she looks like. A child. "Juliet, my *ángel cantarín*."

Juliet is squeezing Violeta's hand and standing very close. They have comparable coloring, being brunettes with olive skin, but the similarities stop there. Their eye colors are different, with Juliet having hazel eyes to Violeta's dark brown.

"Juliet, do you want to have Violeta wait outside so I can introduce you to your new mentoring team?"

Mentoring team. I like the sound of that. After coming off a case of being hired to tear people down, it's exhilarating to be lifting someone up. Especially a girl so young and impressionable, who's embarking on what promises to be a huge career in music.

The small girl shakes her head.

"Um, would it be okay if I stayed?" Violeta asks. "JJ is shy, as you know, Alejandro."

He smiles tightly. "Sure. Everyone, this is Violeta and Juliet Jimenez. Violeta is Juliet's older sister and the reason Juliet was discovered."

"Really? How so?" I smile, trying to make sure our presence isn't frightening the young woman.

"She let me record her singing. It was a ruse. Told her it was for me, for my long trips to Milan and Paris when I travel for modeling."

A model.

I can see that from a mile away. Not only is the sister naturally beautiful, her confidence in herself shines out every pore just by the way she stands, dresses, and looks you directly in the eye.

"Except I sent the sample tape in to a scout a friend of mine told me about. Her recording worked its way up the chain, and now we're here." She hugs her sister around the shoulders. "I'm so proud of my baby sister. She's going to be a star. I just know it!" Violeta beams as though her sister's happiness is all that matters to her.

Juliet's cheeks pinken as Bo stands up. Her gaze goes to him as he does his thing, walking a circle around the pair.

"You wearing anything under that boxy sweatshirt, lamb?" he asks, his tone of voice nonthreatening but still direct.

She nods but doesn't move to remove her hoodie.

"A hair tie perhaps? I'd like to see your beautiful face." He dips down to look into her eyes. Juliet's long brown hair is parted down the center, hiding a good portion of her face, the ragged lengths falling against both cheeks like a veil.

Violeta springs into motion, yanking a brown elastic from her wrist and going behind her sister, where she pulls back Juliet's hair, bringing it into a high ponytail. Juliet's hand lifts to the side of her face. Her sister grabs her hand and gently brings it down. She then moves in front of her sister and whispers something. Juliet slowly unzips and removes her sweatshirt, showing us that she has a very curvaceous form. It's the kind of body Jessica Rabbit has and most women in their right minds would kill for, but it doesn't technically fit the standard size-zero mold an industry like this insists sells a brand best.

"Hot damn!" Skyler says in delight.

"Oh yeah, now this is something we can work with." Bo winks at me and then grins his man-whore grin.

"She's a child, bro," I remind him.

He winces. "Not going there with jailbait, but seriously, lamb, you've got some kickin' curves. Why are you hiding them?"

Juliet looks down and shrugs. "I'm nineteen, not a child." The words lack complete conviction.

"Told you, sis. Everyone loves curves." Violeta dips her knees and knocks Juliet's hip.

"Well, not *everyone*. Our marketing team would prefer Juliet drop at least twenty-five pounds prior to the first large media blitz," Alejandro states methodically.

Skyler stands up, hands on hips, indignation in place and at the forefront, ready to blast this guy into next year.

He lifts his hand. "I mean no disrespect to Juliet or you. I'm only the messenger. I call the shots, yes, but I answer to investors, and the team decides how to best sell a new pop star. We're already at a disadvantage with her height. And of course, she'll need to get the scar on her face smoothed out, along with the protruding bump on her nose." He frowns apologetically.

"Whoa, whoa, whoa." I stand up, an ugly feeling burning in my gut at the same time Bo remarks, "Say what, again?"

Alejandro looks at the three of us and then back to Juliet, who has crossed her arms protectively over her body and is looking at the floor as if the carpeting is the most fascinating thing in the world. When I see a tear slide down the side of her face, I've had enough.

"Violeta, how's about you take your sister back out in the waiting room, and we'll reconvene this meeting in a little bit. Yeah?" I suggest.

Alejandro glances my way, looking rather confused, but nods, apparently going with the flow.

Violeta hooks her sister around the shoulder and leads her out of the room, a deep sadness in Juliet's pretty face. The second the door shuts, Bo loses his shit.

"Are you out of your fucking mind!" he growls, his jaw set in a firm scowl.

I move to him and place my hand on his shoulder and squeeze, signaling I'm going to take over from here and handle this.

"Alejandro, there is nothing wrong with that girl. She does not need to lose weight or have any kind of plastic surgery to look like a different person. All she needs is confidence, a new hairstyle, some time with a makeup team to *enhance* the natural beauty she already has." I state this with the seriousness of a heart attack.

"That's not what the public is used to seeing." He points at the door. "She can be a star if—"

"She can be a star if she has talent and a team of people who believe in her ability. That girl, she is exactly the kind of pop star this world needs. Sky . . . baby, help me out here." I gesture with a wave to my girl, who I know is biting the fuck out of her tongue right now, wanting to ream him a new asshole.

Skyler purses her lips and nods. "Parker is right. From a woman who's at the top: the last thing you need is another one-hit wonder. You want a woman with staying power, like Taylor Swift and Selena Gomez. Sure, both of those women are beautiful, but more importantly, they are *talented*. The songs they sing and the personas they present to the world are not something a mother would be afraid to let her daughter emulate. They are strong women with fascinating songs, and they don't go out of their way to change their girl-next-door appeal. You want to make Juliet a star, so let her be an enhanced version of herself. The IG team can do that for you."

Alejandro rubs at his jaw and then shakes his head. "This would be a major risk for us. We know what's working in the industry right now."

I take a deep breath and lay it out for him. "What's working right now will not work for that girl out there. She is not a diva. Let us bring out her outer beauty so that it matches her inner beauty and the magical voice she has and music she writes. Once we're done with her and you've seen the results, then you can decide. You've got to trust us on this one. You saw what we did with the show in Milan. Let's go big and change the tide here in Spain too."

Alejandro glances at Bo, then me, and finally Sky. "And you'll be here to help?"

Skyler offers a sultry smile that makes Alejandro's eyes flare with interest. She then cuddles along my side, which puts out that small fire instantly. "We're a team. We work together when it's necessary, and I can see with this girl, she's not only going to need the guys' knowledge and expertise, she's also going to need a woman's touch, someone she can trust and be vulnerable with. I'm all in."

Alejandro takes a deep breath and nods. "She is a rare talent. I'd like to try it your way." He goes to his desk and dials the receptionist. "Bring Juliet back in."

Within a mere minute, Juliet and her sister shuffle in. Juliet's eyes are red rimmed and puffy. Skyler walks right up to the girl, tips her chin, and looks into her soulful hazel eyes. "That's the last time you're going to shed a tear about who you are, sweet girl. You and me, we've got work to do with my guys back there, but it's all going to be fun and exciting. No more tears. You are perfect just the way you are. We're just going to spend a little time bringing out your confidence and maybe a little bit of a flirty side. No surgery. No weight loss. Just music, makeup, dancing, and a whole lot of laughter. How does that sound?"

Juliet's pink lips tremble as she swallows. "I don't know how to dance."

Skyler laughs and brings the girl into her arms for a big sisterly hug. "It's okay, I didn't know how to dance either when I started out. That's what they have choreographers for. It's all going to work out, but first, how's about you, Violeta, and the guys and I all go out and get ice cream, get to know each other better. Would you like that?"

Juliet smiles sweetly and nods. Her sister jumps up and down next to her. "JJ, I can't believe we're going to have ice cream with Skyler Paige! Eeek!" She squeals and hugs both Skyler and Juliet at the same time.

Sky tips her head back and laughs beautifully.

Bo nudges my shoulder. "Glad you brought Sky, bro. She's going to be aces on this gig."

"My girl is always aces."

"I heard that," Bo murmurs, and winks at me.

"Come on, ladies, we've got work to do, but first . . . double scoops on me!" Skyler announces to the room, ignoring Alejandro and nudging the girls out the door.

"We'll be in touch." I wave to the man who's smiling and leaning against his desk, watching Skyler with a look of wonder on his face.

Yeah, Skyler does that for me too, I think to myself, *only I get to have it and hold it.*

5

SKYLER

"All right, girls, spill it. Who's your celebrity crush?" I ask, before plopping a large chunk of ice cream in my mouth, practically moaning around the strawberry flavor melting on my tongue.

Violeta's eyes flare with joy. "I'm in love with Justin Bieber. He is perfect," she says with a dreamy look in her eyes.

I cringe and laugh, tipping my head from side to side, thinking about the Bieb's boyish looks and how he is absolutely not on my list of hotties.

Parker crosses his arms over his chest and purses his lips, waiting to hear what I have to say from across the table. I look him dead in the eye. "Not exactly my type. I prefer my men, well, quite a bit older and more manly." I wink.

"Good answer, Peaches." He smirks but turns to look at something Bo is showing him on his phone.

"What about you, Juliet?" I nudge her shoulder and smile, getting closer to her in case she'd rather whisper it.

"I don't know. I haven't really thought about it." She focuses her attention on her gelato, mostly spinning the icy treat in a circle, making a slushy chocolate puddle instead of eating the creamy goodness.

"Sweet girl, what's bothering you?"

Her lip trembles again, and she looks up at me with glassy eyes. "I'm never going to be what they want me to be. I don't know if I can even sing in front of a room filled with people, let alone prance around in front of them. What will they see? A fat girl waddling around like a penguin, screeching out songs they don't want to hear."

My mouth drops open, and my entire body ignites into action. I scooch my chair over to her side right as Parker makes a snarling, animalistic noise across the table. Apparently he heard what she said and is as unhappy about it as I am.

"Look here, we've heard your recording. You're beyond incredible. You have natural talent. It's a God-given gift. Do you believe in God?"

She nods and sucks her lips into her mouth, leaving no pink at all visible.

"Then you need to believe that he wouldn't bring you to this place in your life without a plan. The stage is set. We just have to get you ready for it. And I promise you, we will. Me, Parker, Bo . . ."

"And me! I'm not going anywhere until you are settled and happy in this new phase of your life," Violeta promises. "And remember back when I was scared to model, and get out on that catwalk in the galleria and walk in front of all those people?"

"Yeah," Juliet mumbles.

"And do you remember what you said to me?" Violeta encourages her sister to keep talking.

Juliet bites her lip and nods.

"You said, the first time is always going to be the hardest, but after that, you've already done it so it will be easy. Like me and modeling, each new thing I have to do is hard the first time, but then, once I've done it, it's easy. Piece of cake."

Juliet closes her eyes. "It's different for me." Her voice is so low I have to dip my head even closer to hear. "You're perfect. Everyone wants to look at you. Tall. Thin. Beautiful."

Violeta's eyes go hard, and before she can speak, I shake my head and place my hand on Juliet's back. "You're beautiful. You're small, petite, curvy, and gorgeous. You just wait, I'm going to show you what you don't see, but we do."

"And what do you see, Skyler?" Juliet's hazel orbs seem to dig deep into mine, on a quest for a truth she's desperately needing to hear.

"I see me. The me I was before my mother showed me that I was a talented actress, that I might have been gawky and quirky, but I'd grow with my craft. I'd find the me I was meant to be on the screen. And I did. It took a little while, but with her love and care, I blossomed, and you will too. I'll make sure of it."

Juliet places her hand over mine in a bold move I didn't expect. She squeezes my hand. "Thank you. Even if it doesn't work, it means a lot that you want to try."

"Do *you* want to try? Is this something that you want to do with your life?" If it comes down to her not wanting to do this job, feeling pressured, none of this will work out at all.

Parker leans over the table and rephrases my question. "Do you want to be a singer, sweetheart?"

"It's always been my dream." She swallows and sits up a little straighter.

"Never stop dreaming. Now's your time to shine. To show the world what you've got," I tell her, and believe it straight down to my soul.

She nods and lets out a tortured breath. Her sister puts her arm around her back, showing her support and love.

"Will you work hard with us on making your dream come true?" I ask her. "Because there are three things I know for a fact in this world: nothing is free, nothing is guaranteed, and it takes hard work and sacrifice to make a dream a reality. Are you prepared to work hard?"

"Yeah, but I'm scared."

I smile wide. "I'd be surprised if you weren't. Dreams have the power to become nightmares if you don't work toward making them beautiful. You just have to believe. Believe in us, because we'd never lead you astray. Believe in your sister's love and support. Believe in your gift. Most importantly, you have to believe in yourself."

Juliet takes in a deep breath and pushes her hair back on one side, making the scar around her eye that Alejandro mentioned more visible. It's kind of like a crescent moon around one soulful hazel orb. The shape of it actually gives me some ideas.

She notices my gaze is zeroed in on her scar, and she moves to cover it again with her hair.

"How did you get the scar?" I push her hair back from her face and tuck the strands behind her ear.

Violeta grimaces. "It was my fault . . ."

Juliet shakes her head. "No, it was an accident."

"If I hadn't been messing around, being stupid, getting drunk with that boy, it wouldn't have happened."

"It's no big deal."

"It is a big deal because ever since it happened, you hide your face," Violeta spouts, frustration clear in her tone.

"Tell me what happened?" I ask softly. I don't want to startle them or bring up a bad memory, but it's obviously a bit of an issue between the sisters.

"I was dating a boy. It was stupid. He was in college. Juliet warned me not to go to the party with him and his friends. I did. They got me so drunk I could barely stand up. I had enough sense to call Juliet to come get me. She did. The guy followed us to where Juliet had parked in an alley near the house. When she tried to get him to leave, he punched her. He was wearing a pointed ring that must have had a prong sticking out around the stone. The ring caught her skin, and he tried to shake her off. That's when I hit him on the back with a two-by-four I found in the alley, and we got in the car and left. Unfortunately, the damage to Juliet's face was done."

"Jesus." Parker's voice is a low, anger-filled vibration across the table.

"You know this guy's name? Where he is?" Bo asks with barely concealed malice, entering the conversation for the first time. He grips the table across from us so hard his knuckles turn white.

Both girls shake their heads. "It was three years ago. Juliet was only sixteen. I hadn't turned eighteen yet. We're eighteen months apart."

"You got any name at all?" Bo asks.

"Full name? No. Just Rico."

Both Bo and Parker fume across the table.

I attempt to put out the fire brewing. "Relax, guys. It's in the past."

"But—" Parker starts, and I hold up a hand.

"But nothing, honey. It's over and done with. Anyway, this is what I think would be super cool. I don't think we should hide the scar. We should show it off and tell the story of how you saved each other from a situation that got out of hand. Not only would it help you both let that attack go, it might help other girls who are being unsafe make better choices."

Violeta beams bright as noonday sun. God, she's beautiful and is going to have a long modeling career.

"And you said something about showing off the scar? How?" Juliet traces the jagged skin around her eye.

"Well, it looks like a crescent moon. Let's get you some tiny stick-on jewels to trace the edge. It can be part of your signature if you like it."

"Jewels?" She perks up.

"I can totally see it! A bright-white crystal with some royal blues mixed in with aqua and greens to go with her eyes. I'm also seeing white leather. Sweetheart, stand up." Bo gestures to Juliet, who suddenly looks scared as a baby lamb.

"Just go with it. Bo gets these crazy ideas all the time, but, sweetheart, they always work," Parker adds in a soothing, encouraging manner.

She pushes back her seat and stands up.

"Remove your hoodie, sweet girl." I get where Bo is going with this idea and love every single second of it.

She unzips the large sweatshirt and passes it to her sister. She's now in a black ribbed tank top that accentuates her very large bosom. Girl must be at least a D if not a double D. And on her petite stature— yowza!—the boys are going to go wild for her.

Bo takes off his white leather jacket and places it over her shoulders.

"Oh yeah, I'm seeing this and loving it!" I nod excitedly.

Juliet pushes her arms through the leather as I take off one of my long beaded crystal necklaces and loop it over her head multiple times, making the loops fall strategically over her bare skin in a cascading waterfall of beads.

Violeta squeals. *"¡Estás muy sexy!"*

Juliet's gaze locks with her sister's, and Violeta is nodding and clapping excitedly.

Across the room, there's a half mirror, and I lead Juliet over to it, right in the middle of the store.

Her mouth falls open when she sees herself. I lift up her hair into a sleek, sophisticated ponytail coming to the side. "I'm thinking a cool side ponytail with big curls." I trace the scar around her eye. "Some interesting crystals arcing here with some rockin' makeup and a bright-pink gloss. Fluttering eyelashes and some contouring around the cheeks. Girl . . . you are so gonna rock the stage."

Juliet runs her hands down the front of her chest, glances at herself from side to side, and I can almost see the wheels spinning.

I lean forward and rest my chin on the crown of her head. "Do you like what you see? Can you imagine the rest?"

She nods and sniffs, her eyes getting glassy.

"Ah, ah," I warn. "No tears, remember." I wink, and she grins wide, her big smile making her an absolute knockout just like her sister.

"I like it. I like how you see me."

"Sweet girl, that's not how I see you. That's how *everyone* but *you* sees you. And I'm not going back to the States until you see it too."

Juliet bites into her lip. "Promise?" She frowns.

I loop my arm around her upper chest and hug her from behind. "I promise."

"Thank you, Skyler. I'm not going to let you down." She firms her chin and stands up straighter.

"Oh, you couldn't. Together with this team and your sister, we're going to help make your dreams come true."

Juliet closes her eyes, and when she opens them, I'm hit with a sensation so intense I almost have to adjust my footing for how much it knocks the wind out of me.

"I believe you." Her words dig right into my soul and burrow there in a way I know will never let me forget this moment. The moment I chose to help change someone's life . . . forever.

"And I believe in you."

***

"Peaches, you were amazing with her today." Parker's arm closes around me from behind as I stand in front of the bathroom vanity and pat my face dry after washing away my makeup.

I lean against his warmth, staring at the two of us in the mirror. "Yeah?"

He grins and presses his lips against the spot where my shoulder and neck meet. "Yeah. A natural. I may have to hire you on a more permanent basis." He bites into the muscle there.

I moan and chuckle, laying my arms over his, enjoying his warmth and close proximity. "She just needs to believe in herself."

He runs his lips along my scapula. "Mm-hmm." There's a kiss followed by a little teeth action he knows drives me wild. "You're right, and you're the perfect woman and shining example of what happens when you believe in your gift and work hard."

I spin around, hating that I'm losing his ministrations and what he was working up to from behind, but wanting to be eye to eye. I loop my arms around his neck and focus on his deep-blue eyes, which, right now, look like two endlessly clear swimming pools. "You think so?"

Parker caresses my nose with his, not stumped at all by the new position, just changing his suave sexual tactics, running a hand from my lower back where my camisole sits and teasing the skin there to slip his hand into my bikini briefs and cup a full cheek. "I know so." He places his lips against my neck and grinds my lower half against his thickening erection.

I bite down on my lip and tip my head back so he can get more of my neck. "I'm thinking of taking a much lighter acting schedule after the *A-Lister* movies are filmed." My breath is a sigh when he licks up the column of my neck, making me tingle *all* over.

"Oh yeah . . ." His other hand gets in on the action, pushing at my panties until I wiggle out of them and they fall to the floor. Once they're there, I kick them aside.

"Mm-hmm." I balance my hands behind me on the vanity, knocking a few bottles into the sink.

He chuckles, and I feel it down *there*. Hot and needy between my thighs, aching with every new piece of skin he touches.

"And what do you plan to do if you're not acting full time?" He grips my ass, lifts me up onto the vanity, and spreads my legs wide.

"Um . . . hmm." I lose my train of thought as his chin dips into my camisole and his fingers find my center. He teases between my thighs, never dipping in, but stoking the fire with each feather-light touch. "Honey . . . ," I say as a half sigh, half plea.

"No, no, no. Keep talking, or I'm going to stop." He removes his hand from between my thighs, and I immediately come out of my pleasure daze.

"I'm thinking about opening an acting academy for kids, including a scholarship program for kids that are less fortunate. Even teaching some acting classes myself." I tunnel my hand into his hair as he runs his mouth back down my chest, pressing me back so my head and shoulders lean against the mirror while he keeps moving down. He grips my knees, runs his hands up my thighs, and stares between my legs at my bare sex. His nostrils flare as he inhales, closing his eyes as though he just stuck his nose into the oven while chocolate chip cookies were being baked and got a whiff of sugary heaven.

"Christ, baby, you make me crazy. *Ravenous.* Wild." He cups my ass with both hands, tips my pelvis so that he can get a better angle, and dips his head. Right before he touches down with his tongue, his blue gaze lifts to mine. "Keep talking. I want to know about your plans."

I let out a stuttering breath. "Now?" I cup his head, bringing him even closer to where I want him.

He curls his lip with that sexy-as-fuck smirk I know means business. If I don't keep up the game, he won't give me what I want. Sexy bastard.

"It's all fun and games until somebody gets hurt," he jokes.

I squeeze my legs around him, digging my heels into his lower back. "Yeah, *you*, if you don't put your mouth on me," I admonish half jokingly.

He chuckles and then leans forward, sticks out his tongue flat against my flesh, and gives me one luscious, long lick.

"Honey . . ." I need more, need everything.

"Talk." He cocks a brow and looks at me, his blue gaze swimming with heat when he swirls the tip of his tongue around my clit in maddening, delicious circles, but not enough to take me to the peak any time soon.

"Um, I want to help kids. Give kids less fortunate—" He sucks the entire bundle of nerves into his mouth and grinds his prickly chin against my core. "Oh God." I tighten my legs around his body, lifting my hips to get more of that mouth on me and harder.

He caves for a full minute, going to town on me, licking, sucking, nibbling, until I'm panting, straining, forgetting everything but his talented mouth and devious tongue.

"Give kids less fortunate what?" He pulls back and kisses my thigh.

I shake my head, the haze of lust swirling so intensely I lift my hips, humping the air, wanting that mouth back on me. "Honey, please . . . *I need you.*"

He grins, licks his glistening lips, and hums low in his throat.

Sexy as hell. Tasting me on his mouth like that.

I mewl in protest, wanting that mouth on me, his tongue in me, kissing me . . . anywhere, *everywhere.*

"I know you do. And I like our game, so I need you to tell me what else you plan to do with your life, since I plan to be in that life until you take your last breath."

"Uh, uh, okay. I plan to open an acting academy, teach kids how to act, and give those less fortunate a free ride so they can work on their dreams in a safe place where someone will listen. I want to do that and have my own babies and take them to work if I want or hire people to help . . . and I don't know . . ." His tongue is leisurely delving in and out of me, and I can barely focus. "God, please, just fuck me, honey."

He smiles huge. Stands up, shucks off his briefs, widens my legs around him, centers the glistening wet tip of his cock at my entrance, and eases home. I lock my limbs around him and grind down, making sure he's as deep as he can go.

"Yes!" I cry out, my head falling back as his lips fall against my neck.

"Love your idea, Peaches. Sounds awesome, but I don't want you to give up your dream to be home for me." He eases out and thrusts inside, long and so deep my teeth chatter against one another.

I hold on, getting my leverage on his shoulders. "I won't give up anything. It's what I've always wanted. And when it's time, I want to be with our babies—all the time, not just some of the time."

"Fuck, Sky. Stop talking and let me love you," he growls, sucking on my neck. The bathroom is becoming warm and misty with our combined sweat.

"I'm going to kiss them every day," I promise, and cry out when his cock hits my cervix in a pleasurable, not altogether painless, jab.

"Christ!" He groans, licking my neck where he was sucking.

"Gonna love our children with an intensity they'll never understand until they meet the person they're supposed to spend their lives with and have their own babies. Uh, uh, honey, honey . . ." I cry out, my body flaring in ecstasy from the tips of my toes, up my legs, ass, groin, back, and chest. My nipples are so hard against the camisole I'm wearing that the soft fabric feels like wool grating over them, pinching and pleasurable at the same time.

"Perfect. Fucking. Woman." He hammers into me over and over, sealing every word I said to him with an intense thrust that has my ass slapping against the marble counter so hard I may have a bruise tomorrow. "You come. You come now, Sky. Come all over your man's cock," he grates through clenched teeth, his filthy request turning on every nerve ending, triggering the mother of all orgasms.

My body tightens around his, muscles screaming, burning, the space between my thighs throbbing, wet, and locking around his girth for dear life as I lose myself in his arms. I can fall into the abyss, knowing he'll be there to make sure I have a safe journey.

In my haze, I feel his body jerk into mine a handful of times before he plasters my body against his chest, holds my face to his neck, and bites down on the ball of my shoulder as he shakes. His cock is buried deep when he goes off, coating my insides, touching me everywhere he can. Inside and out.

6

PARKER

The throbbing pain in my head amps up to a thousand tiny men jackhammering against my temples as I watch Juliet fumble her way through the choreographer's dance routines for the fiftieth time today. Over the last two days, we've worked on stage presence and choreography. JJ, who did not lie when she said she couldn't dance, is losing steam in a big way.

I rub at my temples, pressing a forefinger and thumb deeply, and glance at Skyler. She and Violeta have picked up the dance routine by the third attempt. Juliet, I'm afraid, seems hopeless. When she does grasp the routine, she falls off on her singing. The singing only happens at all if the stage is dark and the practice area is closed off for friends and family only. This all means that not only can Juliet not dance, she can't dance if she's singing; she can't sing at all if she's dancing, and she can't sing if there are strangers around. Basically we've encountered the supernova of problems, and that doesn't include how socially awkward she is to start. The four of us as a team have been working with her, and she's definitely making progress, but it's more than pulling one tooth; it's extracting an entire mouthful.

Skyler notes my wince and frowns, stops her moves, and comes over to my side.

"You okay?"

I shake my head. "Baby, I'm not sure she's got this in her."

"With a little more work . . ."

"A little?" My response is unguarded but honest.

"Okay, with *a lot* more work, she could probably get close."

I massage the knots in my neck. "I feel like we're trying to put a round peg in a square hole. This scene is not Juliet."

She purses her lips and glances at the flashing lights, the dance moves, the complete and utter train wreck that is JJ while she attempts to follow along, and eventually her shoulders sag. "It's not. Though I believe in her talent. She's got the singing chops. Maybe this pop star business is not the way to go."

"Sky, she signed a contract. As did IG. We don't want her stuck owing someone for the money they've already put out, and frankly, I don't want to fail at another case."

She places her arm on my bicep. "Honey, you did *not* fail in DC. If anything, you won."

I cringe, remembering what we encountered. The animal torture, political darkness, and legal mayhem were only a few of the things we dealt with that still give me a vibe so ugly it's like bugs are crawling all over my exposed skin. I scratch my forearms and then shake it off with a groan of disgust, realizing what I'm doing to myself. "Anyway, about Juliet, I think we need a new approach."

"Brother, I heard that," Bo agrees, sauntering up from behind us, his black motorcycle boots pounding heavily on the shiny stage floor. "This is an exercise in futility. Two days gone and not much to show for it but a tired teenager whose heart breaks every time she can't get the moves. And this is just the first song. How the hell is she going to do an entire show's worth?" He plucks at his goatee, each arm crossed over the other in his contemplative pose.

"She's not," I state honestly. "We've got to come up with another plan."

Sky pouts, walks in a circle, puts a hand on her hip, and stares out at the empty seats of the practice theater we're using.

"No, no, no!" the choreographer screams for what feels like the hundredth time. "Try it again. From the beginning without the two left feet."

I grind my molars and narrow my gaze at the froufrou dude. He's long and lean, bordering on emaciated in my opinion, Spanish, and flamboyant in his personality and flagrant about his sexual preference. When he's not yelling at JJ, he's hitting on Bo. The first I find aggravating, the latter, hysterical.

"What if she's not the one dancing?" Skyler spins around and rocks from heel to toe a few times.

"How do you mean?" I ask.

"Well, she can't dance. We've established that. Obviously, if she takes a lot of classes, over time she may get better. *Over time* being the key words. That will not happen when she needs to be ready to tour soon. However, just because other pop stars dance all over the stage doesn't mean she has to. Perhaps she can walk around the dancers, singing. If she gets comfortable with them, she'll play along when possible, but for the most part, they'll become her posse in a way. Her friends. They'll make her feel more grounded in her role. I think part of JJ's problem is that she feels she's going to be alone. When in reality there's an entire crew that will be working behind her."

Bo whistles loudly between two fingers, getting the attention of the choreographer. He holds his hands up. "Hey, Pink Flamingo . . ." He waves over the choreographer.

The choreographer stops and cuts the music, then saunters toward us.

"Take a twenty-minute break, ladies. Go get some water, a snack," I call out to Violeta and JJ. Both of their faces take on an expression of relief at hearing of a break. Violeta loops her arm over her sister's sagging shoulders and leads her off the other side of the stage.

"It's Pete Flaco, *cariño*," the choreographer says in a lower timbre, one I believe is meant to sound sexy but only sounds ridiculous coming out of his mouth. And the fact that he called Bo his lover has me chuckling out of turn.

Bo narrows his gaze, not knowing what Pete called him, and I am not about to tell him, because all my fun would be ruined. And right about now, I need a few laughs.

"Whatever, *Pete*." Bo adds the inflection on the man's given name. "Does this production have backup dancers?"

"Oh yes, a team of twenty or so that will be rotating through the production I've choreographed."

I lay it out for the man. "You're going to need to scrap some of it."

"*¿Disculpe?*" His eyes widen in their sockets, reminding me of one of those rubber chickens with eyes that bulge when you squeeze the neck.

"It can't have escaped your notice that JJ is not picking up your very unique and *stunning* choreography." I sprinkle on the sugar as I prepare to flatten his entire cake. "However, this particular star is not a dancer. She's just not, and no amount of yelling or berating is going to make that happen. What we need to do is have her moving around among the dancers instead of doing the dancing herself. Let's focus on getting her singing. Once she's singing, no one will care what the dance moves are, but she will accent your beautiful pieces instead of take away from them."

Pete pinches his lips together. "This is not a bad idea. She is hopeless. The worst I've ever worked with. Even my ninety-year-old *abuela* has some moves, but this girl . . . no. *Cero*. Zip. Zilch."

I inhale slowly, allowing my irritation to seep out before I nail this froufrou dude up by his toes and let him dangle over the stage for the night. Maybe then he'll learn a little more tact and a lot less sass.

"Can you rework your moves? We'll get JJ comfortable singing the songs with people dancing around her."

He stares off at the stage for a full minute before he nods succinctly. "*Sí*, I can do it. I'll get the dancers together, and we can try again tomorrow. Today is . . . uh, how do you Americans say? A bust?"

That makes me smile, so I give him that. "Yeah, it's a bust. We'll work on her makeover and meet back here tomorrow after breakfast."

"*Mañana. Sí.* Bogart, *cariño*, would you like to escort me to dinner this evening?"

"Fuck no!" Bo blurts out, and Pete's head jolts back, clearly offended. "Look, Pinky, I'm not gay. I don't have a problem with people who are. What I do have a problem with is you bugging me about hooking up when I've already told you this. More than once today."

Pete makes a clicking noise with his tongue. "So testy. I like that in a man. I will let you go. I need my beauty rest anyway. *Adiós, cariño.*" He flutters his fingers in a teasing wave.

When he's turned around, I look at Bo, lift my hand, and flutter my fingers at him. "*Adiós*, beautiful Bo," I taunt.

He shakes his head and sucks in air between his teeth. "Not cool."

"Funny though." I grin.

Bo rubs his hands down his face in a worn-out gesture. "Fuck, I need to get me a chicklet tonight. We hitting a bar, club, something? We've been hanging with children for the past three days. I'm due. Hell, I'm overdue for some Bo-style lovin'. You feel me?"

Skyler giggles and wraps her arms around my waist. "Eww, I hope you didn't feel him, honey. I'd have to shower you before I touched you again."

Bo's mouth drops open, and he clutches at his heart with both hands. "That hurt, Sky."

Her laughter continues as the girls make it back to us, each one holding a bottle of water and an apple.

"Girls, we've got a new plan. No. More. Dancing," I announce.

"Really?" JJ asks. "For today?"

"No, sweet girl," Sky adds, walking over to her. "We're going to work something else into the routine that I think you'll like a lot better. We can talk about it on the way."

"Where are we going now?" Violeta asks, then sips her water.

"We're entering my territory. Time for phase one of your makeover. Wardrobe." Bo pushes up the sleeves on his leather jacket.

"Yes!" Violeta fist pumps the air.

JJ crosses her arms over her chest, looks down, and nudges a scuff on the stage floor with the toe of her sneaker.

Sky runs her hand through JJ's ponytail. "Do you not like shopping?"

"I wouldn't really know. I usually wear whatever oversize hand-me-downs Violeta or *mi madre* have that might fit me and the clothes we find at consignment shops."

"Well, JJ, that's all about to change. Come on. This is going to be fun."

***

"Holy shit! Who is that fox standing in the mirror?" Bo howls like the man whore he is when JJ has on a pair of leather pants that show off her sumptuous ass and a high-collared, sleeveless white shirt that he's told her to leave loose over the pants. The shirt hides the small stomach she's insecure about, and the pants highlight one of her best features . . . her bangin' ass.

"Mm-hmm, there is no denying that booty needs to be shown off." Skyler jumps up on the platform and spins her own ass around and checks it out in the mirror. She sighs dramatically. "What I wouldn't give for a booty like yours." She pouts as JJ's eyes go wide. Her glance goes from her bodacious bum to Sky's little one and back.

"You're perfect, Sky. You're what everyone wants to be." Her voice is low and strained.

Sky shakes her head. "You think that because you've been conditioned by the media, but girl, everyone has their own special thing that makes them unique. You've not only got the pipes of an angel, you've got a serious hourglass figure that men will absolutely drool over. I promise you that." She runs her hands in toward JJ's waist. "Look at how much your waist dips in compared to mine." She proves what she's saying by demonstrating her own small curves next to JJ's voluptuous ones.

"And what about me!" Violeta steps up onto the platform that JJ is standing on next to Sky. Her body is a rail next to theirs. She lifts up her shirt so that it shows her abdomen. "I'm straight up and down. Which is awesome for modeling, but not awesome for scoring hot guys." She puffs out her bottom lip.

She is not wrong. Her body is lithe and boyish compared to both Sky's and Juliet's.

"Vi, your face is the most beautiful in the world," JJ compliments her sister, her tone and expression showing her seriousness.

"And this face will pay the bills." Violeta puckers in the mirror. "While I'm doing that, your voice will pay yours. We all have to use our God-given gifts for what we're meant to do. I'm going to use my face and shape while I can, learn all I can about the fashion industry, and take fashion design classes online in the process. Once I've soaked up what I can, then I hope to go into the clothing design part of fashion. My face is only going to get me by while I'm young. Maybe ten years. Tops. Then I'll have to find something else. Your voice, it could last a lifetime. Don't sell yourself short." She looks JJ up and down and then covers her giggles with her hand.

The three of them fall into a fit of laughter while Bo gets more clothes for JJ to try on, and I watch my woman do her magic. The light in Juliet's eyes has already gotten brighter. I can see her starting to view herself in a different way. She runs her hands over the outfit as if the clothing alone has changed her when, in reality, she's just coming to her own personality, no longer stifled by what she believes is beauty.

"I think this look is fantastic and appropriate for a woman your age. Now let's get you in some spiked heels and jewelry." Bo hands her a pair of electric-blue suede stilettos.

Juliet takes them and looks at them as if they've grown scales, a fin, and teeth. "Um, I can't walk in these. I can barely walk in my flats without tripping."

Bo groans and looks up at the sky. "Practice, lamb. Get used to being on stilts, because with your petite stature, you're going to have your dancers towering over you. We need to combat that visual on stage a little. When you're sitting and doing interviews, flats are fine. Otherwise, I'm going to encourage a little height advantage." He winks, and Juliet's cheeks pinken.

She slips the shoes on and instantly goes up three inches, which makes her around five feet six—nowhere near Skyler and Violeta's height, but at least she doesn't look so awkward. Her back straightens, and she looks at herself in the mirror, a flash of pride washing over her face as she studies her appearance. That simple moment is very telling. I think she's finally getting the idea that she really is beautiful and likes what she sees in her reflection.

"Here." Bo hands her a chunky gold necklace and several gold bangles and beaded items. "I'm thinking shiny red nails and bold red lips with this." He assesses her outfit.

Skyler nods. "Totally."

Bo disappears and comes back with some rings, a lipstick, and a clip. He hands Skyler the lipstick. "Make that happen," he says while working Juliet's long dark hair. He leaves a swoop of layered bangs out and wraps the rest up in a twist before clipping it.

"The hair is on the wrong side," Juliet murmurs. Her gaze is hyper-focused on the jagged scar surrounding her eye.

He shakes his head. "Nope. We're accentuating it, remember? You, my dear, are going to show the world that perfection is in the eye of the beholder. You think Skyler is perfect, and because I know her well, I know that her beauty is not only skin deep but all the way through. However, she's one of the most insecure women I've ever met and wacko as a nutjob about her dogs. You wouldn't know that just by looking at her."

Juliet's gaze slashes to Skyler, probably seeking confirmation.

Skyler nods, then playfully smacks Bo's bicep. "Hey, bro, don't be sharing all my secrets!" She smiles. "It's true though. I'm a little bit of a freak about our puppies, right, honey?"

I tug her off the platform and into my arms, laying a hard, quick kiss to her lips. "Yeah, but I love it."

"Who's taking care of the dogs in the States while you're in Spain?" Violeta queries.

Bo straight up starts cackling. "You must not have heard me say she's a nut! She brought the dogs to Spain. One of her bodyguards is walking them around outside while we're inside." He laughs but grabs JJ's hand and pushes a couple of gold bands over it.

Violeta cracks up, and Juliet snickers as Skyler grins, leaves my arms, and opens the lipstick while heading to Juliet. She stops in front of her and pushes out her lips.

"Pucker like this," she instructs.

Juliet does what she says and holds still while Skyler applies the crimson stain to her plump lips.

"There. Beautiful. And sexy." She waggles her brows and gets out of the way so that Juliet can view her entire look.

"All right, what do you think of the full look, lamb? Is it a go?" Bo inquires.

Juliet looks at herself in the mirror, pets her hair, turns from side to side to gauge her body in the outfit. She looks much older and sexy as sin.

"I can't believe this is me." Her voice wavers with emotion.

"Sis, you have always been hot. You've just hid it under baggy clothes and a poor body image. Now look at you. You're smokin'! *¡Muy caliente!*" Violeta smacks her sister's bodacious ass.

"I feel like I'm dreaming," Juliet says as her eyes fill with tears.

Sky loops her arms around me, the lipstick in her hand pressed against my chest. It gives me an idea. I finagle the tube away from my girl, walk right over to the dressing mirror, and write on it:

Never Stop Dreaming

I pull out my phone and wave my hands for everyone to step back. I get behind Juliet and call out, "Pose."

She shrugs. "How?"

Sky laughs, but Violeta goes right to work showing her sis what to do. "Like this. Right hand on your hip, the other at the side of your head. Put the right leg out, showing off the length of your legs in those pants and shoes."

I get out of the way, make sure I have my phone camera pointed at the mirror. The words I've written and Juliet's reflection are both framed to perfection.

"Okay, sis, hold that pose. Now, look directly into the mirror intently, and inhale through your mouth slowly."

The second her lips part in a sexy gasp, I snap the picture.

I look down as Sky cuddles up next to me to check it out. My heart pounds out a heavy beat, and Skyler covers her mouth with her hand. I grin wildly down at the image and then back at Skyler. "Peaches . . ."

"Amazing," she gasps.

"Right?" We both stare at the image for a couple of seconds more while we hear Violeta giving Juliet a 101 on posing.

"Bo, come here. Get a gander at this." I wave my phone in front of me.

He swaggers over in the way only he can, with as much manliness as possible while holding a pair of women's heels and a few items of clothing draped over his arm for Juliet to try on next.

I point to the image so he can see it.

"Fuck me running. Damn, we're good." He grins.

"Uh, sweetheart," I say to Juliet, "you are going to have zero problems getting the world to fall in love with your brand of beauty. It's effortless and smokin' hot." I grin wickedly.

Sky keeps her gaze plastered to the image. "He is not kidding. This needs to go up on your Instagram and that of the music label ASAP. Send that picture to all of us, honey."

I do so, and Violeta pulls her phone out of her back pocket. "¡Vaya! JJ, you look amazing!" She squeals in that way only really young girls can get away with. "I'm making this my Instagram pic of the week! Heck, maybe the month!" She taps at her phone a bunch of times.

Juliet looks over her sister's shoulder at the image, then at the mirror, and finally back to where Skyler, Bo, and I are standing off to the side.

Her expression is one of awe tinged with gratitude.

That sweet face and the meaning behind her gaze have me clearing my throat and wrapping an arm around my woman, wanting her close.

Then Juliet shocks the three of us when she glances at the mirror once more and then back.

She speaks as if the message is three separate words. "Never. Stop. Dreaming. That's going to be the title of my debut album."

7

SKYLER

"Yo, Wendy, what's shakin'?" I hear Parker laugh into his phone a little drunkenly. Eh, maybe more like tipsy. We've had a full dinner inside with the pups and are now to the drinking and kicking-back portion of our evening.

Today was a great day and ended on a high note with Juliet starting to see herself as a young, beautiful woman who has all the potential in the world. I never thought I'd be so enthralled by helping another artist or participating in another one of International Guy's cases, but I've found it's enriching my world as much as I hope to do for Juliet. Truly makes my idea of opening up an acting academy in Boston more realistic and exciting.

Back to Juliet, we're right on target for success.

Goal one: make Juliet see herself as beautiful. Accomplished.

Goal two: get her stage presence up to par, but we'll go back to that after the choreographer changes up the show to make the dancers' routine enhance JJ's performance, allowing her to shine as the star.

Goal three: get her singing in front of an audience without trembling in fear. That's a big one, because her gift needs to be shared, and with her talent, she should feel confident in her ability.

Goal four: media time. Parker claims to have a plan for getting her comfortable in front of a camera and/or the press, though it's last on the agenda. Kind of like the sprinkles on a perfectly baked and frosted cupcake.

Due to the amount of work needed to get Juliet ready, we've extended our stay in Spain to ten days and have already burned through the first four. However, tomorrow Bo is taking JJ for her hair and makeup lessons alongside Violeta, who's tagging along for support, while Parker and I get to have a day in Madrid to ourselves.

I'm dreamily imagining walking through the streets of Madrid, my dogs on their leashes, hand in hand with my man. A sigh slips out as I glance at my hot guy, the phone pressed to his ear. His face has taken on a pinched expression, which usually means something is wrong.

"Read it to me," he rasps into the phone, his voice tight and controlled but with a tinge of anger lacing every syllable.

He narrows his gaze and slams down the glass tumbler so hard, some of the whiskey sloshes out onto the cherrywood sofa table. He doesn't bother with wiping up the mess, and I push aside the part of me that wants to take care of it. "Email me the picture of the note. Send it to Nate too. Any ideas on delivery?"

Parker's jaw firms, and he snaps his fingers at me where I'm sitting and trolling my social media pages at the lone desk in our suite.

"Bring up my Gmail," he demands, and I remove my foot from where I had it hiked up onto the chair and put my fingers to the keys to do as he asks. Parker rarely snaps at me or takes on that tone of voice. I know it's directed by whatever Wendy is telling him and not at me, which makes it easier to hop to action.

Since he's given me his password before, I type it in and bring his account up right away. An email from Wendy is sitting at the top unopened. I don't click on it because it's not my business, even if I'm dying to know what set him off.

Parker leans over my shoulder from behind, reaches for the mouse track pad, and opens the email. He double-clicks the attached JPEG file, which reveals an image of a white piece of paper with black words in all caps typed out and centered.

I read the message, and my heart feels like it has stopped beating as anxiety slithers around the useless muscle, clutching it in a fearsome grip. I hold my breath and read the text more thoroughly.

YOU CAN'T HIDE HER FOREVER.
SHE IS MINE.
WE'RE THE SAME.

"Oh my God, honey." I swallow against the sudden dryness in my throat as Parker's warm hand lands on the space where my shoulder and neck meet. That single touch breathes life into me. I cover his hand with mine and squeeze his fingers.

"Don't worry, Peaches," he states with an urgency that seeps down into my soul. "I'm going to take care of this."

I close my eyes and realize that, whatever is going on back at home, we're thousands of miles away, which is probably the safest place we could be anyway.

"Yeah, I'll get back with you later. Let me know anything you find," he directs, before tapping a button and setting the phone on the table next to his laptop.

He kneels and spins me around to face him, maneuvering his chest between my thighs. I gladly hook my long legs around him and lock them at the ankles. Parker runs his hands up and down my quads, but his gaze is on mine. Those normally deep-blue eyes are filled with fire and intensity when he speaks.

"It's just another stab at us. You're safe with me. I'd never let anything happen to you." The ferocity behind his statement is palpable. I can almost feel the truth of his commitment brushing along my skin like a soft breeze.

I loop my arms around his neck and press my forehead to his. The masculine smell of whiskey mixed with his wood-and-citrus scent calms my frantic concerns as much as his nearness does.

"I know that, but I'm not worried about me. I'm worried about *you*. That note came to you, just like the first one." I bite down on the side of my lip and wait for him to understand the meaning of what I'm saying.

"Yeah, it did, but I'm just the vessel for the message. This person is infatuated with you. By being your man, shacking up, I'm an extension of you. I'm also the person he sees as taking away what is his. It's demented and twisted, but that's the type of person we're dealing with. Someone who's got a screw loose, and that scares the hell out of me when it comes to you being at risk."

"It doesn't make any sense. I haven't done anything to deserve this kind of attention."

Parker runs his fingers through my hair. "Baby, you being you, doing the job you do—it puts you out there to everyone. Any wacko can twist up what they see on the screen and make it part of their reality."

I close my eyes and tighten my hold. "Did uh, Wendy or Annie find anything on the note? A return address or anything helpful at all?"

He shakes his head and grinds his teeth so hard I can hear the noise within our little cuddle bubble. I cup his cheeks and massage the muscle at the hinge of his jaw, trying to work out the tension, even in this small way.

"Guess it's too much to hope our stalker would mess up." I sigh as sadness drips into my soul. I just want this to be over so that Parker and I can focus on what's really important. Us. Our work. Our pups. Our new home. The life we're building together. "What do we know?" I inhale a shuddery breath, defeat clear in my tone, but I need to understand the entire picture so that we can move forward and take action accordingly.

"The envelope had to have been hand delivered or dropped in the mail room at the building for delivery. Annie opened the same type of nondescript envelope we got with the very first message. She immediately took this new one to Wendy. Wendy didn't touch it in the hopes that we find other prints besides Annie's. There was nothing more on the envelope except my name typed on a white label, a red *confidential* stamp on the front, just like last time. Nothing new except there's a more desperate, bordering on threatening, warning."

While I mull this bit of information over, Parker's phone rings on the desk near our heads. He doesn't move out of my arms to answer it; instead, his body language and gaze are focused solely on me.

"Are you okay? Should I not have told you about this? My first instinct was to keep it from you and handle it myself. But I made a promise to keep you in the loop, and I don't want to ever break a promise I've made to you. Not ever. Even if it goes against every male chromosome in my entire body."

I smile even though I want to cry. "I'm okay as long as I'm with you. Answer your phone. I'm sure it's Nate or Wendy with more news."

He grabs the phone, and before he answers it, I can see on the display that it's Nate calling. "What's your take?"

He listens for a bit, then stands up and starts pacing. It's his normal MO when he's worrying a problem or has a bunch of negative energy to burn off. I watch while he stalks the room like a caged animal ready to pounce at the first sign of danger.

"That's true." He frowns and looks at me. "Sky, baby, can I sit there? I need to get to something." He points to the chair and computer.

I stand up, and Midnight wakes from his doggy snooze on the couch across from us where Sunny is still sleeping. I go over to them and sit close, then dig my fingers into their fur. The calming motion of petting my dogs eases the panicked feeling that keeps creeping into my veins at seeing that note and thinking about what it might mean for us.

"Yeah, it doesn't read the same as the letters. Have you asked Tracey if any new letters have come in that are similar to the ones we narrowed down?" He taps at the keyboard and brings up the copies of the fan letters from that person signing off as Your Real BF.

He rubs at his temples and looks up at the ceiling while pressing into them. "The last text I got was before we left. And it was a warning. Let me pull those up." He uses only one hand to work the computer keys, a true pro at the one-handed typing.

He scans the various images. "Yeah, the texts are primarily in caps like the two printed notes. Still, there's something about the cadence that's different."

Parker stands up and moves away from the desk, walking from across the suite's living room into the dining room and back in a long trek, phone pressed to his ear. There's so much power in his movements, I can feel it pumping off him in waves of controlled energy. His mind is likely working a mile a minute, quickly compiling and processing possible scenarios and dropping them to pick up other ideas and moving through those. I'd give anything to catch a glimpse of how his incredible mind works.

"Wendy thinks there's something familiar about the letters. She hasn't been able to put her finger on it, but she's going to review them again tomorrow with fresh eyes. She's also got some type of program she's working on that compares words and phrasing and creates probabilities between unrelated mediums. She's inputting all of the letters, the two notes, and the texts both Sky and I received in order to come up with some new analytics to consider."

Parker inhales and runs his fingers through his hair several times, making the tamed layers and curls on top shift into a sexy mess. This look is usually the one I get to see after a round of raucous sex.

"Okay, let me know if anything else pops up. I want the security camera feed for the entire two days before and the day of reviewed in full. See what you can do about getting those. I'm certain the building owner will have no problem if you bring him up to speed. Nice guy. We've been good tenants. Plus, he's a family man with all daughters. He'll not like hearing about a threat to a woman, but especially not the woman leasing his penthouse."

Parker's entire body jerks and then comes to a dead stop while one of his hands goes into a tight fist at his side. "What! Why the hell didn't you lead with that intel, Nate?" he grates through his teeth into the phone.

Oh shit. I perk up and stop petting my dogs, my own nervous nature starting to prickle at my hairline and make my belly ache.

"What the fuck was he doing there?" he roars.

He listens for a full thirty seconds before he tips his head back and groans. "What is the likelihood that he visits, stopping in to see if Skyler can be reached for a coffee, and all of a sudden Annie has an envelope with a threatening message inside?" he bursts out, anger seeping through his words like venom. "Jesus!"

Parker listens to whatever Nate has to say but chops the air with his free hand in a violent slashing motion. "I want that man banned from even attempting to enter the IG office!" he roars. His barely controlled energy floods the room with an electricity so powerful I press back into the couch cushions, and Sunny, now awake, crawls over her brother and into my lap, seeking comfort. She must know that Daddy is furious. Midnight moves around, his doggy head popping to attention. He must feel the air change in the room, except instead of cowering into me, he jumps off the couch and heads toward Parker.

"We know where he works. That's it. No more playing by the rules. When we get back, I'm paying him a fucking visit!" Parker pulls at his hair, and his gaze lasers mine as his mouth compresses into a flat, angry line.

Midnight sets his doggy booty on the floor right at Parker's feet and looks up at his daddy. Parker seems to sense his dog and looks down, his face softening at the sight. He crouches down to Midnight's level and spears his hand into the pup's ruff until the dog plows his now much-larger body into Parker's chest, catching him off guard and knocking him off his feet to his ass.

Parker smiles for a moment and hugs his boy. "I'm done with Benjamin Fucking Singleton, Nate. Mark my words. That mother-fucker comes even a foot toward Sky, and I will absolutely give the media a show when my fists start flying. Keep that asshole away, or my woman will be bailing me out of jail and we'll be the next piece airing on the nightly news." He smashes the end button and chucks his phone at the single chair in the room. It bounces off the back and surprisingly lands on the ottoman a half foot from the seat.

"Honey . . ."

He picks up Midnight, who goes still in Parker's hold, except for his tongue, which is licking my man's neck like it's an ice cream cone.

Parker comes over to the couch and sits sideways so he can look at me where I've got Sunny cuddled in my lap. Midnight finds a spot next to Parker's thigh and settles in, putting his face in his daddy's lap.

"Benny Singleton apparently visited the IG offices to see about getting your phone number and to inquire on when you'll be back in town."

I frown and make a stink face. "Whyever would he do that?"

"Apparently, Benny Fuck Face can't take a hint. He came to ask you out for another *coffee date*," he snarls unpleasantly, screwing his face up into an expression of utter disdain.

I place my hand on top of his forearm. "You know I've done nothing to encourage his affections, but for some reason he thinks we have this history. As I told you, I haven't seen the man since I was eight years old when we did one commercial together. One." I hold up a single finger to demonstrate the ridiculousness of his undeserved connection to me. "Although, when I ran into him at the coffee shop, I couldn't exactly be rude after I'd spilled his drink. That's not who I am, honey." I frown, but carry on. "I didn't get the impression that he was totally together in the head when he didn't back off after meeting my boyfriend *and* my bodyguards. I mean . . . for real. It's a little crazy."

Parker's eyebrows shoot up his forehead almost comically. "A little? Baby, that guy is fifty-one cards short of a full deck!"

I grin because I can't help it. My man is funny. And he's especially funny when he's being a caveman.

"So, you believe Benny was the one to drop off the envelope? You think he's the mastermind behind all of those texts to you and me, as well as the letters throughout the years?"

Parker runs his hand down his face and eases his head into his palm that he's rested against the back of the couch. "The timing on the note fits. It's not a coincidence. No way."

"Then how would he get our cell phone numbers? Why would he ask Annie for mine if he already had it?"

Parker groans. "I don't know. Maybe he was using that as a ploy to get us off his trail?" he offers.

"Really, honey, you think he's that bright?"

"Again, I don't know. All I know is I'm tired. Tired of not knowing who's messing with us. Tired of feeling helpless. I'm just *tired*. We need some peace, baby. Just me and you."

I lift my hand and cup his cheek. He nuzzles into my hand and kisses my palm before sighing with contentment. When he touches my hand, I feel some of the negative energy coming off him before it quickly dissipates.

"Yeah, we do. And I want to be that safe haven for you, honey. Always." I pick up Sunny and lift her to the other side of the couch. Then I grab Midnight, kiss his furry head, and put him next to his sister, and they cuddle back around one another like they usually do. I snuggle them in their blanket I brought from home so they'd have something familiar. They both close their eyes, their concern washed away now that their dad isn't pacing the floor angrily. Once they're settled, I stand in front of my exhausted guy and hold out my hand. "Come on, honey. You've had enough for one day. Everything will look better in the morning."

Parker follows me without complaint. Once we get to the bedroom, he stands by his side of the bed, just staring at the pretty comforter and mounds of pillows. Hotels always do it up, never going cheap on the bedding when you're staying in the penthouse. I turn Parker around and undo his dress shirt, one button at a time, with no ulterior motive in play. He shucks it off, and I grab it and set it on the chair near the bed. He undoes his belt, pants, and zipper and sits on the bed. I crouch down and remove his shoes and socks, setting the socks inside each shoe before tugging on the hem of his pants. He eases his hips up, and the pants come off, leaving him in only a pair of black boxer briefs. I put his pants next to his shirt.

Without a word, I dip behind him and pull back the comforter and toss several of the pillows to the floor at the foot of the bed. Before I can get him in the bed, he grabs me by the hips and presses his face against my belly. I can feel the warmth and dampness of his breath through the cotton of my tank.

"I can't lose you, Sky. You're my future. The life I want more than anything." He kisses my stomach and rests his head again. "Baby, the fear of losing you eats at me every damn day that we haven't found this person. I can't risk letting my guard down, and I won't until I know for sure you're safe."

I run both of my hands through his hair, scratching my nails down his scalp the way I know he loves. "You're not going to lose me. Between you, Nate, Rachel, Bo, Royce, Mick, Wendy . . . honey, I've got a lot of people watching out for me and looking into this. I'm going to be okay."

He rubs his forehead against my belly and digs his fingers into my hips. "I love you so much, Sky. I can't even imagine . . ." His voice cracks with an emotion so gut wrenching, I need to be near him.

With a little shimmy of my hips to ease his hands off my body, I kneel on the bed and slide onto his lap so he can hold me and, more importantly, I can hold him. He wraps his arms and love around me instantly.

"I love you too, more than I ever thought was possible to love another human being," I whisper while my head is resting against the side of his. "We will get through this. Life is going to throw us some serious challenges, but so far, we've faced them and come out stronger on the other side. It will be that way with this too." I press a kiss to his forehead before he dips his face into my neck and inhales several deep breaths.

He's lost, afraid, a fish out of water, but when we're holding on to one another, it's like a reboot, a reset of our combined strength. Magic takes hold when we're close and pierces through all the bullshit swirling around us.

I stay silent, giving him all that I can, sitting in his lap and holding him. Every so often, I run my hands up and down his back, letting him take what he needs from our connection.

"Baby, I'm so damned tired." His voice is muffled against the skin of my neck.

"I know. Come on." I squeeze his nape. "Tonight, we go to bed and just sleep, then we *sleep in* for once."

"Are you saying I can't perform my manly duties of pleasing my woman?" He pulls his head out of the crook of my neck and pouts.

I kiss his pout and pull back. "Never said that. Wouldn't dream of saying that because you do, and you do so *often*. Tonight, however, it's my turn to see to you, and sometimes that means no hanky-panky."

He looks at me with a blank expression. "Seeing to me would definitely mean hanky-panky," he states with absolute seriousness.

I grin, push off his lap, and strip out of my pants so that I'm standing in a pair of lace-and-cotton bikini briefs. He watches me, but his eyes don't heat as they usually do. I reach up under my shirt from behind and unclip my bra before finding the loop under my tank and tugging my arm through the slip of fabric. I repeat the process on the other side, all without removing my top. The last maneuver, I pull the entire bra through the armhole and toss it on top of my pants on the floor.

Parker's eyes sparkle with interest at that move. "Baby, that was the coolest thing I've ever seen." Though there's a smile on his face, I can tell his heart isn't in it.

I chuckle and move around the bed and pull back my side of the covers. "If that's the coolest thing you've ever seen, you're a lot more wiped than I thought."

He groans and falls back into the bed. Once he gets settled, I cuddle up to his side, hook my leg over his hips, slip an arm over his abdomen, and lay my face on his shoulder and peck it. "Go to sleep. Tomorrow's a new day. We'll figure it all out then."

Parker yawns. "I'll do whatever it takes to keep you safe, Sky."

I kiss his chest and settle back in. "I know you will, honey."

"Whatever it takes," he whispers softly as his body goes lax and he slips off into dreamland.

I allow his body heat to warm my chilled skin as I murmur softly against his form, "I can't lose you either. I won't."

8

PARKER

Skyler and I slept in until ten in the morning and used the rest of the late morning and early afternoon to make love, reconnecting physically, emotionally, and by all things holy, spiritually. Today, Skyler and my love for her are my religion. I want to worship at her altar as often as possible.

While we made love and lay in bed, we spoke in whispers about our new home together, what we're going to do once we move in. How she wants to go with painting the inside in comforting shades of blue, beige, cream, yellow, and white, while I spoke of building her a flower garden in the backyard, plus a horseshoe pit and cornhole setup for the guys to screw around with while drinking the latest brewskis my dad has found.

I expressed how I want to choose the porch furnishings because I fully plan on spending my evenings sitting outside next to her, looking over our land and the view beyond the house while relaxing after a long day on the job. I joked that I want her to buy a full month's worth of bikinis so that during the summer I can have the grand pleasure of unwrapping a naked Skyler in new packaging every day. She laughed her head off but agreed to have her personal shopper get right on it.

Overall the morning and early afternoon were needed, the time together paramount to getting us back on an even keel. Now, we're walking our dogs through the famous Casa de Campo park, having left our woes in the background. Today is about us.

"Did you know this park is five times bigger than Central Park?" I tell her, repeating what I'd learned in my research prior to coming to Spain. I'd hoped we would have a day of fun, and I planned ahead. I even have a surprise for her this evening, one I know she'll love.

She scans the endless number of trees, the lake, the old royal buildings in the background, and inhales long and deep. "It's incredible, being here in the sunshine, holding your hand, walking our babies. I don't think I've ever been this relaxed."

"Especially considering what's been going on," I mumble, but regret it instantly when her lips move into a grim expression and she squeezes my hand. "Sorry, Peaches. Didn't mean to bring it up."

She runs her hand through her long golden tresses. "No, it's okay. We have to be able to talk about it. This is going to seem like a speck in time many years down the road. Instead, let's focus on the fact that we're in Madrid, enjoying the most beautiful park in the world, and not one person has recognized us." She smiles beautifully.

"Got any wood I can knock on?" I joke.

Skyler looks down at my pants. "Not right now, but I'm sure we could rustle up something in a pinch." She winks sexily.

I tilt my head back and laugh heartily. The pressure in my chest eases a little bit more with every step and with every minute I'm with her like this. I hook my arm around her shoulders, and she lifts her chin. I take the advantage and place a slow kiss to her lips, just enjoying her taste and scent, and how it feels to have this woman in my arms, knowing she's all mine.

"I don't think I'll ever get enough of you," I whisper against her smiling mouth.

"Well, I should hope not since you're stuck with me, mister!" she teases, poking at my gut playfully.

We continue our walk until we come to a section of the lake where other tourists are getting into small white-and-red rowboats and pushing off onto the lake. I tug on Sky's hand and steer us in that direction.

Sky skip walks, a huge smile on her face, likely figuring out my plan. My girl is always down for any adventure.

"No. Not a good idea." I hear Nate's rumbling voice from behind us.

Shit. I'd forgotten they were here. A testament to how well they do their job of guarding Skyler without being intrusive.

I stop to turn around and have a chat with the big guy. Rachel is standing a few feet away from Skyler, a smile on her face as she scans the environment. She has a pair of pitch-black aviators in place, hair pulled back in a complicated twist of braids. For the first time, I notice on the side next to her temple she has a portion of hair that's shaved away in a series of razor-sharp lines, making her look edgy and badass at the same time.

"Nate, look, man, we're fine." I glance around the area. "Have you suspected a threat of any kind?"

His lips compress into a flat line. "No, but that doesn't give us the excuse to be lackadaisical. We need to be aware at all times."

"Fine, then you rent a boat and paddle near us, but I'm taking my girl and our dogs on a boat ride. Sky worships the sun, and she needs a little break from it all. That's what today is all about: taking a break from it all. Everything. And sorry, man, but if we hadn't gotten that note yesterday, I would tell you to take a hike because I've got my girl covered. Since I'm a man who loves his woman more than his own life, I'm going to appreciate your presence at all times, but she needs . . . hell, *we* need to be able to do some things on our own, or at the very least, feel as though we are. You get me?"

Nate's jaw tightens so much I can see the veins in his neck bulge a little. "Fine. Carry on. We'll stay close and unobtrusive."

"Much obliged." I place my hand on his shoulder and squeeze, hopefully expressing my deep appreciation for the position he's in. I understand that he has a job to do and it's got to feel uncomfortable at times.

Once I turn around, Sky is practically bouncing in her Converses. She's wearing a pair of tiny black shorts, a light-blue tank, and her hair is flowing in those beachy waves I can't stop running my fingers through. She looks adorable . . . no, *edible* with her long tan legs on display.

"Do we get to go?" She gestures at the boats.

I nod.

"Yay! I haven't been in a rowboat in forever."

We maneuver through the throngs of people, Nate and Rachel following a few paces behind us.

Once I've seen a man about a boat, or two since I rented one for Rachel and Nate to follow us out on, I take Skyler's hand and lead her onto the boat and get her and the pups settled. Sunny is pressed up against Sky's leg, looking very uncertain, whereas Midnight looks like he's about to go on an adventure. He has his tan doggy paws up on one of the wooden boards in the center and is looking out the front of the boat as if he's going to lead the way.

I get into the boat, and the guy pushes us off. I take the paddle and set about bringing my girl and dogs out into the sunshine.

We clear the trees and get out into the open water. Skyler hikes up the bottom half of her shirt to just under her breasts so that her entire midriff is on display, and she opens her tiny shorts and tucks the two corners inside so that her top and shorts become a modified bikini.

I've fucked her three times already today, and if we weren't out in the open, I'd be making a move on her again. When it comes to Skyler, I'm insatiable. She just does it for me. In a big way.

Taking a page out of her book, I settle the paddles in their rings, reach behind my head, and tug off my T-shirt, allowing the sun to kiss my bare chest and back.

Skyler grins behind her Ray-Bans, pulls out her phone from her back pocket, aims it at me when I've got both hands on the paddles, the sun shining down on my bare skin, and captures a picture.

"Honey, you are so fucking hot. If we were alone, I'd jump you right here."

I chuckle, loving the fact that her mind is in the gutter as much as mine is.

"My view is as stellar as it comes." I grin, taking in all that is my beautiful woman.

She smiles, tips her head back, and lets the sun beat down on her body. Sunny settles into a circle near her feet and closes her eyes. Midnight sits quietly and watches the fish in the lake. I'm wondering if he's going to jump in and try to get them. Since we haven't water tested the dogs, I know I'll be taking a dive into the drink if he gets a wild hair.

I pet his soft fur. "That's a good boy. Stay in the boat, buddy."

He looks at me and licks my hand. Sky giggles, eases back, and lets one of her arms dangle over the side of the boat, her hand trailing in the cool water. "This is heaven, honey."

The sun is shining, my pups are behaving, and the water is lapping musically, adding to the serenity we're feeling. My woman's body is on golden display, and I'm working my arms with a beautiful park in the background and a breeze tickling my chest. "Too true."

***

"Tell me what it is we're doing?" Skyler begs for the millionth time tonight.

I shake my head but loop my arm around her waist as we walk the Gran Vía starting at Calle de Alcalá in the downtown area. Rachel and

Nate are following at a much closer distance since this street is busy. And when I say busy, I mean it rivals Madison Square and Broadway in New York City. It's considered an upscale shopping district in the heart of Madrid. "This is known as the street that never sleeps."

"Like Vegas," Sky adds, her eyes alight with wonder as she takes in what the nightlife has to offer.

"Exactly. We have about a twenty- to twenty-five-minute walk. Are you going to be okay in those shoes?" I look down at the chunky wedges she's paired with a flowing little summer dress. *Little* being the operative word. My woman has a delectable body and is not afraid to show a little skin . . . thank God.

"Absolutely. Babe, wedges are like cheating sexy. Most of them have the illusion of height because the entire bottom of the shoe is raised up. However, the actual arch in my foot is only about an inch or two. I could run in these if pressed. Walking is fine."

"Good." I nuzzle her neck where her peaches-and-cream scent is the strongest and give her a few hot kisses there.

She giggles and holds my waist tighter. "What does Gran Vía mean anyway?"

"The great way."

"I wonder what that building is?" She points to a brilliant white one on the opposite corner with the word "Metropolis" in white against a black square background on the front.

"As the sign says, it's the Metropolis building. Built over a hundred years ago, in 1911."

"I love the gold embellishments and the angel statue on top."

I focus on the angel statue. "Actually, that wasn't the original statue that was on top of that building."

She stops where she's standing and stares at the angel, its wings stretched delicately out into the horizon.

"Really?"

I nod. "Really. The first owners had another statue there depicting a phoenix and Ganymede, a Greek hero. They liked it so much they took it with them when they sold the building to Metropolis Seguros."

"Wow, that's interesting. So, the new owner put another statue up. Why?" Her lips tip into a cute little frown as she studies the building and the statue above.

I shrug. "Something about the other statue being so much a part of the history and skyline that they didn't want to leave it empty, so they put something else in its place."

"Cool. Though I think I like the idea of the angel better anyway. A phoenix rising from the ashes with a Greek hero can seem almost foreboding. You know? A struggle, something to fight in the first place. Whereas, to me, an angel represents hope and God's love."

We continue walking as I think about her words. "You've never struck me as being very religious."

She lifts her shoulder and drops it. "I would consider myself more a spiritual person than a religious one. I definitely believe there is a higher power, a God above watching over us. If I didn't, then I wouldn't believe that my parents are watching over me now."

"You rarely talk about them."

She bites down on her lip and swings her arms. "It's still hard. It's been years, but I'm getting to the point where I can think about them now without grief overwhelming me."

"What happened? You said there was a storm and some type of accident?"

"Yeah, I know I told you that the boat capsized in a storm, but that's not technically the truth. It's what I say on autopilot because the truth is much worse."

"How so?" I frown and focus on her pinched, pained expression.

She swallows slowly and runs her fingers along the fabric of her dress. "Because the truth is, their boat blew up."

"Uh . . . I'm sorry, honey. *Blew up?* Like kaboom type of blew up?" Images of a James Bond–type explosion scenario are running through my mind.

She nods. "That's what the report says. Because it sank, they were only able to glean so much, but I paid for divers to get all that they could of the boat, to make sure there wasn't anything left to find. They did find some remains of both my parents, which made it possible to declare them deceased officially. Still the entire thing was fishy. One report said they believed there must have been an explosive device on the boat. Another report said it could have been a mixture of chemicals or fumes leaking in the engine compartment along with a gas overflow. The authorities focused on the second explanation since there was no motive to hurt my parents or the captain and crew. They didn't even make it to their first destination. They got about fifty miles out, and that was it."

"Jesus." I bring her close again and rub her bicep. "Where were you?"

"With Tracey, having drinks at the harbor. Before they left, my mom and I were talking with Tracey and Dad about the fact that I wanted to slow down. It was a common conversation. As my manager at the time, Mom agreed with me. She only ever wanted the best for me. Dad thought I should do whatever I wanted but agreed with Tracey that it would be a waste of my talents to sit back when I was hitting the top. Still, he just wanted me happy too." She laughs dryly.

"Tracey had taken over as my agent a couple of years before. She'd always been good at it, and I liked knowing I had my best friend in my corner, making the deals on my behalf. Over time, Mom wasn't so keen. Told me repeatedly to consider a new agent, one who wasn't so vested in dollars signs but on the roles I wanted to play. But Mom didn't understand Tracey's drive."

"She is definitely a go-getter," I agree.

"Still, a week before they left, Mom and I had a conversation. She begged me to cut ties on a professional level with Tracey and focus on what I wanted. She knew I'd always envisioned myself settling down, finding a good man, creating a family, and living happy. Acting was my job, my craft, and you know I love it . . ."

"Yes, but I've noticed lately your interests are changing." I give her a squeeze of encouragement.

Sky nods. "Because I have something more to live for than the next role. I have you, our new home, the puppies, all our friends . . ." She shrugs. "There's more to life than pretending to be something I'm not. Acting used to be fun, and I know doing this *A-Lister* series with Geneva will be a blast. It will be an ideal finish or, at the very least, a good place to start slowing down. I mean, you're going to be thirty next month. I'm going to be twenty-six a month after. I want to focus on us. Settling down, having kids . . ." She lets that comment just fall off as we continue to walk.

"You want children soon?" I ask, yanking at the top button on my blue dress shirt to give myself a little more room to breathe.

"Yeah, if, you know, things stay the way they are with us, I can see it happening sooner rather than later. I mean, if that's what you want." She nudges my side playfully, easing the gravity of the conversation we're having.

I mull over the idea of marriage and kids. Lately it's been on my mind a lot more, especially with us buying our home, taking that big step. It's only natural to consider the ones after it. "You're right. I'm not getting any younger, and I've always wanted a family. I think us setting up our home is going down the right track. You?"

The corresponding smile she has at my comment is blinding. "Totally agree."

I press a kiss to her temple and keep her moving forward. We have reservations that I don't want to be late for. "One step at a time?" I whisper.

She nods happily. "One step at a time. Now . . . are you going to tell me where we're going or what?"

"No, I'm not." I stop on the sidewalk in front of two large dark wooden doors. "Because we're here."

Skyler gazes at the building and reads the sign. "Cardamomo Tablao Flamenco." Her eyes widen, and an all-white, bright smile stares back at me. "Flamenco dancing!"

"Yep!" I grin. "The only flamenco place recommended by the *New York Times* apparently. It's private, hard to get in, and supposed to be quite the show. We're having dinner here first, and then we've got front-row tickets to the private show."

"This. Is. Awesome!" She screeches in awe, wraps her arms around my neck, and kisses me hard before pulling back and continuing to burst out, "I'm so excited!"

"Come on, Peaches." I hold open the door for her to enter before me.

We're greeted by the hostess, where I give my name and explicit reservation for us to be right up front and the table behind us to be given to Nate and Rachel. She leads us through the throngs of people and into a long rectangular room. Everything in the room is a wild flourish of colors. The circular tables on the ground level are quaint and private. Then a few tables back, the room rises, and there are lines of red booths giving the restaurant goers an unencumbered view, but nothing like the front row. My girl can touch the stage where the performance will be held.

The restaurant fills up as we place our order for the four-course meal. The starter course is an Iberian ham served with toast and tomatoes, reminding me of bruschetta with meat. Sky shimmies in her chair as she enjoys the mixture. Right as we're completing the starter, the waiter delivers what they consider the first course, which is a variety of palate-impressing cheeses and toasted breads.

"One thing I've found in my European travels, they do not mess around when it comes to their breads and cheeses. I don't know what it is. It's like the stuff comes straight from the cheese mill and bakery." Skyler pops a chunk of white cheese into her mouth, then proceeds to lick her fingers. "So good!" She hums, and the sound goes right to my dick, making him take notice.

"I couldn't agree more. My guess is that they probably pick up the bread daily from a local bakery and weekly on the cheese."

She nods, slathers another piece of toast, and holds it up to me. I lean forward, make eye contact, and take a fierce bite. Her pupils dilate, and she licks her lips.

I chew for a few moments and swallow as she watches the movement in my neck. I lift my hand and trace the side of her face down to her jaw with one finger. "You're thinking about fucking me right now." My voice is hoarse, my thoughts going to exactly the same thing.

"Oh yeah. I don't know what it is, honey. Maybe it's just having alone time . . . finally . . . but I'm . . ."—she fans her face—". . . just . . . hot for you."

I grin, leaning over the table, and she does the same until our lips meet in a much more chaste kiss than I'd prefer. "Good. Eat up."

She bites her lip, and I have to grit my teeth to prevent the beast from coming to life. I adjust my cock so that he's got a little more space and take a few deep breaths and a long chug of my ice water, attempting to cool my jets. The last thing I want to do is sit through an entire show with a hard-on.

We pick our second course, which if you include the start is technically the third course, and it arrives shortly after we finish the cheese and toast. I went with the Iberian pork fillet in a black garlic sauce, and she went with the cod confit with salad and roasted peppers.

Every few seconds, Skyler moans around another bite of her fish, which does absolutely nothing for my repeated attempts to keep the beast in check.

Once we've finished eating, I order us some Spanish red wine the waiter recommended to have with our dessert. Skyler scoots her chair closer to mine as men start to line the sides and back of the stage. Four men have acoustic guitars, and another guy is holding what looks like a box of some sort. Another places a few mics where he and two other people sit down, keeping the mics at seat level. The lights dim, and everyone focuses on the stage. It darkens for a moment as a woman dressed from shoulder to ankle in gold-and-green lace appears in the center. The bottom half of her dress has at least ten rows of ruffles. She's holding a bright-red shawl with heaps of fringe dangling from the edge. Her dark hair is slicked back into a tight bun at the nape, where a huge white flower, larger than the bun, is nestled. Her face is focused with a fierce expression, her lips stained a cherry red.

"She's so beautiful." Skyler cuddles at my side, and I put an arm around her chair.

"Yes, she is." However, on her feet are the most hideous pair of black chunky heels I've ever seen.

The acoustic guitar plays out a beat while the woman's body gyrates in a fluid movement, her hands curving in, out, and up along with the melody. The voice of one of the men comes into the song, and the music starts to get louder. As the volume of the music rises, the woman moves faster until she starts to stomp those ugly shoes in a manner that's so kinetic I can feel the thunder in my chest every time her heels make contact with the stage.

Skyler's body heaves along with the music, her shoulders moving from side to side, and her face has a dreamy quality as she watches the woman dance.

The tempo picks up and the volume increases. The entire space fills with the vibrating beat that pounds inside my heart right down into my gut. I feel the music seeping deep, becoming a part of me.

As the music feeds the room with an electric, sensual energy, I lean over to Sky and press my lips against her ear. "It is said that flamenco breathes life, passion, and raw emotion through the skin." I trace her ear with my lips, run my nose down the column of her neck, and press a kiss to her nape. She shivers and sighs at the contact.

The woman on stage pulls the shawl from around her neck and flutters it widely in the air as she spins in a complex series of circles, stomping, and arm movements. Her body flows with the movement in a languid upper-body display, whereas the bottom half is juxtaposed in harsh, hammering jabs to the floor. There's a fiery, almost menacing twist of her lips as she moves like she wants to exorcise the demons floating around her to let the vivaciousness of passion, love, and sex take their place.

I place my hand on Skyler's thigh, teasing underneath the loose fabric of her dress until I secretly slip high enough to trace the lace of her panties. I encounter her arousal coating the flimsy fabric. I trace her slit with an exploring finger.

"Parker . . ." She speaks so softly I can barely hear it over the music; then she opens her legs. It's a silent invitation to touch the heart of her, right here.

I cup her entire sex, grinding the palm of my hand down on her clit until her body goes rigid in shock at the intense, bold move.

Making sure to block out the audience behind us, including Rach and Nate, I curve over my girl's body and whisper in her ear, "Let's go to the restroom."

"Together . . . ," she says breathily.

"Fuck yes," I growl, and nip at her ear.

I remove my hand stealthily and use my white sport coat to cover my very large erection from view. When I stand, both Rachel and Nate stand up.

I hold out my hand in a "stop" gesture. "Just taking her to the restroom. Stay here; we'll be right back."

Nate narrows his gaze while Rachel grins wickedly. That woman sees too much.

"We can follow . . . ," Nate attempts, but I shake my head.

Skyler does the same. "Park's got me. Be back."

I usher her through the crowd, the music thumping a heavy beat in my heart right along to the throbbing in my dick.

Once we make it to where the bathrooms are, I see a door that says "*Salida*," which I know translates to "exit" in English. At the back of the hall, I tug Skyler away from the ladies' room and to the door out back. When I open it, there's a tiny courtyard. In the left-hand corner there's a section of lattice protruding out, almost as if the owner had an inkling that people would get so swept away in their show that the passion would consume them and they'd need a place to relieve that intense feeling.

I note a small rock, which I wedge into the door to make sure it stays open enough that we can go back in. Then I scout the space behind the lattice about ten feet from the door and find just what I'm looking for. It's a smoking section. There's a single wrought iron chair with a canister on the ground filled with cigarette butts. I go over to the chair, and Sky follows, standing a few feet from me, her chest heaving, pupils dilated, and her lips so soft and moist looking, I want to bite them until she screams. Instead, I undo my belt, button, and zipper and pull out my cock. It stands straight up at attention, practically reaching my belly button. Then I sit down, push my pants to my ankles, and point to my cock.

"Sit on it. Now," I grate through my teeth, no longer capable of anything but having her tight, wet heat surrounding me and pounding out this need inside.

She licks her lips, tucks her hands under her dress, and pulls down a tiny scrap of lace, which is a poor excuse for a pair of panties.

I hold out my hand. "Give them to me." I lift them to my face and inhale her musk. It makes my head swim with desire, my mouth water, and my dick weep at the tip.

"Don't make me wait," I grit through clenched teeth.

9

SKYLER

I can't believe we're going to do this, right here, out in the open in a courtyard in Spain outside of a flamenco nightclub. It's so beyond hot, I'm not sure I can make my legs move the three feet needed to get what I want.

Parker doesn't have the same problem, though. He attacks like a python, his movements coiled and tight as he tucks my underwear into his coat pocket, leans forward, captures my hand, and tugs me over his lap. I straddle his muscular thighs and place my hand around his bulging erection like a handle.

"You're so hard, honey." I whimper a little as the walls of my sex contract at the phantom of a cock that's not yet there.

"You make me that way." His voice is strained, a barely contained animalistic sound leaking out the edges of his lips. "Every sigh. Every lick of your lips. Every sway of your shoulders tonight had me burning to be inside of you. I'm not waiting a moment longer." His voice has a ruthless quality while he lifts up my dress, centers at my slick cleft, grabs my hips, and impales me on his length.

"Fuck!" I tip my head back at the intense sensation of taking him in one hard, huge plunge. Everything about it is so raw and unplanned.

Two bodies striving for one another without fear or insecurities. Just our primal, carnal natures oozing out every pore, reaching for the other.

Parker pushes down the front of my dress, his fingers abrading across an erect tip as he forcefully pulls the lace cup of my bra aside, cups my round, swollen breast, and encases it within the heat of his hand.

Liquid fire burns me everywhere. My chest. Between my thighs. Where his mouth is rhythmically sucking at my breast. And it's so good, I can hardly breathe.

"Ride me," he snarls around my breast, biting down until I cry out.

I'm so gone, I get lost in his words, doing exactly as he says. With the power in my legs, and the leverage I've got on his shoulders, I ride him fast and hard, up and down, squeezing his length on every withdrawal, hammering down on each plunge. It's everything and more.

"Hurry, baby. Anyone can come out here and find us," he taunts, and I'm not sure if he does it to scare me or turn me on more. It definitely has the latter effect, my synapses firing all over the place with pleasure.

His cock feels like a velvet-encased pipe, hard and unyielding and soft at the same time. He's powering up as I come down, hitting a spot deep inside me over and over again until I'm chanting, "I'm gonna come, I'm gonna come, I'm gonna come," and then . . . I do.

Spectacularly.

Parker's entire body locks around me, his arms flattening me to his chest, his grip on my shoulders holding me pinned on his cock like a butterfly to a collector's board. "Fuck!" he roars into my neck, biting down on the sensitive tissue so hard my body convulses into another miniorgasm. He licks the space and places soothing kisses there, bringing us both down from the height of bliss. His body jerks in a series of aftershocks, like those after an earthquake, which creates the blessed, amazing sensation of his dick flexing deep inside me.

I run my lips up his neck in a sequence of sweet kisses and sigh into the warmth of his succulent skin as my lips glide along its surface. He does the same using the flat of his tongue, bathing me in his own way. When our mouths finally, expertly touch, we're ravenous, going at one another fervently, kissing deeply, tongues tangling while our arms hold one another tight.

Until the serenity is broken by the back door swinging open, slamming against the brick facade on the other side of it. Through the space in the lattice, I see a large shape and a shiny black gun pointed out in front of the stranger.

I lock my arms around Parker, but it's too late for me to speak or warn him. The dark, shadowy figure moves fast, his bulky frame blocking the small bit of light from in front of us about a good six feet away. I yelp in fear, squeezing Parker like my life depends on it, wanting to make sure that I cover every inch of him with my own body so that he is unharmed.

"Aw, fucking hell! Should have known," a familiar, irritated voice says as the gun disappears from sight and the hulking form walks away.

"What? What is it?" a female voice asks, appearing behind the lattice, her platinum-blonde hair glinting in the low light. "Well, then, mystery solved. See you in the hallway," Rachel announces, barely containing the laughter in her tone. Before she's fully past the lattice, she pokes her head back around. "Nice knees, Parker," she snorts, and then bounds off after her husband.

"Um, honey, did that just happen?" I try to clear the sex haze and fear but fail miserably, my body shaking with the leftover anxiety of seeing a gun right after I had a monster orgasm.

"Yeah, Peaches, Nate and Rachel just caught us postfucking with my pants around my ankles. Second, don't you ever cover my body with your own if you see a threat. You get *behind* me. Always," he chastises in that manly voice that brooks no argument.

I figure to even say anything would have me in a snit with my man, and really, the situation is beyond hilarious. The visual and being caught all starts to hit me, and my body starts to jerk in Parker's lap as the laughter bubbles up out of my lungs and chest. "At least it was them and not the—"

Right as I say it, a bunch of flashes go off from over the fence across from us.

"Shit! Nate!" Parker bellows, and I hear the door to the courtyard fly open as Parker presses up my dress to cover my breasts. "Fence. Paps," Parker calls out.

Nate jumps up onto a crate and hovers over the fence, screaming a bunch of expletives. "Get the fuck out of here. Nothing to see," Nate demands, his arms waving wildly.

While Nate is shooing the two paparazzi away, Parker lifts me off his now softening cock, hikes up his pants, and secures button and zipper before latching his loose belt.

I squeeze my legs together, wishing I had something to use before his essence slides down and out of me in an embarrassing display of our recent sexual activities.

"Rach, can you, uh, take me to the bathroom?" I ask quietly, not wanting Nate or Parker to hear.

Rachel nods silently but doesn't say anything. I know the two of them are unhappy that we put ourselves at risk again, but compromising pictures be damned—I'd never give up that experience with Parker in a million years. It's one of the first times we let loose and were just a silly, lovesick couple getting frisky at a nightclub. I just hope he feels the same way about it. Especially when we see a picture of us snuggling, me in his lap with his pants down around his ankles. At least my dress covered the essentials so there won't be a picture of my bare ass in the papers tomorrow. Though, I know with a sinking heart, the media is going to have a field day with this one.

On second thought . . .

Fuck 'em.

***

The next day, Parker was more dispirited than ever before. His mood deteriorated to surly over coffee when he opened his email and was notified of the hundreds of mentions of his name on every celebrity rag from here to kingdom come. This did not get any better when we showed up at the practice stage to find Bo grinning from ear to ear.

"Quiet day out with my woman sightseeing, he said." Bo grins wickedly.

"Bo . . . ," Parker warns.

"A leisurely stroll through Madrid's nightlife scene, he said." Bo continues his approach, a rolled-up newspaper in his hand.

"I swear to God . . . ," Parker practically spits through clenched teeth.

Behind Bo, Juliet and Violeta giggle like schoolgirls crushing on the high school heartthrob.

"A romantic dinner for two, he said."

"Do. Not. Go. There," Parker growls.

"And what do I find splashed across the front page of *El Mundo* this morning, not that I can read a lick of it . . ." He makes a spectacle of unrolling the newspaper and showing us the front page image, which just so happens to be Parker's face and mine looking over our shoulders, one of his hands wrapped up the length of my back, the other barely covering my bare ass. A little bit of cheek is proving exactly what we're doing, not to mention his bare knees, exposed legs, and pants around his ankles.

"Which doesn't really matter, since the picture is worth a thousand words." He grins like the devil who just got a brand-new, shiny broken soul to play with in his dungeon. "You dirty dog. Banging Skyler out in public, getting caught by the paparazzi." He tucks the paper under his arm and claps dramatically. "Bravo. You win the award for most scandalous sex display. Beats the Ferris wheel story by a long shot."

Parker's body goes completely rigid, and I have to snuggle up to his side and run my hand down his chest in order to get his labored breathing back to a normal tempo.

"Ferris wheel?" I frown.

"You've gone too far, brother," Parker states with barely controlled ire.

Bo's face takes on the expression of one who has been properly chastised. He holds up his hand. "Okay, I admit that last one was bad form, but we're all friends here. Right?"

"I'll think about that," Parker says, his tone matching the surly mood he's in.

I spin him around and pat his chest. "Honey, look. It was bound to happen. We have a lot of sex. We're in love. We can't keep our hands off one another. Eventually the paparazzi were going to get something on us. At least it's not showing any pertinent body parts."

He speaks through his teeth. "Your ass is on display."

"Babe, it's a little speck of cheek that your hand is mostly covering. No one is seeing much of anything. You don't hear me complaining about all the sites that are giving praise to your attributes, do you?"

His eyebrows furrow together. "Da fuck you talkin' 'bout?"

I groan and roll my eyes. "Honey, there are endless sites dedicated to you. Your body. Your sexy hair. Double the hits if you haven't cut your hair in a while and there're some curls visible on top. I even saw one that 'proved' you had a big dick because your feet were so large."

He glances down at his size twelves. The theory is true, but I don't admit it because I'd rather not hear him complain about it. At least on the site they've got it narrowed down to him having a bigger appendage than Johan, which is also true, but secretly I love reading they've come to an accurate conclusion about my man's . . . well . . . manhood.

I run my hands over his shoulders and down his arms until our hands meet and I can interlace my fingers with his. "Nature of the business. There's always going to be someone that wants a piece of me. It's not your fault. One day, when I leave the limelight, it will fade, but now

. . . no way. It is what it is. The picture could have been worse. Besides, I'm fine with people knowing how much we love each other. So what if we show it in a very physical way . . ." I lean my chin against his chest and look up at his beautiful face as he gazes down at me.

He wraps my arms behind my back with his, dips down, and lays a fat kiss on me. Again, we hear a bunch of clicking, but this time, it's Juliet and Violeta and Bo taking the pics.

"Keep going. I'm not sure this image will make me enough to put my pretend children through college one day," Bo says while pushing buttons on his phone.

"Shut the fuck up!" Parker grins, coming out of his funk. "What do we got going today?"

Bo puts his phone in his back pocket and waves a hand in the air. Juliet takes her place in the center of about ten dancers. The stage is set up with brightly colored props that all look like candy.

"I've had an epiphany." Pete Flaco, the choreographer, comes out from behind a hot-pink prop that looks like a wrapped-up lollipop. "It came to me with Juliet's song, 'Your Love Is Like Candy.'"

I know which one he's talking about. The chorus says something like, "Your love is like candy, great tasting but bad for me."

"We've been practicing Juliet singing while walking through the men wrapped up in bright colors that mimic candy. There will be candy props and bright lights bouncing off all of them to create strokes of color. It will be divine. So good you'll want to eat it! Like how I want to eat you, *cariño* Bogart." Pete waggles his brows.

"For fuck's sake, man. I'm never, *not ever* going to go there. I'm straight. I like women. As a matter of fact, I love going down on them and eating their—"

I rush to Bo and cup my hand over his mouth before he can get any crasser than he already has.

Bo licks my hand, and I pull it away as if burned. "Eww! Nasty. You licked my hand." I cringe and wipe my hand on my pants.

He grins. "You put it over my mouth, precious. What did you expect?"

"Remember there are young girls present. Please." I sigh and shake my head.

He glances over to Violeta and JJ, whose cheeks have flushed a rosy pink. He makes a clucking noise and winks at them.

"Oh, for the love—" I walk over to Pete. "What else do you have planned?"

For the next thirty minutes, we discuss the first few songs and the choreography or lack thereof for JJ, but still, it all works. Really well.

"Let's give it a run-through. Sky, Bo, Violeta, let's go down and sit in the audience so we can see it play out. JJ,"—Parker grabs a microphone from the stack at the side of the stage—"I need you to sing the songs along with your music. Remember, it's just the four of us watching. Nothing crazy. Do you think you can do that?"

JJ purses her lips, looks at the floor, and fingers the mic. "Yeah, I think I can do it. Violeta and I have been practicing at home. Our parents are going to come and watch the end of practice today once they get off work. They're so excited." She wrings the mic as if she can twist it into nothing.

I place my hand on her shoulder. "You know you're talented right? You believe in it?"

She licks her lips, straightens her spine, and nods. "*Sí. Mi mami* told me it would be a disservice to hide my gift from the world. She thinks this is my chance to shine, and I really want to make her, Vi, you, Parker, Bo, Alejandro, and the rest of the music people proud." A look of excitement flashes across her hazel gaze. "I can do it," she says with more confidence than I've heard all week.

I smile wide. "Yes, you can. We'll be right down there. And just remember, if you get off tune, or lose your place, just pause, *breathe*, and jump back in when you can. This is not an exact science. Eventually it will become second nature, but right now it's all new, so take it easy and have fun with it, okay?"

She beams, her high ponytail swaying with her acquiescence. She's wearing a pair of ripped-up skinny jeans, a pair of suede ankle boots, and an oversize T-shirt that hangs off one shoulder, showing a neon tank underneath. The shirt is tied in a knot at her back. It's like the eighties called and delivered her clothes, but on her at this age, it works, big-time. Besides, all trends come back around, and Spain is known for being the first to bring a fashion trend back in a new way and with a flourish. JJ is definitely going to rock this new look and more. She looks happy and finally at peace with her curves and her appearance.

Parker holds out his hand for me as he stands at the side of the stage where the staircase is. I walk down and take a seat next to Violeta, grab her hand, and hold it tight.

"I'm so nervous," she whispers, but smiles huge and hollers out a "Woo-hoo!" to her sister as JJ gets into position between some hunky backup dancers.

The music starts up, and JJ smiles into the black abyss of the theater and belts out the beginning notes to "Your Love Is Like Candy." The song carries on, and though she misses a few steps, loses her breath in a couple of places, she does the best we've ever seen her do. She's brilliant up there and so effervescent I know she's going to take the music world by storm.

The song goes into the next tune, and she keeps it up. Parker nudges my shoulder, and I look up at him as he says, "You did that. Gave her the courage and confidence."

I grab his hand. He lifts both of ours, brings mine to his lips, and kisses each fingertip.

"We all did it," I respond, "but mostly, Juliet did it for herself."

***

The second we walk out of the theater, my phone buzzes, and I look down and see Tracey calling for the twentieth time today. I know I can't hold her off any longer. If I do, she'll end up getting on a plane and showing up here. She's not one to be pushed back.

"Yo!" I say into the line.

"What the fuck were you thinking?" she screeches so loud I have to hold the phone back from my ear.

Parker sees the move, and his face hardens.

"Hello to you too, Tracey. How are you this evening? Lovely, I hope," I state blandly, trying to get her to realize her yelling at me is not going to work.

I wait a full five seconds, hearing nothing in my ear but Tracey's angry breathing.

"I'm sorry, Birdie. I've been trying to get ahold of you all day. After that little stunt you pulled in Spain last night, I figured you would have called me, giving me a heads-up so that *I*, your *agent* who runs your publicity team, could get on top of this scandal before the shit hit the fan. Since that did not happen, our office has been fielding calls every twenty minutes from another news source wanting an official statement."

"They're not going to get one." I tug on a lock of my hair and roll it around my finger nervously.

"Excuse me? I'm not sure I heard you right, Sky. We have to say something."

"No," I state flatly. "We don't. Parker and I got a little crazy after some good food, great wine, and even better flamenco dancing, and things got out of hand. I'm definitely not sorry, though I did call the restaurant, speak to the owner, and apologize for our indiscretion outside on his premises."

"You what?" she screeches again, and once more, I hold the phone away so that she doesn't burst an eardrum.

"Yeah, I did. It was the right thing to do. Turns out he didn't care. And the fact that I was seen outside of his establishment—and pictures of me were posted from other patrons who were inside his establishment—meant that everyone and their brother has now bought tickets to the show, and the place is booked out solid for the next six months. He thanked me and offered me a free dinner, drinks, and show any time I happen to be in Madrid again. So . . . no harm, no foul."

Parker puts his arm around me and mouths, "Everything okay?"

I roll my eyes and mouth, "Tracey," back at him.

His jaw tightens, but he doesn't say anything when he moves over to chat up Bo. The girls are waiting patiently to go have our celebratory dinner after such a successful practice.

"I cannot believe you got caught doing that. It's so inappropriate . . ." Tracey continues to bitch. "Another mess of yours I have to clean up." Blah, blah, blah.

"Well, Trace, good thing you get *paid* the big bucks. Now I have to go celebrate with a young woman who rocked the house tonight." I say this loud enough for JJ to hear me.

She beams with joy and pride, looking more beautiful with this smiling face than she ever has before.

"Skyler, you need to come home. Deal with this shit storm, and we need to talk. Things were said between us . . . And, Birdie, we never fight. We love each other. We're sisters. Family. This tension is unhealthy . . ."

The fire in my soul that has been raging for over a week since she told me she was behind helping Johan hurt himself and me in the process comes rushing back to the surface.

"No. I'll come home when we're done with this case and not a second before. I don't care that you're upset we left things the way we did. You. Hurt. Me. Trace! I didn't do shit to you. I'm still not sure how to comprehend what you did to Johan—and *me*, by proxy. It was beyond insane and downright cruel. You took a weak man and made him weaker, and all for what?"

"For you! I do it all for you! Everything I am. Everything I have. I do it to keep you happy. Strong. At the top of your game. Because I'm your one and only. I'm your family. Not Johan. Not Parker or any other man who tries to get between our friendship."

"Ugh, you sound like a lovesick fool. Do you hear yourself? Really, listen to what you're saying. We need a break from each other, Tracey. A big one. Personally, for sure. I'll decide later if I need to do something professionally as well. For now, do what you're paid to do. Take care of the problem. Tell the media we have *no comment*." I say the last part with uncontrolled fire igniting every word. "As a matter of fact . . . tell them Parker and I are *in love* and we got frisky after a few drinks and a great show. Whatever. I don't care! Just leave. Me. Alone!" I grind my teeth, smash the end button, and lift my arm to toss the phone across the street. The anger in my soul is so overwhelming I need to lash out.

Before I can, Parker bum-rushes me, hand to my wrist, and takes the phone, then holds down the off button until the screen goes black. "No more broken phones. Wendy would kill us. She's got tracking devices on these things, and they are not cheap."

"Wendy tracks me?" News to me.

He looks at me as if I've grown two heads. "Peaches . . . it's Wendy. Of course she tracks you. Do you love her?"

I look from side to side. "Well, yeah. She's more a friend than my own best friend now." I scowl.

"'Nuff said. If you love her, she loves you, claims you as her very own, which means you're tracked. And for sure, she's got a lot of other things in your life being tracked."

"Hmm. Should I be worried?"

"Does it weird you out?" He frowns.

I shrug. "Maybe a little."

"She'd laugh hearing you say that but then ignore you. It's just her way. If you're loved, you're part of our crew, you're monitored. I live with it and try my best to fuck with her head."

"Oooh, that sounds like fun. How do we do that?"

Parker presses me along the brick wall at my back, his warm length planted against mine from knees to chest. I can feel his breath caress my lips as he brings his face closer. "We can look up a sex shop and buy some toys, which she'll see when our credit cards ding on her monitoring device, but instead of keeping them, we can have some weird shit mailed to her instead. The whole time she'll think we're into some kinky stuff, when in reality, the stuff will land on her doorstep."

"Ooh, fun! Though I don't think sex stuff would wig her out." Not my BDSM-loving bestie. "We should hit a baby store and buy some random things. That would make her freak-o-meter flag fly like crazy."

"Smart. I like the way you think," he murmurs against my lips, and kisses me.

I forget all about Tracey and her drama llama, focusing instead on my man's silky lips, his cinnamon-gum-flavored tongue, and the heat of his body pressing against mine. Everything fades into nothing when I'm in his arms.

"You make me happy," I whisper.

He caresses my nose with his. "Ditto." He laces our fingers together and tugs me toward our group that is still waiting patiently, Bo included.

Bo probably heard me talking angrily with Tracey and chose to give his jokester nature a break. Which proves that Bo is tuned in to what's going on around him and knows how to cap it when he needs to. When I get close he interlaces his fingers with my other hand and bumps his side against mine as we walk down the street toward the place where Violeta made reservations for our celebratory dinner.

"You okay, Sky?" he asks, his chocolate gaze focused intently on me.

I smile and knock his body to the side in retaliation. "Perfect as a peach."

He nods, brings my hand up to his scruffy face, and kisses the back. "You know I'm here for you if you need to talk to someone other than my brother over there."

Parker ignores us both, but he can hear everything Bo is saying, mostly because Bo's not making it a secret even if he's speaking in hushed tones.

I squeeze Bo's hand in thanks. "I appreciate it. And I do know it."

"And if Parker needs backup, I'm happy to beat down any motherfucker at the snap of your pretty fingers. Even with two bodyguards, you've got more coverage. No one is getting to you here." He tightens his hold on my hand, lets it go, and taps my temples. "Or here. No way, nohow. Family first. Always."

Family first.

Always.

"I love you, Bo," I tell him, because I can't not after how he makes me feel included, part of a team, a real family by choice.

He grins wildly, grabs the side of my head, and kisses my temple. Then the shit talking commences. "Did you hear that, bro? Your girl loves me."

"Did you have to massage his ego like that? Did you?" Park groans, wraps an arm around me, and moves me to his opposite side, farther away from Bo. This has Bo laughing hard.

"That's right, move her far, far away. It won't matter. The love vibes are strong between us. I can feel them from a mile away, bro."

I chuckle as Park and Bo take potshots at each other for the next ten minutes. I just smile and laugh along the way, happy to be right where I am with my all-time-favorite man, his brother, my two friends keeping an eye out behind us, and two girls who are skipping all the way to the restaurant.

No matter what is printed about me in the paper or what Tracey has to say about my reputation . . . I don't care. Because in the end . . . life is good.

10

PARKER

I wake with a twinge of a hangover prodding at my temples and dryness in my throat that a gallon of water will not cure. Yesterday was a long-ass day working with Juliet and the team at the practice stage. After the practice, our little motley crew tied one on. Since the legal drinking age in Spain is a whopping sixteen years old, both Violeta and Juliet put our asses to shame in the liquor-consumption department. They drank all three of us—four if you count the Spanish chicklet Bo picked up somewhere between beers five and six for us guys and sangria for the women—under the table.

Thank heaven we filled up on chorizo, paella, and croquettes along with a bunch of other salami-type meats and a mixture of cheeses or I'd be worshiping the porcelain throne right about now. A headache I can suffer through, a sick stomach, not so much.

My phone buzzes loudly by my head, and the heavy arm wrapped around my waist slaps my belly twice and then stops. A few soft snores can be heard against my shoulder as Skyler falls instantly back to sleep. I ignore the phone, and eventually it stops, only to start back up again with its incessant buzzing.

The hand at my waist does the slap thing again, but has zero result before it stops, the puffs of air coming at my throat once more. I snuggle a naked, warm Skyler and kiss my way down her neck to her clavicle. She doesn't even move.

I chuckle as I open my eyes and look down at my girl. Her mascara is smudged around her eyes, and her hair is a tangled mess of twisted curls from repeated rounds of some pretty energetic lovemaking if I do say so myself. I drunkenly did her up against the hotel door, over the back of the couch, on the floor in the bedroom, and then finally on the bed. All of it messy, sloppy, and so good my teeth ache with the memory of planting my face between her thighs while my cock was in her mouth.

God, my woman is so fucking hot, I'm about to work hard at waking her up for another go when my phone buzzes again. Then it stops, and the hotel phone starts ringing.

Skyler gasps a breath of air, rolls over to her side, grabs my pillow, cuddles it against her chest, and then she's out like a light. In all fairness, I did keep her up half the night. She needs the rest. Besides, we have a meeting this afternoon with Alejandro to discuss where we're at with Juliet and her ability to be the next Spanish pop star.

The phone in the room rings again, and so does my cell. I glance at my cell and see it's Royce calling. I'll have to call him back because the blaring noise of the hotel phone is winning. I pick it up.

"What?" I gurgle into the line, my voice sounding like my throat has been abraded with a cheese grater.

"Finally! Parker, it's Wendy." Her tone is flummoxed, and my head is pounding with the volume of it in my ear.

I spy a bottle of water across the room, so I pick up the entire phone and drag it with me to the holy grail in the form of a Crystal Geyser bottle.

"What's up?" I open the bottle and glug over half of it down while she speaks.

"Did you get my email?" she says, obviously exasperated.

"Minxy, you just woke me up. Royce was calling on my phone, which added to it. Sky's still sleeping. We tied one on last night."

She huffs into the line, which is unlike the normally plucky Wendy. I'd expect a good razzing but not irritation. "Makes sense as to why I couldn't get ahold of Skyler or Bo. I knew you were all in your rooms, though Skyler's phone is turned off. You know I get wiggy when you guys turn your phones off."

I frown and sit down in the closest chair as the world around me wobbles and sways. "Wendy, get to the point. Why did you call?"

"Well, you know how I told you there was something bugging me about the fan letters?"

My head pounds, and I press my finger and thumb to my temples to combat the little man with the sledgehammer doing a number on my dome.

Christ. Where's the ibuprofen?

"Vaguely. I'm a little hungover, if I'm being honest."

"This information ought to wake you right up."

"Lay it on me."

"I recognized the handwriting." She says this as if it's so poignant I should be panting for more juicy gossip. Unfortunately my thoughts can barely catch the train she's on let alone keep up with it.

"Mm-hmm," I mumble, and suck back the rest of the water in the bottle and scan the room, wondering if there's a mini fridge somewhere. If one splurges on the penthouse, there's bound to be a stock of still water. Right? "Why is this important?" I keep my tired eyes peeled for what might be a mini fridge masquerading as a cabinet.

"Because I've seen the handwriting before. Go to your computer," she demands.

I sigh and run my hand down my bare chest and realize I'm standing completely naked while taking this call. "Wendy, I need to call you on my cell. Give me a minute to get dressed."

"Fuck getting dressed! This is important. I'll wait while you grab the fucking computer." She's cursing more than I've heard her do before. Her tone is definitely not one she's ever used with me. Then it dawns on me: She's *scared*. That little crack in her voice is *fear*, not exasperation.

"Okay, hold on." I set the phone down on the chair and move into the living room. I spy the mini fridge and take a detour to grab a couple of bottles of water, because it's the desert in my throat, and if I'm going to be expected to speak, I'll need to drench the dry, cracked surface accordingly. I grab my laptop off the desk and make my way into the master.

Once I get back to the bedroom, I set the bottles and laptop on the table and spy my boxer briefs on the floor and slip into them. I can't keep talking to my technical officer, onetime assistant, and someone I look at as a sister, in my birthday suit.

"I'm back," I say into the phone when I get the laptop settled on my thighs. I bring up my email and click on the message Wendy sent the team. I open the image and see one of Skyler's fan letters from the past side by side with a lined legal sheet. "What am I looking at?"

Wendy grunts, actually grunts like a fucking bear at my question. "Zoom in. I've underlined some of the same words found in the fan letter and the ones on the yellow sheet."

"Okay. I see it now." My eyes and brain are finally working together, though sluggishly, to pick up the similarities. "They're the same. Shit!" I rub at my tired eyes to try and clear the cobwebs of last night's beer and fuckfest. "Where did you get the yellow sheet?"

"Read the fucking note, Parker," she grates, completely exasperated.

From the top it reads:

Wendy,
I've cleaned Zeus's box, refreshed his litter, and made sure
he has enough food for the weekend. The cleaning team
will take out the trash tonight but has been warned not

to let the cat out of our offices for even a second or follow anyone onto the elevator. I'm sure he'll be fine. If you need me to come in on Saturday or Sunday to check on him, you should call me. I wouldn't want Parker or Skyler to feel stuck or worry while on their trip. That would be horrible. I'll pick up more food and litter this weekend, coffee pods, and Post-its while I'm out and submit a business expense reimbursement, if that's okay with you. I wish you a fun weekend. Let me know if you need me. I'm here for you. Thank you.

> *Your assistant,*
> *Annie*

I compare it with the letter Wendy put next to it.

Sky,
I miss you. It seems like forever since you were on the screen entertaining me. I read that you got hurt on set, which pushed production back. You should have called me. I would have been there for you every second, holding your hand, making you laugh, whatever it took to get you better. Instead I'm stuck here with the She-Devil, waiting on the queen hand and foot and taking business classes. She's so horrible. I wish I were with you. You'd make it better. We could take care of each other. Think about it. I'll always be here for you.

> *Your real BF*

"Holy fucking shit." My heart pounds sporadically in my chest, and my pits and hairline begin to sweat. "It's Annie . . ." I gulp, not believing what I'm seeing. I read the letter again and again, trying to unsee what is so very obvious.

"Mick has a friend who's a, uh, graphology expert, a graphologist. When I made the connection, I showed it to Mick. He sent it under the strictest confidence to the guy, who studied it and said within ninety-nine point nine percent accuracy, the two notes are from the same person. He noticed that the first one was many years old, but the new one had the same signature traits, words and letters that are easily unique to one person, much like the whorls and lines in a fingerprint. He also said there's no way this could have been a fake. It's the same person. It's Annie."

"My God. This whole time we've been stressing about who's sending those texts, notes, and letters, and it was *Annie*? Jesus, how fucking stupid could I be?"

"Park, it's not just you. She's fooled us all."

My mind goes right back to when the first note arrived. Wendy was out of the office healing from her gunshot wound when the envelope showed up. Annie was barely on the team at that point.

"Fuck!" I slam the lid on my laptop closed, stand, and toss it on the chair. The seething energy in my body is electric, looking for an outlet to let loose on.

At my outburst, Skyler wakes up, pushing herself to a half-seated position, her beautiful breasts and pink-tipped nipples on full display. Her hair is a golden messy halo in the late-morning light filtering in.

She's my *goddess*, and I let her down.

I run my hand through my hair and tug at the ends while Wendy speaks into my ear, talking about how Royce and Kendra have discussed it but need to find out from me, Sky, and Bo how we want to proceed.

"We need to confront her, but I want to do it in person, when we're home," I say with a conviction I haven't felt about anything other than Sky and my love for her in a long damn time.

"Honey . . . ," Skyler calls to me. Her worried, dreamy gaze narrows as she watches me pace the floor.

"It's okay, baby, I'll get you up to date in a minute," I promise, not liking what I'm going to have to tell her at all.

"Talk to Sky. I've also sent the documents to Nate and Rachel. They've already touched base but felt it would be less of a blow coming from me instead of them."

"Yeah, less of a blow. I can't fucking believe this. She was under our noses the whole goddamned time." I clench down on my molars and grind so hard I may crack a tooth.

"Go to Sky, tell her what's happened, and we'll reconvene. Until you get back, we can keep everything quiet, not let on that we know. Continue business as normal."

"Normal." I shake my head. "I don't think anything's normal about this situation at all. Later," I say flatly, and hang up the phone.

"Honey, what's wrong?" Skyler has the coverlet now clutched to her chest, her shoulders closing in on her ears in preparation of bad news. It's a protective pose that she shouldn't have to resort to at all.

I inhale a long, slow breath, willing my heartbeat and anger to dull to a simmer while I tell my girl the bad news.

"Turns out we know who was sending those fan letters to you throughout the years."

She frowns. "Who?"

"Annie."

This time her brows rise up into her hairline. "Annie Pinkerton. Your meek assistant, Annie?"

I clench my hand into a fist. "Yeah. She's been right there the whole time."

"How did Wendy figure it out?" she asks, not even a speck of anger in her tone, which surprises me because I'm ready to break anything and everything in this hotel room. Though I won't because it wouldn't even put a damper on the level of hatred I have swirling in my gut right now.

"Handwriting analysis. Mick has a friend. Wendy sent one of the letters along with an office memo Annie wrote to Wendy last week. It's a ninety-nine point nine percent match."

Skyler runs her finger along the quilting in the comforter. "Huh. I mean, I can't say that I'm shocked she sent those letters. She's always had a bit of a fascination when it came to me. I noticed it early on when she would come to work wearing something I'd worn on TV or was seen wearing in the celeb mags. It was more noticeable when she bought the same shoes I'd worn out with you and again when she adopted a golden retriever."

Her words are a bucket of boiling-hot water tossed over my head, burning from the outside in. "Fuck me! Why didn't you say anything?"

"Besides the fact that it was rather obvious?" She blinks and keeps her face set at an expression that's devoid of emotion, one I can't comprehend right now.

I tilt my head to the side and level her with invisible daggers. "Baby . . ."

She purses her lips and gazes out the window. "It's sweet. And honestly, a lot of it stopped after I started going to lunch with her and chatting her up about clothes and movies and such. She's kind of my friend now, honey." Sky plucks at her bottom lip. "I mean . . . I can totally see the letters, but the texts?" She shakes her head. "I don't know."

"You see what she wants you to see. We all have. This woman is not sane. She's a head case who's obviously smarter than we realized, because she's been able to keep this under wraps for years. Then she gets a job working in the same company as your boyfriend? There's no way that's a coincidence. She staged that shit. How? I don't know, but don't think for a minute that Wendy is not already digging deeply into Annie's background, financials, living situation, credit, everything there is."

Sky continues to worry her bottom lip, but she doesn't seem angry, when I feel like I'm going to explode.

"It's odd. I wouldn't think she'd have it in her to taunt us the way she has. Those texts . . ." Her face shifts into a grimace. "They're creepy."

"Her dressing like you, getting the same dog, working at your boyfriend's work to be close to you, keeping tabs on you for over a decade . . . *that's* fucking creepy!" I practically bellow because I'm having a whole helluva lot of trouble keeping my anger inside.

Skyler grabs my arm and runs her hands up and down the length in a soothing manner that does ease the tension . . . slightly. "I guess I just think imitation is the sincerest form of flattery, is it not? I mean she's never made a play for you, said or done anything to warrant your anger . . ."

My rage explodes.

"Are you fucking kidding?" I burst as I stand, no longer able to keep my cool. "She's been sending texts, rather threatening ones. Notes to the office that she *pretends* to deliver. That. Is. Twisted. Skyler. How can you not see that?"

She frowns and shrugs while picking at a thread in the comforter.

"It's obvious we're processing this in a different way," I say. "We need to get ready, meet with Alejandro, and finish this job so we can get back to IG and deal with this traitor."

She nods. "Okay, honey. Whatever you want."

Whatever I want?

I want *my woman* to realize the severity of this threat. I want my woman to be as angry as I am.

Why isn't she?

Knowing I need to get a move on, I push it all to the background so we can get ready and meet with Alejandro and the other bigwigs at the music label. Maybe if we're lucky, we can finish this up early and head out on the next plane to Boston. Better yet, Skyler can call her fancy jet so we can get home even faster. Money finally has its advantages.

***

"*Hermosa.* You look enchanting, Juliet." Alejandro kisses both of JJ's cheeks.

His eyes travel down her body from her white leather bomber jacket, over her tight-fitting tank that shows off a healthy dose of cleavage, and down her skinny jeans to her royal-blue suede stilettos. Bo did an amazing job getting her hair layered so that it's a wild mane of curls down her back. It's pulled up on each side and accentuates her face and the crescent arc of crystal gems surrounding her scar, making her look like the total package. They went with bold red lips, smoky eye makeup, and a ton of silver jewelry at her wrists, fingers, and neck.

Alejandro smiles at us and nods his appreciation. "Shall we see a preview of your show and hear your singing?" he requests.

Juliet looks right at him, lifts her chin, and says, "Absolutely. Pete, can you set the dancers? I'm ready to perform."

"Definitely, Ms. Juliet." He bows as if she's a royal. Dramatic, but effective.

Bo groans at the move while Skyler snickers. I'm still pissed off at finding out Annie is our superfan/stalker and can barely restrain myself from lifting Skyler over my shoulder in a fireman's carry and whisking her back to Boston on her jet. I want this situation dealt with. Now.

The IG team takes their places in the second row of the theater while the music label reps sit up front. Juliet faces backstage and holds a position with her body that puts all of her curves on display in the best possible way. The girl has a banging body, and every media outlet from here to the States is going to pick up on it when they see her and, better yet, hear her sing.

The music picks up, and Juliet starts shaking her ass. One of her arms goes up, and she counts down *"Tres, dos, uno . . ."* with her fingers, spins around, and belts out a note that I've only heard from the likes of Christina Aguilera, Whitney Houston, and Mariah Carey.

My mouth drops open as I watch while Juliet moves across the stage, singing her heart out. There are no missteps, no breathy pauses, just a girl up there who knows her moves, is comfortable in her body, and is using the voice God gave her.

I peer over to the side to watch Alejandro take in Juliet on stage. He, along with every man in the front row, has his eyes glued to our girl strutting her stuff.

The dancers flow around Juliet in a whirlwind of movements. At one point, they come at her in a provocative move, but she lifts a foot and mimics kicking one away, then pushing another, and both artfully fall to the ground as if wounded by her rejection while she sings the chorus about how their love tastes good, but it's bad for her.

I glance to my side where I can see Skyler holding her hands to her chest in a prayer position, the tips of her fingers touching her smiling lips. She's watching Juliet as if her baby sister has just graduated high school.

A pang picks up in my heart as I see the joy and beauty plastered across Skyler's face. She deserves this. Needs this type of feeling in her life. The shit with Tracey second-guessing our relationship, her parents dying, the drama with Johan back then, and more recently with her stalker/fan . . .

I shake my head.

Skyler deserves more.

She deserves the world, and I'm going to be the man to give it to her. This freak situation with Annie is going to stop. We'll confront her and discuss a legal restraining order, I'll have the pleasure of firing her, and it will be done. If she so much as attempts to send Skyler another letter or reach out to her, we'll take her to court for harassment.

Skyler's problems are over. My girl is going to breathe easy and live every moment with that beautiful happiness plastered across her pretty face.

I'm going to make sure of it.

While I watch JJ do her thing, I can finally catch my breath. I've got a plan for Skyler, and as seen on the stage, our job here is done.

If Alejandro doesn't love the progress made by International Guy, he's going to have to shove it.

Juliet is a star up there, and as I look at each of the bigwigs' faces, the awe clearly visible in every person who's watching her, including Alejandro, I know we've succeeded once again.

Our job in Spain is over.

I grab Skyler's hand, interlace our fingers, bring them to my lips, and kiss each tip. She turns toward me, eyes swirling with delight. Then, my love smiles at me, and it's everything.

Time to go home.

11

SKYLER

Leaving JJ and Violeta was difficult, but we exchanged numbers, and both girls promised to let me know when they were in the States and keep me in the loop on what's going on in their lives. I warned JJ about being a celebrity and not to fall to peer pressure or into traps of any kind. I stressed that I was only a call, text, or email away at all times. They swore they'd be smart and stick together as much as possible, but I still warned them I'd be checking in . . . regularly. Now I'm exhausted, coming off a long-ass flight with a man who was so fidgety I couldn't handle sitting next to him. So, instead of talking it out like I thought we would, he decided to strategize with Nate and come up with a plan for taking down Annie.

Taking down Annie.

Like it's really a thing. It's absurd. I'm not convinced she's actually done anything wrong. So she sent a bunch of fan mail over the years. Technically for more than a decade, but none of the letters were threatening. Sweet, if anything. I just can't comprehend that Annie was the same person sending all of those texts, unless this entire situation just turned into one of those freaky afternoon TV specials where the bad guy actually has two personalities and you're being threatened by both.

I guess it's possible. Unlikely, but possible.

Parker grabs my hand once we step off the plane and leads me straight into the back seat of Nate's SUV. Officially my SUV, but it's dedicated to my security team to keep me protected.

"Stop yanking on me." I pull my hand away, and Parker's shoulders drop as he goes around the car and gets into the other side. He sits close, our legs touching, and turns sideways toward me.

I make a shocked face. "Oh, you're finally going to talk to me? You know, *me*. Skyler. Your girlfriend. The one you just sat on a plane ignoring for the better part of eight hours?" I blink a bunch of times to make my point.

He deflates before my eyes, his entire expression becoming one of unrest and apology. "I'm sorry, baby." He holds my hands and rubs both of his thumbs over the top of mine. "I'm unhappy. Angry. And this entire situation is unsettling."

"Yes, it is. But you can't shut me out to make it easier for you to deal with. Remember, we do everything together. You and me against it all."

Parker closes his eyes and dips his forehead so that it presses against mine. "You're right. I'm sorry. Can you forgive my brooding, petulant, caveman ways?"

I smile, lift my chin, and kiss the tip of his nose. "Always. Just don't shut me out. I can handle anything but that. If you're angry, tell me you are and that you need some space. I'm not ignorant to the fact that a man needs to process things in his own way. A woman does too. Usually it involves ice cream or wine and a bestie. Sometimes all three at the same time, but in the end, she always needs her man by her side."

"I need you too. That's why I'm so angry. I need you more than I want to need you. You've gotten so far under my skin, baby, there's no way out. Not ever. We're a part of one another. I have to do whatever it takes to protect you. Protect what we have."

Before I can respond, Nate opens the door at my side and places Midnight on my lap, who goes directly over to his daddy and settles by his side, and then Sunny, who immediately licks my neck and cuddles in.

Both Parker and I smile at one another and pet our babies. Until my phone begins buzzing against my ass, and I start wiggling around. Parker's squawks similarly in his coat pocket, and he reaches for it at the same time I reach for mine.

The display sends a chill down my spine.

From: Unknown

LESSON 1: YOU WERE WARNED.

Under the text is a picture. I click on it and gasp, covering my mouth with my hand. Parker goes silent at my side. The image is of the bed in my master bedroom in the penthouse. The entire thing is engulfed in flames.

"Oh my God, honey." I reach for Parker's hand, and he holds mine tight, his eyes focused on his own phone.

Another text comes in as tears prick the back of my eyes, fear digging into my chest.

From: Unknown

LESSON 2: YOU CAN'T HIDE.

"Fuck!" Parker's voice is an avalanche of icy-cold rage.

He presses a few buttons and then puts his phone to his ear, his other hand not leaving mine for a second.

"Wendy, where the fuck is Annie right now?" he blasts, that chill now directed at our friend.

I can't summon the urge to freak out about it too much since my teeth are starting to chatter, and I can feel the cold filling my bones as he speaks.

"What? That can't be. We just got two texts in a row. Does she have her phone on her?" His voice is harsh and unrelenting, his jaw a chiseled stone as he scowls.

Parker lets out a fast breath. "We were just sent two threatening texts along with a picture of Skyler's master bedroom . . . ablaze."

As he says that, I can hear alarms blaring through his phone.

"Get the fuck out of there, but do not take your eyes off Annie! I want her by you and Royce at all times. Handcuff her if you need to. Don't lie and say you don't have a pair on you." He pauses and clenches his teeth. "That's what I thought. Meet you at the front of the building. Go now."

"Park?" The one-word request from Nate comes out more as a demand.

I hand over my phone to Nate when Parker puts the phone to his ear again.

"Roy? You got Kendra, Zeus? Okay, Wendy has both? Yes, get out of there, but do not let Annie out of your sight. Call Mick. He'll lose his mind when he finds out there's a fire in the same building Wendy's in. I do not need him on my ass right now."

Nate makes a low, animalistic sound deep in his throat as he scans the texts and image. He hands the phone to Rachel and slams the door to walk back to the car where Bo is waiting for us to head out. I turn and look out the back window as Nate tells Bo the bad news.

All I can think is I hope they've got everyone out of the building and the fire department is putting the fire out before it reaches any other floors.

My hand trembles in Parker's, but he drops the phone, turns toward me, and cups both of my cheeks. "Nothing's going to happen to you. You hear me?"

I nod, but the trembling inside turns into a full-body smackdown. The fear is crippling in its intensity. "Wh-what a-about the other p-people in the b-b-building?" I stutter through my chattering teeth.

"Baby, it's going to be fine. The firefighters were already heading up there when Wendy and the team were heading out." He caresses my face. "We're going to go there right now. Speak to the cops and Annie. Find out what the hell is going on."

"B-but how could sh-she start a f-fire while in the of-of-office?"

He shakes his head and brings me against his side while Nate hops in the SUV and fires the engine, and we're off.

"I don't know. Doesn't look like she started it." He makes a snarling, discontented sound.

"Or the t-texts?" I suck in a big breath, inhaling Parker's citrus-and-earthy scent. Breathing in his familiar smell along with feeling his hand running up and down my arm helps the shaking subside, and my heartbeat goes back to a more even pitter-patter.

Before long, we're screeching up to the building but are stopped by a barricade the cops set up. Nate gives our credentials, and the cops let us pass through. We park across the street, out of the way. Out in front of the building we see Royce standing close to Kendra, Wendy, and an obviously frightened Annie. Annie has Zeus in her arms and is petting him methodically while staring up at the building. Heavy black smoke is billowing out from my balcony doors on both sides.

Once we make our way to the group, Annie's eyes light up. "Oh, thank goodness you're both okay! I was so worried because I didn't know when you two were coming back. Skyler, Parker, I'm so sorry about your home." Her eyes fill with tears, and a few fall to the sides. "I got Zeus, though. Please tell me your puppies weren't in there?" She hiccup sobs.

I shake my head. "Uh, no. They are in the SUV with the windows down, sleeping."

"Another miracle." Annie looks up and wipes at her eyes, then continues to snuggle Zeus, who genuinely seems to enjoy the cuddle time.

"Where's your phone, Annie?" Parker asks, malice filling his tone.

She looks at Parker and blinks a few times. "Uh, I don't have it. It isn't working. I need to get a new one."

"Convenient. It's broken all of a sudden," he sneers.

She takes a jittery breath. "I um, because I broke it two days ago. Dropped it into the fountain over there when I was having lunch. I like to eat out here in the sunshine."

Nate comes up behind Parker, and I hear him whisper near his ear, "She does eat her lunch there daily."

"And I called my provider, and they said I wasn't due for an upgrade, and I couldn't afford the extra insurance, so I have to wait for my next paycheck to get another. Don't worry, though, it's not going to affect my job. At all."

"Do you have a burner phone?" He continues with the questions.

"A what? I'm not quite sure I know what that is. Is that a new name brand, like Apple or Samsung?" she asks with such innocence I can't help but nudge Parker's shoulder, wanting to get his attention. This is all wrong. Off in a really bad way.

"Honey—" I try again, but he cuts me off.

"Annie, do you or don't you have a phone?" Parker grates through clenched teeth, his shoulders and body so tight where he stands that if Nate tried to bodycheck him, he'd bounce right off as though he'd run into a freestanding brick wall.

Annie shakes her head. "No, but like I said, it's not going to hinder me in doing my job . . ."

Wendy cuts in. "Park, she didn't have a phone on her when you got those texts because she was sitting right in front of me going over the schedule. And although I'm tech savvy enough to pull off sending a text at a specific time from an alternate location and number, Annie is not. I've been looking into her the last two days since we figured out the connection to her and Skyler, and it's just not possible. I'd stake my life on it," she insists, but it's as though Parker doesn't even hear her, his anger fueled by his fear and lack of control.

Annie's eyes widen. "What . . . what do you mean you've been looking into me?"

"You have been sending fan letters to Skyler for over ten years," Parker spouts, his face a mask of frustration and arrogance. Not a good look on him.

She frowns and cuddles Zeus closer, pushing her chin into his ginger-colored fur. "Yeah, because she's my best friend," she says so sweetly I can smell the sugary scent from a few feet away. She glances at me, frowns, and then looks back at Parker.

"No. You're her stalker." Parker lays it out in a brazen tone.

Annie's expression flutters from confusion to concern. "Wh-what?" She shakes her head a bunch of times. "No. We're pen pals. We have been for years. I even have a card with a headshot that she signed. I have several actually. I have them all framed. In my house. We're friends. *Longtime friends.* I just thought Skyler maybe didn't recognize it was me because we always corresponded by mail, and since she meets so many people, I'm sure it's easy to get confused."

"I sent you a card and a signed headshot?" I close my eyes and remember back when I was a teen signing hundreds of headshots for my mom. She'd fill out these multicolored little cards that she wrote on my behalf.

"Yes, of course." She smiles brightly. "You wrote the first one on a pink card, I'd say about eleven years ago. On the inside you said—"

"My fans are my friends." We both say it at the same time.

Jesus. I forgot about those days. They stopped once Tracey took over and hired a publicity team.

I reach for Parker's arm and curl my hand around his bicep. "Honey, I used to do that with Mom. She'd have me sign five-by-seven images, and then she'd send them to my fans whenever we had a little downtime. I must have had five different cards and images over the years."

Annie nods wildly, her blonde hair shaking with the effort. "I have all five! I did think it was odd that you'd say the same thing." She frowns. "I just figured it was our special thing to one another. You sent it to others?" Annie looks crestfallen.

My goodness, she really believed we were longtime pen pals . . . friends.

"Uh, yeah. I'm sorry, Annie," I say softly, not wanting to hurt the poor, misguided woman.

"So, we're not friends?" Annie's voice quavers, and her bottom lip trembles.

"We are . . . ," I say at the same time Parker blurts out, "Fuck no."

Annie swallows, and tears fall down her pearlescent cheeks. Her eyes are the size of dinner plates, looking wide and afraid. "But I thought . . . You were there during all the bad things. When she hurt me over and over, and you'd send me pretty cards, and I had nothing else. Nothing else to look forward to. No. My God. It was all a lie. Just like she said. Always told me you'd never be my friend. But . . . but I believed. And your cards . . . I-I have to go."

"I don't think so, Annie. The jig is up. You can play coy and innocent all you want, but that doesn't change the fact that you've been sending threatening texts . . ." Parker continues to nail her when she's clearly hurting.

"Parker, no," Wendy butts in. "I haven't been able to trace any of those texts back to Annie. A lot of those were delivered at times where I was able to verify she was in the office, and the signal the text came from was not bounced off our towers or anywhere close. Annie didn't send the texts." She bites into her bottom lip.

He scowls. "Where there's a will, there's a way."

Wendy puts both of her hands on Parker's biceps and looks him straight in the eyes. "Parker, she goes from work to the bus stop, to the convalescent hospital where her only relative—her dying stepmother—lives, and then home, and back to work to repeat the process again the next day. From my digging, the stepmother has been her only parent for the last fifteen years. The same woman who was visited multiple times by child services after repeated trips to the hospital for Annie's suspicious falls and accidents. The poor thing has had more broken bones than an NFL player. It's no wonder she's awkward and has an unrealistic relationship with Sky. In all likelihood, being Skyler's friend was the only escape the poor, abused child had. It kept her hope alive."

My stomach twists, and my heart squeezes as though there's a vise around it. I reach out to touch Annie, but she jerks back.

She shakes her head and holds Zeus close. "You're researching me. Looking into my past!" Her voice is but a whisper when she looks at me, tears filling her frightened eyes. "You're *not* my friend. Y-you, you just think I'm a crazy fan. Oh my God!" She bursts into tears, dropping Zeus to the concrete, who lands perfectly on his feet without a problem and goes straight over to Parker's legs, where he proceeds to spin a circle around them. Parker picks up his cat at the same time Bo makes his way to us.

"I'm guessing you've already had it out with your stalker?" Bo adds to the conversation with the most shit timing in history.

Annie hears his words and starts wailing. Wendy leads her over to a nearby bench and sits her down, an arm around her back, comforting her. Kendra moves in to assist.

"I wanna go home. I don't want to be here. I have to go. I . . . I . . ." She bursts into tears and covers her face with her hands.

I don't think the situation can get any worse. My heart hurts, my mind is in a tizzy, and I've just broken an already-fragile young woman.

Parker's phone buzzes as I lean against his side. He hands me Zeus, letting out a long, tortured breath before lifting the phone and staring down at the message. I hover over his shoulder and read it along with him.

From: Unknown

DID YOU LEARN YOUR LESSON?

Another one pops up while we're reading the first.

From: Unknown

BREAK UP WITH HER OR SUFFER THE CONSEQUENCES.

With the last text, Parker yanks me to his side, his embrace so tight I worry we're going to squish his cat.

From: Unknown

YOU CAN'T KEEP HER SAFE.

I rub my hand up and down his back. "Honey, whoever it is, they're messing with us."

"You think?" he says flippantly.

"Park, the police want to speak with you and Skyler. It's time we give the entire load to them. This latest threat was premeditated and could have hurt a lot of people. It's arson with an intent to harm." Nate's voice is low, because what I didn't notice before but do now is that the paparazzi have rolled up and are taking picture after picture of us standing in a huddle while the firemen and cops clear the building.

"Sky, Sky, what happened? That's your penthouse, right?" one says, breaking into my thoughts.

"Was the fire an accident?" another calls out.

"Is someone trying to hurt you, Skyler? Parker!" A female this time.

"Parker, is she in trouble?" One of the males tries to appeal to my guy, but Parker expertly ignores him.

Nate takes the phone when Parker holds it out.

"More?" Nate's low rumble is as heavy and thunderous as a summer storm.

"This time, they gave us an ultimatum with a very clear threat," Parker says, hooking his arm around my shoulder. I snuggle Zeus and go with him toward the group of cops who are waiting for us. I glance over my shoulder at Wendy and Kendra, who are comforting Annie.

The letters, our response, it was all a misunderstanding but one I know Annie will never forget and maybe never recover from.

Silently I swear to myself that I'll fix things with Annie. She never threatened me. She's fragile, sweet, and innocent, but she was swept up in all this crap and got hurt in the process. My mother always told me to make amends if I harmed another, and my behavior and Parker's toward Annie just crawled to the top of that list. Right after we deal with the current threats to our safety.

I let out a long sigh and stay close to my guy as we make our way to the cops.

This entire thing is right out of one of my fictional movies.

When will it stop?

When is enough going to be enough?

What can we expect next?

12

PARKER

Longest. Day. In. History.

I curl my arm around Skyler's sloped shoulders when she gets out of the SUV in front of my apartment complex. The paparazzi have already figured out that we'd be here since her apartment caught on fire and is unavailable.

Rachel moseys over to them and whispers a bunch of words. Shockingly, they look properly chastised, and all of them put down their cameras. I don't spare them a further glance, focused only on getting my girl and my dogs properly fed and put to bed.

For a week.

The cops and arson investigators said they'd be going through Skyler's penthouse for a few days, taking evidence, before we are allowed to go and see if anything is salvageable. Skyler is mostly worried about some mementos and pictures she had of her parents. Many of them were in her private quarters, her bedroom, but a lot of them were also in the living room. There's hope that she'll have some of the past to take with her. The good news is that a lot of her stuff hadn't been moved from her home in New York, so the most valuable pieces are secure in the penthouse she hasn't sold yet.

Briefly that reminds me to ask what her plans are for that place, though now is definitely not the time. Once we've gotten deeper into my complex and around the corner, out of view of the paparazzi, I try to grab her hand. Skyler stumbles, but I react fast and get a good lock on her and am able to keep her standing. She stops where she stands, her body vibrating with barely controlled anger, her face a tight mask of unfiltered rage.

"I'm so fucking tired of all of this!" she screeches like a banshee, her arms flailing in the air as though she's pretending to fly, but she's mostly just waving them frantically.

I stop her movements by placing my hands on her shoulders and dip toward her face. "I am too. The cops have a lot to go on with all of our texts and the notes. When we left, they were heading to Benny's address. They'll find him. Question him, and God willing, he'll admit to it all."

She frowns. "And in the process, we *destroyed* Annie. A sweet girl who never did anyone any harm. All she did was think we were friends, and without knowing it, I perpetuated that scenario with the fan response mail I sent over the years and recently with our lunches. But what's worse, I was really beginning to think of her as a friend. Sure, she's strange, socially awkward, but when you've spent years taking care of a woman who beat the shit out of you, I imagine that's got to do some damage to your confidence."

I run my hands up and down her arms and settle them against her neck. "We'll fix it. I fucked up more than you. One and one added up to three, and I . . ." An exhausted breath slips past my lips. "I didn't want to see the mistake in the logic. It's my fault."

She shakes her head, wraps her arms around my waist, and presses her cheek against my chest. "It's not your fault. You can't take on the blame for the world. There is someone seriously jacked up in the head doing all of this. And I just . . ." She sighs against my shirt. "I want it to be over, honey. I want to make my movie with Geneva, go home to my beautiful house where my man meets me after a day in his office and I can play Frisbee in my yard with our dogs. We should be able to have that life. We work hard. God, I just want to be fucking normal for once!" She pushes away from me and runs her hands through her hair, holding the lot of it against her nape before curling it over to one side.

"One day, we'll be past this, and we'll have exactly what you're dreaming of. I swear it." And I will do everything in my power to make it happen.

Nate comes up with the dogs and passes the leashes to Sky. She kneels down and coos at our dogs, rubbing their heads, then leads them over to a patch of grass and bushes.

"I'm going to go in first, check everything out, do a walk-through," Nate says, moving toward the entrance to the hallway of my apartment.

"Thanks, man."

"It's my job," he says in response, and walks with a purpose toward my door.

Rachel comes up behind us.

"We need a moment," I tell her, and she nods, moving in the direction her husband went, eyes shifting around the area, but there's nothing to see. We're in a gated complex, and this section leaves nowhere for a person to hide.

"It's going to be okay." I go over and take Skyler's hand and lead her toward my apartment.

Skyler interlaces our fingers as the dogs straggle behind us, sniffing the grass and doing their thing.

Once we're about thirty feet from my door, I hear Nate scream and see him coming our way at a dead run. It's like watching an action hero, only his face is a twisted grimace.

"Go back!" he roars.

His wife turns around, everything moving so fast. She runs at a mighty clip and literally jumps into the air, bum-rushing Skyler and knocking her down to the ground at the same time I watch in horror as

Nate's six-foot-plus form catapults into the air and an explosion pierces my eardrums. A wave of fire rolls toward me, and I'm tossed back by a wall of heat so intense I smell the scent of burning hair before my back and head smash to the concrete in a powerful blow.

***

Alarms are blaring, and I think I hear a woman screaming as I blink in the black smoke and taste ash on my tongue. Nope, not a woman. My ears are ringing, screaming inside my head, but then I see an angel. My angel. Skyler runs her fingers along my face, her mouth moving, but I can't hear anything except the ringing.

I try to sit up, but my entire chest feels as though I've been hit by a car. I grit my teeth as Skyler helps me to a seated position. Fresh air stings my lungs. I look around and note the burning hole that was the front of my apartment, fire and smoke still seeping out of the open wound at the front of the hall.

Neighbors I barely recognize are scuttling around, but it's the still form about fifteen feet from me that has me struggling to stand. Skyler's hands are all over me, her hair a mess, soot on her face, but she looks no worse for the wear.

Nate's form is unmoving on the concrete, Rachel at his side, performing CPR.

Oh Jesus, no.

Fuck no.

Absolutely not.

I roar out a war cry, but I can't hear it. I can't hear anything but the incessant ringing in my ears. A sticky substance is running down the side of my face from somewhere at my temple. Skyler is trying to press her sweater to it, but I push her arm away and limp toward Nate's body. She follows, her mouth moving, no sound reaching my ears.

Rachel continues compressions as I move to the top of Nate's head. I tip his head back and hold it straight so Rachel can work. Her powerful muscles undulate with her efforts as she performs CPR on her unresponsive husband. His massive, muscular chest looks odd, one side sunken in, and I fear he has a collapsed lung. I press my fingers against his neck and find a tiny pulse. It's weak, very weak, but he's alive.

"He's alive. I can feel his pulse." I say the words but don't hear them. "Keep doing what you're doing. I think he's got a collapsed lung." Again, I say words I cannot hear as the alarm in my ears doesn't stop, and a pounding in my head picks up the tune. It feels as though my thoughts are moving slower, sluggish. I blink a few times, trying to clear the extreme exhaustion I feel threatening to take me out.

There's blood pooling at Nate's back, staining the concrete a deep, sickening red, flowing toward my knees. The puddle is getting larger too fast.

"He's bleeding somewhere!" I yell, but I'm not sure if they hear me. Still Rachel scans her husband's body. She must have turned him over, because I can see little bits of rock and debris imbedded in his forehead and the tip of his nose and chin.

The pool gets so big it paints my khakis red where I'm kneeling. I lift his body to the side and find the cause of the bleeding. There's a metal spike of some sort that must have shot out with the explosion and is impaled in his lower back. The metal is wedged at an odd angle, leaving a gaping wound at the bottom half. I grab the sweater Skyler is holding and press it around the spike to stanch the flow of blood.

Rachel reaches for the metal, and I shake my head, staying her hand.

"Leave it; we don't know if it's pierced something vital or not."

She nods and puts her hand to his neck. Her eyes are wild but relieved when she must feel his pulse, though if he doesn't get help soon he's going to bleed out, not to mention that collapsed lung and concave chest are seriously problematic.

I'm debating lifting him when another small explosion goes off, sending more debris flying and ash raining down.

"We've got to get out of here," I say, but right then the cavalry shows up, and first responders in blue uniforms come barreling around the corner with a stretcher. "Yes!" I scream, and Rachel's eyes go toward the spot I'm looking at, and an expression of gratitude fills her face.

It's the last thing I see before I black out.

The end . . . for now.

RIO:

INTERNATIONAL GUY

BOOK 11

To the team at Verus Editora.

You brought me to the Christ,
one of the most profound experiences of my life.
You believed in my stories
and shared them with your country.
I cannot thank you enough
for the passion you, your country, and the Brazilian readers
have brought into my world.
I hope this book brings some of the beauty of Brazil to life.

1

SKYLER

"Please wake up, honey. Please, *pleeeease*. I need you . . . *so much*." I lick my dry, cracked lips and focus with everything I have on Parker's face. His striking bone structure, the cut of his chiseled jawline with two days' scruff that abrades my hand, yet I can't seem to stop touching him.

I *have* to touch him. Losing that link now will ruin me. I'll tumble into a twisted ball of despair on the spot. "You have to wake up. I-I can't do this alone. And you prom—" I swallow down the emotion as tears flood my eyes and fall down my cheeks in a river of feelings I can no longer hold back.

"Honey, you promised. It's you, me, and the pups. They miss you, but they're okay, no harm done from the explosion. Wendy's got them at their house—Mick called in a vet to look them over. Wendy's taking really good care of them. And baby . . ." I run my fingertips across his brow, noting the large bandage on the side of his head where he received eighteen stitches. That's in addition to the giant egg on the back of his skull where his head slammed to the concrete, giving him a concussion. He fell the second time when he blacked out, and he's yet to wake up six hours later. The local anesthetic and painkillers should be wearing off soon, and the doctors assure me it's only a matter of time before he wakes up. His brain scans were excellent, but there's always concern when a concussion is involved. His chest and ribs are seriously bruised, but internally, he's fine. Rest and taking it easy are on the agenda for my guy.

If he'd just wake up!

I take his hand and pet his arm from elbow to fingers in what I hope is a soothing, comforting gesture. He needs to know that I'm right here, ready for him to open his eyes. Never leaving his side.

The door behind me opens up, and Wendy enters. "Hey, how is he?" Concern and sadness mar her usually perky features.

I shake my head. "No change. Why won't he wake up, Wen?" I choke out, covering my mouth when the emotions overwhelm me, and a sob slips out.

She rushes to my side and wraps an arm around my shoulders, easing into the chair next to me. "His body and mind have to be ready. He took two nasty hits. One to the temple and one to the back of his head. The brain and body are in protection mode. Just give it a little time. The doctors said he'd wake up, and you yourself said he was up and helping with Nate before he conked out. That's a good sign." She squeezes the ball of my shoulder. "It's going to be okay."

I close my eyes and nod, saying a silent prayer to God that he'll take care of Parker. I've lost so much already; I can't bear to lose him too.

"Any news on Nate?" Wendy asks.

An intense wave of sorrow crashes over me, forcing me to buck in her arms, the sobs wracking my frame. "I don't know. He's in surgery. And it's all my fault. He was protecting me . . ."

Wendy cups my cheeks. "Look at me. What happened is not your fault. He was doing his job. He knows the risks. You had no idea this demented person was going to set fire to your home or set a device to explode in Parker's."

"Is that what happened?" I narrow my gaze and focus on Wendy's crystal-blue eyes and fiery-red hair against her pearlescent skin tone.

Wendy bites into her bottom lip and looks over at the door as if she's making sure no one else can hear.

"I did a little hacking of the police department's computers. The fire in your penthouse was set using an accelerant on the center of your bed. Parker's apartment was far more complex. In layman's terms, according to the bomb squad's report and evaluation, the person who set the bomb was very knowledgeable. And for some reason, they're theorizing that the person has government experience. Apparently, the configuration of the bomb is something that's taught in black ops training with soldiers and a division of the CIA."

"CIA? Black ops?" I press my hand to my forehead. "You've got to be kidding me. I don't know anyone in the government, nor do I have any idea why someone in a special operations position would want me or my boyfriend dead!" My voice rises as the panic sets in. My heart is pounding; the blood rushing through my veins feels ice cold, and my entire body starts to shake.

"Oh no, no you don't! No freaking out on my watch!" Wendy rubs my arms and back. "We're going to figure this out. I've uh, actually called Paul, Park's brother, to review the information. He's the one who figured out the police talk regarding the black ops, and that the person involved has government or high-level-military connections."

"Is it . . ."

"A hit? Maybe. Paul says he can't be sure, but it's not looking good. As a matter of fact, he's so concerned, he's outside watching Parker's door. I gotta say it: that boy is fiiiine. He's wearing camo pants, combat boots, and a black T-shirt that fits like a second skin, with his dog tags hanging down his chest." Wendy bites on her knuckle. "I would eat that boy for breakfast, lunch, and dinner. My goodness, he's hot." She waves a hand at her flushed face.

"Are you kidding me? You're talking about how fine Parker's brother is right now? When everything is ass up? My life is crumbling around me; everyone I love is either dead, at risk, hurt, or fighting for their lives." My voice cracks. "The fucking CIA spooks are after me; someone possibly put a hit out on me or Parker or the both of us . . ." I start to lose it. Straight up. Lose. My. Shit. I stand up and screech, my hands in fists at my sides, and I'm so blazing mad I can hardly see straight. "And you're talking about how hot Parker's brother is!"

Wendy smiles huge. "All right!" She smacks her thigh. "Now *there's* my fighter." She wipes at her brow dramatically. "Whew! I thought I was going to have to bring in reinforcements to get you out of your pity party and back into fighting Irish form!" She fist pumps the air, then puts her hand out for me to high-five.

"I'm not Irish!" I tunnel my fingers through my hair and tug on the ends as I spin around in a circle to move away from the bed so I can pace. It works for Parker, so maybe it will work for me. "Okay, okay. Who do I know in the government?" I lift my hand up and point at Wendy. "We know Kendra!" I fire off, as though I've just won the jackpot in a million-dollar lotto.

Wendy frowns. "Nope. Quizzed her. She doesn't have any connections to the CIA."

"The CIA. Does Parker's brother?"

Her mouth contorts into a funny expression. "Uh, yeah. He was special ops for years."

"Could the bomb be related to Parker and not me?"

Wendy's shoulders fall. "We don't think so. All signs point to your freaky texter. The cops have a profiler on staff who reviewed the texts and gave his assessment."

"Did the police find Benny?"

"Singleton? Not yet, but since he was a suspect and there was a bomb involved, not to mention the fire in a public building, they got a warrant and raided his place. Didn't find anything bomb related, but they did find a ton of pictures of you at various stages in your life all over his walls. The dude was definitely stalking you. They've got units out looking for him."

"So, he could be the bomber and is definitely my stalker."

She shrugs. "Looks that way. Until the evidence says otherwise, that's the angle the cops are looking into at this point. They'll want to speak with you and Parker again once he wakes up. The doctors have put them off for the time being."

Once I've paced until I've calmed down, I go back to sit at Parker's side. "This is all such a mess. I don't know how this can even be my life. Everything just escalated."

Behind us, the door opens, and Mr. and Mrs. Ellis enter. The second I see Parker's mother, I burst into tears all over again. "I'm sorry, I'm so sorry!" I sob into my hands, but before I know it, I'm surrounded by warmth and love. The scent of wildflowers filters around me, and I breathe it in while clutching the woman who's slowly becoming a female figure I look up to.

"Sunshine, you get that nonsense out of your head right this instant." Cathy rubs the back of my head while I snuggle right into the crook of her neck and cry big, heaving sobs.

For a long time, this amazing woman holds me and fills my mind with whispered words of comfort and love. She expresses repeatedly that it's not my fault, that bad things happen to good people all the time. Cathy tells me she loves me and that we'll get through this hard patch as a family.

A family.

There's that word again. The one word I've not known in far too many years. Now I have it in spades. With Parker, his parents, his brothers, Wendy, Mick, Rachel, and Nate . . .

Another sob wracks my frame. "Nate might die." I continue crying into her shoulder.

"There, there," she coos. "We'll pray real hard to the Heavenly Father that he will take mercy on that strapping young lad and heal him from the inside out. That's all we can do, my dear Sunshine."

I pull my head out from the comfort of Cathy's hold. "W-will you pray with me? For Nate? For Parker?"

She smiles softly and cups my cheeks. "Of course I will, my dear." She brings my head toward her and places a kiss on my forehead. I close my eyes and let the serenity that is a mother's love seep into my soul.

Wendy moves aside so that Cathy can sit at her son's side. Cathy grabs his hand, reaches for mine as I sit in the chair right next to them, and closes her eyes.

"Heavenly Father, we come to you today to ask for your love and mercy. We ask that you spread your healing powers to my son Parker and our dear friend Nathan as they try to come back from this horrendous attack. Let your will be the outcome, and let us as your children have the capacity and understanding to accept whatever decision is made. We pray to you in the name of the Father, the Son, and the Holy Spirit. Amen."

"Amen," I whisper, holding Cathy's hand tight because I'm afraid to let it go.

"Mom?" A croaky sound comes from the bed. "Baby?" Parker's voice sounds like his throat has been put through a meat processor. "Why you prayin' over me? I'm not dead."

Before I can even react, Cathy squeezes my hand, looks at me, and says, "God works fast." She smiles up at the ceiling and then back at my man. "You scared the living daylights out of our girl here, not to mention your momma."

"Sky, baby," he croaks, and tries to clear his throat but can't.

I move so fast I think I may knock Mrs. Ellis out of the way in my need to express my relief and love. I put a knee on Parker's bed, lean over, grasp his cheeks, and kiss his dry lips hard.

He accepts the kiss, but I'm not done. I press my forehead to his and breathe deeply. "Don't you ever scare me like that again, Parker James Ellis," I whisper against his lips, and then proceed to kiss every inch of his face I can touch that's not covered in a bandage with a series of "I love yous" mixed in between kisses.

"Sunshine, my goodness, give the boy some room to breathe!" Cathy pats my back and helps me ease off the bed, but I don't take my eyes off Parker.

He drowsily smirks and accepts the pink cup of water his dad brings near his face. He sucks down the water as though he's a man who's been stuck in the desert for a few days, not lying in a hospital bed for the last several hours.

"Thanks, Pops."

His dad's voice is thick when he pats him on the shoulder. "Good to see you awake and on the mend, son."

Cathy leans over the bed and kisses her son on the forehead. "My boy." She sighs and caresses his cheek. "Happy to have you back, darling."

Parker pushes on the bed with his fists and shifts his body up with a massive groan and a wince. "Jesus Christ, that hurts. I feel like I've been hit by a truck, and a band of horns is blaring in my head." He lifts one hand to touch the side of his head that's covered by a bandage.

"Nope, explosion. Concussion. Two head lacerations with eighteen stitches just above your temple and into your hairline." Wendy states his medical ailments like she's listing out the ingredients for the dinner she's about to cook. "Oh, and your ribs and sternum are bruised, but nothing too serious there."

"Is that all?" Parker asks dryly.

She grins. "Happy to see your face, Bossman."

He sighs and smiles, leaning his head back against the pillow his mother is fluffing for him. "I'm happy it's here to be seen. Now who's going to update me on Nate's condition?"

2

PARKER

Skyler's beautiful brown eyes glaze over with tears when I ask about Nate.

"Fuck no," I grate out, barely able to recognize my own voice through the incessant ringing in my ears. At least I can hear everything, unlike before. All I can imagine is the worst, that we lost a friend tonight. A man who was protecting me and what's mine.

My girl reaches for my hands and shakes her head as twin tears fall down her cheeks. "No, baby, he's not gone. He's in surgery, but that's all we know. It's been just over six hours since we arrived."

I grind my teeth and breathe through the pain in my chest and head, letting the fear recede and reality weave in. "I've been out for six hours?"

Sky bites down on her bottom lip and nods.

"Did the cops catch the guy?" I ease my pounding head back against the pillows. My mother runs her fingers through my hair, and it feels so damn good I could almost squeeze out a tear. She hums softly, and that sound is as familiar as my favorite song and drowns out some of the ringing. My mother is one of the most comforting people in the world. Her touch, the sound of her voice humming a tune, remind me of when I was sick as a boy and she took care of me.

Wendy steps up and puts her hand on my toes above the covers, shaking my foot a little. "They're looking for Benny Singleton to question him. The cops want to talk to you more about uh . . ." She looks from my mother to my father, and her voice falters enough that I know she has more to say but doesn't want to in mixed company. ". . . the explosion and the fire."

My father, ever aware of the situation becoming heavy in the room, takes that moment to announce his need for coffee. "Come on, Cathy, let's give them some space to get up to date while we grab a cup of joe."

Mom runs her fingers along my brow, and I close my eyes. "You're perfectly capable of getting coffee by yourself. You don't need me—"

"Woman." My father's tone brooks no argument. "Can't you see they want to talk alone? Without their parents hanging over their shoulders?"

I open my eyes in time to see Ma looking affronted, her head jerking back with the drama of a woman who's about to lay a person out with a piece of her mind, none of it good.

My father takes her hand and tugs her toward the door. "Come on, my love, you can yell at me on the way."

"Don't think for a second I won't." Her gaze narrows at my father with laser-like accuracy.

"Wouldn't dream of it." He grins and winks at me, then smiles at Skyler and Wendy.

"Sweetheart, I'll be back soon. Do you want anything from the cafeteria? You must be hungry . . ." Before I can answer, she waves her hand as if to cut me off. "I'll just get you a little something. Maybe a sandwich, or a slice of pie. I'll bet they have a good soup."

"Jesus, woman. He just woke up from being tossed by an explosion. I think the last thing on his mind is food."

My mother narrows her gaze, and her mouth tightens into a firm white line. "Food is the cure-all for everything, dear. You'd think you would know that since you own a pub. Sweet heavens above." She shakes her head and walks through the door my father is holding open, murmuring heated words under her breath at him.

I smile and watch them leave, but once the door shuts, I reach for my girl's hand. "You okay?"

Skyler swallows slowly, her eyes filling with tears once more.

"Baby, don't cry. I hate seeing you cry. It breaks me wide open."

The tears fall, and she sits by my side, close enough for me to cup her wet cheek and wipe away her tears with my thumb. She holds my hand against her cheek, turns her head, and places a kiss in my palm. "I love you." She whispers the words, but I can hear them clear as day, each syllable coating my soul with a much-desired healing balm.

"I love you too, and baby, I'm going to be fine. Stop fretting, okay?"

She nods but continues to hold my hand to her face, her breathing evening out as if simply touching me is easing her pain. I know that's what it's doing for me.

I turn my gaze to my feisty redheaded friend. "Wendy, tell me what you know. The whole truth."

For the next twenty minutes, Wendy updates me on what she found through her hacking and going over the information with my brother.

"Bring Paul in," I snap, my frustration getting the best of me.

Instead of blistering me with a bitchy comeback, Wendy hops to it. She knows this situation has hit DEFCON 1, and no amount of ribbing or humor is going to ease the strain.

Paul enters, looking as though he's ready to go into battle. Fatigues, sans the jacket, black tee, boots, and his tags clearly visible. He crosses his massively muscled arms over one another. "Glad you're awake, bro. Knew you'd be okay."

"You been watching the door?" I ask while cocking a brow.

He nods. "Keepin' an eye on your woman too. Reporters and paps have already tried to sneak in. Hospital security is keeping the riffraff out, but they still attempt to disguise themselves."

I nod and squeeze Skyler's hand where she's now holding mine.

"You think this is a black ops job?"

Paul simply nods. No words are needed.

"You on this?" I grit my teeth, the pounding in my temples increasing as my heart rate doubles.

Another nod.

"My gratitude," I grate out, and clear my throat as best I can.

"Not necessary. I've got some of my friends working intel with Wendy. The cops are scouting for one Benjamin Singleton, but, brother, I've gotta say, I'm not liking him for the explosion or the fire."

A battering ram could have struck me and it would have hurt less.

I grit my teeth and breathe through the pain engulfing my frame as I get angrier by the second.

Paul continues his theory. "Naw. My gut—and I'm usually right or I'd have been dead a dozen times over—"

"How comforting," I snark, wanting him to get to the point.

"My gut says Benny's not your guy. At least not for this. Doesn't have what it takes to pull an operation of this magnitude off. I mean the guy's been following Sky around like a long-lost puppy for years but just barely made a move. And a poor one at that. Delivering that second note, making a point to see her in the elevator, at the coffee shop. That's child's play, crush-type bullshit. This . . . bro, this shit is close to high level, but there's still a naivete about it. It has all the signatures of true black ops or spec ops, but my gut tells me there's only one person involved, and this is *personal*, not business or even a hired hit."

"Fuck!" I lean my head back as Skyler runs her hands down my arm.

Paul continues. "And I don't know if you're aware of this, but every bomb maker has their own signature. The type of wire, the twists, the metals used, the soldering method, the device—everything is planned out, and there are parts that are generally specific to one person. A calling card if you will."

"Okay, so how does that help us in this instance?"

"For one, whoever did it set the bomb in place prior to the fire. It was set on a ten-second delay. A few moments after the key entered the lock and turned, it triggered the bomb, which was taped to the other side of the door. That means whoever did it would have expected you to be hit first. Unless they knew you and Skyler were together. If that's the case, it would make sense that either Nate or Rachel would check the apartment before you entered. Taking out one or both of the bodyguards would hurt Sky but not kill her. If it were you who went there alone, it would take you out. Either way, both scenarios would break Skyler but not get her killed. Whoever it is wants you dead and her alive."

Skyler's hands strangle my arm at the last part of my brother's info dump.

"What's the next step?"

"I've got one of my boys working on the bomber's signature. That's the best way to track the creator."

"And the cops?"

Paul snickers. "You think they have the ability to hunt down a black ops bomber?" He shakes his head. "Nuh-uh. I've got this on lock. I'll have more information in the next couple of days, if not sooner. And you"—he points to Skyler—"I'm on like flies on shit from here on out. Where you go, I go. Period. You feel me?"

Skyler frowns. "But what about Nate and Rachel?" Her voice fills with emotion, and she gets choked up.

"They're out. I'm in. No one is going to blow up my brother's apartment, set fire to his woman's home, and try to take either of you out. Not on my watch. No way, no how. You gotta problem with that, sis?"

"Sis?" She swallows, the word coming out a whisper.

"You buying a house with my brother, adopting dogs, shacking up for the long haul?" he asks flatly.

Her eyes are wide innocent pools focused on my brother's scowling face. She nods and murmurs, "Uh-huh."

"Welcome to the family." He grins a fox-like smile as the door opens, and a man in a white coat walks in.

Before the doctor can say anything, Paul is in his face, a hand to his chest pushing the flustered man back toward the door.

"Credentials. Now," he growls.

"Uh, uh, Dr. Perenski . . . ," the man babbles, and tugs at his lapel where he has a picture of himself on a badge clearly listing his name and title.

"Show me a second form of ID," my brother demands in his scary-as-all-get-out bear growl, and I don't stop him. Because for the first time ever, I realize that my apartment fucking *exploded* because someone wants me dead.

***

Later that evening, I'm slurping down soup and chowing on a sandwich, staring into space while Skyler is in the window seat, curled in a little ball, finally asleep. My mother and father left with my assurances that I'd eat everything and do exactly as the doctors say. They also practically demanded Skyler and I stay with them once I get out, but I explained that, as much as I hate to admit it, their place isn't secure enough for Skyler. Not to mention, if someone is out to kill me, the last place I'm going to lead them to is my parents'.

Since the doctors are holding me overnight for observation, I have a little time to think about our next move. If I don't do that, I'll obsess over Nate. We still haven't heard anything, but a couple of hours ago, Royce, Wendy, and Bo couldn't find Rachel in the waiting room, which likely means they called her back. Either that or they gave her concerning information. The doctors were mum about it, which put Wendy in a tailspin. Last I heard, she was having Mick bring her "red" laptop. The red one is the one she uses for all her funky poaching that she doesn't talk to us about. Says it's safer the less we know.

I take the last sip of the cooling chicken soup I can choke down and push the tray to the side as the door opens and Rachel enters.

"Hey . . ." I'm shocked to see her in the flesh. Her eyes are red rimmed, her hair back in a messy knot on her head. She's wearing the same pants she wore earlier today, but her top is a bright-pink hospital scrub. It looks so out of place on her that I almost laugh. Except my heart is pounding so hard I can feel it throughout my entire body. Even the pain meds can't dull this ache.

She licks her lips and comes over to my side. "Nate survived." Her voice is scratchy, and her gaze scans the room, noting Skyler asleep before she takes in my form. "You're okay?"

I nod. "How is he?" I whisper as her gaze jumps up to meet mine.

She closes her eyes, and I can tell that she's trying to be strong, but she doesn't have to be. Not now. Not with us. Not when her whole world is lying in a hospital bed in the ICU.

I lean far enough forward to reach her wrist and encircle it with my hand before tugging her closer. She starts to shake her head, but I bring her to sit on the side of my bed by my hip and wrap my arms around her. For a moment she's as stiff as a board; then something inside her must crack, because her body convulses. Her head falls near my chest, forehead against my neck, and she clutches my sides as though her life depends on it. A keening cry leaves her, muffled by my neck as her tears soak my skin and hospital gown.

Skyler wakes up from across the room and jumps to attention, then rushes over to us and, easing down next to Rachel on the bed, puts both of her hands on her friend's shoulders. I hold Rachel as she cries hard. The pain in my chest is blistering, my head ready to burst with each throbbing pulse of my heartbeat, but I don't care. I'll take every inch of pain if it helps get her anguish out.

"Nate?" Skyler mouths to me.

"He's alive," I say out loud, and Rachel jolts and sobs against my neck.

After a few minutes, she finally eases her face back, wipes at her nose and eyes, and clears her throat. "I'm sorry."

I frown. "Sorry for what? Being human? Needing your friends?"

Skyler runs her hand up and down Rachel's back. "We're here for you. I'm just so, so, so sorry this happened . . . It's all my—"

"Don't you dare say it's your fault," Rachel snaps, her tone filled to the brim with anger. "The only person responsible for my husband being hooked up to machines fighting for his damn life is the evil that created a bomb and attached it to your man's door. Nathan and I take risks in this job. Every day we are committed to taking a hit if that's what's needed to protect our charge. We take all the precautions possible, which is why he's still alive." She looks down and away as if she's seeing something off in the distance or remembering something.

Her gaze unfocused, she continues. "He must have heard the click of the timer when he unlocked the door. If he hadn't run, all of us could have been dead or hurt far worse. My husband took the brunt of that explosion . . . and I'm proud. I'm *so proud* of him for doing what he could to warn us, to give us the time to react." Her voice shakes, and a tremor wracks her frame. She sniffs and lifts her chin up in a move showing her strength and resolve.

Skyler bites her lip and nods, obviously so overcome with sadness she's unable to respond.

"What did the doctors say?" I grab Rachel's hand and hold it between both of mine. Skyler grabs her other hand and mimics my gesture.

She inhales fully and then lets it out slowly. "They said he arrested twice on the table, but they were able to bring him back. He had a collapsed and punctured lung they needed to repair but that wasn't the biggest problem. It was the shrapnel in his back and the blood loss. It perforated one of his kidneys, the intestines, and a small portion of the stomach, plus demolished his spleen. They removed the spleen, patched up the stomach and kidney, and had to remove a section of his intestines. What we didn't realize was that his back was burned pretty badly as well, so they treated those wounds and have him in a medically induced coma. They don't plan to take him out of the coma for at least the next couple of days. His body needs the time to heal."

"So, he's going to be okay?" Skyler asks with a hint of hope in her voice.

Rachel shrugs. "They told me it would be touch and go for the next forty-eight to seventy-two hours, but they're doing everything they can." She swallows, and her voice shakes as she continues. "They said he's a fighter . . . and he is. He'll fight to come back to me."

Skyler pulls Rachel into her arms and holds her as she breaks down once more.

"Do you need us to call anyone?" I feel useless lying in a hospital bed like an invalid.

Rachel sits back up and wipes at her tears. "I've spoken with his mother. Their clan will be flying to Boston tomorrow."

"What about you?" I ask.

"I'll be fine." She continues to wipe at her tears. "The nurses rolled in a cot for me. I'm going to watch over him, sleep by his side so he'll know I'm there."

I nod. "Skyler could come with you," I offer, even though I don't want Sky anywhere outside of my line of sight.

Rachel shakes her head. "No. No. Sky has to be watched over too. Paul is still out there holding court. Big guy." She smiles briefly. "He said he'll be taking care of you while Nate and I are laid up."

"Yeah, is that okay?" Skyler says, always worried about everyone else over herself.

Rachel chuckles through her emotions and cups Sky's cheek. "Nate would be so angry if anything happened to you. The best thing you can do for Nate or me right now is to stay safe. And that guy out there"—she points to the door—"is a professional. I have no worries with you under his watch. How about you, Parker? What did the doctors say?" She glances at the bandage on my head. "Skyler screamed her lungs out when you blacked out and hit your head."

I lift my hand and rub my fingers over the goose egg I'm sporting. "Yeah, well, my head is harder than it looks." I wink at her, and she nods.

"Now that I believe."

"They're just keeping me overnight for observation. Concussion, stitches, a knot on the back of my head, and bruised ribs and sternum, but because of your husband and his heroics, I'm going to be fine."

Rachel's jaw firms, and there's a tic in her cheek. "He'd be happy to know he gave us the time to back up."

"We'll visit with him tomorrow when I'm set free."

On that note, Rachel stands and rubs at her arms. "Thank you, guys. I'm really glad you both are okay. It's a small comfort knowing that we did our job."

Skyler hugs Rachel again and whispers something in her ear. Rachel nods and looks Skyler in the eye for a long time before she squeezes her hand and slips out of the room.

"What did you say to her?"

"I told her that once Nate is back in top form, we'll be celebrating at our new house and that I fully expect to have Nate and Rachel back as my security team the moment he's better. Told her to look forward to moving into her own new home."

"Good." I reach out, and Skyler moves into my space. I scoot over to the side the best I can and pat the empty space at my hips.

Skyler grins and eases onto the bed, gets under my crappy hospital blanket, and snuggles against my bruised chest. I bite back a groan until the pain subsides once she's settled. I suck in a large breath and rest my chin on the crown of her head.

We stay that way for so long I think she may have fallen asleep until a tired yawn escapes her lips and she says, "Speaking of homes . . . we no longer have one."

"Sure you do!" a chipper voice says from the doorway as Wendy saunters in, carrying a bag. She ignores our confused faces as she pulls out a bundle of clothing from the bag. Once she's laid out the items, I note a pair of jeans and a T-shirt that I recognize. She puts them in the cabinet along with what looks like a pair of burgundy boxer briefs and a rolled-up pair of socks. Then she hangs a flowery sundress that I know I saw Skyler wear on our trip to Madrid. "Hope you don't mind that I had our housekeeper go through your bags. She washed all your clothes except for the unmentionables, which she washed by hand, then took the dry-cleanable items out for cleaning. The rest she unpacked in one of the suites in our McMansion." Wendy closes the cabinet and wipes her hands like she's dusting them off. "There. All situated for release tomorrow. Our driver will be here at the ready to bring you home."

"Home?" Skyler drawls, sleep clouding her tone as Mick saunters into the room.

"You're moving in with us until your house is ready. It makes the most sense. We have tons of room, and as you stated, the security in our community is like Fort Knox. I have also contacted your Realtor and asked what it would take to speed the process up. They've agreed to get you in the house within the next two weeks. Since you're paying cash in full, the escrow process can be sped up."

Skyler sits up, sleep leaving her instantly. "Really? We're going to move into our home in two weeks?"

Wendy grins huge and loops her arm around Mick's waist. "My man is the shit."

"Cherry, how many times have I told you that the colloquialism *the shit* makes absolutely no sense. To be the shit you'd have to be shit, which therefore makes the entire statement a false positive. Essentially meaningless."

She pouts. "Then you're the bomb!"

Skyler cringes and I wince.

"Oh . . ." Wendy's expression falls into one of chagrin. "That wasn't good timing."

Mick turns her chin and kisses her lips softly before tapping her nose. "You're adorable. And your friends get the point. Alas, they are probably very tired. You've dropped off their clothes, told them about their home, settled where they will be living as of tomorrow—I think it's time you give them space to rest."

"But . . . I don't like being away . . ."

He holds her chin. "Cherry . . . Parker and Skyler are fine. See." He eases her face toward us using one finger. "They are right there. They have a very large soldier guarding their door. One I'm confident could do severe damage when pressed. You have nothing to worry about."

Wendy pouts, and I can see her bottom lip tremble. Ah, my minxy is scared. "Are you sure you're okay?" she asks me.

"I got my girl with me; you've provided us with a place to stay. Thank you for that."

"Yes, thank you so much," Skyler adds.

"We'll be fine, and we'll see you tomorrow."

Wendy nods, and Mick leads her toward the door. "Sleep as well as you can. I'm very glad to see you are both safe."

On his words, Wendy breaks from his arms and rushes over to the hospital bed, where she leans over and kisses me on the forehead and then does the same to Skyler. "Don't freak me out like that ever again. I don't do well with getting phone calls saying my friends were blown up."

I grab her hand and squeeze it, letting my eyes tell her how much her concern means to me. "We don't like it either."

"Try not to do that again," she teases as she walks out the door, her man's arm hooked around her waist.

Skyler chuckles and cuddles back against me. I groan and hiss when she digs her shoulder into my sternum but hold her tight until she settles once more.

"I'm hurting you," she says tightly, her body a live wire ready to snap.

"You're doing no such thing." I rub my hand up and down her arm until she relaxes. "You being close, my skin touching yours, inhaling your peaches-and-cream scent, *heals me*. Don't ever doubt the power you have over me, Peaches. Now go to sleep. We have a lot to deal with tomorrow."

"Okay, honey," she says against my chest, and I can feel the exact moment her body fully relaxes. My girl is out cold, exhaustion taking over.

Closing my eyes, I ignore the ringing that has definitely lessened since I've been awake but not gone away completely.

With Skyler in my arms, my brother at my door guarding us, and Nate looking like he'll make it, I let the pain meds and fatigue take me off to dreamland too.

3

SKYLER

Motion in the room has me opening my eyes. A nurse is adjusting something on a stand next to Parker's bed. It looks like she's changing out one of the clear bags that are giving him fluids.

The nurse smiles softly and puts her hand up to her lips, making the universal gesture for keeping quiet. I nod and ease up and away from the bed. Parker's hands tighten around me, and he wakes instantly.

"Where you going?" he mumbles sleepily.

"Gotta go to the bathroom."

"You'll need to use the restroom outside." The nurse points to the door. "We're monitoring his urine output, and the bathroom in the room is for patients only."

I roll my eyes and maneuver out of the bed. "I'll be back."

Parker yawns. "Make my brother go with you."

"'K, honey." I run my fingers down the bandage-free side of his face, loving more than anything that he's alive and I can do this. After almost losing him, I know with every fiber of my being that this is the face I want to wake up to every morning, the face I want to fall asleep by every night. He's it for me.

Parker James Ellis is the one.

He may not be perfect, but he's perfect for me. I smile as he closes his eyes, and I leave the room, blinking at the brightness of the hallway.

Paul is standing guard, his hands behind his back clasped at his crossed forearms, legs apart in a wide stance, looking positively menacing . . . and sexy as all get-out. The man absolutely knows how to work a pair of camos.

Instead of speaking, he does a chin lift that basically asks "What's up?" without having to actually say it. Totally hot-guy soldier. I get how that vibe would work for a lot of women . . . or in his case, his *man*, Dennis.

Before I can say anything, I hear someone yelling, "There you are! My God, Sky! What the hell!" I turn and see Tracey storming down the hospital hallway, almost as loud as a bullhorn in the middle of the freakin' night.

As I'm about to approach her, mostly to get her to be quiet so as not to wake the ailing patients, Paul maneuvers me behind his back with one muscular arm, his other hand on the holstered gun under his arm. "Stay back," he growls.

I'm not sure if that is meant for me or Tracey.

"Back off, *Rambo*; that's my best friend you've got."

"Stop right fucking there or I pull my gun. Do not test me, lady." His voice is a deep rumble, like thunder announcing an impending storm. Paul is an impenetrable wall in front of me, his body language threatening and every muscle strung tight as a drum, ready for any action.

Tracey's eyes go wide, and she stops in her tracks. I come up behind Paul's back and tap his shoulder. Without looking at me, he rumbles, "You got somethin' to say, sis, you say it, but you do so from behind me. Got it?"

"Sis? She is not your family, *Sylvester*. Back away," Tracey demands, and tries to go around him. Bad idea. Paul is unfazed, both protective and foreboding at the same time when he extends the beefy arm that was holding me back, stopping her with his hand on her chest.

"Paul, honey, she really is my best friend and agent." *For now.* I think that part in my head but don't say it. Now is not the time to deal with my rocky relationship with Tracey.

"I don't know; she looks a little wild eyed. Don't go too far." Paul removes his hand from his gun and moves to the side but remains close enough that he can react if there is a problem.

"I'm fine." I wave him off, but he doesn't look convinced.

"What the hell is going on? I texted you fifteen billion times," Tracey says sourly.

I pull my phone out of my back pocket and note the multiple texts and voice mails, the first around the time of the explosion.

"How did you find me?" I frown, my head buzzing with the need for more sleep, and my bladder screaming, reminding me why I got up in the first place.

"Are you kidding me? Your penthouse catches fire, your boyfriend's apartment blows up, and you don't call your best friend? I've been here for hours trying to hunt you down, but no one would say a thing. I just happened to get up to use the restroom, and there you are." She puts her arms around me. "It's okay, Birdie, I'm here now."

And it does feel good to be in my friend's arms. I hug her back.

"I'm so sorry for your loss," she says while rubbing her hands up and down my back. "It will be okay. I'll take care of you. You know I'm always going to be here to take care of you."

God, I'm so tired, I can barely follow what she's saying. "Wait . . . What? My loss. You mean my house?" I struggle to put two and two together as I pull away.

She grabs me back and holds me tighter. "No, your man. He died in that explosion, right? I'm so sorry. I know how much you cared for him."

I shake my head, feeling like cobwebs are coating every synapse that's trying to fire. "No. No." I push back. "Parker's fine. I mean . . . he's hurt but he's fine."

Her eyes narrow for a moment before she smiles wide. "Oh, thank God! I'll bet you're so relieved. Then . . . oh my, did your bodyguard die? That was one hell of an explosion. I saw the hole it left behind."

"No. Nate's . . . Well, he almost died. Technically did die in surgery a couple of times, but we're hopeful that he's going to pull through."

Her lips tighten as she nods. "Yes, yes, that's so good. Still, Birdie, I'm here for you. We can fly you back home to New York and get you settled once again. And I'll be there. Staying with you until everything goes back to normal."

My bladder takes this moment to remind me that I really do have to *go*. "Follow me to the restroom." I hook my arm in hers and head down the hall. Paul follows close behind until I hear a snapping sound behind me, and all of a sudden, there's Bo, jumping out of a blue cushioned hospital chair in the waiting room.

"You've got the door," Paul rumbles, and gestures to Parker's door. Bo promptly goes over to Parker's room and leans against the wall outside.

"Paul, we're in the hospital; it's two in the morning. No one is going to get me here. You don't have to follow me to the bathroom."

He huffs. "I'm not the one who almost got blown up. How's about you start to understand the phrase 'I'm on you.' Which means, you don't go *anywhere* I don't know about, with anyone I don't know. This woman, I don't know, but since Bo didn't balk at the two of you arm in arm, it means he does know her."

"I told you, *Private Ryan*." Tracey uses another mocking name for Paul that makes me grind my teeth in irritation. "I'm her best friend. I also happen to be her agent. Which means you can run along." She tries to wave off Parker's brother, a huge mass of sinew and muscle. A special ops soldier who I know does all kinds of scary things that most people wouldn't dream of.

"You have no clue what you've stepped into, lady." Paul narrows his gaze at Tracey, and I can see things are getting well and truly twisted between them.

She laughs haughtily, takes two steps forward, and gets in Paul's face, her voice dropping an octave. "You think I don't know what you do, who you are? I can see it all over your face. Career military. Probably special ops. I know the type. My father *was you* forty years ago. And I was a daddy's girl. He taught me everything he knows. I'm sure you're running through all the possible scenarios on how you could break me using only one hand so you could get Skyler out of reach with the other. You're a meathead. A gun for hire. A trained killer. The difference between me and everyone else you attempt to scare is this: I'm. Not. Afraid. Of. You."

Whoa. Where the hell did *that* come from? My mind is spinning so hard I can barely see straight. I remember from when we were little that Tracey's dad was in the military or something, gone for long periods of time, weeks, sometimes several months. He had a giant safe in his office where Tracey told me he kept tons of guns. She used to brag that her daddy taught her how to shoot and how good at it she was. I just figured she needed to boast whenever possible because her dad was rarely around, unlike my dad, who was always there for me.

"Damn, Tracey, I know you're pissed I didn't call you, but you don't need to take it out on Paul. He's doing me a favor by watching out for me, and he's Parker's brother and a *veteran*. I'd appreciate if you'd show him the respect he's earned."

Tracey looks at Paul and then back at me before she inhales long and slow. "I'm sorry for my outburst. I was worried about my best friend. You got caught in the crosshairs."

Paul doesn't say anything, just nods, his jaw looking tight as he tips his head and looks Tracey up and down as if he's analyzing her. I wonder if he does that all the time to people or just to people who are connected to me because I'm his new charge.

Finally he breaks his silence. "Hurry up. I prefer you locked in tight with my brother for the night, and pretty soon, he's going to start worrying."

He's right about that. If I don't get back to my man soon, he'll cause a ruckus by getting out of bed and coming after me.

Behind me, Paul pokes his head into the women's restroom, crouches low, and stands. "You're safe." He nods at the bathroom, and I want to roll my eyes but realize again, he's just doing what he feels is necessary to keep me safe.

"Well, pretty soon she'll be getting on a plane and going home to New York, and you and Parker won't have to worry about anything. Right, Birdie? We'll get you back safe and sound." Tracey's tone drips with annoyance.

I blink at Tracey a few times in utter disbelief as Paul's lips thin into a hard flat line.

"This true? You bailing on my brother and going to New York?" Paul's voice is suddenly filled with emotion, and not the good kind.

"Of course," Tracey says at the same time I respond with, "Absolutely not."

"Trace, we need to talk about what you think is happening, because there is no way I'm going back to New York. I'm moving in with Mick and Wendy for a couple of weeks until our house is done and Parker and I can move in together."

Her nostrils flare, and her face flushes red. "You could have been killed tonight! Someone wants your boyfriend dead, and they'll kill you in the process! You have to come home where I can take care of you!" Her voice is strained, bordering on hysterical. She's two clucks from the cuckoo's nest, proving how much this is freaking her out. She's never experienced me being at risk like this, and regardless of our fight about Johan and everything else, she loves me and wants to see me safe.

I run my hand down her arm in an attempt to comfort and soothe. "Flower, I'm fine. You don't need to worry about me. Paul has me covered. The cops are working on this. They're going to find out who planted that bomb and set the fire and bring them to justice. In the meantime, though, I'm not leaving Parker's side. He's all that matters to me. I love him more than anything. He's my entire world."

Tracey's expression goes blank, and I watch as tears fill her eyes. "What about me? I love you. I want you safe. I couldn't bear to lose you, Birdie."

I shake my head. "I'll be fine. Trust me. It's all going to be okay."

"You're putting yourself at risk for a man who will probably hurt you in the end. Just like everyone else has. I'm the one who's been there for you."

I grab both of her arms and force her to look into my eyes. "Trace, you are my best friend, and I love you, but you need to understand, I'm choosing to spend my life with Parker. If it ends up being a mistake like you think it is, it's my mistake to make. Except I know what I see when he looks at me and when he tells me he loves me. I see our lives together playing out in my mind, and honey, it's beautiful. So damned beautiful it brings tears to my eyes." Which is happening at this very second.

"You are in so deep you can't see the forest for the trees. He's going to fuck you over. Mark my words." Her voice is dripping with acid.

I grit my teeth. "I can't hear this right now. I have to use the facilities and get back to my man, who's lying in a hospital bed because of me, not the other way around. Someone wants to hurt me by hurting the people I love. That's my cross to bear, but right now, I'm tired. I'm so damn tired, Tracey. I can't listen to you second-guess my relationship another minute. Just go home. Go back to New York. Once this is all over, we'll find the time to talk. Right now . . . I don't need you."

Her eyes fill with tears, and her mouth drops open.

"Go. Not only do I not need you, I don't want you here. Just go. Let me deal with my life. I don't need you, Tracey. Not anymore."

On those parting words, I turn around and go through the door to the bathroom. If she can't understand how much Parker means to me and be a part of that, I'm going to have to let her go.

I take care of business, and when I leave the bathroom, she's gone and Paul is waiting patiently. I expect him to walk behind me; instead, he loops his arm over my shoulder and tucks me close to his warm, massive chest.

The tears don't come.

I'm done crying.

Paul squeezes the ball of my shoulder and kisses the crown of my head. "It will be okay. That life you want with my brother? You're gonna have it. I swear."

I pat his stomach and kiss the underside of his jaw. "Thanks, Paulie." I use Parker's nickname for him.

His chiseled features gentle, and he smiles, kisses the crown of my head one more time, and opens the door to Parker's room.

I can see my man is awake and frowning. "Peaches, you took a long fucking time."

"Yeah, I had a chat with Tracey."

Paul pats my shoulder and leaves us alone, closing the door behind him.

"What was she doing here?"

I shrug and run my hands through my ratty-ass hair. "I don't know. She must have found out about the trouble somehow and then came here. She'd been texting since it happened, but I had my phone on silent."

"So, she tracked you down here?" He frowns.

"Yeah, said she was waiting for me for hours. Probably saw one of the guys or whatever." I yawn, my entire body feeling heavy.

"Get in bed, baby. You're dead on your feet."

I kick off the slippers the nurse gave me earlier and get back into bed with my man. The second his arms tuck me against his solid chest, I hear his heartbeat and start to drift.

"We're going to have a beautiful life together . . . ," I murmur against his heated chest.

"Yes, baby, we are. No doubt about it. This is just a rock in our path," he whispers, and kisses my forehead.

"More like a boulder." I sigh.

He chuckles, and the comforting feeling of his warmth, the sound of his breathing, and his hands holding me close take it all away.

***

Two days later, and I'm snoozing on the chaise lounge in the large suite in the Pritchard McMansion when I'm awakened by the sound of Parker gleefully booming, "Finally!"

I push up onto my hand as Parker comes around the chaise and eases down slowly, his body still recovering from the explosion. He rubs a hand down my calf. "They got him, baby!"

Fully coming awake at his smiling face, I sit up and tuck my feet underneath my ass. "Got him?" I push the hair out of my eyes and focus on my guy, who has his phone pressed to his ear.

"Benjamin Singleton. Five-O picked him up trying to sneak back into his apartment. Dumbass." He grins. "What else you got for me?"

And as suddenly as that grin appeared on his face a second ago, his expression falls flat. "You're kidding me."

I reach for Parker's hand, but he's already up and pacing. He winces and tucks one of his hands around his sore rib cage. We have it wrapped for stability to help keep the pressure off the bruised ribs, but that won't do much if he's jumping around or moving too quickly.

"He's a fucking liar!" he roars.

I stand up and come to a stop at his back and wrap my arm around his waist to remind him of his injuries. I press my forehead to his warmth so he'll feel my presence, hopefully grounding him through whatever is setting him on a tirade.

"Seriously? This is a joke! I can't believe this shit. That's all you can get him on?"

As he's barking into the phone, there's a knock on our door, and without me saying a word Paul and Wendy walk in.

Parker turns around and scowls, his face a mask of rage and pain. He looks at Paul, and his mouth tightens. "Yeah, Paul's here now. Fine. Thanks." He says this as if it hurts him to say it. "He's not the guy?" He stares at Paul.

Paul shakes his head once, obviously knowing exactly what they're talking about. Wendy must know too, because she looks as though she's smelling something rank right at this very moment.

"Honey, tell me what's going on," I prompt softly.

"He's. Not. The. Guy." He twists his lips into a snarl, and his voice rises, rage so clearly displayed across his handsome face, I'm worried steam is going to come out of his ears.

"Had a gut feeling, brother. Told you that." Paul shakes his head in obvious apology.

"You told me that. What the fuck, Paul! You said you'd *handle this*. Get your guys on it."

"And I am, brother. If you'd think clearly once you cool down, you'll realize that it was *my* guys who tipped off the cops to get Benny in the first place."

Parker's head jolts back, and his jaw locks. "Cool down? How the hell can I cool down when my woman and I are not safe? We're hiding out in our friends' house waiting for the shit to go down. And this guy is out there waiting for us to make a move! And you're telling me and the cops are telling me that Benjamin fucking Singleton is not our guy!" he roars, and tosses his phone on the couch.

Wendy glances at the phone and then back at Parker and finally at me. Her eyes are pools of sadness and concern.

Benny is not the guy.

"So what did Benny say to the cops?" I ask.

Parker huffs, tosses his hands up in the air, and lets out a pained groan, hunching over as if he's just been sucker punched in the gut. He pulls in quick bursts of air as I rush to his side.

"Honey, you've got to sit down, take it easy."

"Tired of takin' it easy, Sky," he says through clenched teeth as he hobbles to the nearest love seat.

"Can one of you three tell me what's happened?"

Paul takes a wide-legged stance and puts his hands behind his back as if he's addressing a superior officer. "Benjamin Singleton was picked up and questioned at the station. He copped to writing and hand delivering the two letter-sized notes to Parker. He says he's in love with you, and he was attempting to warn off Parker. He admits to following you around New York and securing a job in the building where your boyfriend works so he could be closer to you."

I can't stop my mouth from dropping open and my blood from boiling. He followed me? Around New York?

Paul keeps hammering the nails into the coffin. "Then when you moved here and leased the penthouse, you basically made all his twisted dreams come true. He told the cops you were considering dating him but Parker was in the way. Which, of course, had the cops believing he was your texter, as well as the person who set the fire in your penthouse and the bomb in Parker's home."

"Makes sense." I sit next to Parker and rub my hand up and down his thigh, trying to calm him as much as myself. He covers my hand with his own, brings it up to his mouth, and kisses my fingertips. I take a slow breath, getting my bearings as best I can.

"Yes, it does. Only he's got several alibis for the time frame of the fire. Also, he took the week off when you left to go to Spain. One of those days he came and visited the IG offices and dropped off note number two, which we have on the security feed. It's the note that says, 'You can't hide her forever. She is mine. We're the same.' Which is very similar to the first one that said, 'I am her. She is me.'"

"I don't even know what those mean." I frown and squeeze Parker's thigh.

"Apparently, he meant to remind you that you were both child actors, grew up in the business, and had done that one commercial together, making you"—he motions air quotes—"the same."

"He's nuts," I whisper.

"He proceeded to tell the cops that the second note was to warn Parker off and remind you of your connection. He denies having anything to do with the fire or the explosion and has been able to provide proof of his location during the time frame the fire was lit. He's spent the last week visiting his mother in Hoboken, New Jersey. Repeated toll images show him driving in and out of the city, and there were several credit card charges this past week. He's also given the cops a list of people to confirm his whereabouts in New Jersey."

"And all of this means . . ." I let the thought dangle, hoping one of them picks it up and goes with it.

Parker turns toward me, grabs my hands in both of his, and holds on to them. "Baby, it means the bomber is still out there, and right now, we have very little to go on."

I feel as though I'm shrinking, and I pull my hands away, curl my legs up into my chest, and wrap my arms around them. Sunny notices my movement and wiggles her doggy body up to the love seat and hops on it to snuggle against my side. Midnight had at some point placed his booty next to his daddy's feet and stuck himself there to watch the show.

"Which brings me to why I'm here," Wendy chirps, effectively lessening the blow of Parker's explanation.

She moves around the room until she finds my purse and holds up her finger, showing me a tiny square the size of a Chiclet piece of gum.

"This is a tracker. It's going inside the lining of your purse. I've already put them on all of your vehicles, and of course your phones."

"Great. I'm being tracked by a psycho and by one of my best friends. Awesome," I announce flatly.

Wendy comes over to my side and gets down on her knees. "Sky, I get that this shit is extreme. No one should have to deal with it. Especially not someone as kind and sweet as you. Since it is happening, we have to be smart. This is the only way I know to make sure you're safe at all times. Are you okay with it?"

I shrug. "It's fine. Whatever."

I can't tell her right now that I do not want to deal with any of this. It seems like every time we take two steps forward, we have to take four back. Benny's not the bomber. Great. Fantastic.

Then who is?

Wendy pats my knees, and I curl myself into an even tighter ball.

"Sky, I've got my men on this," Paul says. "Skilled men. Experts. Trained in this type of scenario. They're tracing the bomb's signature now."

"And why haven't they found it?" Parker asks in an accusing tone.

Paul's jaw tightens as if on reflex. "It's tough to narrow down. The bomb has all the benchmarks of someone who's in government. Black ops as we said, only it's so closely linked to what they're trained on, it's hard to decipher the calling card from that of the instructor who teaches the coursework." He tilts his head, and his lips compress. "My guys are on it, though. Very close. It won't be long now before they can narrow it down more."

"I get you. What I'm upset about, and I'm certain you can understand, is that I don't know how to keep my woman safe. I feel like we're sitting ducks, and the last thing we want to do is bring any trouble to Wendy and Mick's door."

"Oh please. You're family! Don't you ever worry about putting us out. You're in trouble, we're in trouble. That's how family works, right?" Wendy says.

I watch Parker as he offers a small, sad smile. "No, Wendy, that's not how family works. We protect one another; we don't bring more harm. Skyler and I need to get out of here. Disappear for a while. Let Paul's team do their magic." He glances at Paul before tugging my wrist and pulling it from around my legs so he can slowly unravel my little cocoon of safety. "Come here, Peaches."

And without even blinking, I'm cuddling up to his side, letting his warmth invade the chill that crept over my skin as the situation seemed to get more bleak by the minute.

"You feelin' the need to escape?" Paul asks vaguely.

"Yeah, man, I think it's the best plan." His voice comes out tired and ragged. My poor man is aging a year with each day that we don't have a resolution.

Paul smirks. "I may just have a stellar idea for that. You're going to need your passports and a jet."

Parker smiles at me with one eyebrow cocked. "Looks like we might be needing that fancy jet of yours again, Peaches."

I nudge his shoulder and snort. The ease with which this man can bring me back from the brink of despair is mind-boggling. Still, I need to give as good as I get. "Told you it was a good investment."

4

PARKER

"I cannot believe you talked me into this, Paulie." I wince and hold on to my sore rib cage as I maneuver into the now familiar camel-colored lounge seat in Skyler's jet.

Skyler hovers over me like a momma over her baby chick. Making sure I have a pillow behind my back, running her fingers down the side of my head to check the stitches that are currently uncovered.

"Well, I simply cannot wait to introduce you to my beautiful country," Dennis announces with a huge smile on his face.

My brother grins and runs a beefy hand down his boyfriend's arm. It's sweet and a bit odd to see my brother so affectionate. Sure, he's a back-slapping, shoulder-squeezing type guy. Also shows his love for our mother and father when expected, but I've never seen him with a mate. Ever. And definitely never expected my big, burly, special ops, alpha brother to fall in love with a sweet, shy man like Dennis. Or any man at all for that matter. I'm still tripping off the fact that my brother is bisexual, not that it offends me. I firmly believe love is love, and any way it comes is a good thing for the person receiving it. It's just been a surprise, and having met Dennis and seeing the way he dotes on my brother, overall it's been a pleasant one. Plus, Ma *loves* that Dennis is in touch with his feminine side. He's always open to talking about clothes and style, books, cooking, decorating—basically all the same things she enjoys.

Dennis pushes his glasses up his nose and starts to remove his sport coat. Underneath he's wearing a mint-green polo tucked into a pair of chinos and a nice leather belt that goes with his very trendy loafers, sans socks. A very put-together look. All of that the exact opposite of my brother, who's wearing cargo pants and a tight-fitting navy tee that looks like it's seconds away from shredding at the seams of his bulging biceps. On his feet, a pair of lace-up boots. He and Dennis couldn't be more different, but somehow, they work perfectly.

"And the fact that you're going to help me with my little problem, Parker, means the world to me and my family," Dennis gushes.

It's not his gratitude that sets off all kinds of alarms in my head; it's the mention of a problem that I haven't been apprised of. "Problem?"

"Yeah . . . uh, about that," Paul says. "When I asked you and Skyler to come to Brazil, the request was twofold. The first was to get you the hell out of Dodge and somewhere safe while my guys work on the bomber and arsonist, and the other was that Dennis's family has a corporate and financial issue at work I thought you could take a look at. You know, with your experience . . ."

"If it's a financial problem, you've asked the wrong guy . . ." I start to object; then in my periphery, I see another person boarding the plane. My one and only big, black, well-dressed, smiling brother.

"Royce?"

He holds out his arms, palms out, his wingspan almost touching both sides of the plane, the guy's so huge. "In the flesh."

Skyler claps where she's sitting next to me. "Yay! Cool surprise!"

"Surprise?" I narrow my gaze at Paul.

"Well, I had to ask for reinforcements regarding the money concerns, and Royce offered to help a brother in need. Especially since most of the work for IG is suspended right now until your problem is solved."

"'Sides . . . you think I'm going to miss a free trip to Rio de Janeiro, God's country? And you know it's God's country since they have a giant Christ statue standing on a mountain looking over its people. You're lucky I didn't tell Momma Sterling, because Rio is on her bucket list . . . same as mine. Sho'nuff I'm gonna be sitting my ass in this swank jet on our way to paradise, seeing the sights and helping a brother out. Two birds, one stone, yeah?" Royce lifts his fist to Paulie, who knocks it.

Tension builds in my temples, and I press my thumb and index finger into them. "All I know is I'm in no position to do a lot of work. My body and my mind are mush right now. I'm concerned about one thing and only one thing: keeping Skyler safe."

Skyler runs her hand down my forearm and interlaces her fingers with mine. "Honey, I'm fine. Look, I have four guys around me right now to keep me safe, and besides, it's you the bad guy was after, so the more of your brothers here, the better."

"Bo and Wendy taking care of the office?" I ask Royce.

He nods. "Yeah, and Kendra's there." His nose crinkles at the mention of her name. "They said they're going to work on getting Annie back in the office. Once everything went down, she sent an email to Wendy, saying she quit. They're going to try and reverse that."

I clench down on my molars, and Skyler grips my hand tighter. We both feel awful about what happened to her, but it was me who laid into her repeatedly and wouldn't see reason. I'm going to have to do some groveling to make it up to her when this is all said and done. Just another to-do on the never-ending task chart of making things up to people that is currently my life.

I take in a long, deep breath and ease back as much as I can in my seat. Skyler lets go of my hand and fiddles with our dogs. Once again, she's decided they cannot be left with Wendy while we travel.

Royce takes a seat across from Paul and Dennis on the left side of the plane while Sky and I are on the right. The dogs are situated on the love seat in the same spot they were when we flew to and from Spain.

Once the captain announces we're ready for takeoff, the crew gets into position, and I wait to pick up the conversation until we're forty thousand feet in the air.

"Now that we're going to be here for a while, why don't you tell us what's going on back home that needs our attention, Dennis? Bring us up to date?"

"*Sim.* You know we're in the international import business and looking to expand to the States."

I nod as Paul reaches out an arm and extends it behind Dennis.

Dennis continues. "I've been receiving the financial statements from our accountant back home, and there are things that concern me." He frowns and runs his fingertips over his clean-shaven chin.

"Okay, do you own the company?" I need to know a bit more about the legal specifics.

"My brother, Fabian, and I each own half of the company. Our father left it to us when he retired. He's still involved in the day-to-day operations on a very limited basis and mostly just as a resource for Fabian. I do most of the international contracts, traveling, and making deals, which takes me out of the office and plant. Fabian runs the warehouse back home and handles the distribution and fulfillment. Another person does the buying based on the contracts I secure. It's been going great. Really well. And as I told you, we've been meaning to expand to the US and Asia for quite some time, but there have been discrepancies in the books that we can't always nail down, which concern me."

Royce leans forward. "Can you give us an example?"

Dennis pushes his thick black-rimmed glasses up his nose. "Financial discrepancies mostly. I'd set contracts for the client to purchase certain things at a certain price, and then I'd see it listed much lower from the supplier than the per-unit price I'd negotiated. When I checked with the team, they had no idea why it was like that. After it happened a few times, I contacted one of the suppliers and they didn't know what I was talking about since they were being paid based on their contracted amount. But the funds from the price difference weren't showing on the books."

Royce's mouth goes tight, and he rubs his hands together slowly. "Anything else?"

"Lost inventory. Shipping errors that would ultimately cost us tens of thousands in lost dollars on product or shipping alone. I understand that there are times when things get damaged, but we're talking full shipments disappearing. Never arriving where they're supposed to, forcing us to declare a loss."

"And the shipping company?"

"Claims they never got the product in the first place."

"But the inventory is gone?" I confirm.

Dennis nods.

Royce licks his lips and sucks them inside his mouth until I can't see them anymore before he shakes his head and runs a hand over his bald head. "Brother, sounds like you got an embezzler."

Dennis frowns, possibly because the word isn't translating since English is his second language.

"A thief. Someone on the inside may be stealing money. Noting in the books that the product costs less, then pocketing the difference," I clarify, and Dennis's eyes go wide.

"On top of that, an individual could possibly be selling the supposedly lost product to someone outside, under the table, and making that money without anyone being the wiser while the company chalks it up as a loss. You getting what we're sayin'?" Royce asks.

Dennis's expression is awash with what I can only interpret as sadness. "I don't know how what you say could be possible. All the people I work with are family or distant relatives and friends. My brother would have to know, and he says he thinks it must be an error in reporting and that there is no problem at all."

And there go the alarm bells ringing in my ears. His brother says there isn't a problem. Refutes the issue as an error in reporting? Hmm.

"I guess we'll have to take a deeper look, so I'd like to get Royce digging into those profit-and-loss statements."

"Damn straight. I'm 'bout to become best friends with your accountant and your financial team," Royce promises.

Dennis nods and his shoulders slump. Paul curls his arm closer to Dennis and grips his shoulder. He leans into his guy. "Hey, me and my brother are gonna figure this out, yeah?" He tips Dennis's chin and looks into the saddest brown eyes I've ever seen. And under Dennis's gaze, my big, badass brother melts.

"I've got you, Denny. You're my guy, right?" He taps him under the chin until Dennis smiles dreamily at my brother.

And then my brother does what I've never seen him do. He kisses Dennis. At first, I thought it would be weird, seeing my brother kissing a dude, but it's not. Dennis raises his hand and holds Paul's arm while Paul teases his lips in a series of nibbles and pecks.

"Eu te amo, pistola," he says softly against my brother's lips.

Paul grins, squeezes Dennis's neck, and kisses him lightly once more. "I know. You better?" he asks in a low tone that shows my bro can actually be tender.

"Olhando em seus olhos, sempre serei perfeito," Dennis says.

"Oh man, I wanna know what he said." Sky sighs dreamily, her body hanging over my chair so she can get closer and hear better.

Paul chuckles, and Dennis blushes but says, "At first, I told him I loved him. Second, I told him, 'Looking into your eyes, I'll always be perfect.'"

Skyler's mouth drops open, and her eyes become glassy.

"Don't you start crying, Peaches. You know what that shit does to me," I warn while tunneling my fingers through her hair and holding her at the nape until she looks at me. She clamps her lips flat, and her chin wobbles. "Don't you do it," I tease, before lifting her chin with my thumb and kissing her hard enough to make her forget her teary response.

Once I pull back I see the same dazed look on her face that Dennis had on his.

"Looking into your eyes is perfect too, honey," Skyler whispers.

"Baby, that was totally fuckin' cheesy, you repeating that." I chuckle, and she snort-laughs in response as the rest of the guys join in.

The rest of the flight, we have easy conversation, play cards, watch a movie, eat, and snooze. We refuel in Miami, but overall, I get better rest on the plane with my chair tipped back, my girl's hand in mine, my dogs sleeping across from us, and no threat to be had while up in the air.

***

When we arrived last night, it was dark as shit. Nothing to see, not to mention the five of us were seriously jet-lagged. Dennis and Paul got Royce, Sky, and me settled into a Hilton right next to the Copacabana Beach. Of course, the moment we walked into the hotel with our two dogs, the hotel staff looked at us funny until we upgraded our normal room to the penthouse for the week. Then, suddenly, they were fine with our two pups. Once we were situated, Dennis and Paul left to stay at Dennis's apartment in the city with the promise to come back late this morning to meet for breakfast.

I sit on the side of the bed and watch my beautiful girl sleep. She's absolutely gorgeous all the time, but when her eyelashes are fanning her cheeks, her hair is a wild lion's mane all over the pillowcase, and her bottom lip puffs out with each breath she takes, I'm stunned stupid all over again by her beauty. I run my finger down her arm, bringing the sheet with it as I go. My girl stirs but doesn't wake, even though her bare tits respond to the cool temperature of the room, tightening into hard little points before my eyes. My dick hardens in my briefs, and I move the sheet all the way down, exposing her entire naked body. We were too tired last night to do anything about the small dry spell we've had since our trip home from Spain a week ago and my recovery. My body isn't 100 percent, but my dick doesn't know that. He's standing straight up, rip-roaring and ready to go.

I use one finger to tease a pink nipple. Skyler turns her head to the side, moving her arm above her head, her back flat and her body open to my gaze. Easing over her form, making sure not to put any pressure on my sore ribs, I swirl my tongue around one succulent peak. Skyler sighs in her sleep, and her legs shift. I smile and suck her nipple into my mouth at the same time I lay my palm flat against her belly and slip my hand down until my fingers encounter her thin line of blonde curls that's like a little landing strip, showing my fingers, mouth, and cock just where to go. When I get my hand between her thighs and cup her mound, her body tightens, and a moan slips from her lips. I suck her nipple harder and glance up to gaze into two shimmering, lust-filled caramel-brown eyes. Skyler licks her lips as I open my mouth and worry her nipple with my teeth just enough to cause her to bite down into her bottom lip.

I release her nipple but grind the edge of my palm against her clit while I pierce her center with two fingers. She gasps.

"Morning, Peaches. I got a taste for something this morning, woke ravenous. I'll give you one guess what for, and it's not pancakes." I finger her harder, swirling my index and middle fingers, searching for that spot inside her that will curl her toes with pleasure.

"Uh, um, mmm . . . honey." I see I've got nonsensical Skyler this morning.

I slowly remove my hand, and she pouts. I'm not talking a little lip; no, my girl's entire face pouts. Getting off the bed, I gaze at her fuckhot body in utter appreciation while slipping off my boxer briefs and kicking them to the side.

"Honey . . . why'd you stop?" She brings her fingers to her thighs and grips the flesh as if she's trying to work that ache I started inside by rotating her hips.

"Told you I was hungry, baby." I get to the bottom of the bed and kneel at the edge. "Scoot your ass down here and open wide. If I don't get my mouth on you in the next minute, my dick might possibly explode."

She laughs and pushes her ass to the edge of the bed, lifts her knees shyly, but I can still see the V at the top of her luscious little cheeks. With my thumbs, I trace the crease of where her ass meets thighs, and gooseflesh breaks out against her skin.

"You cold, Peaches?" I taunt, petting what I can of her lower lips near her behind.

"No."

"Open your legs, Sky. Give your man what he wants. Offer it up to me on a silver platter, baby."

Her entire body trembles at my demand. The caveman talk works for my girl. Turns her way the fuck on.

"I won't ask you twice. I want to see that pretty pink pussy opened up and wet for me."

"Parker . . . ," Skyler says, but opens her legs about a foot.

"Knees to the mattress, baby, I'm ready to eat," I growl, seeing nowhere near enough of her pink flesh, until she does what I ask and spreads her legs wide, her knees resting against the white sheets.

"Fuck!" I dip my head close and inhale the scent of her honey until my mouth waters with the need to get in on the action. With as much restraint as I can, I run my hands from her knees up the inside of her thighs.

Her body is electric, her breath coming in heavy pants. "Look at you. So fuckin' pretty. My dream girl. Open for the taking, and only for me. Such a gift. The best present I've ever gotten was the day you became mine."

Skyler undulates, her body arching, tits pointing up like two sharp arrows ready to strike. "Touch me. Kiss me. Honey . . . I need you."

I use both of my thumbs and ease the lips of her sex apart, opening right to the soft heart of her before I delve my tongue as deep as it will go. I don't stop. Her body jolts and jerks, but I keep moving.

Drinking.

Licking.

Sucking.

Taking.

Until she's digging her nails into my scalp and screaming out her orgasm. And still, I don't stop. I keep at her, but this time, I use two fingers hooked deep as I lay my mouth over her clit and alternate between sucking and swirling my tongue in circles until my girl is going off like a rocket again.

When she's out of breath, panting like she's just run a marathon, I get up, go around to the side of the bed, and lie down. Before I can even tell her what to do next, she's straddling my hips, centering my cock, and slamming down.

"Fuck!" I roar, gripping her hips.

"Oh shit! Did I hurt you, baby?" she asks, pushing her hair out of her face.

I shake my head. "No, it just feels so fucking good I almost shot off in one go. Taking you there twice made me a hair trigger, baby. I suggest you take a slow ride this round."

She grins, eases her hips up, and slides them down. Then she lays her body over mine and works my neck, ear, nipples, and back up to my mouth, all while her hips are moving at a leisurely rate.

I run my hands up into her hair and bring her lips down to mine for a long, wet kiss. She takes it deeper, slanting her head left, then right, before sucking my tongue and nibbling first my top then bottom lip.

"You feel like heaven raining down on my skin, Sky. I want to drown in you, taste your soul when you make slow love to me."

She smiles wide and lifts up using her legs, making sure to avoid putting pressure on my chest and ribs as she moves up and down a little faster.

"Play with yourself. I wanna watch you worship your beautiful body."

"Honey. . . ," she whimpers, still riding slow, but now one hand covers her breast, and she uses her thumb and two fingers to pluck and pinch her nipple.

"That's it. Put your other hand where we connect. Feel where you're making love to me."

She slides her hand seductively down her body until her fingers separate around my aching length as I slip in and out of her wet heat.

Watching the combination of her playing with herself and touching the two of us between her thighs has my balls drawing up. My gaze is locked on the carnal display of her teasing her tit and clit. Electric tingles start at the base of my spine and work their way down my legs, up my chest, and out my arms. I can feel the pleasure she's giving me in my fucking fingertips.

"Peaches, you're everywhere, *all over me*. I feel you in my blood, owning every inch of my body. It's yours. I'm all yours."

Her back arches farther, her breasts jutting out, but she keeps her pace even as her sex locks down around my dick in a fist so tight I have to hold my breath.

That's all it takes. The fire inside of me shoots off, and I hold her hips down, grinding her clit against my pelvic bone until we're both crying out, and my release bursts from my body, mixing with hers.

When her body stops pulsating over mine and "the beast" is fully satisfied, she looks down at me with a sex-induced dreamy gaze. "You okay? Your ribs, chest?"

I ease my hand up her hip, ribs, and back down. "Yeah, Peaches, I'm perfect. I got your taste on my tongue, my dick is happy, and we're hidden away in Rio."

She giggles and eases off my softening cock. Right when she makes it off the bed and into the bathroom, the doorbell rings. Yep, that shit is fancy when you've got the penthouse, and if Sky wants to spend her money on the best, who am I to say she can't? We've already had that argument, and I lost, so I'm just along for the ride when it comes to her hotel stay preferences.

I maneuver out of bed, my ribs and chest more sore than they were yesterday, having been worked even though we were careful.

My underwear is near the end of the bed, so I toe it and lift it to where I can better get into it. I forgo anything else because the only people who know we're here are the hotel staff, Paul, Dennis, and Royce.

I leave the bedroom and close the door so Sky can have some privacy. Trailing through the living area, I make it to the door, check the peephole, and find Paul and Dennis standing outside. Without thinking twice, I open the door and let them in.

"Morning, guys. We just got up."

Paul walks in with a frown on his face, looking me up and down. Dennis, on the other hand, checks me out from head to toe and back, his entire face flushing a pink hue.

"P-Drive, really? You're fucking naked."

"So? You came to my room."

"Bro, my brother is practically naked in front of my boyfriend," he growls. "Put some goddamned clothes on."

It finally hits me what he's saying.

"Oh, you don't have to get dressed on my account." Dennis waves his hand over his still cherry-red face. "Wow. You Ellis brothers are genetically put together very well." He looks his fill until Paul wedges his entire body in front of Dennis like a six-foot-two wall of muscle.

"You like that when you got all of this keeping your bed warm?" He runs his hand down his chest and grips his crotch.

Dennis grins and puts a hand to Paul's chest. "Relax, *Paulo*. No need to be green. I am in love with you, my feisty *pistola*. Though it must be said that *seu irmão fica muito bem nu*. I cannot tell a lie." He grins, and his gaze shoots to me.

"I'll be getting ready for the day. Feel free to make coffee or continue bickering. Whatever floats your boat."

When I walk back into the bedroom, Skyler is standing with a towel wrapped around her body, her hair wet from the shower. "Was that Paul and Dennis I heard?"

"Yeah, and get this." I walk over and stand behind her where she's digging in her suitcase. She pulls out a pair of lacy underwear, and the beast takes notice. I grip her hips and rub up against her from behind.

She laughs and slaps at my hands, trying to remove her booty from having contact.

"Get what?"

"Paul got jealous. I answered the door like this, not thinking it through because, you know, it's just the guys. He got a little pissed that Dennis drooled a bit."

Skyler laughs. "Can't blame him there." She spins around, wraps her arms around my neck, and lifts up onto her toes. "My man is freakin' hot to trot! Naked or clothed but especially *naked*," she says, before kissing me silly. "Although, now that your brother has a boyfriend, you should probably be a bit more discreet."

"True." I kiss her once more, swiftly, before smacking her on her towel-covered ass and heading to the shower. "I'll be fast, and then maybe we can get them to take us down to the beach."

"Before you start looking into his company?"

"Definitely. There's no way I can work today. I need some time after that travel day. And we all need to take a load off."

"Yay! The pups will love that! Speaking of . . . I best go make sure they peed on the puppy pads and not on the carpet. You want me to grab you a cup of coffee?"

"I'd love that, baby."

For a moment, I watch Skyler shimmy into her lace panties and matching bra before tossing a short sundress over her head. It falls down to her midthigh in a flare of wild blues, purples, greens, and yellows, accentuating her honey-tanned skin and spectacular legs. She's a ball of light and color. That's what Skyler Paige does for me. Puts color into my world.

5

SKYLER

The water at Copacabana Beach is a startling deep blue with twinges of a dark moss green at the edge where the waves crash against the crescent shape going as far as the eye can see. We've just finished brunch, and I'm filled to the brim from eating fried bread, chicken and cheese croquettes, and scrambled eggs and tuna. At first, the last combination did not sound appetizing at all, but Denny, my new gay BFF and self-designated Rio guide, required that we eat it. He assured us it would be *"felicidade na minha boca."*

He explained that it translated to "bliss in my mouth," to which Parker immediately joked that I was bliss in his mouth and went on to state he'd proven such a thing that very morning. Everyone had a great laugh at my expense, and I blushed profusely at his candor, while he and Paul knocked fists like alpha hotheads.

Now we sit, full bellied, staring out over the ocean. I smile at Dennis. "Your city is beautiful, Denny. I wish Royce could have joined us."

Parker tucks me against his side while Paul loops an arm over Denny's shoulder to cuddle his guy.

"Peaches, Roy was wiped. He hasn't done international travel in a long time and doesn't sleep well on planes. Besides, Dennis gave him some of the newest financials, and he's going to get a bead on those later on this evening after he's slept and eaten off his jet lag. We'll catch up with him tonight for dinner."

I pout but nod. I'd hoped to spend a little time with Royce once I found out he was coming along on this trip. Most of the trips we've been on were with Bo, so I feel as though I have a deeper connection to him. I want the same thing with one of the other men Parker holds high in his life.

"Okay. What are we doing first?" I flick my gaze to my sleeping dogs where they wait patiently under the table for another walk. I smile and focus on Dennis and Paul.

"First and foremost, Sky, you are safe here, and you aren't," Paul announces. "Just because we're thousands of miles from home does not mean we're going to be completely lax. I'm still on you and Park. Yes, you can feel freer here. The likelihood that the person who's trying to hurt you knows where you are is slim to none. Which means I want to make sure you don't make that easier on the individual. No posting pics on your social media feeds or talking to folks back home. The people who know where you are, are trusted and vetted. Mom, Dad, Wendy, Pritchard, and Bo. That's it. No one else."

I tense up at the mention of the trouble back home. Parker presses his lips to my ear, his breath hot against my skin as he whispers, "You're safe. My brother and I are going to make it so."

My hand rests on Parker's thigh, and I squeeze in acquiescence, but turn my head to look into his sky-blue gaze. "I'm not worried about me, honey. If I lose you, there might as well be no me. After everything I've lost, losing what we have, what we're building together . . . I couldn't hack it. And I'm woman enough to admit it."

He cups my cheek, then tunnels his fingers through my hair until he's holding me at the nape. "You're not going to have to. It's you and me against it all. Remember?"

I lick my lips and swallow down the sudden emotion. "Yeah, honey. You and me."

"Against it all," he repeats, but takes my lips in the softest kiss. That single kiss tells me everything I need to know. He's aware of how important he is to me; he understands it and feels the same way. We're truly in this together.

"All right, you two, I think we're good. Just remember, I'm going to be around, keeping an eye out, but be wary. Enjoy yourselves, enjoy my man's home, but don't be stupid."

Parker tosses his napkin at his brother's face. "Shut up, bro. We got the message." He stands up, grabs the leash we had wrapped around his chair arm, and holds his hand out for me to take. Midnight and Sunny both bang around between the chairs until they rest their booties at their daddy's feet, tongues lolling out, ready for whatever is next on our agenda. "Now if you don't mind, my girl worships the sun, and my dogs need some exploring time. I'm going to take my woman for a stroll along the beach. You gonna give your man a little of your time too, bro?" He lasers his sardonic gaze on Paul, who scowls but stands up to follow.

"Come on, baby. Let's go get our feet wet." Parker holds my hand, and I follow him off the side steps of the beach restaurant and stop at the bottom to remove my flip-flops and take Sunny's leash while he has Midnight's. He removes his thongs too, the two of us letting the warm sands of Rio de Janeiro slide between our toes. I tip my head back up toward the sun and soak in the golden rays.

Parker waits silently until I'm done giving the world a hug, and we tread with our pups through the sand toward where the water is breaking against the shore. The dogs are excited but leery of the crashing waves and water running up and back.

We get to the water's edge and walk hand in hand, letting crisp waves slap against our feet and ankles as we go, watching our dogs chase the water in and out again playfully. I scan the horizon and see endless blue until it meets the earth, highlighting Sugarloaf Mountain and the city and mountain range beyond, where the Christ the Redeemer statue stands, arms stretched wide, overlooking God's country.

"Did you know that the Christ statue was designed by a Frenchman?" Parker mentions conversationally as I stare at the statue way off in the distance. I really want to see it up close and hope that Dennis plans to take us there while we're here.

I stop where I stand and press my sunglasses up into my hair. Parker is devastatingly handsome in his black aviators, his hair a bit curly on top, fluttering teasingly in the light breeze.

"For real?"

He nods and grins a pearly white smile.

God, thank you for bringing me such a beautiful man.

"Yeah, some say that's why the face of the Christ and Lady Liberty seem so similar. I think it's the fact that both are huge statues that make incredible statements of peace, love, and unity, regardless of the Christian nature of the statue here."

I grab Parker's hand and swing it, thinking about what he said. Our position, hand in hand walking along the beach, reminds me of our time in France. "I loved our time in Paris. Speaking of, have you talked to Sophie lately?"

He shakes his head. "No, but we've texted. She's a busy woman, and now she has a man she's committed to having in her life for the long haul. I'd like to invite her and Gabriel out once we're settled into our home. What would you say to that? I know before you didn't want to stay at her home, but I was hoping, after everything, you'd see there really isn't anything at all to be worried about. I'm all in with you, baby. There's not another woman for me."

I smile huge, turn toward him, plaster my chest to his, and wrap my arms around his neck. Sunny's leash creates a bit of resistance, but I hold strong. "I'd love that, honey. I know you care about her, and I'm no longer threatened by the fact that you once had a physical relationship with her. If you want Sophie to come visit us, I'll happily open my home."

He grins and squeezes my ass before nuzzling my nose. "That's good, baby, because I already told her that, after the new year, she and Gabriel can come visit and check out the house, meet my parents and the pups."

I slide my nose against his and press my lips to his before speaking softly. "You are too much."

"Hopefully just enough for you." He wraps his hands around my waist and spins me around in a circle. The dog leashes quickly tie us together, and we both laugh at our misfortune, kiss several times in quick succession, and maneuver out of our silly predicament.

When I turn around, I notice Paul and Denny about twenty to thirty feet behind us, wrapped in one another's arms. Paul is kissing up Denny's neck while Dennis laughs joyfully.

I nudge Parker's shoulder. "Did you ever think you'd see that?"

He glances behind us and watches as Paul cups Denny's face and lays a demonstrative lip-lock on him. One of Denny's feet playfully rises in the classic lovers' pose as his hands grip Paul's massive biceps. The man really is built. The two of them, standing together, having a private moment on a beach in Rio, are absolutely beautiful. So different, yet it works for them. Dennis is everything Paul is not. Quiet, charming, eloquent, and sweet to Paul's brooding, built, gruff, no-nonsense way. What Paul hides from others is openly visible when he's with Denny or Parker, and now with me: his heart is made of pure gold, and Dennis Romoaldo has captured it completely.

"Honestly? I had no clue my brother was into men. More and more, I'm getting used to it, but it's never bothered me. More revealing is that I've never seen him happy romantically. My money is on Dennis being the person Paulie settles down with."

I bite into my lip and squeal under my breath. "Righteous!" I blurt, and Parker chuckles, looping my waist with his arm so we can continue our walk.

"Yeah, it is. I'm happy he found something he loves as much as the honor and duty he fights for being a soldier. I worried like fuck about him. Last I heard, he's thinking about not reenlisting."

I tilt my head and glance over my shoulder back at the two men. Paul's gaze is on us, so I wave.

"You're a dork." Parker laughs.

"I'm just thinking . . ."

"Uh-oh. Nothing good ever happens after a woman says that." He brings his hand up to curve around my neck.

I growl playfully. "Seriously, I have an idea about what your brother can do if he chooses not to reenlist."

"Yeah? Lay it on me."

"Well, since he's made himself my protector until we figure out who this psycho guy is, what if he did that job for a living? I mean, Nate was military prior to owning Van Dyken Security. Maybe he could go into business with them, or start up one of his own?"

Parker nods. "Could work. Guess it depends on what he wants to do."

"Yeah."

"I'll mention it to him. Even when we get this situation on lock, I still want him on you until Nate and Rachel are a hundred percent."

"I'll make sure my accountant has his info, so he can issue payment every two weeks."

Parker stops and smiles wide. "Good luck with that, Peaches."

I frown and stand next to him, letting the wet sand suction around my feet up to my ankles as the surf splashes in and retracts.

He shakes his head. "Baby, he's never gonna let you pay."

I jerk my head back. "That's absurd. He has to let me pay him. I'm not a charity case—" I continue to argue, but I'm cut off.

"No, babe, you're my woman. His sister. *Family*. You need the services of someone like him. He isn't working. He'll provide that service. Period."

I grit my teeth. "Honey, listen to how crazy that sounds in your own head and hear it from my perspective. Really listen." The independent woman inside me is bristling with one helluva complaint.

He shrugs. "It's the way it is. You're family. Regardless of what you might think, your job makes you a target. My brother deals in neutralizing enemies. If he thinks you're in danger or unsafe, he's gonna step in. It's his way. It's who he is. You're now an important part of his world."

I wiggle my feet until I break up the sand that's built up around them up to my ankles and stomp closer to Parker and look up into his handsome face. "He will be paid," I clip, then turn and march off down the beach, taking my irritation with me.

Parker's laughter echoes from behind me until he and Midnight run past us, which immediately gets Sunny moving at a trot, so of course, I follow them.

***

The wire cable threading through the box above the cable car is the only thing I can hear inside this see-through box as it sails through the air, thirteen hundred feet above water and land toward Sugarloaf Mountain. As much as I want to take in the beauty that is Brazil from this height, I can barely breathe. I close my eyes and burrow against Parker's chest and hold on to my man as though my life depends on it. Probably because it does. Because we're going to fucking die out here. Those tiny wire cables are really thin. One of them is going to snap, making the weight distribution all jacked up, and it's going to toss us from side to side until the entire thing falls off and we end up in the South Atlantic Ocean or the forest-filled mountains directly below.

I can imagine the headlines and the story:

Actress Skyler Paige Dies a Horrific Death After Falling over a Thousand Feet Trapped in a Glass Box. She plummeted to her death, and it is surmised that she hit trees and jagged rocks until falling off a mountainside into the ocean and drowning. Unfortunately, her body was never recovered because it was trapped in a crushed glass box at the bottom of the fucking ocean!

I'm so glad we dropped off the pups with Royce in the hotel to relax and rest while we went to see the sights.

"Sky, baby, you're shaking." Parker rubs his hands up and down my back. "You're afraid of heights?" he asks with a hint of surprise.

I dig my fingers into the muscles of his back, and he grunts but doesn't push me away. Not that he could; I'm practically glued to him at this moment.

He chuckles. "Talk to me."

"Um, is it over yet?" My voice is flat and guarded.

"We're hitting the top soon." He whispers into my hair, "Why didn't you tell me you were afraid of heights?"

"Because I'm not," I lie. "Not really. Dangling a thousand feet over mountains, trees, cliffs, and water in a flimsy glass box?" My voice takes on a soprano quality as the fear digs its ugly claws into my psyche. "Yeah, scary."

He tucks me against his chest, arms fully wrapped around me, and kisses the crown of my head. "They take a couple of thousand people a day up and down this tram. There's nothing to be worried about."

"Mm-hmm. Just tell me when it's over."

"Okay, Peaches. I will. We're almost there. Another three minutes. You can handle that." He presses his lips to my temples. "My brave girl."

I close my eyes and let those words sink in and blanket my fear, breathing deeply until his arms tighten and the entire box jolts and locks into place.

"Hallelujah! Let me off this thing!" I blurt, and he snickers but leads me through the double doors and onto terra firma. I could almost flatten my body and kiss the solid surface if we weren't in public. Instead I attempt to play it cool.

"Heights, huh? Thought you were a tough girl?" Paul winks with a sexy smirk as he passes me.

I scowl and make a face. "I am tough!"

"Uh-huh. You lost some serious street cred there, sis."

"Whatever," I grumble, but all thoughts of my fear of heights and the desire to maim Paul leave me at the stunning view beyond. Without speaking I walk to the metal railing until I'm finally capable of creating words. "Oh, my heaven . . . it *is* God's country."

Parker comes up behind me and places his hands on either side of mine on the railing. He rests his chin on my shoulder, and together we look at the extreme beauty. The entire city of Rio is below us, the crescent shape of Copacabana and Ipanema a blip on the horizon. Sailboats and yachts dot the cove in their white brilliance, looking like polka dots against a startlingly deep-blue ocean background. Behind the city is the sprawling mountain range that fills the panorama with lush green tips and ridges that give the viewer an intense desire to explore its wonder. And sitting at the top of the tallest and most pointed is the Christ statue. He looks like he's watching over his people, arms spread out, expressing his unending love and guiding presence.

"Do you see that jut in the mountain over there where the *Cristo* is?" Dennis asks, standing to our right while pointing out over at the mountain range beyond.

We nod but stay silent, content to just learn from Dennis about his home.

"That's called Mount Corcovado, which means in English 'hunchback.'"

"Interesting," I say, while soaking in as much of the view as I possibly can.

We stand there for at least ten full minutes, not speaking, just taking it all in until Dennis breaks the silence. "Have you ever had *ah-sah-ee* before?"

Both Parker and I turn from the view, me rather regrettably, and focus on Denny. "I don't know what word you're saying," I say.

He frowns, and Paul laughs from behind and spells out the word. "*A-c-a-i*, you know, the berry?"

"Oh yeah, of course! It has a ton of antioxidants and is used in a plethora of health drinks and fat-burning diets," I inform them, because as the girl who's been on one diet or another her entire life, I could practically be an expert.

"It comes from Brazil." Dennis preens proudly. "You must have it, frozen." He waves us toward a little cart that's making fresh acai berry in a frozen-yogurt-type fashion but with nothing else but ice added.

Dennis places his order in rapid-fire Portuguese, pulls out some multicolored bills, and passes them over before either Parker or Paul can say a word.

"We're paying for dinner," Parker announces unnecessarily.

One of Paul's eyebrows goes up as though he can magically prevent that from happening through a single look. He obviously doesn't know my man. One thing Parker never allows me to do is pay for a meal. Ever. I think it goes against his alpha male code of honor or something. I think it's gallant, and after spending a year and a half with a man who expected me to pay for everything, including his clothes, food, and everything in between, I'm happy my boyfriend is chivalrous.

I don't get involved in the daggers the two men are sending through their gazes but, instead, focus on Dennis and the cup he's handing me with a purple frozen substance inside.

"Taste it. Americans go crazy over this. For us, it's really normal, but your country thinks it's very exotic."

I plunk my spoon in and scoop up the frosty purple sludge. "Bottoms up." I place the frozen morsel on my tongue, and the berry lands in an explosion of flavor. Tart, sweet, not quite sour, but incredibly refreshing. It reminds me of a blueberry but not. A blackberry but not. A strawberry but not. There really is nothing on earth like the taste of pure acai berry, and I freakin' love it!

Parker takes his cup and watches me while I moan around my second and then third bites. He plops a bite in his mouth, and I watch while my man's eyes go wide and his lips pull together. "Shit, this is good."

"Told you. Americans love it." Dennis takes a bite but doesn't seem all that impressed. "Honestly, I don't get it, but I'm happy you enjoy the fruit of my country."

Paul smirks and shovels in some frozen goodness.

"What's next?" I ask, and then scoop in more acai.

"Why don't we go to the very top, sit and have a glass of wine with our treat, and then discuss dinner?"

We follow Dennis up another set of stairs, bringing us even higher, where there are souvenir shops. I immediately walk toward the trinkets and notice these little trees with different-colored gemstones on them.

Parker follows me into the store as I pick up one of the small trees. The base is about an inch thick and made up of tiny colored rocks pressed together. In the center of the base is a gold twisted wire that leads out to a dozen or so branches, each with a crystal or gemstone intertwined.

"What is this?" I hold it up to show Dennis.

He enters the store while Paul stands outside being large and in charge. I place the item in his hand, and he presses up his black Buddy Holly glasses in that way I find completely endearing and adorable. "These are Brazilian wishing trees. You see how many of these have the same-colored stone?"

I nod and finger one that has all amethyst stones.

"The trees are meant to be given to someone you wish to give that specific stone's trait to. The amethyst stones are for strength and purity.

If you give that tree to someone, your wish is for them to have an abundance of those things in their life."

It's as if he's speaking right to my soul.

"Aw shit, I think we're going to be here awhile. Paul, maybe you should go up and order us some drinks while Sky shops?" Parker suggests dryly.

Paul shakes his head. "I'm good right here where I can see you both. Carry on. I've got nothing but time."

"Humph." I huff and narrow my gaze but turn back to the beautifully handcrafted souvenirs, and I'm immediately drawn to a tree that has turquoise stones. "What's this one?"

Dennis smiles sweetly. "That one is for healing."

Instantly I picture Nate lying in his hospital bed. We received a text after we got off the plane that Nate was awake and would be moving out of the ICU at the end of the week. Maybe this little trinket could be a totem to help him heal even faster, as it is my greatest wish.

Next, I point to one that has red-orange stones, gold wire, and a multicolored base. "And this one?"

Dennis smiles wide. "That is carnelian and most often is given to someone who you wish to have a baby. It is a fertility stone."

"For fuck's sake, Sky, don't even touch that one." Parker grabs for my hand before I can touch it. "You don't want to mess around with that kind of thing."

"But, honey, Wendy wants a baby, and after losing one, maybe this could help."

Mentioning what Wendy lost has my guy wincing and cursing. "Fine. Just make sure you're wishing for *her* to get pregnant, not you." He places his hand over my belly. "It's not our time. Not yet, yeah?" He kisses my neck and gives my belly a squeeze.

"Yeah, honey. As long as it's down the road, I'm good to wait awhile."

He takes a full breath and lets it out. "Perfect. Fucking. Woman," he says, then winks.

I grab the healing tree and the fertility tree and point to one with pink stones. "And that one?"

Dennis grins. "Pink quartz. *Amor eterno.* Eternal love."

Fingering the pink stones, I say my own little wish under my breath. "I wish to be with Parker for eternity."

Once I have all three trees, I take them up to the front. I'm about to use my credit card when Paul is suddenly behind me. He grabs my wrist and shakes his head. "No, sis. Your cards can be tracked."

"But we haven't gotten any *pesos.*"

His mouth twitches. "Sweetheart, the currency in Brazil is called the *real. Pesos* are Mexican currency."

"Shit. I'm sorry." I frown at the checker as Paul pulls out a wad of Brazilian cash and pays for my gifts. "I'll pay you back," I promise, and he winks but doesn't say anything, tucking his roll back into his cargos and moving back to Dennis.

"Instead of wine, shall we go to this incredible place down the hill that serves . . . What do you call"—he frowns and speaks in Portuguese—"*carne no espeto?* It is like the meat cooked on a metal spike."

Paul nods. "It's like meat on a stick. It's a Brazilian steak house. He's taken me there, and it's incredible. Finest cuts of meat you've ever had. You'll be stuffed. Roy will be all over it too."

"Sounds incredible, and by the time we get down the mountain in the death trap, I'll be starving."

"You ready to hit it?" Parker asks me, as if this entire day is about me and my comfort.

I hold on to my purchases and think about my wish and how I'm going to put that little Brazilian wish tree on the mantel in our brand-new living room when we move into our home together.

"Yeah, honey, today's already been one of the best days we've had in a long time."

He kisses my temple and loops his arm around my shoulders. "Good food, the beach, excellent views, my brother, his man, and the love of my life sharing an incredible experience . . . Yeah, baby, it's been a great day."

6

PARKER

Unfortunately we had to skip "meat on a stick," as enticing as it sounded, because Royce called the four of us back to the hotel. He'd found something in the financials that was unusual. Now the four guys are sitting at the dining table in our penthouse suite since it has the most room to work. Skyler is placing cocktails she's concocted in front of each man, humming happily as she does so.

"Thank you, baby." I glance at my drink. It has some bits of crushed lime and lemon and is clearish in color. I hold up the glass and sniff it before taking a sip. "What is it?"

"*Caipirinha.* It's the national cocktail in Brazil," she says with obvious pride. "I found a note in the bar on how to make it. Mostly it's rum and *cachaça* and crushed fruit."

"And . . . what's *cachaça*?"

"It's fermented sugarcane juice. I had to GTS it, but honey, I don't really know—I just followed the directions. Figured when in Brazil, go Brazilian." She smiles wide, tipping her head from side to side as she assesses her own before tasting it. "Pretty good. A lot of liquor, which isn't exactly a bad thing."

I take a huge glug. "No, it is not." The sweet of the cachaça and sour from the lime mixed with the white rum makes me crinkle my nose. It's not unpleasant, but not necessarily something I'd drink more than one of. She is not wrong; there's a healthy dose of rum in it, which is a *good* thing.

"Girl, this is the shit!" Roy sucks down half.

"Easy, brother, you're jet-lagged," I warn.

He narrows his gaze. "You think I can't hold my liquor, bro? Let me remind you who drinks the most actual liquor in our band of merry gentlemen." He reminds me of his predilection for whiskey neat with a subtle curve of his full lips. His black goatee is trimmed neatly around his mouth and jawline, his bald head particularly shiny in this light. He's wearing a tight-fitting burgundy T-shirt that probably cost more than my entire outfit and a loose-fitting pair of gray pajama bottoms. My brother Roy likes his fabric to be *soft*—"the underside of a woman's tit" type of soft—and pays dearly for such threads.

Royce grabs the pages he has in a stack in front of him and passes out a set to Dennis and another to me. Paul eases back in his chair next to Denny and puts his arm around his guy in a move that shows he's there for support, but he won't get his nose dirty in this business if he's not asked.

"I'll order us up some food. The menu talks about something that looks like breaded cheese balls . . . definitely getting those." My girl scans a menu card.

"*Pão de queijo*, Sky. It's Brazilian cheese bread. You'll have nothing like it in all the world," Dennis says. "If they have it, order with *feijoada*, which is a pork and black bean stew. Excellent together."

"Mmm," Skyler agrees, rubbing her belly. I chuckle but can't take my eyes off her. She's silly, sweet, and so damned golden she makes my eyes hurt if I stare too long. It's times like these I have to remind myself that she's all mine, and I'm one lucky bastard to be able to make that claim.

"And, baby girl, if they have those chicken and cheese balls . . . ," Royce rumbles, and licks his lips making an *mmm* sound of his own.

"*Coxinha,*" Dennis provides helpfully.

Royce points at Dennis. "Yeah, those. Hook a brother up with those."

My girl nods and scans the menu.

"Also, some *pastel*, sis. Love those breaded things. Meat or cheese doesn't matter to me, but those things are delicious."

Skyler grins wide. "It seems we're having bread, cheese, beans, and stew."

"When in Brazil, baby . . ." I remind her of her earlier statement so she doesn't get hung up on the fact that probably everything but the stew she's going to order is loaded with calories and high in fat. Not that she's dieting, but she did mention she needs to get in fighting shape for the *A-Lister* series. "Don't worry, Peaches, we'll work it off between the sheets," I say with a sexy grin.

Her mouth drops open, and her eyes go wide with shock.

"I heard that!" Roy chuckles deep as Paul laughs and shakes his head. Dennis's cheeks blush a solid pink.

Skyler purses her lips and narrows her gaze at me.

"Love you, baby." I kiss the air in her direction.

She doesn't lose the fire in her gaze, but I know her too well. She's not mad, just not altogether pleased that I'm making sexual innuendos in front of others. My girl may be a freak between the sheets, but she's a bit of a prude when it comes to talking sex outside of the privacy of our bedroom.

"I'll just be ordering the food now," she says. "Anyone need a refill on their drink?"

The three other men hold up their glasses, but I push mine aside. "I'll switch to beer if they have it."

"Gotcha." Skyler spins around, her ass swaying delectably in the process.

"Brother, you've got your hands full with that one." Royce watches her hips and ass sway and laughs heartily.

I grin. "Two perfect handfuls at all times."

Royce cracks up, smacking the table. "Jeez-us. You best be thankin' the good Lord above for that windfall."

I hold out my fist. "Fuck yes, I am."

He knocks it and picks up the papers. "All right, how's about we get to the shit I found. Straight up, Dennis, it doesn't look good. You've got a few shady accounts that aren't adding up. I need to get in the office tomorrow to dig through more records and request some additional data, but from what I can see, fifty and fifty is not adding up to a hundred. You feel me?"

Dennis bites into his bottom lip, pushes his glasses higher on the bridge of his nose, and nods.

"From what I can see here . . ." Roy points to an item on the page. "Line number thirty-two, that account is suspicious. What the fuck is *product reserve*?"

Dennis scans the paper in front of him and shakes his head. "I don't know. Maybe it's an account that holds money for product purchases?"

Roy frowns. "Nah, man, those accounts are clearly labeled in line items four through ten. The money goes in and out of those accounts regularly, but for some reason, quite a lot of money keeps getting shifted into this product reserve account, and I can't find anything in your financials so far that gets paid out of that account. Turn to the third page. Note how money from that account dwindles down every two weeks, always leaving roughly four thousand *reais*, which is roughly a thousand American dollars?"

Dennis studies the flow of the money and flips back to the account, goes through a couple of pages, and settles back. "Where does this account go if it's not going against product payments and accounts receivable and payable?"

Royce taps the stack of papers. "Exactly. It empties down to that exact amount every two weeks. I need to go into the office to see what account that money is being transferred into, but it's not in any of these accounts on the books, which means it's dumping the money into an untracked bank account. I've seen this many times before, man. Usually that account is owned by one of the staff in a high position, if you get my drift."

"Puta que pariu!" Dennis booms angrily.

I don't need to speak Portuguese to know that whatever he said was seriously profane.

"I need to call my brother!" He stands up, pushing his chair back so hard it almost falls before Paul catches it smoothly.

Paul stands and puts a hand to Denny's shoulder. "Denny, cool it. Let Roy go over it all before you jump to conclusions."

Dennis's breath saws in and out as he breathes deeply. He nods jerkily, attempts to slow down his labored breathing, and settles back down, pushing up those glasses again. "Is there more?"

Roy licks his full lips. "Yeah, man. The worst part, I found two more accounts just like it. Hidden in plain sight. Those issues you were talking about, overpayments . . . the payment differences look like they're paying against those charges that don't exist when in reality, they're dumping into those reserve accounts, which also get drained every two weeks."

"How much money are we talking?" My chest squeezes at the thought that my brother's mate is getting swindled.

"In Brazilian dollars, for the last three months alone, just over four hundred and fifty thousand *reais*, which is roughly a hundred and twenty thousand US dollars. About forty grand a month is disappearing. With your import business, the money in and out is shifting between *reais*, US dollars, euros, *pesos*, *kroner*, *yen*, the English pound, and a host of other currencies across the globe. There's a lot of money moving, which makes it hard to trace if you don't know what you're looking for. Plus, whoever's doing it knows that the people looking at these financials must not understand every line item."

"Me." Dennis hooks a thumb at his own chest. "I'm the person who doesn't understand every line item. However, my brother, our accountant, and the financial officer should. Though each and every last one of them answers to Fabian."

"Shee-it." Royce runs his hand over his head in a move I recognize as discomfort.

"You're going to tell me that you think my brother is stealing from us. *From me.* From the *entire family*, as my parents still get a percentage of the profit so they can live the life they worked so hard for."

Royce sucks in both lips and nods solemnly. "I can't prove it just yet, and I would suggest you not approach him until we get more of the facts. Park and I will go in tomorrow, get the goods, talk to some people, do what we do best, and hopefully have a better answer for you."

Dennis nods as he runs his fingertips along the stacks of papers, seemingly adrift in his thoughts even though he's sitting right here. "My mother and father are hosting a dinner tomorrow for me and my *friends*." He places special inflection on the word *friends* and looks at Paul, whose jaw goes so tight the guy could break concrete between his teeth.

"Friend, huh?" Paul grumbles, a note of scathing irritation lacing his words.

"*Pistola . . .*" Dennis puts his hand on Paul's. "*Por favor . . . ,*" he pleads.

Paul's eyes turn hard, flashing with what I know to be anger and maybe even a little bit of hurt. He stands abruptly, and this time *his* chair does slam back and down to the floor as he kicks it out of the way. Skyler walks over holding two more cocktails, and he turns to her. "Sis, I need something a little fuckin' stronger."

She responds instantly. "Rum shots?"

"Marry her, bro," Paul growls over his shoulder, looking at me with a vicious anger marring his features. I can tell from his gaze and the way he glares at Dennis and back to me before scowling and turning away that his frustration is pointed at his man and not at me.

Skyler, however, misses the entire exchange and smiles like a loon thanks to the compliment my brother gave her. She shimmies her way over to the table to set down the drinks in front of Dennis and Roy. Dennis grabs the drink and swallows down half in one go, ending with a wince and letting out all the breath in his lungs.

"Your brother likes me . . . ," she teases, then flips her hair over her shoulder confidently and moseys back toward the bar. "Come on, Paulie, let's get you liquored up!"

"Thank Christ!" he grates through his teeth.

I look at Dennis. "What the hell was that all about?"

He closes his eyes and bites down on that bottom lip, holding something back. "Just a repeating argument. My family hasn't accepted my sexuality yet. I believe more time seeing Paul and me together will help them understand, but . . ." He shakes his head. "He'll cool down . . . eventually."

"Okay. . ." I glance at Royce, and he shrugs. Paul is very clearly pissed off. Dennis looks over at Paul, who—I've noticed out of the corner of my eye—has already slammed back two shots of straight rum. Skyler tips the bottle near his glass, and he nods, so she fills it again. He pounds *número* three back without so much as a reaction when the liquor hits his throat.

Definitely something going on with my brother. I add that to the ever-pressing list of shit to figure out about Paul. With him gone over the years, we lost that brotherly connection, the "end each other's sentences" thing a lot of blood relatives have when they're close. Our inside jokes are few and far between, and there's a distance in my brother's eyes I don't know how to breach. If he sticks around this time, I'll make a point to repair that gap and bring us back to the way we were as kids, which was *inseparable*.

The doorbell rings, and Paul's head jerks to it as if someone just cocked a shotgun.

Sky places her hand on his shoulder. "Food? Room service," she reminds him.

His jaw tightens, and he nods curtly, moving toward the door outside the living area. "Stay here. You're outta sight at all times." He points to her, and she lifts her hand to her forehead and gives him a silly salute.

"Aye, aye, Captain."

I chuckle. Fuckin' goof. And all mine.

***

Last night we ate, we drank, and when everyone left—Roy to his own room, Dennis and Paul, not speaking to one another except in clipped little whispers, back to Dennis's home—Skyler and I hit the bed and made love. Most of today was spent at the international import business, going through files and financials and meeting with staff. To say English being a second language for the employees was a severe impediment to my process is putting it lightly. After a while, we agreed that Dennis needed to get us an interpreter who was not him or a member of his family in order for me to grill the staff accordingly and get some real answers that weren't filtered through the fear of saying something to one of their bosses.

Unfortunately the account information was also more complex than what we'd gathered last night. The accounts feed into alternate accounts and keep going down the line. At the end of a long, tiring day, we had to call in Wendy to do her hacking to figure out where the accounts finally landed and in whose hands. Since we dumped all of this on Wendy just today, she informed us that she needed at least twenty-four hours to do her thing, whatever that entails. We didn't ask and prefer not to know.

I let out a jagged breath as Skyler laces her fingers with mine and we follow Dennis up the concrete steps of what he told us is his family home. It's palatial. All one story, dark mahogany trim mixed with an eggshell-white stucco surface. Big pots filled with palm fronds and exotic flowers at the base burst with vibrant colors, adding a welcoming feel. The home is sitting high up on a hill that overlooks a lot of the mountain range we visited yesterday.

Dennis knocks on the door, which I immediately find strange. Back home, Paul and I just walk right in. Maybe it's a cultural thing. Even stranger than that is the fact that Paul is standing behind Royce, Skyler, and me, instead of at his man's side. Not something I'd expect for a meet and greet with a family he says he's met before.

Skyler clutches a bouquet of flowers as I hold on to the bottom of an expensive bottle of wine we picked up at the store. Royce has a white, string-tied box that contains a variety of rich desserts he had the hotel make up for us to offer Dennis's family. Paul, however, is standing back looking surly even though he dressed up for the occasion, wearing a pair of fitted slacks and a button-up short-sleeved dress shirt. Skyler is in one of her many vibrant dresses, this one a mixture of green, purple, and yellow. She switched out her shoes from flip-flops to high-heeled, cork-soled wedges. Royce, as ever, is dressed to the nines in a fucking linen suit with a pair of stylish men's leather sandals. He skipped the tie and opened the top two buttons of his pristinely pressed pale-yellow dress shirt. Me, I went with what I've dubbed "tourist chic." A pair of tan chinos, a white fitted shirt open at the collar, and my navy sport coat, paired with canvas slip-on white boat shoes.

The door flies open, and a petite, round woman opens her arms and embraces Dennis. Her features are similar to Dennis's; the dark hair and eyes, the shape of her nose and cheekbones clearly make this woman his mother.

"Meu bebê!" she squeals in Portuguese, hugging him tight.

"Mamãe." He switches quickly to English after his greeting, which I imagine is for our benefit. "It's good to see you."

She smiles wide and switches also, her dark gaze coming to our crew. "Welcome, everyone, to our home. I hope you are wanting full bellies!" she says kindly.

Paul makes a snarling noise from behind me, but when I turn around to catch his gaze, he shakes his head and looks off into the distance.

It seems whatever crawled up his ass yesterday, the thing that had him doing shots and chatting up my girl last night, has not yet worn off this evening.

Dennis and his mother lead us in, and I'm taken aback by the unique beauty of his childhood home. Wild colors, textures, and patterns fill the rooms from floor to ceiling. It's clear to me that they definitely take advantage of their international import business. They have interesting pieces of furniture and sculptures that I've seen in different European countries, as well as items that have to be considered Asian inspired—not to mention the interesting mix of tapestries hanging on the walls that I'd venture to guess came from the Middle East and India.

We walk down a few steps and are met with a dozen faces, some standing and holding drinks, others stuffing their faces with what I now know is *pastel*, and two sitting on the couch. A group of children race between us and off through the rest of the adults, squealing and laughing as they go. Overall, it looks like a family barbecue back home. The scents of fresh-baked bread and grilling meats permeate the air, making my belly growl and my mouth water.

Skyler eases an arm around my waist and waits for Dennis to make introductions.

"Everyone, these are my friends from America. Last few times I was home you met my *friend Paulo*; this is his brother, Parker, and Parker's girlfriend, Skyler . . ." One of the females in the group gasps, her eyes going wide as she covers her mouth. Dennis continues undaunted. "This is Royce, a friend and business partner of Parker's. They are also here to look into some issues at work at my request."

Dennis points at the different people in the room, going over their names, but my mind is on repeat, stuck in a loop on the word *friend* as he referenced Paul. He didn't say *boyfriend*, *mate*, or *partner* as I would have expected. Back home, Paul introduced Dennis as his boyfriend and made it very clear they were in a relationship, a very serious relationship. My parents were shocked, as any parents would be when their child suddenly announces they're bisexual, and not only that, but they're bringing home a partner to be introduced into the family. It was different, but what I'm seeing here is making my spidey senses flare.

I'm getting the feeling that either Dennis hasn't come out to his family, or he hasn't told them that Paul is his boyfriend yet.

But why?

Once introductions are made, a woman who looks similar to Dennis and his mother but is definitely older than Dennis by a good decade comes and takes him into her arms. *"Meu irmãozinho,"* she says against his hair. The woman is lovely, her dark hair streaked stylishly with blonde highlights, beautiful with her tanned, honey-brown skin tone. She moves out of Dennis's arms, still cupping his cheeks as she switches to English. "I see you are very happy." Her gaze goes to Paul, who's standing at the edge of our group, shrinking into the background. "Might I believe it has something to do with your handsome man?" She gestures with her chin to Paul.

Okay, so he's come out to the family, but something's not adding up.

Dennis looks over his shoulder at Paul. "He makes me the happiest man in the world, Raissa."

She pats his cheek lovingly. "That's good. My baby brother deserves happiness, regardless of what *Mãe e Pai* have to say about it. You know I'm always here for you."

"*Sim, irmã.* I know you are. *Obrigado.*" He repeats the word I know means "thank you."

She moves out of his arms, hugs Paul, and whispers a few words into his ear. He nods, but a flash of pain and hurt moves across Paul's normally stoic face. He's hurting, and he's not talking about it.

Skyler nudges me. "Honey, something's wrong with Paul."

I wrap my arm around her shoulders and bring her close to my chest. "I know, baby. I'm going to get to the bottom of it, but I have a sinking feeling in my gut about what's going on."

Once Dennis's sister shakes Royce's hand, she comes over to me. "Parker, Skyler, in case you didn't catch it in introductions, I'm Raissa, Dennis's big sister. I'm very glad to meet you. And Skyler, I'm a huge fan of your movies. They are given subtitles here, and I've seen them all. You are a true gift to the acting world." Skyler beams and shakes Raissa's hand.

"Come, let's get you all some food and drink. We Brazilians have the best food," Raissa says with a whopping dose of pride.

"Oh, you are not kidding. Dennis took us out on Copacabana Beach yesterday for breakfast and later for treats on Sugarloaf Mountain, and last night, we had room service . . . my goodness." Sky rubs her belly. "We've had a wide range of amazing Brazilian dishes, each one better than the last. I'm going to gain five pounds at least."

Raissa smiles sweetly. "Well, if you do not gain *ten* during your time here, we have done you a disservice."

Skyler and I both laugh and follow the classy lady into the kitchen. Once there, we're introduced once more to their mother, Lucia, and father, Cadu. I watch closely as Dennis interacts with his family, but he stays a good distance away from Paul. When we were in Boston, they were nearly inseparable; here they're acting as though there's an ocean between them.

Paul follows the group around from room to room silently, not partaking in any conversation. This, in and of itself, is not unusual with

Paul because he's generally more of a listener than a talker, but it's as if he's purposely trying to avoid bringing any attention to his presence.

Being a family man and not liking the vibe I'm getting between Paul and most of Dennis's family, I enter into the fray boldly, inserting myself right next to Skyler, who's talking to Cadu and Lucia on the expansive deck outside. Currently they're asking Sky about her latest film.

I wrap an arm around her shoulders and wait for my time. It happens quickly when Raissa enters the conversation and asks how things are back in Boston. Instead of telling her that there's a psycho trying to kill me and keep Skyler as his love slave or whatever it is the fucker wants, I turn the subject to Paul and Denny.

"Really good. Though I will say my mother and father are so excited that Paul is settling down with Dennis. They worry about their boys, and knowing Dennis is taking care of Paul while Sky takes care of me has my mother practically planning our weddings." I laugh jokingly.

Paul's entire body goes tight. Dennis lets out a long breath and frowns.

Still, I continue. "I mean, sure, it was weird at first to find out that Paul had a boyfriend, but we all love Dennis so much, we couldn't be happier."

"Park!" Paul barks, but I ignore him and carry on.

"And of course, seeing them in love is such a joy for my mother and the entire family. Dennis is amazing. You've raised a great man. I'll be lucky to have him as my brother-in-law one day."

The entire deck goes completely silent. Every member of the Romoaldo clan stops what they're doing and stares at Cadu and Lucia.

I can almost hear crickets singing in the landscape beyond before his mother tenses, her expression devoid of emotion, as she looks right at me and breaks my fucking heart.

"Dennis will marry your brother over my cold dead body." Her words are seething with intensity. "They are *not* a couple. They will *never* be a couple. Bite your tongue with your blasphemous allegations. My son may have been confused over your brother's charms, but we have worked this issue out within the family. He would never disgrace our family's good name or go against our God with such depravity."

"*Mamãe*, stop. Please." Dennis attempts to get her to calm down.

She squints and narrows her gaze even more. "I thought we agreed you would not bring that man into my house again. I detest everything he stands for. Attempting to turn my boy into something he's not."

"*Mamãe*, Paul is in my life. I agreed not to bring up my sexual orientation and *pretend* in your presence, but nothing is ever going to change. I am a gay man."

Lucia covers her ears. "I'll not hear such disgusting words in my home!"

Her husband scowls and puts his arms around her, speaking in rapid-fire Portuguese under his breath while moving her from our small circle and taking her into the house.

"What the fuck just happened?" I growl, eyes on Dennis. "You brought us here, knowing that they hate my brother? Why would you do that?" Skyler places her hand on my back and runs her hand up and down in a soothing gesture. She knows me well.

At my tone, Paul approaches and places both hands on Dennis's shoulders in what I assume is a gesture of support. "It's no big deal, Park. This happens every time we come. We just don't engage with one another much, which usually keeps the peace."

"I . . . I . . . This is bullshit!" I let go, my anger ripping through me at a hundred miles an hour. "You can't pretend you're something you're not. That's ludicrous. And they despise you, Paul. That's why you've been so surly since we found out last night we were coming here." I splutter out my words. "Why are we even here?" I shake my head and slice the air with my hand. "Dennis, I'm sorry, but your family is jacked up."

Dennis's eyes get bright with unshed tears, and his entire face turns a dark shade of pink. "You don't understand. They just haven't been able to accept my sexual orientation yet. I still have hope that one day they will. I figure the more they see Paul and me happy together, they'll accept it, like Raissa does." He points to his sister, whose sorrowful gaze is on her brother. She blows him a kiss but stays out of the conversation.

Fucking bigots!

"I don't like this. I won't be around people, break bread with a family who *loathes* my brother because he's in love with their son. Nuh-uh, no way." I breathe deep several times, look out over at the mountain range, and catch a glimpse of the Christ statue standing tall, spreading love and unity over the land, just *not* in this household.

"One thing I know to be true in this life is that each and every one of us has to be honest with ourselves. Leave family obligation at the door. When you take the hand of the person you're meant to be with, the person you love with your entire being, that person becomes your *family*. Everyone else, that's icing on the cake of your life, man."

"Parker . . . in time they'll understand," Dennis tries again.

I'm not having it. "Sorry. Until that day comes, I can't be here. I won't support it. *You be you*, in all things, Dennis. That I will support. Not this. There will never be a time where I can sit back and accept the hate I just experienced directed at my brother because of your love and your relationship. It took a Herculean effort for Paul to come out to me that he was bisexual and was in love with you. He did it again when he introduced you to my family. They may not have understood this new development right off the bat, but they never spread hate or treated you poorly. As a matter of fact, they rolled with this information about their son and opened their arms to the man he loves. You need to think about that. Your family needs to think about that. Right now, we're outta here. Baby?" I take Skyler's hand in mine, and she holds on tight.

"We love you, Dennis," Skyler says, but follows me toward the entrance to the house.

When I reach the door, I hear Royce's voice and glance over my shoulder. He's got Dennis in a man hug and is smacking his back hard, the sound echoing over the angry bees buzzing in my head.

"You got some soul-searchin' to do, my brother. See you tomorrow." He gives one last slap, and his big form twists, heading our way. I wait a moment while my brother stands in front of Dennis.

"I'm going with them. Are you coming with me or staying here?" Paul asks his man, the love of his life.

He holds out his hand for Dennis to take. Dennis looks at the many faces watching him. I hold my breath and grit my teeth, waiting to see if Dennis makes the right choice, all in front of his family.

Dennis glances at my brother's hand, closes his eyes once as a tear slides down his face. Then he puts his hand into Paul's, his other one reaching up to cup my brother's face.

"*Paulo*, I go where you go. *Minha família.*"

7

SKYLER

The warm body lying next to me shifts for the *millionth* time. A heavy sigh leaves Parker's lips while his fingers slide along the fleshy expanse of my thigh. I'm not sure he even realizes he's doing it, but something is definitely bothering my man. It's still early, and sunlight is barely peeking through the slit in the curtains. I ease my hand over Parker's chest slowly, kissing his chest where my head has been resting while my hand maps the planes of muscle and smooth skin.

For a couple of minutes, I wait to see if he'll say anything, ease the burden that's stealing his sleep. When he doesn't, I figure it's time I wade in. "Honey, you've been restless all night. You want to talk about it?"

The arm that's around me tightens, and he brings his other arm up and over until I catch what he's trying to do and shimmy to the side, both of us facing one another.

"Last night was a shit show," he grumbles tiredly, his voice scratchy and uneven.

"Agreed," I whisper, but wait for him to open his heart and mind and let all the nasty out that's plaguing him.

"It's not right. Paul and Denny shouldn't have to hide their relationship from the people who are supposed to love them the most."

Parker is such a good man. Worrying his night away about the situation regarding his brother and his chosen mate. I reach out and trace Parker's plump lips with two of my fingers. "You're right. True love is unconditional. Unfortunately, people can be very closed-minded. It sounds to me like his parents are having trouble reconciling to the idea that their son is gay."

"But why? Who he sleeps with, who he gives his heart to, is none of their fucking business."

I run my hand through Parker's sleep-tousled hair. "Except, when you're in a tight-knit family, it seems that everything is open to judgment and conjecture. The downside to having a loving, involved family is that they believe they *do* have the right to express their likes and dislikes about your life. Not that I have much experience, other than Tracey." I frown, thinking about how I left things with her at the hospital. My heart sinks knowing that our relationship has been seriously damaged, and I'm not sure how to deal with the blows it's taken.

Parker takes me out of my own pity party for one. "My parents have always been involved, or at the very least on the sidelines, cheering us on, making themselves available if we need them, but they would never force their viewpoints on us. We make our own decisions."

A small chuckle bursts from me as I think about Momma Ellis. "I'm not so sure that's entirely true, honey. Your mother is all over your and the guys' lives, as is Pops. They're just more supportive and intrusive in an acceptable way than Dennis's family. If something doesn't hurt you, the Ellis clan will step back and let you deal. However, when you were in the hospital, your mom made some pretty hefty waves, pushing the staff around, sometimes even me around." I laugh. "Definitely nagging your dad. And she had all of the guys running whatever errands she deemed appropriate. She even sent home chicken soup with us when Wendy and Mick brought us to their home, as if they didn't have a full kitchen staff or weren't capable of taking care of us."

He grins, and the sunlight coming into the room hits his face, making those blue eyes sparkle. "You've got a point there."

"I know I do. And she's completely inserted herself into the planning for Wendy's wedding, along with Momma Sterling. Those two together are like double trouble."

Parker frowns. "My mother is a woman with no daughters, and Wendy is a woman with no mother. She's stepping in, helping out."

"Mm-hmm. Which could be considered intrusive and annoying if Wendy didn't eat up the familial attention like a dog to a bone. It happens to be something she wants and needs in her life, and your mother is happy to give it to her. Which is probably how Lucia feels about Dennis. She thinks he's doing something wrong, and she's stepping up with a firm hand to express it. You see, honey, you can say whatever you want, but families are families. They have their own methods."

Parker flinches. "What happened last night was cruel. Are you telling me you think she was in the right?"

"Heck no! She was way out of line. In fact, she erased the line altogether. What I'm trying to say to you is she probably felt that it was within her right."

"And that brings me to my next issue. Why would Dennis bring us there in the first place? It makes no sense."

I nod. "Do I agree with how they're acting about Dennis and Paul being a couple . . . *absolutely not*. The things she said were horrifying. However, we can't blame Dennis for his desire to have his family accept the man in his life. My guess is that he brought us all there hoping that it would somehow soften them to the idea. See how easily Paul's family accepts them, and maybe it would rub off."

"You think?"

I shrug. "It's possible. Just please, swear you won't have a go at Denny, okay? He has enough emotional baggage to fill up a fleet of planes. Besides, practice what you preach. If you don't want them involved in your brother's relationship and how he lives his life, you need to respond the same. We lead by example, right?"

Parker smiles, hooks me at the waist, and rolls on top of me. I open my legs as he settles between them.

"Damn, my woman is smart." He slides his nose along mine, holds his upper body aloft by his forearms, and drives his fingers through my hair to cup my head. A warmth settles all over my body now that I can see Parker's worry slipping away.

I chuckle, and he pecks my lips.

"And staggeringly beautiful . . . ," he continues, and kisses me again.

"Generous and insatiable in bed . . ." He waggles his brows and nibbles on my lips.

He kisses me deeply when I start to laugh against his parted lips.

"And she loves me." He closes his eyes and rests his forehead on mine. "You really love me. I can hardly believe it's true."

I smile wide. "Straight down to your bones, honey."

"Speaking of boning . . ." He prods against my panties with his steely length, and I'm incapable of ignoring the immediate arousal shooting through my body and settling between my thighs.

***

Much later, Parker is donning his professional gear with the intention of meeting Royce at Denny's family business when I hear my phone buzzing on the dresser across the room. The type of buzz is announcing a new text. I get out of bed, my limbs feeling languid, my entire body well sated. I smile at Parker as I walk by him completely nude.

"Christ!" He groans, his gaze all over my form.

"Remember that word. You promised we'd go to see the real deal before we leave. It's on my bucket list, so you can't back out."

"Peaches, looking like that, you could ask me for just about anything and get your way." His eyes blaze with renewed heat and desire.

I grin as I dig through my purse, searching for the blasted phone. I pull it out and notice a series of texts and voice mails that I've missed since yesterday.

The first is from Rachel, and I move quickly to open it, wondering about Nate's status. Leaving only a few days after the explosion stressed me out, but I knew it was for the best. If we're far away, the person who's trying to hurt me and Parker won't have a sitting target.

From: Rachel Van Dyken
To: Skyler Paige

Nate's awake. Feisty as hell. Hates that you're away and he's not there for you. Be safe. Tell your soldier you better not come home with a scratch or he'll be dealing with us.

My chest tightens as I reread the message, my belly fluttering with happiness at seeing he's on the mend. I feel an intense relief in the portion of my heart that was hurting for Nate. Knowing he's awake and giving his wife trouble is a great sign. You don't keep a man like Nate Van Dyken down for long.

"Nate's doing good, honey!" I call out to Parker, who's standing at the vanity in the bathroom brushing his teeth. He turns my way and grins a foamy, toothpaste-filled smile, toothbrush caught between his teeth as he gives me a thumbs-up.

I move back toward the bed and find my man's dress shirt from last night and slip it on over my naked body. Scanning the room, I see my panties peeking out from the coverlet at the end of the bed. With a quick wiggle and a hop, I've got them on under his shirt. The next text has my attention as I sit on the bed and run my fingers through my sleep- and sex-mussed hair. The message is from Tracey. I inhale a full breath as the thought of her makes tears prick at the backs of my eyes.

From: Tracey Wilson
To: Skyler Paige

I hate that we're fighting. I went to the IG office to see you and no one will tell me where you are. I'm worried about you, Birdie. Call me. Please.

There's another text from her right on the heels of the last one.

From: Tracey Wilson
To: Skyler Paige

I took your advice and went home. I'm back in New York. You have all my numbers. Please call me. I need to know that you're okay. I love you.

She loves me.

My throat feels dry as I attempt to swallow down her words. If she freakin' loved me, she would be more understanding and supportive about the man I intend to share the rest of my life with. We're buying a home. We've adopted animals. He's never, not ever going away. Why can't she see that and be happy for me?

Tracey has been the only family I've had most of my entire life, and especially after my parents died. When their boat exploded, I thought I'd lost everything. My best friend didn't lie when she said she picked me up and put me back together. Well, she and Johan.

Johan.

The woman I trusted most in the world was feeding my boyfriend drugs and women. All because she believed he wasn't worthy of me. Now she thinks Parker's going to do the same, or something similar. There's nothing she could offer him that would make him take a penny or cheat. He had the opportunity to bed Alexis in Montreal, and he didn't take her up on the offer. And technically, at the time, he thought we weren't together. Still, he stayed true to me and our love. He was hurt, broken up about what he assumed I did with Johan, or rather what Johan alluded to doing with me, yet he was faithful. Why can't Tracey see that he loves me fully and completely? That our future is together? I'm happy because of him. Blissfully elated, with nothing but a beautiful life ahead, and my best friend can't wrap her head around it.

Why?

My phone buzzes in my hand, and I look down. My heart begins to pound, ice filling my veins at the name of the caller. I tug the coverlet toward my chest and read the message.

From: Unknown
To: Skyler Paige

Come out, come out, wherever you are.

"Parker!" I cry out, and hear something fall to the vanity in the bathroom before he's coming my way at a dead run. The pups see the action and think it's time to play, running after him and nipping at his heels.

"What's wrong?" he says as I jump up from the bed and wrap my arms around him, my entire form shaking like a leaf.

"He's back."

"Who's back, baby?"

I release the Superwoman hold I have on his form and hand him my phone. He takes it and reads the message, his jaw turning to stone along with his gaze. He presses a few buttons and puts the phone to his ear with one hand, the other wrapped around my waist. Parker leads me back the few feet it takes to get to the bed and sits us both down.

"Skyler just got another text. Can you trace it?" he barks into the phone. "Conference Paul in, Wendy," he demands. He turns his face to me. "It's okay, baby. You're safe here. We're far, far away from Boston. Nothing's going to happen to you."

I nod but lock both of my arms around his waist and press my face against his chest. His heart is beating rapidly, but hearing it settles me some.

"Yeah, she got another text. I don't know; let me look. Give me a minute." He presses the speaker button and curls his fingers around my hand where I'm gripping his lapels. "Sky, baby, you gotta let me get to my phone."

"Oh, sorry."

He smiles and kisses my forehead. "Never be sorry for holding on to your man like your life depends on it." He winks and grins one of his sexy-assed smiles. It helps ease my fear but doesn't completely relieve the anxiety. What he doesn't realize is I'm not scared for me. It's him. I couldn't handle it if something happened to him because some freak is obsessed with me.

Parker shuffles me around a little, pressing me more to his side than his chest, and tugs out his phone from his breast pocket. He slides his thumb over the imprint, and the display comes to life, showing he's got a handful of messages. My heart pounds and my freak-o-meter flares when I see the telltale "Unknown" in his list of received texts.

I wrap my arm around his abdomen and take in a full breath, holding it when he clicks on the text and reads it to Wendy and Paul.

From: Unknown
To: Parker Ellis

You didn't learn your lesson. Now I hurt you the way you hurt me.

"What the fuck does that mean?" Parker grits through his teeth, taking the phone off speaker and plastering it to his ear. "He blew up my apartment, set fire to Skyler's penthouse, almost killed Nate, and is scaring the fuck out of my woman!" His voice is a bearlike roar into the phone. "Fuck!"

I close my eyes and say a little prayer that whatever this person is threatening, he's not capable of getting to the man I love. What the entire team doesn't know is, if given the chance, I'd willingly serve myself up on a silver platter if it means no harm will come to Parker.

"Another goddamned untraceable burner? Great. Attempt to get the cell towers it pinged. Yeah, that got us nowhere last time." His tone is sarcastic, bordering on condescending.

He listens for a moment; then his shoulders slump, and he tucks me deeper against his side. "I'm sorry, Wendy, I don't mean to ride your ass. You're doing all you can. Ignore me. I'm just frustrated." His voice softens. "Yes, we've got all our trackers in place. Taking every precaution." His lips twitch into a slow grin. "I don't know when we're coming home. Best guess, a few days. Paul, anything from your friends?"

His body stiffens, and his spine straightens. "Really? That's interesting. Who do you have talking to him? Excellent. Text me the person's name and photo if you've got it." He chuckles. "Of course you have it. Stupid me. Sorry, minxy. Yeah, yeah, I'll tell her. Just get me the info. Paul, you'll meet us here in thirty?" he asks. "See you then. I'll be in touch, Wendy."

Parker presses the "End" button on his phone and turns sideways so he can cup both of my cheeks and look into my eyes.

"First of all, it's gonna be okay. You believe me?"

I lick my lips and nod, searching his clear-blue eyes for any hint of doubt, and find none.

"Second, Wendy and Paul are on the hunt. Wendy will forward the text information to the police so they have everything."

I let out the breath I've been holding.

"Third, they were able to locate the instructor at the CIA whose work has almost the exact same signature as the bomb that was used at my apartment. He agreed to take a look at what we have and see if he can give us anything to go on."

A thrill of excitement rushes through me, easing the fright that was clawing at my insides.

He runs his hands down my shoulders and arms to my hands, which he clasps with his own. "The instructor is actually retired, living in Florida of all places. Paul's team is sending the information down to him as we speak. We should have more very soon."

"This is awesome news, honey."

Parker leans forward and takes my lips in a soft, meaningful kiss. It's all too brief when he pulls away and touches his phone.

He scans the information and frowns. "The instructor's name is Trevor Wilson. Retired five years ago. He and his wife—"

"Laura . . . ," I say in a choked gasp.

Everything in the room starts to fade to black at hearing that name, my vision narrowing on Parker's blue eyes. Stars flicker in my peripheral vision, and my heart pounds so hard and fast I can't catch my breath.

Parker's gaze narrows, and he cups my cheek. "Breathe, Skyler. Inhale fully. Look at me. Look into my eyes." I can hear his clipped request, but it's muffled, as if he's speaking through a pillow over his mouth.

I can't breathe! I'm drowning, and I'm not in water.

The blackness wobbles in and out, and I blink several times, my body feeling weighed down, heavy, as though a ton of bricks is sitting on my chest.

"Skyler, look at me. Breathe!" His mouth is moving, and I hear it far away as an intense dizziness comes over me.

"Breathe, dammit!" His voice is getting louder, one hand rubbing at my chest, the other holding me upright.

"Come on, baby, come on back to me!"

The blanketed dark edges of the room slowly recede, and I can see more of the space clearly.

I gasp, sucking in air, and grip Parker's shoulders with both hands, digging my fingernails in for purchase.

"That's it . . . there's my girl," he coos, one of his hands holding my cheek in place. "*Breathe*, Sky. Nice and easy. Focus on your breathing. In and out, nice and slow."

With my eyes on nothing but him, I do as he says, letting precious air flow in and out of my lungs until the dizziness subsides and my heart rate slows to a more normal pace.

"I'm sorry . . ." I gulp as tears make it hard to see. They fall down my cheeks as he lugs me into his arms, tugging me until I'm straddling his lap, legs wrapped around his waist, ass on his thighs.

"Jesus, Sky, you scared the fuck out of me." He rubs his hands up and down my back and buries his face against my neck, kissing me there several times. "You had a panic attack, baby, but fuck all if I know why."

I lick my lips and center my breathing like I've been taught in my yoga classes. I need to pick yoga back up. It will help me deal with this crazy crap going on in my life.

"Sky, baby, you need to tell me why you freaked out."

"I don't know."

"Then can you tell me how you knew the name of Trevor Wilson's wife?" he asks low against my ear, our faces pressed cheek to cheek as I hold him tight.

"Honey, Trevor and Laura Wilson are Tracey's parents."

He pulls his chest back a bit so he can look me in the eyes. "Say what?"

"Those are her parents' names. Her dad was military a long, long time ago, and I knew he took a job for the government, but no one ever said he worked for the Central Intelligence Agency. I just knew whatever he did, he made good money, and Tracey's mom didn't have to work."

Parker just stares at me, his mouth opening and closing dumbly, but he doesn't say anything.

"Honey, what if . . . what if whoever is doing this to us, is doing it to hurt Tracey! Oh my God!" I put my hand over my mouth and choke back a sob. "I told her I didn't need her in my life. We had a huge fight before we left for Spain, and then she came to the hospital and I was mean to her, honey . . . so mean. And now she could be a target! Because of me."

Parker grabs the back of my head, pulls me against his chest, and holds me while I mull over the ramifications of this situation.

"We'll figure this out too. Don't worry about Tracey. We'll get with her, especially after we talk to her dad. In the meantime, we'll touch base with her. Let her know what's going on so she can take precautions."

I nod against his neck, lift my head, and wipe my nose with my shirtsleeve.

"Baby . . ."

"Yeah," I mutter, worried like crazy that whoever is after me and Parker is after my best friend too.

"That's my dress shirt you're wiping your snotty nose and tears on." He grins and raises his eyebrows until I laugh out loud, releasing some of the stress racking my body emotionally and physically.

"Ah, there's my beautiful girl. You're pretty all the time, Sky, but you light up the world when you smile."

"I'm scared for Tracey, honey," I admit on a shaky breath.

He hugs me again and kisses my lips. "Don't be. I'll contact Wendy and Paul with this new intel. Wendy will reach out to Tracey."

I frown. "Shouldn't I?"

He sucks in air through his teeth, making a whistling noise. "Actually, we're targets. I'm not sure it's a good idea that we make her one too by staying in close contact. We'll get Wendy to reach out, warn her. Then when we know it's safe, we'll contact Tracey directly."

Instantly it feels like the weight of the world is upon me. "Okay. Please tell me the moment I can reach out."

"Just whatever you do . . . don't tell her where you are. The less she knows, the safer she is."

I nod. "Okay, baby. Call Wendy and Paul. I'm going to take a shower. Can I come with you to the offices today? I don't want to be alone." I attempt to stand up, but Parker holds me tight.

"You're never alone, Skyler. Not anymore. Not ever again."

8

PARKER

The shower is running, and I can hear the shower door open and close.
I press my fingers to the phone and call Wendy.

"You got the info, Bossman?" she asks instantly.

"The instructor is Tracey Wilson's father."

There's no sound on the other end of the line.

"Wendy?"

"Uh, yeah, just processing. That's some heavy shit you just laid on
me, Bossman. You'd think you could have warned a girl. I mean, damn
. . . her best friend's dad? Do you think he's the one who created the
bomb?"

I clench my teeth. "Do your checks; find out if he's been in Florida
the last few months. I want to know every time he left his city. Check
his phone calls, credit cards. The whole shebang."

"On it."

"And do the same for Tracey. I want to know everything. She told
Skyler via text that she's gone back to New York. Follow up on that too.
However, I need you to call the woman and tell her that the person
after Sky and me used her father's signature to make the bomb. Gauge
what she has to say about that, but also record it. I want to listen to it."

"Parker, the way you're saying this and what you're asking . . . Do you think Tracey has something to do with all of this? Those texts. The fire. The bomb?"

A vision of Tracey's smug expression the last time we saw her before we went to Spain flutters through my mind.

"Honestly, at this point, anything's possible. All I know is she had access to Skyler's penthouse and phone number, even when it was changed, and her father's signature is on that bomb."

"Yeah, but to play devil's advocate, Wilson taught a lot of CIA operatives who might still use his techniques. The bomb could have been built by anyone."

"Maybe she hired someone to do it for her?" I spit out angrily, and realize how loud I'm speaking. I glance at the bathroom to make sure that Skyler didn't hear. The shower is still going, and steam is billowing out of the open bedroom doorway.

Wendy makes a humming sound. "This is true. I guess she could have. The real question is: Why would she?"

That's the problem. They're best friends. Tracey has no reason to want to hurt me or Skyler. She's constantly telling her how much she cares about her . . . loves her.

"I'm working through the motive. Something doesn't add up. I need to think about it after hearing about this new connection. In the meantime, warn her. Do your funky poaching on Tracey and her father, Trevor. Let me know what you find. I'll update Paul when he gets here."

"You got it, Bossman."

"Hey, have you uh, talked to Annie?"

A groan-like sigh pierces through the phone. "I tried. Kendra tried. Bo went to her apartment. Did you know she lives in a shitty little apartment in a not-so-good side of town?"

"No, I didn't."

"Yeah, well, he did, and she wouldn't talk to him. And apparently most of her earnings go toward her stepmother's convalescent home.

According to the woman's medical files, which I hacked, she's cantankerous and mean as hell. Throws things at orderlies and nurses. Spits on people. And Annie dutifully pays the half that the woman's retirement doesn't cover and visits every week."

"Jesus."

"It's so sad. The woman treated her like garbage, physically and mentally, throughout most of her entire life, and she takes care of her as though it's her job. Ugh. I guess some family is better than no family, but man, for me, family is what you make it. You gotta get good to give good."

I sigh and run my fingers through my hair just as the bell to our suite rings. "You are not lying. I gotta go. Paul's here."

"I'll hit you back when I know more about Tracey and her father."

"Perfect. Also, keep me posted on any progress you make with Annie."

"Yeah, I'm thinking the only person who's going to make progress on that front is Skyler. Annie's embarrassed and hurt. And when a shy little thing like that loses the one person who made her feel like a somebody, it's not easy to brush that under the carpet and go back to the way things were."

The bell goes off again, so I head toward it, shutting the door to the bedroom so Sky can get ready in private.

"I understand. Just keep trying. I'll send a text and have Sky send one too saying we want to meet with her in the coming weeks when we're back in town."

"That sounds like a good idea, boss. Be safe, take care of our girl—and yourself while you're at it." She chuckles.

"Bye, minxy." I end the call while opening the door to our room.

Paul's larger-than-life body is poised at the door, and his expression is as craggy as a jagged cliff over deep water.

"Hey," I say, and hold the door open.

Paul just tips his chin and enters stiffly.

"I got some news I need to share with you about the instructor. The plot thickens, brother."

And for the next ten minutes I go over what Skyler told me and the state of her relationship with Tracey right now.

"You think she's good for it?" Paul asks, his voice a muted rumble.

I glance at the bedroom door to make sure it's still securely closed. "Maybe. She has the access to our phones, Sky's penthouse, her schedule. Hell, she can probably track the jet we took."

Admitting that out loud has an electric sizzle burning at the base of my neck. I curl my hands into fists and breathe through the anger and fear for my woman's safety. She's here; Tracey's there.

"There was something off about that woman when she came to the hospital after you were hurt. A remark she made that didn't make sense then but makes a little sense now, given this information."

"Yeah? What did she say? And how the hell did she know we were there, anyway? Skyler said Tracey had been waiting hours and texting her, but Sky ignored them. How did she know what happened or what hospital we were at in the first place?"

"Unless she was watching her handiwork go down in person?" he offers.

"Maybe. Now what did she say to you?"

"When I was keeping her back from touching Skyler—and brother, I've seen women who are close—this woman acts like Skyler is her child or mate, not just her best friend."

"Well, they're close. She's all Skyler had for a long time. She's also one of the only constants Sky's had in her life, especially when Skyler's parents died three years—"

"Sky's parents are dead?" Paul interrupts.

I tip my head. "Yeah, why?"

"How did they die?"

For a split second, I can't breathe. I can't even form the words as the disconnected pieces start locking together, creating a prospective picture that's incomprehensible.

I lick my lips and mutter, "Boat explosion."

Paul's jaw goes hard, and a muscle flexes in his cheek. "Park . . ."

"Fuck!" I rake my fingers through my hair and start to pace the length of the living space and back to Paul. "A fucking explosion. That can't be a coincidence."

"What did the police report say?"

"I don't know exactly, only what Skyler told me. They didn't have a definitive answer. They blamed it on a possible combination of leaking fuel and other chemicals mixing and reacting in an explosive manner. The yacht was small, got out into deep water before the thing blew, taking both of her parents, the crew, and the captain in one go."

Paul pulls out his phone and taps the screen while looking at me. "I need to see that report," he growls, and points at me before he places the phone up to his ear. "Yeah, it's Ellis. Need you to look up a police report." He looks at me. "When did it happen?"

"Uh, three and a half years ago, close to four now. Parents' names are Jill and Steven Lumpkin."

Paul repeats the names and time frame into the phone. "Get everything you can on their deaths. I want it all, man. No stone unturned."

The second he ends the call, I stop pacing and lean against the back of the couch, bracing myself or holding myself up, I'm not sure. All I know is, if what we're thinking is true, my woman is going to be a fucking mess. "You gotta promise to keep this under wraps."

Paul frowns. "Which part?"

"*Everything.* Until your guy interviews Wilson Senior and you're able to analyze that report, I don't want Sky in on this."

Paul narrows his gaze, and his voice drops with a tone of warning. "P-Drive . . . it's not a good idea to keep things from your woman. I may have a man in my life, but it's the same damn thing, and it never works out in our favor, bro."

"She had a full panic attack this morning when she thought that Tracey could be in trouble."

He rubs at the back of his neck and sucks a breath through his teeth. "That can't be good."

"No, it's not. I'm not going to add weight to her worry if we're thinking the worst of her best friend. If Tracey is in on this in any way, shape, or form, we'll take her down. That alone is going to crush Skyler. If the woman called a hit on me, has been sending those texts, and had anything to do with her parents' deaths . . . brother, Skyler is going to lose it. I want her home, back where we have all of our friends' and families' support and love at her back. She's going to need Wendy, Ma, and the rest of the team to help her come to terms with something of that magnitude. You feel me?"

"Yeah, man, I feel ya. I don't like it . . ."

"I don't like that we fuckin' suspect her best friend of trying to kill me and possibly be responsible for killing her goddamned parents! We need more intel. We need fuckin' proof before a word of this is breathed to Sky. Believe me, I know my woman. I know what she can and cannot handle. This will tear her up. We have to be a hundred percent."

Paul nods, and a river of relief settles in my chest. "All right," he says. "We'll take it day by day until we know exactly who the perpetrator is."

"Deal." I hold out my hand, and Paul shakes it.

Right then, Skyler walks in, wearing a smart-fitting pencil skirt, a sleeveless blouse, and a pair of stiletto sandals. She looks good enough to eat.

The beast takes notice, and I have to bite my cheek not to get hard at the sight of my woman in her version of professional work attire.

"Hiya, Paul!" she says happily, then shimmies her tight ass over to my brother and flings her chest against his to give him a warm greeting.

Paul grins over his shoulder at me and blatantly kisses my woman's cheek. "Hey, sis, how you doin' today?"

She pulls back and makes a face, her lips moving into a crooked snarl. "Crummy. As Park probably told you, now my best friend could be in trouble. The stakes are getting higher, and it's freakin' me out," she confides, as though she's been telling him her secrets for years. My brother has that effect on people. They just want to spill their guts about all of their woes. I think it's part of what makes him so good at reading people. Half the time they give it all up after only a few meetings with him.

"Aw, sweetheart, she'll be fine. We'll make it so. Don't worry your pretty head, yeah?"

"Why is it that you both say that? If I were a different woman, telling me not to worry my pretty head would piss me off. Since I know both of you are alpha possessive badasses who don't mean it in a bad way, I'll let you off the hook. Though you should be careful. A lot of women could take that kind of thing poorly and rip your pretty little heads off!"

Paul looks at me, grins, tips his head back, and laughs hard. "Damn, sis, you are too much. You've got a live one with this woman, brother. All kinds of trouble."

I grin, take my woman's hand, and pull her against my chest. "And all kinds of possibilities. I'm a very happy man."

Skyler slides her hand down my chest in a petting gesture. "Well, now that my personal soldier is here—thank you very much, Paulie—I think we better head out. Royce and Dennis have to be waiting for us."

At the mention of Dennis, Paul scowls.

"Bro, I want to say I'm sorry for last night," I say. "It really wasn't my place to go off like that. Even though I could make a hundred excuses why I feel I was right, it really comes down to the fact that none of us, our family included, has any say in what you and Dennis do. I should have been more supportive. Sky really helped me see that

Dennis didn't mean you any ill will; he just wants his family to get to know you and, by extension, us. See that we're all accepting and maybe they'd be accepting too."

"Parker—" He attempts to cut me off, but I don't allow it.

"Naw, man, it wasn't cool of me to state my opinions, though they are one hundred percent right; it still wasn't my house or my place. Sky made me realize that I was doing the same thing they were doing to you and Dennis. Judging you. I don't agree with anything they said, and it feels ugly in my soul, man, that they're unaccepting of Dennis's choice, you being the biggest part of that choice, but in the future, I'll stand down or talk to you first."

"Park . . . if you'd shut up . . ."

I close my mouth and zip it tight. Skyler cinches my waist, and I can tell she's holding her breath again. Always worried for me but still standing by my side, being my anchor.

"What I wanted to say to you is thank you. You stuck up for me, put me and Dennis first, and not one person in that house besides Raissa had thought of either of us last night. That's the fourth time I've been there and been given the cold shoulder and ignored. Dennis keeps trying to get them to like me, but it's never going to happen. Until they change their way of thinking, I'm always going to be a sore spot, a stain on their family."

A stain.

"You are a fucking hero. A man who fights for people's freedom. Everything you stand for is good, honest, and caring. If they don't want to have a person like that with their son, they can fuck off!"

Paul chuckles and grins. "Glad you think so, bro. I'm pretty proud of my little bro too. Still, this whole thing is hurting Denny, and that's something I can't sit by and let happen. We're working through it, but so far, I think the only thing to do is for Denny to move to the States. First, though, we've got to figure out what's going on at his company and get your little problem solved, yeah?"

"Yeah. Fine. I'll leave it be. For now."

"Appreciate it." He grins and glides to the door.

Skyler grabs her purse and hands me my sport coat. She goes to the bar area and pours two bottles of water into the bowls and refills the dog feeder with kibble we brought for the pups. They dash from their spot on the couch to their bowls.

Paul waits at the door as Skyler pets our dogs. "Bye, babies. Mommy and Daddy will only be gone for a few hours. Try not to destroy everything," she says.

That is one thing we've gotten very lucky on. The dogs really haven't chewed up too many things. They mostly play with each other and sleep when we're gone. Then they're balls of energy when we come back.

"Can we take them for a walk along the beach tonight?" Sky asks as we get to the door.

"Yeah, baby. We can take them out."

"Yay!" She claps just her fingertips together.

I loop an arm around her waist and lead her to the elevators, Paul at our back. "My silly girl."

***

"Bia Acosta. I don't know that name. I've never heard it before." Dennis pushes up the black rims of his glasses as he scans the account name and the pages Wendy sent over to us via email.

Wendy is on speaker as Royce, Dennis, Paul, Skyler, and I hover around the conference room phone. "Looked her up, and she has two small children. Clarissa, a two-year-old girl, and Fabian, a five-year-old boy. Guys, I hate to say it, but it gets worse." Wendy's voice sounds strained, maybe even pained.

"Ms. Wendy, please continue. I am fine. Confused, but fine." Dennis swears under his breath and continues looking at the black box on the table and no one else.

Paul places a hand on his man's shoulder. His body is a veritable pillar of strength while Dennis braces himself against the top of the table.

"Uh, well, it seems that the two children were born to a Bia Acosta. The other name on the birth certificate is . . . Jeez, I'm sorry, Dennis. The other name is Fabian Romoaldo."

"What!" Dennis screeches, his voice so loud I'm taken aback, as is Skyler, who reaches for my hand instantly.

"Fabian has *three* children, Andreia, Brigada, and Able from his wife, Izabel. They've been married for over ten happy years. You must be mistaken."

I close my eyes, knowing that Wendy wouldn't have dropped this bomb if she hadn't checked and triple checked the information before bringing it to our attention.

"I'm sorry," she whispers into the phone. "The three dummy accounts feed into several other accounts and then route fully into one account. The sole name on the account is Bia Acosta. I have her address, image, and phone numbers. I've sent those in a separate email. Her home and expenses are all paid out of those accounts. I'm sorry, Dennis. I'm so sorry."

"Baby girl, we'll handle the rest. Thank you," Royce says, and hits the button to end the call.

"I don't understand. My brother, Fabian, is married to his high school girlfriend. They have three children. He can't have a mistress. And two more children. *Meu Deus. Isso é loucura.* This is crazy," he repeats in English. "No, no, it is not possible."

"Call him in," I state flatly. "Let's get this out in the open."

"My father and mother are here, walking the floors! Greeting the workers like they do every month!" Dennis responds, his tone filled with misery.

"Bring them all in. Let's get this settled. Royce, can you bring up the images that Wendy also pulled off social media?"

"There are p-pic-tures?" Dennis swallows slowly and reaches for his chest; his hand covers his heart.

Royce hits a button on the phone, dialing the receptionist. "Yes, thank you. This is Mr. Sterling in the conference room. I'm with Dennis, and he'd like to see his brother, Fabian, and his parents. Last we heard they were on the warehouse floor. Can you page them and have them meet us in the conference room?" He smiles. "Excellent. *Obrigado.*"

Paul leads Dennis into an empty leather chair. The conference room can seat a good twelve people at the large table. Once he gets him settled, we all take seats and wait the ten minutes it takes until Dennis's brother and his parents enter.

"What is the meaning of this?" Cadu says with a hint of anger in his tone.

"Have you finally come to your senses, *meu filho?*" Lucia says to Dennis, but her eyes are invisible daggers directed at Paul.

I want to rip her a new asshole but know how hard the next few minutes will be on the family as it is. They don't need strangers getting more involved in their business than we already are.

"Mom, Dad, Fabian, have a seat," Dennis says with more confidence than I would have anticipated. It seems he's found his strength.

When the three sit down, Dennis stands up. He walks over to Royce, who hands him the extra sets of documentation we put together.

"I called you in to show you some unsettling things that I've uncovered about our business and family."

"There's nothing wrong with our business," Fabian blurts. "You're looking for errors when there aren't any. Mom, Dad, you know I run this business as well as you. I was taught and trained by the best."

Lucia pats Fabian's hand. *"Nós sabemos, meu bom menino."*

"English, please." Dennis frowns.

"Son, we are here to help you deal with the demons inside of you. The ones that are telling you to do wrong." Cadu's expression is one of fatherly concern as he focuses his gaze on Dennis.

Dennis's lips flatten into a thin white line. "This is not about me. I know you think I'm the black sheep of the family. That my body is filled with demons and the devil because I'm attracted to men. I'm in love with a man! I know the God I worship loves all his children, gay or not! This is about the fact that your other son has been stealing money from this company for the past two years!"

Fabian smacks the table. "You're insane! He's crazy, *Mamãe e Papai*. You're just trying to make me look bad because you're letting down your family by being with"—he gestures to Paul—"that man! It's against your parents and against God! You're in the wrong, Dennis!" He blathers on and Dennis loses steam, the blow of Fabian's words hitting him dead in the chest. He winces, and his shoulders sag.

When I see he's struggling, I stand up. "Actually Mr. and Mrs. Romoaldo, Dennis is not lying. Royce, give them the data." Royce does as I ask, taking the three stacks of paper back from Dennis that prove what Dennis is saying is fact, not fiction, and handing them to his parents.

"Follow the money. Note the three accounts we have highlighted . . ."

Lucia looks down at the paperwork. "What is a product reserve?"

"Or a disability reserve?" Dennis's father adds.

"Um, *Mamãe e Papai* . . . uh, those are just for extra savings," Fabian attempts.

His father and mother both stare hard and flip pages, obviously familiar with how the accounting works since they ran the company from its inception until their retirement.

"Actually, there are three accounts, the two you mentioned and the last one I've highlighted. Money is deposited into each of those accounts and transferred out every two weeks. The monies are moved into a series of other random accounts, which are again drained and the funds deposited into the personal checking account of a woman named Bia Acosta," Roy confirms while I focus my gaze on Fabian.

His mouth drops open, and his face turns a ghostly white. He shakes his head and looks at Dennis. "No. Don't do this," he pleads with his brother.

"You already did. When you decided to steal from me and this family." Dennis's voice is hoarse and filled with unchecked emotion.

"Dennis, *meu irmão*, I beg of you—" Fabian tries again.

"Who is Bia Acosta?" Cadu demands angrily. "And why is she getting close to a hundred and fifty thousand *reais* a month?"

Apparently Cadu is a financial guru in his own right since he was able to pull up the exact amount so quickly.

Dennis closes his eyes. "Royce, please put the images on the screen."

Royce pulls up the first picture, which is an image that Wendy must have taken off Bia's social media feeds. The translated caption below reads *Our happy family. Me, Fabian, Fabian Jr., and Clarissa.*

Lucia's eyes go so wide they look like an archery target, the dark of her pupils a perfect circle surrounded by a large white one. She raises her hand and covers her mouth.

"Fabian has two families. The money is going into his mistress's account to take care of her, their home, and his two other children."

"Fabian!" Cadu stares at his son.

"*Papai* . . . I'm . . . I don't know what to say other than I know I messed up . . . ," Fabian whispers, his face filled with fear and what I hope is self-loathing.

Lucia looks at Fabian and then at Dennis, her eyes filling with tears. "Both of my children have shamed this family. *Não vou permitir!* I will not have it!" She smacks the table as if her physical action can somehow change all that's come before.

Dennis shakes his head and laughs dryly, but I know by the look in his eyes that it cost him. "After what happened last night and what I have found today, I want to dissolve this partnership and sell off my half of the import business. I'm going to start up my own, in the United

States, Boston to be specific, where I'm moving to be with my boyfriend and his family."

"Son . . . ," Cadu starts.

"Brother . . . ," Fabian croaks.

"Dennis . . ." Paul puts a beefy hand on his man's neck.

"This is it. I will no longer be a part of this family. You are a cheat, Fabian, and deserve whatever hell you're going to go through with Izabel and Mom and Dad. And the two of you: I'll always love you, but until you can love me unconditionally, even though I'm gay, even though I'm going to move away and live with my boyfriend, then you can carry on with having just one son in your life."

"How dare you . . ." Lucia growls, stands up, and places her hand in a fist at her heart. "You'd sacrifice this family—for him!" She points at Paul. "We are your family!" She hits her own chest several times.

"I don't need a family that doesn't love me for who I am and won't open their hearts to the most amazing person I've ever known." Dennis wraps his arm around Paul's waist in a possessive move. "I'll be here while I pack and sell off my half of the company. If you open your minds and find you can let go of the hate in your hearts, call me. For now, my sister, Paul, and his family are the family I choose."

With those words ringing in everyone's ears, I grab Skyler's hand and follow Paul and Dennis out of the conference room, Royce bringing up the rear.

"Are you okay?" Paul asks Dennis as we make our way through the company and out into the open air.

Dennis smiles wide, loops his arms around Paul's neck, and lifts his face to the sky. "For the first time in what feels like forever, I'm finally happy. I know I made the right decision."

"Yeah?" Paul asks with a small smirk.

Dennis looks at my brother deeply, their noses almost touching. "I choose you. I choose to live free. There's nothing more important in life than to live free."

Skyler hugs me around the waist as we watch my brother wrap his big paws around Dennis's neck and seal their love and his profound statement with a long, deep kiss.

9

SKYLER

The bus ride up Mount Corcovado is bumpy, humid, and scary as hell. Buses coming down the mountain and the one we're on going up pass one another with an inch of distance to spare between them.

Fear ripples up my spine, and I close my eyes as another bus passes us. I can imagine the screech of metal on metal in horrible clarity as one driver or the other makes a fatal mistake. It doesn't happen. I'm greeted by only the sound of people inside the bus talking, my own breath coming in and out of my body, and the soothing beat of Parker's pulse where my thumb is resting on his wrist in a death grip.

Feeling ridiculous but still needing him to know, I lick my dry lips and nudge his shoulder until he looks at me. "Honey, if we die in a bus wreck on the mountain the Christ sits on top of, I think we'll definitely get into heaven. Regardless, I just want you to know that I love you, and so far, you're the best thing that's ever happened to me. I wouldn't take back a day we've had together."

Parker chuckles jovially and tucks me closer to his side, making the already steamy ride sweltering hot and not in a good way. "Peaches, we are not going to die. The drivers do this trek up and down all day long. You have nothing to worry about."

"Just tell me you love me . . . just in case."

He shakes his head, smiling. "No, because that's bad juju. How's about I tell you that we're going to see one of the seven new wonders of the world together. Now that's beautiful, baby."

My smile is wide when I look up at him and take in all that is Parker Ellis, the man I'm going to spend the rest of my life loving. His hair is combed back, but his curls on top are making an appearance in the humid weather. He's wearing his black aviators that shade the prettiest blue eyes I've ever seen. None of that is what steals my breath, however. It's his lips. When he smiles. When he looks at me with curious interest. When he's about to kiss me. The little dip at the top fits perfectly against mine. No man has ever had a better set of lips in my opinion.

He runs a finger along the ball of my shoulder. "Oh fine . . . I love you, baby," he acquiesces, then nuzzles my nose and kisses the tip.

When he pulls back, the van comes to a stop in front of what looks like a normal building set on top of a giant mountain.

"All right, all right, let's go see big Jesus!" Royce licks his full lips, then claps his hands and rubs them together before standing.

Our squad leaves the vehicle, my knees squishy sponges barely able to hold me up since I've spent the last thirty minutes clinging to the hope that we'd make it to the top alive. I'm getting my land legs back while being guided through an air-conditioned restaurant/souvenir shop.

"Now why would I want to buy something before I've seen the Christ?" I ponder out loud.

Parker shrugs, leads me out to where people are congregating, and flips his specs on top of his head, looking utterly edible. Damn, my man is fine. If he hadn't given me the *business* this morning, I'd be tackling him where he stands. For now, I can just simply appreciate his good looks and preplan my evening's activities.

He must sense my admiration because his chin dips down, and his gaze rests on mine. A well-shaped eyebrow rises as he purses his lips.

"Peaches, if you keep looking at me like you want to take a bite out of me, you're going to be screaming Jesus's name instead of visiting a statue in his likeness."

I move to chastise him, but he takes my mouth in a blistering, wet kiss, cutting off any retort or argument. His tongue tangles with mine, one of his hands moving against my ass, the other cupping the back of my head while he deepens his taste.

"Would you two give it a freakin' rest. *Shee-it.* We haven't even seen the big guy, and you look like you're planning to sin right here on the good Lord's mountain!" Royce huffs but does so while smiling good-naturedly. "Come on, I've got a date with a deity."

He moves ahead of us, his long legs eating up the concrete as we follow the crowds of people moving in one direction. Paul and Dennis follow us from behind, and even though there's a heaviness about them, they seem even more connected after yesterday's horrible meeting with Dennis's family. The two are clinging to one another, hands never leaving the other's. It's sweet and a good sign.

Last I heard from Parker before bed was that Dennis's parents wanted to talk to him about not selling his half of the business right away. I'm not sure what, if any, decisions were made, but I have high hopes that it will all work out as it should. Dennis is an intelligent man, and Paul will do whatever it takes to keep his man happy and protected.

For what feels like a solid twenty minutes, we hike up stairs that lead to walkways that lead to more stairs, all ascending to a breathtaking height.

I squeeze Parker's hand on my right and the railing on my left in equal grips. Thankfully I had some flat sandals that are comfortable, because this is one serious trek upward.

It feels like we're climbing forever until the shaded pathway filled with an overhang of trees parts, and there he is. Larger than life.

Christ the Redeemer.

The sheer size of him is breathtaking, but the open arms do me in. Tears prick at the back of my eyes as my heart pounds a heavy beat in my chest.

I swallow down the sudden emotion, my throat feeling tight and restricted.

Parker leads me around the base of the statue to the front. Once we're standing right at the foot of the statue, I look up and take in his face. Deep slashes with high, rounded edges make up his cheeks, a strong, square nose, and a natural-sized forehead. His lips are thin and unremarkable, hair parted down the center in what seem to be soft waves. Even in stone, it's as if the wind is blowing it back from his face. The chin is a handsome, chiseled square with an iconic dip in the center, proving strength without being too bold. It's the eyes that get me, though. Open, rounded voids that stare right through to the heart of me where my soul resides. They know all. They see all.

"He's magnificent," I whisper with the utmost respect, though it's not warranted, but somehow it *feels* warranted.

"Awe-inspiring," Parker agrees, also in a lower volume. He interlaces our fingers. "Let's sit."

He brings me over to a couple of open mats randomly placed on the concrete and helps me get settled. I glance around and note several people are sitting cross-legged behind me, praying, gazing up at the Christ in all his glory.

Even surrounded by people, it's peaceful here.

Parker holds my hand and together we gaze up at the Christ.

"Would you pray with me?" I turn to Parker, a profound sensation coming over me, like being wrapped in a cashmere blanket.

"I'd love to." He smiles softly and maneuvers his body sideways on the mat. I follow his movements and do the same. He removes his sunglasses and I remove mine, setting them inside the crook of my crossed legs.

Parker pushes up a few inches until our knees touch. "Come here, baby." He cups my cheeks and leans slowly forward until our foreheads touch.

Instantly it's just he and I, surrounded by nothing but the feeling of warmth, peace, and light.

"Close your eyes and press your hands together at your heart," he suggests softly.

We close our eyes, and with our heads pressed together and our knees touching, our hands keep the connection of energy running between our bodies. A magnetism that's unlike anything I've ever felt circles through me. It's like a bolt of electricity encircling our forms, filled with power and vitality.

Parker's voice when he speaks is soft but holds a hint of respectful compassion I haven't heard from him before. "Lord, please keep Skyler safe from harm. Protect her when I can't. Let me love her our whole life long. In the name of the Father, the Son, and the Holy Spirit, amen."

Tears fill my eyes with his words and fall down my cheeks. I gulp a breath of air and wrap my hands around Parker's neck, making the connection between us more intense. He cups each side of my neck as I whisper my prayer for him.

"Dear Lord, please give me the strength to always walk by Parker's side. To lift him up when he needs it and support him in all things. And please, please don't take him from me. In the name of the Father, the Son, and the Holy Spirit, amen."

Parker eases back, opens his eyes, and wipes the tears tracking down my cheeks with his thumbs. He leans forward and kisses each cheekbone before gifting me the saddest smile. "I'm never going to leave you, Skyler." His eyes are a glittering sapphire blue under the cloudless sky, holding truth and resolve within their depths.

I lick my lips, tasting the salt from my tears. "Sometimes people don't intend to leave, but we're powerless when it happens."

He presses his lips together and lets a full thirty seconds of silence sit between us before he speaks. "You've had a rough go, I know this. What you have to understand is that our life together, what we're building, it's gonna last. I'm not going anywhere. You need to believe in that. Believe in me. Believe in us."

I nod and bite down on my bottom lip. Silently I look up at the Christ, stare into his soulful eyes, and offer a silent prayer of my own.

Please, Lord, let him be right.

***

After another harrowing ride down Mount Corcovado, Dennis piles us all into a taxi van and takes us to Fogo de Chão, the Brazilian steak house he had raved about.

The place is packed with early dinner goers, but we're led to a beautiful semiprivate patio seating area outside that has a perfect view of Sugarloaf Mountain and the harbor. The water softly laps at the side of the building and base of what the patio sits on. Boats majestically dot the waters, resting prior to taking off to the call of the open sea.

"Wow, Dennis, this is incredible." I brace my arms on the metal railing and let the slight breeze whip my hair and kiss my face with its gentle caress. Some of the humidity has subsided, and the air feels much cooler, comforting in degrees versus the sweltering temperature of before.

Parker comes up from behind and wraps his arms around my chest. I lean against him and take in the view while he rests his chin on my shoulder. "Not as incredible as my view of you taking in this view."

I bump my booty into his groin and chuckle. "You're a dork."

"Maybe, but I'm your dork." He kisses the side of my neck and sighs, holding me close while we take in the view.

"Would you two like a table to yourselves?" Royce's deep voice rumbles from the seating area behind us.

"No," I say at the same time Parker says, "Yes."

I turn around in his hold and smack his chest playfully. "Honey, we're here to have experiences with our friends."

"I'm not. I'm here to help my brother out and keep my woman safe at all times. Best way to keep you safe is to keep my hands all over you." He nips at my lips and kisses me briefly.

"Skipping right to dessert, I see," Paul hollers out.

I crack up and push my guy out of the way so that I can go sit with our friends. He follows me and holds out my chair, adjusting it like the gentleman I know he is when it comes to certain things. Definitely have to thank Momma Ellis for teaching her son to be chivalrous.

Once we're settled and the waiter takes our drink order, he explains the layout of the restaurant. Apparently you can order your main cut of meat and do open salad bar and hot buffet, or you can do the whole deal and take cuts of meat on a stick.

"When in Brazil . . . ," I tease Parker.

"I think we'll all do the self-serve salad bar, the buffet, and meat on a stick," he tells Dennis, who orders for us all in Portuguese.

Once the waiter leaves, a team of people brings us breads, fresh plates, and a variety of sauces to dip in as desired. We take our plates and fill up with salad and a mouthwatering mixture of hot and cold side dishes to go with the meats. The second we sit down, a man with a long skewer comes over to the table and offers us a cut of prime rib. He shears it right off the giant piece of meat, shaving a perfectly thin slice onto each one of our plates.

We're barely biting into the succulent rib when another man comes up offering a cut of filet mignon. No one turns down the filet either.

Throughout the next hour or so the five of us sample the best meats I've ever tasted, all seasoned perfectly and complementing the sauces and sides we've chosen.

"How are you enjoying Brazilian food, Skyler?" Dennis asks.

I rub my very full protruding belly. "Too much! Dennis, you have to find us Brazilian food in Boston."

He smiles. "How about, instead, I cook for you all when we get settled into our home."

Parker jumps right in on this tidbit of information. We knew it was coming, and everyone's talked about it peripherally, but Paul hasn't said the words "I'm moving in with my boyfriend" yet.

"So, Paulie, you and Dennis are officially shacking up?" He loops an arm over the back of my chair and teases the curve of my shoulder with his fingers. It's a comforting gesture he's always done and makes me feel special and loved.

Paul smirks, wipes his mouth with his napkin, and leans his big body back, relaxing his legs out in a wide V before taking Dennis's hand and holding it on one of his enormous thighs. "Yeah, P-Drive, I am. We've been talking about it for the better part of six months, which is why he came to Germany with me when I finished my last contract. We wanted to take in the lay of the land with family by meeting up with you first, then Mom and Dad. With the way Denny's parents haven't accepted us, I didn't want to bring him into another uncomfortable situation. Now that he knows what I always knew, which is our family is perfectly accepting of the two of us, he's eager to get settled, set up a house and an import business of his own."

"That's fantastic. I'm happy for you both, bro." Parker smiles at Dennis, who blushes a pretty pink up his neck and into his cheeks.

Feeling this is my moment to approach Paul about working for me and the ideas I have, I choose to test the waters. "And what do you plan to do, Paul? Go back for another four years?"

He shakes his head. "Naw, Denny and I talked about it. When I'm gone, I'm gone. He'd only hear from me rarely, and that's no way to live. If he's taking the leap of moving to another country to be with me and my family, I'm officially retiring."

"Then what will you do?" While waiting for his response, I take a sip of an awesome cabernet the waiter suggested.

He shrugs. "Not sure. Got plenty of money in savings. Been working twelve years, not spending much since I was never centered anywhere for any length of time and lived on bases all over the world when I was in between missions. That's a lot of dough. Thinking about investing it in Denny and his new business since he'll likely be doing everything from scratch."

"Would you consider personal security?" I smile.

"Sis, you're not going anywhere in public without protection until you've got the Van Dykens back. Don't you worry." His tone is forthright and commanding, leaving no doubt he's personally planning to keep me safe.

"Ugh," I groan. "I'm not talking about me! Well, I am, partially. Obviously, for the immediate future, I want to hire you to stay on as my personal bodyguard, even when our little issue is over."

"Pay me?" He scoffs before continuing with, "Babe. That is not happening." He chuckles.

"Of course I'm going to pay you." I use my most forceful tone. "If you are acting as my security, I pay. That's how it works."

Parker snickers and reaches for his beer. Royce rubs at his goatee and chuckles behind his hand. Dennis just grins, his gaze going from me to his man.

"No, sis. I'll tell you how this works. You need to be safe. I keep my family safe. End of."

A fiery heat enters my veins and works its way through my system. "That's absurd. You are not gifting me your personal security services."

"Watch me," he states flatly.

"I won't have it."

He grins. "You will."

"I won't!" I stiffen my spine and straighten in my seat, narrowing my gaze at him, making sure he knows I'm 100 percent serious.

"You my family?" he asks randomly, breaking up the flow of our little contest.

"Well, yes. I'd like to think so."

"Baby, you're family." Parker runs his hand down my stiff back, which soothes the burn of my irritation just a bit.

"Case in point." Paul gestures with his hand toward his brother.

I shake my head. "No, no, case in nothing! If you are acting as my personal security, you get paid, and I'm *generous*. My safety is important to me and my man, and it's not very fun dealing with paparazzi, or crazy fans, or the crush of bodies at an event. I'll be working the *A-Lister* series well before Rachel and Nate come back on. Those will be long days on set. Usually I'm able to let my security guy go while I'm on set, but that still means you're on call, all day. That's expensive in the security industry, and I'm more than happy to pay for that service. Therefore, you get paid," I state adamantly and definitively.

"We'll discuss it later," Paul says, blowing off my very informed stance on how this situation will work between us.

I narrow my gaze at him.

"Sis, let's enjoy our dinner before some other shit storm hits us, yeah?"

He should have knocked on wood, because the second the comment passes his lips, Parker is reaching for his cell phone in his chest pocket.

His face is all smiles until he looks down and reads the display. All hints of today's happiness and the lightness we let in today are gone in a flash.

I look over his shoulder and see the message coming from "Unknown."

This time it's not a text, it's two images. The first is the sign outside of Parker's father's bar, Lucky's. The second image is Mrs. Ellis sitting on a stool in front of the bar at Lucky's, laughing at something Mr. Ellis is saying. Mr. Ellis is grinning, towel hung over his shoulder, arms braced on the bar, eyes sparkling as he takes in his wife.

"Oh my God, no!" I gasp, covering my mouth, fear and dread tingling all over my nerve endings.

"Park, what is it?" Paul growls.

He doesn't respond. He hits the contact list on his phone until the name Lucky's comes up. Before he can even press to call, the display flashes again and the "Lovemaker" title comes across the screen.

Parker answers the phone on a bark: "Bo."

I can't hear what Bo is saying, but Parker closes his eyes and runs his hand over the back of his neck. He stands up abruptly. "Are they okay? Fucking hell, Bo, tell me if my parents are okay!" His voice is rough, thick with emotion.

"Jesus! Fuck. We'll get on the first plane back home." Paul is up and at Parker's back when he says, "Call me the second you know my father's status."

He ends the call, and Paul puts his hand on Parker's shoulder. I watch in horror, holding my breath.

"Mom and Dad were in a hit-and-run car accident tonight in the back parking lot at Lucky's. They were walking to their car when the car gunned for them. Mom . . . uh . . . Mom just sustained a series of bruises, a sprained wrist, cut knees and elbows, because Pops pushed Ma out of the way."

Tears fall down my cheeks as I imagine Mrs. Ellis being flung out of the way of a car barreling toward them. Mr. Ellis would sacrifice himself for the woman he loves. Absolutely.

"Pops . . . fuck." His head falls forward, and Paul braces both hands on his brother's shoulders.

"Hold it together, Park."

Parker nods, seeming to take strength from his brother's clipped demand.

"Pops, uh, was rushed to the hospital. His lower half was hit by the car. Bo doesn't know how fast the car was going or what the prognosis is. He's with Mom. She's lost it, Paulie. We have to get home. Now," he croaks.

Hearing Parker's need, I wipe my tears, swallow down my upset, and brace my heart and soul to take on whatever pain Parker is dealing with. It's my time to be strong for him, put on my big-girl panties, and ride this wave as the strong woman he needs. I grab my phone and pull up the number for my charter jet and schedule an immediate flight out. The earliest they can get a flight plan and fueling stop approved is four hours from now. This will give us all enough time to get our stuff, pile up, and head off to the airport.

"Royce, will you pay the bill?" I ask.

Roy nods, walks over to the two Ellis brothers, and smacks a hand on each man's shoulder, gives a squeeze, but doesn't say a word. He knows there are no words of comfort when you're almost five thousand miles away from home and your family needs you.

"Dennis, can you seek out the valet immediately and wait out front for the taxi?"

He nods, his gaze flickering to the two brothers, heads together whispering quietly to one another. "I'll do that right away."

"Thank you. I'll round up our boys."

He glances longingly at Paul, but instead of interrupting, he presses his lips together and leaves them alone, heading to do as I asked.

When he's entered the main restaurant, I walk over to the two men and place a hand on the shoulder of each one. "We've got the jet leaving in four hours. Royce is paying the bill, and Dennis is getting the van. We need to go back to our hotel, pack, head to Dennis's to pack, and then get to the airport. There isn't time to waste."

Paul nods and lets his brother go but squeezes his bicep. "None of this is gonna fly, Park. We'll get the fucker. I swear it on the Ellis name." He slams his fist against his heart, turns on his booted feet, and exits the patio. It's the first time he's left us alone when we weren't locked away in our hotel room.

Parker watches his brother leave, grabs my wrist, and yanks me into his arms. I hold on for dear life. He puts his face against my neck and breathes deeply, soaking up my scent, his hands gripping my back and hip, connecting with me physically. It's something he's done from the start of our relationship, and I love it more than anything else . . . his need to physically connect to me.

"You ground me, baby. When the entire world goes to hell, and all I want to do is fly off the handle, you bring me back to reality. You save me from myself."

I tunnel my fingers into his hair and scratch my nails over his scalp several times until I can feel his strength seeping back in, his muscles tightening where he stands. When I feel his heartbeat is back to a more normal rhythm, I cup his cheeks and pull back so that I can stare into his eyes.

"We'll deal with it together. Don't think the worst. We don't know much. Let's focus on one thing. Getting back home to them."

10

PARKER

If someone asked what happened in the past eighteen hours of my life, I couldn't tell them. Although I could hear and see everything happening, it all felt like it was in a dream state. Skyler and Royce led both Paul and me through the process of getting all of our things from the hotel, including our dogs and bags, as well as stopping at Dennis's and picking up Paul's stuff. Dennis and Paul had some heated words because Dennis wanted to accompany his man to Boston. However, doing so would have severely changed the plans they had of him closing his end of the family business and packing up. Paul and Dennis battled it out, but in the end, Paul got his way. Dennis would stay behind with the promise that Paul would call the moment he could to update on our parents' status.

We were whisked through an airport, Paul's eyes watchful, his expression so hard everyone kept their distance from us, even when some recognized Skyler and me. Royce got us to the jet, and we took off without any additional fanfare. We stopped once to refuel in the States before landing in Boston a whopping eighteen hours from the time we got the call that my parents had been targeted and attacked. My mother was banged up; my father was in surgery from the injuries he'd sustained in the accident, of which I don't know anything more to date.

I'm exhausted, but at the same time wired for sound when Paul stops the SUV Skyler had waiting for us at the airport in front of the hospital doors. The four of us jump out, and Royce circles the car.

"You guys go on ahead. I'll handle the car." He lifts his chin.

I wave a hand in the air, clasp Skyler's fingers in a death grip at my side, and run into Bo in the lobby.

"Fuckin' hell, bro. Glad you're here." His expression is relieved, but there are deep bags under his eyes, proving he's been here the entire time.

"My father?" I grate through clenched teeth.

"He's going to be fine. Messed up, but alive and out of recovery and in his own room. Your mother's with him now. I'll take you there." Bo turns around, and we all follow him at a fast clip through the halls of the hospital, up an elevator, and down another white-walled corridor.

Standing in front of what I assume is my father's hospital room door are a couple of burly-looking fellas wearing black T-shirts and black cargo pants and boots, one Caucasian, one African American.

Paul skirts around us and lifts a hand, grasping one man's meaty paw and squeezing his shoulder, then repeating the process with the other. "My gratitude, brothers." His voice is thick. "Anyone come through that wasn't approved?"

Both shake their heads.

"Friends of yours?" I lift my chin to the two heavily muscled giants with buzz cuts and bulging biceps.

Paul grins. "Brothers in arms."

"Some of the best to have, I imagine." I smile weakly.

"Damn straight." Paul turns to the two men. "You're relieved. Marker whenever, no question."

The black man scowls, his face turning to stone. "Fuck the marker. This one's on me. We keep family safe."

The other soldier nods. "Our families don't get threatened on our soil and come out harmed. You need us for anything, we're there, brother. Speaking of . . ." He shifts his hand to behind his back and pulls out a Sig Sauer, then passes the weapon to Paul.

Paul inspects it, checks that the clip is full and a round is in the chamber, flicks the safety, and tucks it in the back of his own pants.

"My thanks." He claps the man on the biceps, nods, and ushers me, Skyler, and Bo into the room.

The image of my father lying prone in a hospital bed, his head, cheeks, and arms cut up as though he'd been pulled along gravel at a high speed, not to mention his unmoving lower half wrapped in a variety of things I can't see, burns like icy-hot pokers in my eyes.

"Boys!" My mother stands and opens her arms.

"Ma," I say, and get to her embrace first. Her wildflower scent seeps deep into my nose, bringing with it comfort and solace. She pats the back of my head, squeezes my neck, and then shifts so she can bring Paul into our huddle. I'm loath to let my mother go, so I don't, but I do move to the side. She loops her free arm around Paul and kisses his forehead.

"My babies are home. Sweet, sweet heavens above, you're safe."

I close my eyes and grind my teeth, not wanting to let my emotions take over. Not now. I can do that later. Much later, when I've ascertained whether or not my father is okay. "What about Pops?"

Ma swallows, eases back, and wipes at her tears. "He's got a long road ahead, but he's alive. The car that hit us shattered his hips and broke both legs. He had to have full reconstructive surgery on the hips and setting of the bones in his legs. This caused a great deal of internal bleeding, but the doctors assured me they have it under control. He's on heavy painkillers, blood thinners, and a mess of things we don't need to go over right now."

"Christ, Ma." I rub at the back of my neck. "He's going to need a lot of physical therapy."

She stands up straight, shoulders back, and lifts her chin. "And he'll have it."

"The pub . . ."

"Got a plan worked out for that, brother," Bo says softly from the wall at the back of the room. Royce is standing next to him. He must have sneaked in when we were huddled with Ma.

Bo continues. "Gonna take over running the bar for the next six months or so until Pops is back on his feet. He needed help before. A manager eventually. A waitress, definitely. Gonna make that happen. I'm sure you, Royce, Wendy, and Kendra can manage IG without me for a while, yeah?"

I close my eyes.

"Course we can. It's a good plan, and I'm happy to come in the evenings, manage the money. Whatever it takes," Royce puts in.

Fuck, I love these guys. My heart pounds, and my throat goes dry at all they're offering.

"I can help." Paul's voice is so harsh it's like boots scraping over rocks.

Bo shakes his head once. "Man, you gotta protect Sky. Unless you want to find another set of security."

"I'll be fine," Sky whispers, close to my side but not intruding in my brothers-and-mother huddle.

"Paulie, you gotta stay on Sky. I can't . . . She's my . . . Fuck . . ." I choke on the words, not able to express how much him protecting my woman means to me.

Ma pats my cheek. "Yes, we know she's your world. Just like your father is my world. And Dennis is Paul's world. Bo's plan is perfect. We have the cook to take care of the food. Bo is perfectly capable of running a pub. He said he worked in one in college."

Which he totally did. It was how he tagged so many women. A new one every night back in those days. Hell, he'd be doing that now if we didn't have so much work.

Ma looks to Royce. "With Royce's help managing the books, I can take care of your father. It's time I leave the library anyway. We've saved enough, and well, it's time."

I look at Paul, whose jaw tightens, but he nods before I move my gaze to Bo. "I'm gonna owe you a lot, brother."

He grins, a twinkle in his eyes. "I know. Looking forward to making you pay up . . . huge. Not sure what it's gonna be, but it will be awesome!"

"You too, Royce," I state.

"Nah, man, family is family. 'Sides, Momma Sterling is gonna be all over helping Momma Ellis." He reminds me how much our families are intertwined where it counts most.

Skyler comes up behind me and wraps her hands around my waist, pressing her chin against my spine, where she kisses me. "Owing Bo doesn't sound like a good thing."

A smile threatens my lips. "No, baby. Owing Bo one is never a good thing."

Bo grins. "I'll leave you guys to it. Gotta call Tink. She wanted to know the moment you were back. She's itching to be here but says she's watching the team that's meeting with Mr. Wilson."

"Shit, that's going down today?" My gaze shoots to Paul's.

"Yeah. I'll check in. Ma, you okay? Need anything?" he asks, a deep rumble in his voice.

"Now that my boys are home, no. I'm good. Let's just get your father up and at 'em, and the world will tilt back on its axis as it should."

I suck in a huge, calming breath, hold on to Skyler's hands where they are wrapped around my waist, and finally exhale, my gaze on my father. He's sleeping soundly, the heart monitor beeping along melodically.

"Peaches, you want to go with Royce and get us some coffee? It's gonna be a long day and night."

"Sure, honey. We'll find some food too. It's been a while since any of us have eaten."

The thought of food makes my stomach growl heartily. I didn't realize we'd forgone food, but it makes sense. All of us were focused on one thing: getting home. Now that we're here, I can see Pops is going to make it. Ma is shaken but in charge as usual. I can relax a little. We will get to the bottom of who hit my parents with their fucking car.

Royce and Skyler leave as Paul twists to the back of the room, phone to his ear. I move to sit with my father and take his cool hand.

"We're here for you, Pops. We've got a plan in place, and we will get justice for what was done to you. I promise you that. Paul and I won't sleep until we do."

After about ten minutes of staring at my father, cataloging his features, from the salt-and-pepper hair to the wrinkles framing his closed eyes, I begin wishing he'd wake up and start complaining about how uncomfortable the bed is, or how he can't sleep due to the nurses checking on him a hundred times. Basically anything keeping him away from home and being in front of his TV, watching his teams play and bickering with my mother.

Behind me, Paul ends his call, grunts, and gestures for me to move to the door.

"Ma, we're gonna step out for a minute, yeah?"

"I'm not an invalid. I've been taking care of your father for thirty years; I think I can keep doing that without assistance."

I can't help grinning. My mother is a freakin' warrior. She takes a hit and keeps on going.

Once Paul and I get out into the hall, Paul's face turns hard. "We've got a fuckin' problem."

"You mean besides the fact that our father is in a hospital bed after someone ran his ass down?" I clench my teeth and cross my arms over my chest.

"The security footage outside of Lucky's shows a black SUV. Plates clearly visible."

"Excellent. That means they know who the fucker is?"

He licks his lips. "Plates circle back to a car rental company. And Park, you're not gonna like who rented that car."

I close my eyes, already knowing in my heart the name he's going to say.

"Brother, it's Tracey Wilson. She rented that car. Wendy's been trying to get in touch with her. No dice. She's not answering. I know she told Sky she went back to New York, but there's nothing on record that says she booked a flight or train out of Boston. Woman's still here, man. Wendy can't find her, but says it's only a matter of time before she shows up."

I spin around and press my thumb and forefinger into my temple. "Fuck. This is gonna kill Sky."

"There's more," he grumbles.

I close my eyes, lick my lips, and lean against the wall opposite my father's hospital room. "Lay it on me before Sky gets back."

"Her father . . ."

"Trevor, retired CIA agent."

"Yeah. My guys grilled him. An experience he did not find pleasant. Turns out his daughter not only was Daddy's little girl, she'd read all of his course curriculum and was taught how to make a bomb. Her dad was thorough. Didn't think she'd ever use it since she talked about becoming a talent agent after meeting and becoming best friends with the girl next door, who was a burgeoning actress. Says all she ever wanted to do was work with Skyler. So, she did it. Guy said Skyler was the best thing that ever happened to his girl."

"Say what?"

"When they were kids, before Skyler and Tracey met at age ten, Tracey had a baby sister, Staci. Died a year before they moved to that house and Tracey met Skyler. Trevor said Skyler coming into Tracey's life was a godsend. Tracey was grief-stricken to the point where she stopped talking altogether when her sister died. Trevor told my guys that Skyler took all Tracey's grief away. Said she focused all her attention on Sky and none of it on the loss of her sister. They've been inseparable since."

"Jesus, you think Skyler is kind of a replacement for the sister she lost?"

Paul shrugs. "Maybe. Probably. Fuck if I know. I'm just telling you what I got from Wendy and my guys."

"How did she die?"

"Leukemia," Paul says flatly. "Not pretty or quick."

"So basically, young Tracey watches her sister die a slow, painful death, meets Skyler, and what, sees it as her job to take care of her? To protect her?"

"Has she told you anything else about their relationship that would strike you as overbearing and suggest such a scenario is in play?"

All of the shit that involves Tracey is overbearing, most specifically how focused she is on Skyler's career and her romantic relationships. "Uh, yeah. You could say that. Hell, she encouraged Skyler's last boy-friend to do drugs and cheat on her. So much so, she provided the access to easy women and handfuls of drugs. He took her up on that offer, proving to Tracey he wasn't worthy of Skyler's affection. Then of course, she was the one who was there on a white horse to sweep in and fix the problems when Skyler was heartbroken."

"And what about her parents?" Paul circles back to the first people Skyler lost.

"Did your guys find anything conclusive or new to investigate about that accident?"

He shakes his head. "Not yet. The case is old, and so much of it was handled poorly. We might not ever know what went down on that boat, but it can't be a coincidence."

"What did Trevor say about the bomb?"

"At first, he was baffled because not only did it have the markings of what he teaches his agents, it had his own *private* signature he'd never told anyone about, mostly related to the delayed detonation. He's a master at setting bombs that are detonated by the turning of a door lock. There's a sensor that's unique, and the bomb used on your apartment had a sensor. It wasn't the same as the ones he's used, but that could be because decades have passed since he's made one himself and the manufacturers no longer offer that specific type."

Paul continues. "At first he thought someone was trying to frame him. Then we started asking about his daughter, and when we made the connection between his bomb and the fact that his daughter could have been the perpetrator, he clammed up real fast. Started asking for legal counsel, which stopped any further questioning, and he demanded the chance to call and check on his daughter's safety. This, of course, was denied, and law enforcement is holding the guy based on the evidence that the bomb is so closely related to his own signature. He has a pretty strong alibi, what with being in Florida when it all went down, but that doesn't mean he couldn't have created the bomb and given it to someone else to place. We're using that to hold him, so he doesn't get ahold of Tracey and warn her that we're on to her. We don't want the bitch fleeing before we can get our hands on her."

"Jesus, this is going to hit Sky like a tsunami hitting Boston and destroying everything in its wake."

"Yeah, figured that."

I slump against the wall, my mind spinning on how I'm going to break this news to my woman. She'll be devastated to say the least.

"Do they have a bead on Tracey?"

He shakes his head. "That's the problem. No one has seen her."

"The rental? Someone has to have seen an SUV with a seriously damaged front end."

Paul rubs his hand over his cropped hair. "They found the car abandoned not more than ten blocks from Lucky's. She's in the wind, brother."

11

SKYLER

"Baby girl, how much food you think your man can sock away?" Royce gestures to my tray.

I glance down at my tray filled to the brim with four different sandwiches, chips, drinks, a couple of apples, two slices of pie, a handful of protein bars, and six cookies.

"Um, maybe Cathy wants something."

Royce grins that super-big, all-pearly-white smile at me. "You'll be lucky to get him to sit down long enough to eat a sandwich, let alone all of that."

"I just want to help."

He squeezes my shoulder with his free hand, a bottle of OJ, the car key, and a banana in his other hand. "You being here, supporting him, is all he needs. I'm gonna surf the salad bar while you check out, yeah?"

"'K, Royce. Here, give me the key, and I'll put it in my purse." I smile, gesturing to my bag hanging in front of me. He hands me the key to the SUV we took from the airport, and I tuck it into my purse and push my tray along the long line ahead of me. There are about eight people waiting for the slow-as-molasses cashier to ring everyone through.

My cell phone rings in my back pocket, and my heart stops as I frantically pull out the phone to make sure it isn't Parker needing me back immediately because something's taken a turn for the worse with his dad.

The screen says Tracey is calling, and with everything happening, I'm so relieved to see her name I hit the answer button.

"Trace, oh my God! Are you okay?" I breathe into the phone, pressing it hard against my ear.

"Birdie . . . ," she gasps, her voice sounding pained and small.

"Tracey, what's going on?"

"He has me." Her voice shakes and wobbles as if she's speaking through tears. "He says . . . says he's gonna kill me."

Oh. My. God.

Chills erupt all over my body, and I leave my tray and walk away from the line and toward the door of the cafeteria.

"Tracey, who has you?" I ask frantically.

"He's hurt me, Sky. So bad." She coughs and cries out in what has to be pain.

"Where are you? Tell me where you are? I'll get Parker and Paul and Royce and Bo. We'll come get you."

"No!" Her voice is panicked, choked with fear. "You have to come alone," she whispers, and whimpers. "He . . . h-he says if you come, he'll let me go. I wouldn't ask you, but he, h-he . . . he's used a knife. I'm bleeding bad, Birdie."

"Oh my God, oh my God . . ." I spin around in a circle and look down one hallway and the next, searching for the exit sign. I see the green lights above one of the doors and head at a fast clip in that direction. "Okay, okay, fine. Where are you? How do I get to you?"

"A-a-re you a-alone? He says he'll kill me if you're not alone. Birdie . . . I'm scared. So scared!" She cries and then screams out, and a banging sound like metal hitting concrete fills my ears.

"Please, God, no. Please. Tracey! Sweetheart, talk to me!"

"Come to Lucky's." She moans as if in pain.

"Lucky's?" I repeat as I push through the exit door before flying down three sets of stairs until I come out at the parking lot. It's the opposite side of where we entered. I glance around, not knowing what to do or where to go. I have no car . . .

Wait a minute. I do! Royce just gave me the key. I dig into my purse and pull it out and notice a panic button on the fob. I press the button frantically with my fingernail. For the love of all things holy, karma is smiling down on me, because I hear the alarm sounding off two lanes away.

"I'm coming for you. Just do whatever he says. I'll be there soon. So soon."

"Alone. You have to come alone, or I die." She cries out in what sounds like excruciating pain.

Tears hit the back of my eyes, but I tighten my fist, digging the keys into my palm to cut the emotional response with pain instead. "I'll be right there. Do what he says . . . Tracey?"

"Sky!" she screeches, and then the phone goes dead.

No, no, no, no, no.

I run as fast as my legs will carry me to the SUV, unlock the door, hit the panic button to stop the alarm, and get in. I've got the ignition turned and am barreling out of the parking lot when I see Royce alight from the stairwell exit I came out of. He's waving his arms.

I don't stop.

I can't.

He'll kill her.

***

The drive feels like it takes hours but probably only takes twenty minutes. When I pull up to Lucky's, there's only one car in the parking lot. I bail from the SUV, leaving the door wide open, and scramble to the back door of Parker's father's pub. I know it's unlocked because I can see from ten feet away that it's open about an inch. I curl my fingers around the heavy wooden door, and as quietly as I can, pull it open just enough to slip through.

Once I'm inside, I make sure it doesn't slam closed as my eyes adjust to the dark. Tiptoeing, I move down the dark hall to the front of the bar. When I get there, the backlight behind the liquor display is on, but nothing else. There, sitting atop the bar, legs dangling over the edge, is my best friend.

I glance to the left and right, trying to ascertain where the bad guy is, but find no one. Then I hear a tapping sound, and my head jerks back toward Tracey.

"Birdie, there's no one here but you and me."

Her words hit me like a smack to the face. "What?" I whisper, still looking for the threat, then snap my gaze back to Tracey and realize she's smiling. I scan her body from the top of her honey-brown hair to the bottoms of her sandal-covered feet.

There's not a scratch on her.

What the fuck?

"I assume you came alone." She smirks.

"Tracey, we have to get out of here. If he comes back—"

Tracey tilts her head back and laughs. Hard. "God, you really are helpless. It's a wonder I've been able to keep you alive and functioning all these years. Not that it didn't take a ton of effort. Sky, you are a handful."

I curl my hands into fists, my nails digging into my palms. "What are you talking about, Tracey? We. Have. To. Go. Now!" I move toward her, but she puts her hand up in a *stop* gesture.

"Don't come a foot closer. It's my time now, and frankly, I've gotten real tired of your bullshit." She lifts her other hand. She's holding a black square box with a red button. "See this? It's the detonator for an explosive device." Tracey nods in the direction of a table in the center of the room, where a bigger black box and various items sit with something bright yellow wrapped with black tape. "That's a bomb. The same one I placed on your boyfriend's door. Not that it did any damn good."

Bomb.

Placed on my boyfriend's door.

The pain of what she admitted blasts my soul. It feels like I've been hit by a Mack truck barreling at sixty miles an hour. I gasp and reach for my throat.

"I told you he wasn't good enough for you. For the longest time, I believed you'd get tired of him. Come to the realization that he'd never be good enough. Then he goes off to Montreal believing you'd cheated, and I was thrilled. Thrilled!" she seethes through her teeth. "Until you forgave him. After his dalliances with that blonde, big-boobed girl." Tracey shakes her head. "Have I taught you nothing, Staci?" She calls me by a name I've never heard her use before.

"I am the only one who cares about you. Me. Your big sister. I'm the one who protects you. Loves you. Not Parker or his band of lame asses. Not Wendy, the skanky redhead who wears a collar like a dog. Like a dog! And you took advice from her? Over me!" She makes an ugly, bloated sound and continues. "To think I got rid of Johan and made sure you got all the best parts in the acting industry and became ridiculously rich. Beyond what you'll be able to spend in your lifetime. And for what? For you to toss me aside like yesterday's newspaper? I don't think so."

"Tracey . . . please. I don't understand."

"Shut up, Staci! You will understand once and for all. Unlike those pathetic people you called your parents. Ugh! It was nothing to do away with those pesky people. Trying to talk you out of moving into the big-time roles and leaving me in the dust. That woman . . . the one who claimed to be your mother. Obviously not, since you and I have the same mother and her name is Laura, not Jill."

"Jill is my mother—" I attempt to butt in, but her eyes cut to mine, and they're filled with rage. White. Hot. Rage. So intense I fear what's behind them.

"Don't. You. Dare. Forsake our mother. She took care of you, Staci. For *years*. Wiped your tears. Fed you when you didn't have the strength to hold up a utensil. Wiped your body clean of bodily fluids when you couldn't get up to use the restroom as the cancer ate away at you. But . . . I *saved* you. Prayed and prayed and prayed God would be merciful. Then you left. For a while, I thought you were gone forever. I vowed then and there that I wouldn't speak a word until you came back. A year went by. Then one day, I looked out my window, and there you were. Playing in the neighbor's yard." Her entire face lights up as she must be remembering.

"You had come back to me. A different name, but I knew. I *knew* inside my heart"—she thumps her chest with her free hand—"that my very own baby sister had come back from death's clutches and had been delivered to me. I knew that day I had to take care of you. Protect you from the evil of the world. Provide for you. Make sure you had the best life where no one, no one could hurt you. And here you are . . . Staci, my Staci. Except you told me you didn't need me anymore. That you only needed that man!" She sneers, and it's so ugly I don't even recognize her, just see this vile casing of what I'd always thought was my best friend.

"Trace, it's me. It's Skyler. I don't know who Staci is, but I'm not her." Tears fill my eyes and start to fall down my cheeks.

"Don't. Lie. To. Me!" she screams as loud as she can, and I take a few steps back and bump into a chair and table set.

"I'm not lying. Tracey, I don't know what's going on. I don't know what's the matter with you, but I'll get you help. I swear—"

"Help!" She hops off the counter and takes a step toward me, waving the black box with the red button in the air. "I don't need your help. I've taken care of *you*. I've taken care of *everything*. Blew up your so-called parents' boat when they told you to stop working with me."

My parents.

Tracey killed my parents.

"No. Oh my God, no." My stomach twists and churns, violently quaking. I want to vomit. Tears fill my eyes and fall so fast I can barely see while my heart pounds so hard in my chest the edges of my vision start to blacken.

"And Johan . . . You know what I did to him. For you. All for you." She waves a hand flippantly in the air.

"Tracey . . ." I choke out a sob, thinking of my poor sweet parents boarding that boat, waving to Tracey and me standing at the harbor, me waving wildly, my mom blowing me kisses I pretended to catch. And she'd killed them. "Tell me you didn't kill my parents . . . please," I beg. I cannot make myself believe she's capable of something so horrendous.

Her face contorts into a confident, evil smile. "Oh, I made sure they were very dead and couldn't mess with my plans for you anymore. Of course, in all of this, I made one mistake."

A sob rips through my body. I close my eyes, the black threatening to take me.

"I hired that man. But I had no choice! You needed to get your acting muse back, and I was right. He did help you. What I didn't plan for was that he would fall in love with you. Not that he's worthy of your love. I'm the only person worthy of your love. I'm the only one who makes sure you're taken care of, right, Staci?"

I shake my head. "Tracey . . ." I can't even form the words there is so much fluttering through my mind. All the vile things she's done. Killing my parents. Hurting Johan. The texts. The threats.

"You set my apartment on fire?" I swallow, and she smiles.

"You needed to come home. To New York" is her flat, emotionless reply.

"And you set the bomb on Parker's door. The one that almost killed Nate and Parker."

Her face contorts into one of malice. "Should have planned for a larger boom. Then it would have done what I'd wanted and taken them both out. Damn bodyguard. Smart, that one," she sneers.

"Jesus, Tracey. You sent those texts. Scaring me. Warning off Parker. Why?"

Her head jerks back so violently it's as if she's taken a blow to the face by an invisible man. "To turn him away from you. He did a good thing by bringing back your muse, so at first, I wasn't intending to hurt him. Just get him to back off. Since you apparently have a golden pussy, the man wouldn't leave. That's when I needed to ramp things up." She runs her fingers through her long hair and sighs.

"And Mr. and Mrs. Ellis?" I gulp down the bile that's creeping up my throat.

Tracey smiles wickedly. "Chivalry is not dead, it seems. He pushed his wife out of the way of my car so fast I couldn't even swerve to hit her too. He took the brunt of my anger all on his own. I have respect for a man like that. I do hope he makes it." Her response is nonchalant and lacking any humanity. The Tracey I thought I knew is gone. Maybe she never existed. It was all a big act.

"Oh God," I whimper, and wipe at my nose. "Why did you hurt them? They did nothing to you."

"You left. He stole you away from me to Brazil. I couldn't get to you fast enough. Take care of you. I needed you home." She shrugs.

"This is all my fault. Everything. You did this all because of me."

"Staci, I'd do anything for you. I told you that when you took your last breath all those years ago. I'd bring you back. Take care of you. Be there for you forever. And you did. You did come back."

"I'm not Staci. I don't know who Staci is!" I scream, and pound the table. "Tracey, you are insane. You need help. You've lost your mind!"

Tracey smiles and starts to laugh. "Oh, Staci, dearest, you were always a funny girl. Now that you know everything, we can get on with it. I've been siphoning off a portion of your earnings for the past five years. I've got fake passports, and our travel destination is all mapped out. We're headed to the South Atlantic Ocean to the tiny island of Tristan da Cunha. It has harsh weather but is so remote they say fewer than three hundred people live on it. Perfect place to live out our days in peace. No one can get to you there, Staci, I'm certain of it. There, I'll be able to protect you forever. And you'll never have to worry about that man again."

"I don't think so," a voice I love more than anything booms from the same hallway that I came through, attached to the one person in all the world I need more than my next breath. My guy. Parker.

Tracey spins and points the black box at Parker, placing her thumb over the red button. "Ugh, you again. Why won't you die? I've blown up your house, run over your father, and taken your girl, and you still come back for more!"

Parker slowly enters the room, Royce and Bo behind him, but I don't see Paul.

Tracey's gaze narrows at the three men. "Great, the whole gang is here." Her head moves my way. "You said you'd come alone."

"I did! I have no idea how they found me."

Parker lifts up a single finger with a little black square that looks like a tiny microchip on it. "Trackers."

"The redheaded skank, I assume." Tracey sighs and rolls her eyes. "Whatever. Doesn't matter. My Staci, the girl you think is Sky, and I are leaving. Without you three." She moves over to me so quickly she's practically a blur as she grabs my bicep, her fingernails biting into the flesh.

"Over my dead body," Parker growls, and my heart clenches.

"Honey . . ."

"Great! Funny you should mention that . . ." Tracey backs us up toward the front of the pub where the main entrance is. "This little box is attached to that there bomb." She gestures to the table where the scary-as-fuck number of bomb-like things is sitting. She puts her hand and arm straight out. "I press this button and you are all dead."

"Then you are too," Bo states.

She grins. "Yeah, but I don't care if I die, as long as my sister, Staci, goes with me."

"Staci?" Royce rumbles. "Who the fuck is Staci?"

Tracey shakes my arm. "This is Staci. My baby sister!"

"Uh, what you been smokin', sugar?" Bo says dryly. "That's Skyler. Your friend. Your best friend. A woman who trusted you."

Tracey looks at me and back at Bo, then scans the room before she looks at me again, shaking her head. "No. No. No. This is Staci. She pretends to be Skyler. She's an amazing actress. Extremely talented. She's been acting since we were kids!"

Parker lifts his hands. "Tracey . . . I know you don't want to hear this, but your sister, Staci, died when she was eight years old. She's gone. You met Skyler a year later. If you look at her closely, you'll realize that's not Staci. It's Skyler . . ."

Tracey stomps her foot. "Shut up! Just shut the fuck up! You don't know anything. This. Is. Staci. Pretending. To. Be. Skyler!"

Parker shakes his head but approaches one slow step at a time.

"Tracey, I'm not Staci. I'm sorry. I'm so sorry you lost your sister," I say, but her hand cinches my arm so tight I cry out.

"Shut up. None of you know what you're talking about! Keep your mouths shut, or I'm going to blow this entire place up with all of you in it! Now, I know Staci doesn't want that because her heart is pure, but you so much as move one more step and I'll do it. You know I will."

"No. You. Won't," a deep voice booms from directly behind us, and a gunshot rings out.

I barely have a chance to see Paul standing at the entrance to the bar, gun pointed out in front of him, when Tracey roars out in pain and drops the black box to the ground. Parker jumps forward, knocking

Tracey down at the same time that Paul catapults over his brother and Tracey, scrambling for the black box and securing it across the room.

Tracey is on the floor screaming in pain, her hand holding her other limp wrist, blood pooling all around her, until her cries stop and she passes out.

Paul grabs for the mutilated wrist that looks to be hanging on by a thin string of skin and tissue while I stand stunned in the center of the pub watching the guys tend to Tracey.

"Get a fucking towel!" Paul hollers, and Bo moves into action, grabbing one off the bar and rushing to his side. "Call the police!" he continues.

"On it." Roy's deep timbre enters the fray.

Parker leaves Tracey in Paul's capable hands and moves directly in front of me so that I can no longer see the hideous vision of what was once my best friend now bleeding all over his father's bar. He curls a hand around each side of my neck. "Sky, baby, you okay?" He dips his face down so close I can smell the mint on his breath as he invades my space.

"Uh, uh . . . no." I shake my head, staring numbly at my man's blue eyes.

"That's okay. I've got you," he murmurs softly.

"Um . . . Paul shot her?" I repeat what I saw, looking over his shoulder to watch Paul and Bo move around Tracey in what seems like slow motion.

"Yeah, babe, he did." He wraps his entire arm across my back and tucks my cheek to his chest. My body starts to shake violently, or maybe it was always shaking but I'm just now noticing it.

"That was . . . that was . . . a g-good sh . . . sh . . . shot." My teeth are chattering, and I can't stop them.

Parker rubs his hands up and down my back and arms. "Shit, Sky, you're going into shock. I want you to breathe with me. Okay? In for four beats . . . out for four . . . Focus on my breathing." He breathes in deeply for four counts and then lets it out for four beats. I follow along with his breathing pattern as a whirlwind of facts sprints through my mind . . .

My parents being murdered.

All of those vile texts.

Johan. The drugs and women.

Nate being blown up.

The attempted murder of Parker's parents.

My best friend planning to take me away to a remote island.

"Stop, baby. Let it go for now. Just breathe. That's all you gotta do right now." He presses his forehead to mine and inhales. It sounds overly loud, so much so, it's all I hear for what feels like a few minutes as I pair my breathing to his. The panic slowly subsides.

Vaguely I begin to become aware of the barrage of sirens and the sound of boots stomping along the wooden floors. Parker adjusts our position to hold me full against his chest, my cheek pressed over his heart, and my focus is solely on him. The smell of citrus mixed with wood, the extreme warmth and safety that can only be found within the circle of my man's arms.

He is alive.

He is holding me.

He is telling me it will be okay.

I close my eyes, breathe in his scent, take in his warmth, and let the sound of his heart beating against my ear settle the hurricane inside my soul. His words seep into my conscious mind.

"It will all be okay. I swear it, Skyler. It's over, baby."

I lick my lips and squeeze my man with all of my might. "It's over."

12

PARKER

"Baby, you have to get out of bed." I cup Sky's chin and caress the apple of her cheek with my thumb. It feels like velvet against my skin.

She pouts and squeezes her eyes tightly shut. "I don't want to. Everything bad happens when I'm awake."

I lean forward and kiss her temple, dragging my lips to her ear. "All the good things happen when you're awake too." I nibble the edge of her ear.

She snickers briefly, but all too quickly the smile is replaced with the deep frown she's had for the last week.

Seven whole days have passed since her former best friend was shot, rushed to the hospital, and treated, only to end up losing her hand. They had to amputate it.

The good news is my father is awake and cantankerous as all hell, demanding to see Skyler and be discharged to go home. Nate, who has done remarkably well for all the injuries he sustained in the blast, is pushing to be released as well. Now that his vitals and levels are back to normal, he's set to get his wish today. Which is part of the surprise I have planned for my girl, if she'll ever get out of freakin' bed.

"Peaches, I know you're hurting, but staying in bed and avoiding life is not the answer." I curl my hands around her and lift her up.

"Hey! What are you doing?"

With a slight twinge in my ribs, which have mostly healed, I haul her body up and over my shoulder, stand, and smack her ass.

"Ouch! Parker, let me down!" she hollers, but I ignore her.

"No. We're all done with this pity party for one." I smack her ass again. "It's time to shower and enter the world of the living again."

"Let me go!" She pounds on my ass, but I ignore it. "I mean it, Park! Let. Me. Down!"

I enter the en-suite bathroom and mess with the shower dials, and the water shoots out. With her in her tank and panties and me in my pajama bottoms, I walk right into the warm water. I slide her down my body, then press her up against the back of the shower wall, caging her in.

"Listen to me," I demand.

"I can't believe you would do that!" She growls, her face filled with anger. Hell, I'll take the anger. It's the first emotion besides sadness I've seen in a week.

"Shut it!" I growl back, my nose almost touching hers. "You do not get to hide under the covers for more than a week. I will not see my beautiful girl sink into a depressed oblivion one more fuckin' day." I use so much inflection in my words that the water running down my face splatters against hers as I speak. "You. Are. Better. Than. This." I smack the wall of the shower behind her, and she flinches. "Come back to me, baby. I've been waiting patiently, but no more." I run my nose along hers. "I need you back."

Tears well up in her eyes and fall down her cheeks. Her lips tremble. "Honey, she killed my parents."

I tunnel my hand into the back of her hair, cupping her nape and pressing my forehead to hers. "I know, baby, and I'm sorry. I'm so fuckin' sorry."

"She killed my mom and dad." Her voice is tortured, filled to the brim with sorrow.

"Yeah." The word comes out a guttural, mutilated sound because her pain is shooting out of her and right into me. I'll take it all to bring her back from the depths of her grief.

"And she hurt Nate."

"Not your fault; she's whacked in the head."

"And your dad. Baby, she almost killed your dad." Her voice comes out a sob.

"They're on the mend, Peaches. And no one blames you. They blame *her*. She did this. In her own fucked-up brain, she created a reality where she didn't lose her sister. The pain she felt with that loss had to be enormous, and it messed her up bad, Sky."

Her fingers grip my biceps so hard I can feel her nails digging in.

"For some jacked-up reason, you became the sister she lost. And she became some kind of twisted protector. I'm not saying that's an excuse, but what I am sayin', baby, is you had no part in that. You are loving. Kind. Generous. Sweet. And your heart is so fuckin' huge, it shines light on everyone who comes into contact with you. She took advantage of that. She hurt you and hurt the people you loved, but you can't let her win by not living. What would your mom and dad say about that? If you let her break you? Take away the life they gave you? Huh, Sky? What would they say?"

Her body convulses, and I wrap my arms around her to hold her up as she sobs in big heaving jolts against my form. I take it all. I'd take anything for her. All her pain and grief. Anything to make her happy again.

"Th-they . . . they'd hate it."

I nod against her shoulder. "Exactly. So, how's about we clean up. Wendy is worrying herself ragged about how you're doing, which makes Mick an absolute dick to deal with. She needs to see you're all right."

She squeezes me tighter. "I'm not all right."

I rub my hand up and down her back slowly, wanting her to feel our connection. "I know, baby, but you will be. I'll make it so."

"I love you," she whispers against my ear.

I wrap my arms around her tighter. "Christ, I needed to hear that. I love you too, Skyler. So fuckin' much it hurts sometimes."

For a long time, we stand there just holding one another, letting the water beat down on our combined forms, sealing our physical connection as much as our mental one.

I lean back and look into her swirling brown eyes. "We're going to choose to live. Put all of this behind us and live free, right, Peaches?"

She nods, lifts up onto her toes, and kisses me. I delve into her kiss with relish, letting her lead, and thank God I've got a piece of my dream girl back. It's going to be a long road, but I know we can do it together.

Once we've removed our sodden clothing, I take my time washing my girl. Then I make slow love to her in the shower while she cries. It's cathartic and one of the most beautiful moments of my life.

When we get out and I've dried her off, I pull open the drawer and rummage through her makeup, finally finding a red lipstick. "Ah, perfect!"

She comes up behind me, strokes my dripping back, and kisses me there. "You're perfect."

"I'll remind you that you said that the next time I fuck up."

She chuckles and kisses my shoulder blade again. "What are you doing?"

"Putting up a reminder for you . . . and for me."

I take the cap off the lipstick, twist up the stick of red, and point it toward the mirror. There in big capital letters I write the one thing we both need to remember after everything we've gone through.

LIVE FREE
Love,
Us

Skyler smiles against my skin, and I watch her peeking out from behind me to stare at the words I scrawled in red across the corner of the mirror.

"Like I said, perfect, honey." She wraps her arms around me.

I cover hers with my own before bringing one of her hands up to my lips and kissing each fingertip and then the center of her palm. "Yeah, it is."

***

Hand in hand we walk down the road, our dogs on leashes in front of us. Everything excites our pups these days. A bird, a squirrel—all of the nature around us makes them pounce and jump.

"Obviously we're walking toward our house, but why?" Skyler asks.

I grin down at her and waggle my eyebrows. "It's a surprise. I told you that."

She crinkles up her nose. "Lately, surprises have not been very good."

I roll my eyes and squeeze her hand. "Just let me have this, baby."

Skyler shrugs. "Okay."

We make our way to our beautiful home. Skyler sighs. "It's magical, isn't it?"

I grin, taking in the landscape, the trees beyond the acreage, and the wraparound porch. I lead her up the walk, and she stops, tugging on my hand.

"Honey, we can't. They haven't given us the key yet."

I dig into my pocket and pull out the shiny brass key. "You mean this key?"

Her eyes widen, and her mouth opens in a cute little O shape. "Honey . . ." Without as much as a smile passing between us, my girl wraps her arms around my neck and hops up in the air. I catch her ass as her legs wrap around my waist and her lips slam down on mine.

She kisses me hard and for a very long time. I hold on and kiss her back with everything I have until she pulls away and laughs out loud, her head tipping back, the golden waves of hair moving in the slight breeze.

God, her laughter is the most beautiful sound in the world.

"This is so awesome!" she squeals, and slides down my body.

"Good surprise?" I smile.

"Best-ever surprise!" she says, and grabs my hand, this time pulling me toward the door.

When we get there, I open it, swoop her up into my arms, and sloppily whisk her over the threshold and into the entryway, our dogs in tow. She giggles as I kiss her neck several times then set her back down. We both let the dogs off their leashes. I hit the lights at the entry, and the simple chandelier with its crystals hanging down sets off sparkles on the walls around us.

She spins around, her arms out. "Honey, we're home."

"Yes, we are!" I grin wide. "Come, I have one more surprise for you."

"Really? There isn't anything better than entering our home for the first time. It's going to be hard to beat."

I chuckle and interlace our fingers while leading her to the farthest end of the house, where the master suite is. When we get to the double doors, I drop her hand, take both handles, and open them wide. Inside is a huge handmade wood sleigh bed. The headboard is high and thick, etched with delicate swirls I thought she'd like, but the heavy oak color and shape still give it a touch of manliness. On top is a heavenly bright-white down comforter that Wendy found for me as well as the softest sheets in the highest thread count she could find. I spent a mint on it, but with the look of complete awe on Sky's face, I know I've done well. My dream girl is happy.

"You like it?"

She looks at the bed, the only thing in the room because I told her I wanted to buy the bed, but I wasn't kidding when I said she could decorate the rest of the house.

"Like it? Honey, *I love it!*" Wonder coats every word. "It's the most beautiful bed I've ever seen."

I grin and wrap my arms around her from behind while she stares at the bed as though it might get up on its legs and walk away at any moment. "I'm glad you love it, because I love you!"

She spins around in my arms, kisses me once, and backs up with a sexy smile on her face. She lifts a hand up to the halter tie at the back of her neck that holds up the flirty little dress she's wearing. In a moment, the tie comes undone and the dress falls to the floor.

My girl is standing in front of our new bed wearing nothing but a pale-pink strapless bra and matching panties. She kicks the dress and her flip-flops aside.

"I say we christen it right now." She smirks, one eyebrow cocking up sexily.

I lick my lips and take in all the beauty before me; then I spring into action, removing my shirt. Her eyes light up with desire while she runs her fingers down her sides. I kick off my sneakers and toe off my socks as I undo the button on my jeans, shove them and my underwear down in one go, and kick them to the side. Her eyes go to my crotch, and she grins wickedly.

"You see something you like, Peaches?" I smirk.

"Oh yeah, something I like very much." She reaches behind her, flicks the hook on her bra, and it falls to the floor, her succulent tits bouncing free.

"I think it's time to get a little wild." I stalk toward her.

She pushes down her panties, and they drop to the floor. "And I think it's time we live free."

When I reach her, I wrap one hand around her waist, tugging her to me, and cup her gorgeous face with the other.

"All day, every day, baby."

That's when I prove to her what living free with me will be, in our brand-new bed in our forever home.

The end . . . for now.

LOS ANGELES: INTERNATIONAL GUY BOOK 12

To Jeananna Goodall.

A year. We made it a full year on this project.
You are my biggest cheerleader, my strongest support,
the person I can lean on when I fear it's not enough.
You remind me every day why we work so hard.

It's all about the story.
It's all about friendship.
It's all about love, light,
and living our best lives.

Together, we continue to live our truth.

1

SKYLER

Wendy flutters around her master bathroom, adjusting her boobs in her strapless, corset-style wedding gown, touching up her hair, and prodding at her unmovable hairdo. I made sure that hairstyle will not so much as shift in a harsh breeze by hiring the best celebrity hairdresser in the business. Those fiery short locks are not moving from the super-badass bouffant look she's sporting. The longer hair on top is raised in what can only be described as a stylized pouf, sleek on the sides, looking like nothing but hair magic, the kind my girl wanted on her wedding day. It's a little punk rock, a little fashion model chic, and a whole lot Wendy Bannerman, now Wendy Pritchard.

"So, when are you and Bossman getting hitched?" Wendy asks while touching up her bright cherry-red lipstick.

I mull over her question while checking out my sexy-as-sin strappy Valentino Garavani Rockstud heels. They're gold with studs all over the T-strap style and a full four-and-a-quarter-inch spike. Parker told me this morning that these shoes were staying on while he fucked me tonight. I cannot *wait*.

Wendy's question is deep, though, and since my ex-best friend has been confined to a mental facility to await her final sentencing, I've had two months of nothing but loving, recovering, and spending time making a happy home and building a life with my man.

I know without a doubt Parker is my forever. I go to sleep cuddling against his warm chest and wake up to smiles and "I love yous" every day. More than that, he *shows* me in all the little things and special ways of his. He makes my coffee every morning and serves it to me. He kisses me the moment he sees me and before he leaves my side each day. Even if it's to go throw the ball for our dogs, he always gives me a moment of affection, which lets me know that he's committed to me. For the long haul. Forever.

"Hello! Earth to Sky. I said . . . When are you and Parker gonna make playing house more like prepping for a family than sharing space?"

I frown and tip my head, taking in all that is Wendy in her beautiful wedding gown, hand on her hip, sassy expression plastered on her features.

"You're one to talk. You've been with Mick what, four years, and are finally tying the knot."

She waves her hand. "Technicality. He collared my ass in six months. In our world . . ." She tugs on the new, one-inch platinum choker at her neck. The new one has a black diamond heart dangling from a ringed loop at the center. Mick privately presented her with this piece last night. Once it's put on, the lock disappears into the design, and it can't be removed. The only way to remove it will be to cut it off. Wendy was beside herself with glee when she showed it to me this morning prior to the ceremony outside on their estate. Apparently Mick got a tattoo that matched the design of her collar but on one of his wrists. I couldn't see it under his dress shirt, nor did I ask to see it, because it's not mine to see. If he wants to share that piece of his commitment to his wife, he will. Though the concept of her man branding himself to only her is not lost on me. It definitely makes the ultimate statement.

"In our lifestyle, the collar is the highest form of commitment. We didn't initially need the rings or the public statement. We committed to one another in the way that means the most to us. However, once we decided to have children, it made sense to seal the deal legally." She winks.

I nod and pluck at my lip, thinking about Parker and me walking down the path of marriage and children. He knows I want to cut back on the number of acting jobs I take on after the A-Lister Trilogy is filmed. We've talked at length about me opening up an acting studio for kids, especially children who are less fortunate and wouldn't otherwise be able to afford professional classes. First, though, we'd need to commit to one another completely.

"Honestly, Wen, we haven't talked about it. Our future is always just there. *When* we have a family, *when* we get married . . . it's not like he's made any overtures that he plans on us tying the knot any time soon."

Wendy pouts. "Hmm. Well, then, you're just going to have to do it yourself."

I frown. "You mean, ask *him* to marry *me*?" The idea forms and lights up like a freakin' halogen bulb over the top of my head.

Wendy smiles huge. "Whoa. Now that's an idea. I was thinking maybe you need to push him toward the concept by leaving wedding magazines around, dropping hints and stuff. But I like your idea way more! It's perfect. Who says the woman can't ask the man?" She rubs her hands together and nods. "Yeah, me likee this idea a lot. It's not as though he'd turn you down. The man is over-the-moon in love with you. I just imagine with all that's happened, the fact that you're dealing with a lot and just coming over the top of that hill, it might make him leery to make any new life changes."

"True," I murmur, knowing Parker worries about me more than anything.

"Which means it's up to you to do it!" She claps. "Woo-hoo! Operation SkyPark Proposal commences now!"

I groan. "Wen, let's not forget that we're at *your* wedding right now. Your husband is probably pacing the floor wondering why you're taking so long. My guy is probably getting smashed with his brethren, and you need to prep for your honeymoon! And the whole reason we came in here was because you had to pee!"

She crosses her legs and wiggles her hips. "Yikes! Yeah, still gotta go. Wanna hold up this end of my dress so I can take care of that?"

I chuckle, grabbing for the hem of her shockingly poufy-as-all-get-out dress. The top is totally kick-ass rocker girl with a lace-up corset, but the bottom is straight-up princess, over-the-top, and all Wendy.

Once she's done her business and washed up, we walk out, arms linked at the elbows.

"Your wedding was perfect." I nudge her shoulder and smile.

"Yeah, it was. Now it's time to get rowdy and start Operation SkyPark Proposal." Her bright-blue eyes seem to sparkle with white-hot fire at the mere idea.

I shake my head. "One-track mind."

She shrugs. "When something is good, it's good. When it's right, it's right. Why not move on it? There's no reason to weigh all the pros and cons. Don't even allow the negative in. That's what Mick has taught me. Just roll with life as it comes. Stop letting fear drive your decisions. It's time to let love take the driver's seat."

Her words sink in, and I nod. "Girl, you are wise."

She grins wickedly. "A wise*ass* most of the time, but I have my moments."

"Like now." A growly voice breaks into our chatter. "You better get your perky ass to your husband's side right this *instant*, or that ass will no longer be wise, but *red*."

Wendy smirks, winks at me, and then sashays over to Mick. He watches her movements like a hawk scouting his prey. When she stands right in front of him, she lowers her eyes. "Sir . . ."

A throaty growl leaves his mouth as he loops a finger through the ring on her collar and tugs. She gasps, her blue eyes darkening at nothing but that simple touch. Damn, Mick has some mad skills when it comes to his woman. Then again, all Parker has to do is skim my neck with his nose and inhale my scent, and I'm a puddle at his feet.

Wendy has an excellent point. When it's right, it's right.

"I'll leave you two alone." I grin and move around the two locked in a stare-down.

"That's probably a good idea," Mick says to me, but his gaze never leaves Wendy's.

I skedaddle along the hallway, down the long staircase, and past several more rooms before finally making it to the backyard where the fun is happening under massive white tents, each column dripping in flowers and twinkle lights.

When I enter the main area, I catch Parker's gaze. He's talking to his dad and mom but waves them off to come to me. His dad is in a wheelchair but smiling jovially today. I love seeing a smile on his face. With his therapy bringing him down, we don't see a lot of that grin, and it's definitely a sight to behold.

"Everything okay, Peaches?"

I nod and take him in as if it's the first time I'm seeing him. He's wearing a brilliant pitch-black bespoke suit, a yellow satin tie, and a golden paisley pocket square. The dress shirt under his jacket is a crisp white and paired with a gray vest that goes perfectly with my pale-yellow slip dress. The smile adorning his ruggedly handsome, clean-shaven face is wide and heartfelt as he approaches. It's like I'm watching the other half of my soul lock into place right before my eyes. It all seems so very clear to me.

It's him.

Parker.

It's always been him.

It will always be him.

It's up to me to make it forever.

"How's my dream girl?" He grins, looping a hand around my waist, bringing our bodies together and dipping his head to plant his nose at the crux of where my shoulder and neck meet. He inhales deeply, and I close my eyes, memorizing the very moment when I decided I would make this man, the other half of my soul, my husband.

As Wendy said, Operation SkyPark Proposal commences now.

2

PARKER

"Damn, baby, you smell so good," I murmur against her skin, then place a few sloppy kisses there. She giggles, and it's music to my ears. Hearing her laugh has been rare these past few months. Her doing it more and more eases the vise of worry squeezing my heart. Every day she seems to smile more, and along with that comes a little more pep to her step. This wedding has gone a long way in helping her heal, by spending gobs of time with Wendy. Sky's focus on something beautiful has been a godsend.

Skyler snuggles closer as I run my hand up and down her exposed back. "Have I told you today that I fuckin' love this dress?"

She laughs out loud and tips her head back, which gives me the opportunity to layer a line of kisses up the delicate column of her neck, landing at her mouth. Once I've kissed her softly, she pulls back, her forearms looped around my shoulders.

"You may have mentioned your appreciation for this dress a time or two, yes."

I grin like a devil who's just been granted another soul for eternity. "And the shoes . . . You remember what I have planned for those fuck-hot spikes?"

Skyler flushes a pretty pink at the cheeks. "Mm-hmm . . . something about having them digging into the back of your thighs while you fucked me into next week, if I remember the conversation correctly."

I run my hand down to the exposed skin above her ass and flutter my fingers there, knowing it's a sensitive location for her. Usually when I have her belly and tits to the mattress, and I put my mouth on that spot, she goes wild. It's not exactly the same when I use my hand, but the intention is to remind her of what's to come.

She shivers in my arms, and her brown eyes dazzle and darken to a rich espresso color as lust invades her senses.

Message received.

Sky rests her head against my chest as I hold her close, soaking in her essence and warmth. "I'm so glad Wendy and Mick pushed their wedding a couple of months," I murmur into her hair.

"Me too. Everyone is happier now that things have settled down."

I inhale fully, letting out what feels like a ton of emotional weight filling my heart. "Exactly. Having the IG team back in full force, being in our home, having you to wake up to every morning . . ."

My girl lifts her head and smiles beautifully.

"That part *is* awesome," she agrees. "And I'm thrilled that Bo got Annie to come back and that we had the opportunity to mend fences over some beers and food at Lucky's."

"Definitely. She seems to be coming out of her shell and truly becoming part of the team. I'm glad to have her back too."

I stare down at the woman who owns my soul. "You are so damn beautiful, Sky. I'll never tire of looking at this face." I cup her chin and run my thumb over her cheek before dipping down to take her mouth. Right when our lips graze, I hear Royce's voice roar above the music and the other partygoers.

"Woman! You make me chase that sweet ass one more yard and I'm going to lose my damn mind! Shee-it. Give a man a break, why don'cha!"

Both Sky and I turn to the side and watch Roy grab Kendra's hand and spin her around until she's in his arms. Her mouth opens to say something, and based on her twisted facial expression, that something is *not* going to be pleasant, when he cups the back of her head and smashes his lips to hers. He kisses her hard, taking a long drink from the well that is her mouth. She gives as good as she gets, rubbing her lean body against his. He slants his head one direction; she mimics the move, tilting to the other side, both going full blast on the kiss.

I swear I've seen men come back from war and not be able to match this level of intensity, and those men have waited months to see their women.

This kiss, however, is one for the books.

I watch Sky as she pulls my phone out of my jacket pocket and takes a handful of photos of the kissing duo.

"What are you doing?" I whisper.

"Honey, we need proof of this. If I didn't see it with my own eyes, I wouldn't have believed it!"

I shake my head. "This is not going to be an easy road . . . for either of them."

She frowns. "Why would you say that?"

I don't have the chance to answer because Kendra pulls back, her eyes looking wild and frightened, before she whips her hand out and lays a wallop of a smack on Royce's stunned face.

I cringe. "Ouch. That had to hurt." I suck in a sharp breath.

"I told you to keep your hands off me!" Kendra growls low in her throat.

Roy doesn't so much as move to cover the cheek that has to be burning like fire. His mouth twists into a snarl. "Stop running, goddamn it! You have to talk to me. This is not over."

Kendra glances around and notes that pretty much everyone is watching their passion come to life. "It was a handful of really bad decisions. We agreed!" she insists, practically stomping her foot in her small tirade.

"Well, I reserve the right to"—he gets into her face—"change. My. Mind."

Her features contort into an expression of frustration and anger. "Let it go. I mean it, Royce. This time around, what we had was over before it ever even started." On that note, she twists in her unbelievably tall stilettos and races off, leaving Roy breathing heavily, his gaze seemingly lost, eyes locked on her retreating form.

He hangs his head and runs a hand over his bald dome.

"Not again," I groan. My spidey sense is working overtime; this is going to be a shit show of epic proportions.

"Maybe we should, um . . ." Skyler lifts her head toward Roy.

"Yeah." I sigh and lead my girl over to my brother.

"Roy . . ."

Royce's head snaps up, his dark eyes filled with nothing but heart-ache. I shake my head. "Brother, let's see a man about a bottle of whis-key. You look like you could use a drink."

"Damn straight." He half groans while adjusting his wide shoul-ders. The guy played college football back in the day and hasn't lost any of that bulk even at thirty. He's big. He's black. He's badass. Until now, he didn't take any shit from anyone. Then again, not everyone is a tall African American beauty with light-hazel eyes, long dark hair, and naturally full hips on a body that won't quit.

No matter what she'd like to think, Kendra's the one who got away, and if that kiss was anything to go by, even followed by that smack, she's moved right back into Roy's heart with a vengeance. Seems like he's got a major challenge on his hands. She doesn't act as though she wants to go the distance, no matter the fireworks we all just witnessed.

We reach the bar, and I order up three fingers of whiskey neat for us both, taking a tumbler for myself and passing the other to Royce.

Skyler and I can crawl home since our house is just a few acres down the road from the Pritchard McMansion.

Royce lifts his glass to his lips and takes a healthy swig, knocking a full finger back in one gulp.

Skyler gets a glass of wine and leans next to my side, her arm wrapped around my back, her other hand holding her glass in front of her, where she sips silently.

"You wanna tell me what all of that was about?" I gesture with an index finger to the area we just left where Royce and Kendra had their blowup.

"Not particularly." He takes another big swallow and sucks in a harsh breath after.

"Brother . . ." I let that word hang out to dry, an invitation and an admonishment at the same time.

"Fuckin' woman won't listen to reason," Roy snaps.

I cock a brow and wait it out. He obviously needs to vent, and since I don't know what the hell is going on between the two of them, I need him to lead this charge.

He shakes his head and looks out over the small reception of people milling about. I've been told most are people from Wendy and Mick's private lifestyle. I don't know if that means they're all kinky or just friends we've never met before, or both. Either way, Skyler and I have enjoyed meeting some of their friends outside of our little world. They mostly seem to be closer to Mick, as though they are his side of the wedding party and the IG people and my family as well as Royce's mom and sisters are Wendy's side.

"I messed up, brother." Roy rubs his hand over the back of his neck and squeezes. He uses his free hand to chug more whiskey until there's nothing more. He turns around and slams the tumbler to the bar. "Another."

Guess someone else will be crawling back to our house with us tonight.

"How did you screw up?" I ask softly, not wanting to make it too much of a big deal that we're talking about him and Kendra, even when it is. In the past, she was his *everything*. Then it all went to hell; one day she was there, they were planning their future together, and the next, gone. Poof. Disappeared.

Of course, I was dealing with my own shit with Kayla cheating on me, our ex-best friend, Greg, being the douchecanoe that did her. We lost both friends, so I wasn't really up to snuff on the comings and goings of Royce and Kendra. At the time, Royce only told me that she said she was ending things and leaving. Then before I came out of my Kayla-induced pity party for one, Kendra was gone, having moved to Washington, DC, leaving Roy and the life they were building in the dust.

"We hooked up, man. Several times. Each time better than the last." He looks down at his feet. "Being with her is like soaking in a natural hot spring. Everything just feels right, warm; your senses and mind are finally at peace for once in your life. Except, the second you lift out into the open air, you get nuthin' but ice-cold chills all over your body." His dark gaze lifts to Sky then back to me. "You ever feel that? A cold you can't escape?"

I shake my head. "Nah, man, I just wrap myself up in my very own Skyler blanket and keep my ass warm."

He huffs and points a finger. "Attaboy. That's the way it should be. And you, baby girl, you ever feel cold?" He turns a steely-hard gaze Sky's way.

Skyler frowns. "Not when I'm with Parker. He'd do anything to keep me warm. Always." She bites into her bottom lip, clearly knowing where this conversation is going.

"Exactly. When we're together, we burn so hot it feels like no storm could break us. But each and every time . . . it ends. And that end is harder to accept than the last, because every fuckin' time, I fall in love with that woman a little bit more. One taste of her and I'm gone. Can't get that taste out of my mouth, and I don't fuckin' want to. What I want is that sweetness that is all her, on my tongue, forever."

"Jesus, Roy." I lift my drink and swallow down half of what's in my glass, letting that shit burn a hole through my gut to distract from the pain of knowing what my brother is living through: not having the woman he needs by his side. I couldn't take it. Even that brief time between the San Francisco and Montreal jobs that I didn't have Sky officially in my life shredded me. I don't think I could live with it if I lost Sky now that I know the beauty of all that is her.

Roy grabs the glass the bartender has refilled. Thank God it's an open bar, because the shit Mick and Wendy are pouring is the tippy-top shelf that's usually fifty dollars a shot at my father's bar, and this guy tending bar is generous. I suck back the last of mine and lift my chin to the server. He takes the hint and fills my drink another three fingers.

Roy takes a smaller sip this time. "It's all right, man, I'll be fine. Just need to get my shit together and figure out my next step."

"Are you going to let her go?" I ask, and Skyler stiffens at my side.

"Fuck no! I'm going to lick my wounds and regroup. She's it. My endgame. I just have to find a way to convince her I'm hers."

I grin and lift my glass between us. "To creating the future we are meant to have, with the women we're meant to have it with."

Skyler leans her head against my shoulder and nuzzles closer as I clink glasses with my best friend. He'll find a way.

Love always wins.

***

After Momma Sterling intruded into our male brooding, I left Roy in her very capable hands. The last thing I heard was, "And that Kendra is running her brand of damage on my boy all over again. Stupid witch." At that point, I steered Skyler and myself out of the conversation and toward the dance floor.

"Will you dance with me?" I twirl my girl around and bring her back into my arms.

"Anytime, every time." She smiles wide, placing one arm around my back and her free hand securely into mine.

The music swirls and dips around us, and before long, I see Bo with a buxom brunette I recognize very well in his arms.

"Geneva! I had no idea you were here." I maneuver Sky and myself over to where Bo is dancing with our old friend. She's been in Boston for the past month, meeting with the movie people, running lines with Sky and Rick before shooting starts in another three weeks. When she heard about what happened to us, she met with her people and pushed the entire movie schedule back three months. Skyler was in no position to act the part in a very beloved romance, and Geneva would have no one else but Sky since the character was practically crafted in her likeness.

Geneva smiles and runs a hand down to Bo's ass, where she cops a feel right on the dance floor. "Couldn't attend the ceremony, but I wouldn't miss the reception. I'm here as this wild one's date in the hopes of getting a little bit more than a twirl around the dance floor. What do you say, cowboy?" she coos in her lovely British accent, though her innuendo is anything but lovely. It's downright naughty.

"I say giddyap, ma'am." He swings her out and brings her back, dipping his hips and rubbing his body all over the wanton author.

"My goodness . . . you two need to get a room!" Sky giggles, her cheeks firing red for the second time this evening.

I love how my woman still blushes. She's so beautiful when her face takes on that rosy hue.

"Why, that's an excellent idea. Wha' d'ya say, cowgirl? You want to take a ride?" He rolls his hips in a blatantly sexual manner.

"I just got here!" She chuckles and swats his ass. "Behave."

Behind them, I see Baylee pacing in the background, her thumbnail resting between her teeth, her eyes flickering to Bo and then back to the room at large as if she's debating interrupting his dance. The woman is new to our fold, doesn't actually come around much, but I know since she started working at Lucky's a couple of months ago, Wendy and Sky have spent some time with her. From what I understand, we don't know a lot about her, just that she needed the job and started work immediately. The holidays had hit right around the time the shit went down with Tracey, and with Pops being laid up, Bo hired a couple of people, Baylee being one of them.

Seeing her pace the floor in a royal-blue dress that reaches about four inches above her knees and a pair of nude platform pumps is a side to her we haven't seen. Hell, I knew the woman had a nice shape and a gorgeous face. In all honesty, Bo wouldn't have hired her if she weren't easy on the eyes. It's just not in his makeup. Still, I don't think any of us knew the bombshell she was hiding behind those shapeless T-shirts, jeans, and sneakers. Looking at her now, the woman is a freakin' knockout. Long legs that seem to go on for days. Tanned skin. Long, wavy sandy-brown hair, and a fuckuva lot of it too. Normally she's got that mane in a ponytail or pinned in a messy bun on her head. Hanging down and styled, not only is it eye-catching, it looks shiny and soft, something that makes a man want to run his fingers through it . . . after he fucks the shit out of her. Her dress is rockin', showcasing her large breasts, and it glides along her flared hips. The woman is the epitome of an hourglass figure. Yep, definite knockout.

"You can stop licking your lips now, honey." Skyler dips her face in front of mine so all I can see is her and not Baylee.

"Peaches, I would never—"

She places two fingers over my lips. "Relax." She smirks. "I was just joshing you! Though I did catch you eyeballing the new girl."

"Sky, baby, I can't help it. I've never seen her look like . . ." I scan her sexy-as-fuck body and blink a few times, making the image go away before my woman clocks me the way Kendra clocked Roy earlier.

"Like a *Sports Illustrated* swimsuit model?"

I blink dumbly and focus on my golden girl. "Yeah. Pretty much."

She snickers. "Honey, she's wearing my dress."

I can feel my eyes trying to bug out of my head as I maneuver her around so I can get a better look. Shit, yep. It's one I've drooled over Sky wearing.

"Though I will say, her female attributes have been highlighted to their fullest possible extent." She smiles, taking in the woman.

"I didn't say anything," I blurt defensively.

Skyler grins. "I know you love me and only me, but you're not dead. You're allowed to look and appreciate a beautiful woman." She leans into my space again, bringing her lips to hover just over mine. Her peaches-and-cream scent fills my nostrils, and I'm drunk on her all over again. "You're just not allowed to touch." She kisses me softly, touching just the tip of her tongue to mine before easing back and smiling.

"You do not play fair, woman." I pull a move like Geneva's and get handsy with my girl's ass.

"Hey! Pretty boy. Hands off," she admonishes, and after a playful squeeze of the tightest, most perfect ass I've ever seen, felt, or bitten into, I move my hand to the center of her spine, where I can trace the velvet surface of her skin at my leisure.

"What do you think she wants?" I watch her focus completely on Bo and decisively nod, her hands rounding into fists at her sides.

She's about to approach Bo, her finger reaching out to tap him on the back, when Bo growls and crushes Geneva's lips to his in a searing kiss that rivals the one Royce gave Kendra earlier. Not quite as heated as theirs, but definitely holding promise of something more carnal at a later hour in the evening.

Baylee sees the kiss, backs up several steps, bumps into someone, and steps on a man's foot with the spiked heel of her stiletto.

"Ooowee! That fucking hurt!" the man roars, spinning around and grabbing Baylee by both biceps and shaking her. "Watch where you're fucking going, you idiot!"

Oh *hell* no. I move to approach, but at this point, Bo's already turned around and jumped into the fray before I can even situate Skyler behind me and back up my buddy.

"Watch how you talk to a lady, asshole!" Bo spits with a growl, and yanks Baylee out of the man's hold. "Are you okay, Lee?" He slides his hands soothingly up and down her arms, which I can already see have red blotches marring where the fuckface grabbed her.

She looks at him, then at the furious man who's shaking his sore foot, her eyes filled to the brim with tears. "I'm sorry . . . so, so sorry. I didn't mean to hurt you." Her face is a mask of remorse and apology. "And, Bo, I didn't mean to interrupt. Um, I didn't know . . . uh . . . that you had a girlfriend. I'm . . . I'm . . . It doesn't matter what I am. I need to go." A tear slips down one high cheekbone before she dashes it away with her hand, steps back out of his hold, turns on her tall heels, and takes a runner.

What is it with women and running off?

"Christ! Baylee! Come back, sweetheart!" he calls out, and then, without another word, jets off after her.

Geneva crosses her arms and pouts. "Well, bloody hell. Looks like I'm going to have to find another bloke to warm my bed this evening. Pity," she mumbles.

Mick approaches with a stern face and his wife holding his hand and trailing just a step behind him. Her fluffy dress is bouncing all over the place as he moves at a fast clip.

"What is the meaning of this debacle?" Mick's voice is hard and cold. "Are you starting trouble again, Uncle Neil?"

The older man, who carries a remarkable resemblance to Mick, blusters and straightens his coat as if he's been in a full tussle. "Out of nowhere this bumbling woman crashed into me and speared her stiletto into the top of my foot! She may have broken a bone! I'm going to have to see a doctor," he tuts, as if Baylee planned to run into him.

Mick's mouth quirks for a moment before he gets control of himself.

I wrap my arm around Sky's shoulders as she adds, "That may have happened, but you didn't need to manhandle and yell at the young woman who accidentally bumped into you and stepped on your foot. I saw the entire thing."

"I see the drunken, bumbling twit has friends," the man barks.

That makes my hackles rise. No man treats a woman like that, especially a sweet girl like Baylee.

"Jesus. She didn't do anything to you. Man up," I bark back, standing up straighter while taking a step closer.

"Well, I've never been treated such a way in my entire life." He raises his chin haughtily.

Mick's nostrils flare, and he narrows his eyes. Unfortunately he's too late, because Wendy takes the torch, pushing herself in front of her husband. "Sounds to me like you're overreacting—"

"Cherry, quiet," Mick growls, but lovingly wraps an arm around her chest from behind.

"Are you going to let your new wife talk to me like that, son?" the man asks, seemingly affronted.

"I am *not* your son, and I'll let my wife speak however she wants to the guests at *her* wedding in *her* backyard. Do remember who controls this family. You do not want to get on my bad side, or the family business we actually do together, *Uncle Neil*, will dry up. Keep that in mind. Now if you'll accompany your date to the receiving room, I'll have the doctor on call here evaluate your injury."

"Good," he sneers, and grabs the arm of the woman he's standing with and storms off. I assume she's his wife, although she's at least half his age.

"If his foot were broken, he wouldn't be able to walk." Wendy watches his retreating form.

Mick chuckles softly against Wendy's neck and kisses her there right at the sparkling collar.

"Just sayin'." She snickers.

Mick turns his wife around and brings her into his arms against his chest. "And I am saying that my wife is the most beautiful woman here, and I shall request the honor of our first dance together as husband and wife."

"I shall accept your request and return that my man is a stone-cold *fox,* and I'll dance circles around you all night just to see you smile like that at me." She bats her eyelashes and shimmies her hips and chest in a sultry display that gets all of Mick's attention.

He grins wide, his eyes sparkling blue and his smile only for Wendy as he captures her against his chest and sways to the music.

I watch as Geneva moves off the dance floor, likely to find a new guy to keep her entertained since Bo disappeared after Baylee.

Following Mick's lead, I curl my hand around Skyler's and bring her back into my arms. "Wow. A lot just happened," I murmur in her ear.

"Totally weird. First, we've got Royce and Kendra in a kiss-off ending in a fight. Then we've got Baylee acting strange about approaching Bo and then running away in tears. And Mick nearly duking it out with his uncle Neil, which I didn't even know he had! Then to hear the way that Mick feels about his uncle . . . yikes. There is some family drama all over that. I'll have to find out the goods from Wendy."

"Sky, don't get involved in their drama," I warn.

She frowns. "Why the heck not? Wendy has half her body stuck in everyone else's lives. Why can't we poke around a little? Hmmm?"

I chuckle. "It's none of our business, and we've had enough of our own drama to last a lifetime; we don't need anyone else's."

Her smile falls. "This is true. I hate it when you're right."

I rub my cheek along hers. "It's not that I'm right; I'm just protecting what we have. We've been through a lot, and I don't want to get involved in anything else that's going to shake our lives up again. I want just you, me, our home, our dogs, and living the good life. Can we just do that for a while?"

She kisses my cheek and wraps her arms tighter around me. "Yeah, honey, we can do that . . . for a while. At least until Wendy gets back from her honeymoon."

"Christ. Whatever am I going to do with you."

She shrugs and grins as her eyes light up with a sensual flicker I'd recognize anywhere. "I can think of a few things."

"Mmm . . . I bet you can."

3

SKYLER

Not long after the debacle on the dance floor, a surly Bo flops down in the open seat next to Parker and me. He reaches for the huge slice of wedding cake in front of my guy and slides it in front of himself. Without a word, he picks up the fork, digs a big chunk out of the cake, and shovels it into his mouth. Frosting rings the hair around his mouth of his mustache and goatee.

"Hungry?" I ask with a grin.

His lips twist into a snarl while he tips his fork sideways and cuts another large helping of cake.

"Brother, what's up with you and Baylee?" Parker asks gruffly.

"Nuthin', man. I got it under control. It's all good," Bo half growls, but focuses on the stolen cake and not my man.

Park nails him straight out. "Then why the hell are you avoiding eye contact with me?"

Bo drops the fork on the plate with a clank, grabs the linen napkin in front of him, and wipes his mouth with it. "I tagged her, all right? It was a one-time thing, we both agreed. No biggie."

"Nuh-uh!" My mouth drops open of its own accord as shock—and a little bit of excitement—skitters down my spine. I twist my seat a couple of inches closer as Bo crosses his arms and leans back.

"Then why did she look like a little kid whose ice cream had been taken away when you were dancing with Geneva?" Parker asks, a curt and protective note to his tone.

Bo sighs and plucks at his goatee. "Hell if I know. When I caught up to her, she said she was feeling out of sorts, was sorry she bothered me, and bailed again. That time, I didn't chase her. Not gonna play games. If the woman doesn't want to talk, give up what has her ass in a snit, who am I to push?"

Parker purses his lips. "Bro, she ran off after seeing you with Geneva."

"Nah, man. She ran off because she was embarrassed."

"You're wrong. I *know* women; you know I do. That woman had hurt plastered all over her face. That hurt was directed at you, not at the fuckwad extended family of Mick's."

Bo shakes his head. "You're wrong. Me and Baylee, we're tight. Work together at the bar five, six nights a week. She's solid. Works hard, keeps her head down, never complains."

"Yeah, but you just said you slept with her," Parker adds.

"It was two months ago, right after all the shit went down with Tracey and Pops. I was working the bar; it was Christmas Eve. All of you had plans, and I had the bar on my own. It was busy as fuck. She came in, having seen the 'Help Wanted' sign. Hired her on the spot. She worked the tables, took orders, and served, and we made the bar a shit ton of cash. After, we were tired, dead on our feet, so we took the solo couch in the place, turned on the TV, and sat and watched Christmas movies while doing shots. We got shit-faced. One thing led to another. Hooked up. One-time deal. We agreed. She says she's good and has been at work every day since. I have no idea what was up tonight, and she didn't want to share. End of. Now can we move on from this?"

Just as Parker's about to say something, we see Mick approach the stage where the four-piece quartet is, standing about ten feet in front of us with a mic in his hand, his beautiful bride at his side.

Wendy is beaming from ear to ear as Mick puts his arm around her waist.

"My wife and I would like to thank everyone for coming and sharing this day with us. The past year has been a whirlwind of activity."

Mick grins and glances down at Wendy's smiling face. "My woman became the sister to a brotherhood of men we couldn't imagine our lives without." Mick's gaze roams to our table where all of us are sitting.

He then turns and cups Wendy's chin and caresses her cheek with his thumb. "We suffered a crushing personal loss and helped our friends overcome crippling tragedies . . . and yet here we all are, celebrating an *unbreakable* love. One that I will never take for granted." He wipes away a tear that slides down her cheek.

My heart stops, and I grip Parker's hand in mine, squeezing it tight. He lifts our hands and kisses each one of my knuckles as we watch stoic Mick worship his woman with his words.

"Wendy, you are my entire world. Without you, I have no compass. No path to follow. No goals to achieve. *Nothing.* I will live every day of my life attempting to give you all that I am, and all that you could ever dream of. In front of all of our family and friends, you are my love and my life." He gifts her a rare, full, even-toothed smile, but it's not enough for our quirky girl. No, she wraps her arms around his neck and smashes her lips to his in a heart-melting kiss. He cups the back of her head and kisses her more deliberately to the hoots and hollers and tinkling of glasses from the entire crowd.

Wendy eases back and rubs away the red stain on Mick's lips. He grins, takes his pocket square, and wipes his mouth as she finagles the mic from his hand.

"Hi, everyone . . ." She waves cheekily at the crowd, including our table as we laugh at her cuteness.

"I want to reiterate what Mick said. We're very thankful to have each and every one of you in our lives." Her facial expression becomes serious. "You know, I grew up with nothing. No family. No friends. Looking around this room, I know how very blessed we are to have all of you. From my guys"—she gestures toward our table—"to my best friend, Skyler, who helped me make all of this happen, and my new adopted parents, the Ellises and Momma Sterling." She gestures to the table next to ours where Parker's parents are sitting alongside the Sterling clan of Royce's mom and sisters. "As well as all of you, our friends from all over the globe. We thank you."

She turns her body toward Mick and brings the mic toward her face. "Mick, you're the first person I ever loved. I didn't even know what the word meant until I met you. Our love story moved at the speed of light. Some people say when you meet the person you're supposed to be with, you just know. The day we met, all you had to do was look me in the eye, and I knew there would never be another person on this earth who could move me the way you do. You smile, and I melt. You kiss me, and I die a thousand beautiful deaths. You make love to me, and the entire world stops. The day we met, my life started over. You're the man of my dreams. And you're going to be the world's greatest father."

The entire room goes dead silent as Wendy reaches for Mick's hand and places it on her belly.

Mick cups Wendy's face with his other hand as she holds the first to her abdomen.

"I'm going to be a father?" We can hear him through the microphone, only it's softer since she has it held down at her hip.

"Yes, sir." She lowers her gaze.

"You're pregnant with my child. My *son*." His voice is strained and thick with emotion.

"Or baby girl. We won't know for another two months what we're having." She smiles, lifting her gaze to his.

He squints and shakes his head, but he moves both of his hands down to her waist. "I'll never be happier than this moment." He dips down and presses a soft kiss to her lips. She closes her eyes and wraps her hands around his neck but turns to the side, bringing the mic up to her mouth.

"Sir Mick knocked me up, everyone! Time to party!" she booms into the microphone.

I stand up and cry out, "Woo-hoo! Right on, Mick and Wendy!"

Parker follows me by standing and clapping. Our table, along with most of the crowd, does the same thing. I watch as Wendy hands the mic back to the musicians; then Mick loops his arms around her waist and spins her around. She tips her head back and laughs as he kisses her neck, clearly overwhelmed with her news.

I turn to my man. "This is awesome! I know after their loss, this is the absolute best news ever!"

Parker pulls me into the warmth of his arms and nuzzles his chin against my neck and shoulder. "It really is. I knew they were trying, but she hadn't mentioned anything since they lost the baby in Montreal, and that feels like an eternity ago. I'm glad they're getting their happily ever after. As Mick said, their love is unbreakable."

I smile happily, watching my friend's man dote on her. He leads Wendy over to their table, kneels at her feet, bringing her belly right in front of his face, where he traces the outline of her stomach. His eyes are filled with wonder as he looks up at his wife with absolute pride. I melt on the spot and even more so when he does the ultimate, pressing his face to her belly, hands spanning any leftover space. He seems to be speaking to their unborn child. Wendy runs her fingers through his hair as he kisses her there several times and then leans his forehead against her body for a long time.

Parker turns us to the side so he can see what has my attention. A soft smile spreads across his lips. "That's one grateful and happy man right there."

323

"Yeah. He's almost as awesome as my man." I wink and point my best cheesy grin up at my guy. "I want that, honey."

"What . . . a baby?" Both of his eyebrows rise up toward his hairline as surprise coats his expression.

I chuckle. "Yeah, eventually. Just all of it. Marriage, babies, family. Being settled in our life."

Parker stares at me, an intensity in his blue eyes I've never seen before. "Peaches, we don't need to rush anything. We've got all the time in the world now. You're safe, and we *are* settled in a way. We've got our house that we're making a home. You've got the new role coming up. International Guy has never done better. I don't want you to make any rash decisions because you've had a tough year. I wouldn't want to put that pressure on you or me."

I frown. "What if it's what I want?"

"Baby, you've had a lot happen to you this past year. I need to know that you're healed inside and out before we make any more massive changes about our future."

I tip my head and run my hand down his lapel, straightening out nonexistent wrinkles. "Are you saying you don't want to marry me?"

"Whoa, whoa, whoa . . ." Parker grabs my hands and interlaces our fingers. "I'd marry you in a second if I thought you were truly ready for it. Sky, you've just come off of a seriously traumatic experience. I want you to give your mind the time to heal from that."

I laugh stiltedly. "So what you're saying is that you'll marry me when *you* think I'm ready?"

He purses his lips. "Yeah."

"That's a bit high-handed of you." I cock an eyebrow, trying to make my point but still not take offense.

"That may be, but I've got your well-being at heart." He brings our hands around his back so that our chests are flush against one another. "How's about this. You and I spend time living the boring life for a while. You continue your therapy, and then we'll see what the future brings. When the time is right, we'll both know it. Yeah?"

I crinkle my nose, not at all agreeing, but nodding anyway. Wendy was right. I'm going to have to take my future into my own hands.

"Come on, Peaches. Let's go congratulate our friends and let loose on the dance floor." He steps away but tugs my hand as he does.

I follow him, though my mind is no longer on dancing or Wendy and Mick but on how in the world I'm going to get my guy to see that I'm ready for the next step in our relationship.

***

"Don't even think about moving that perfect ass," Parker growls from his position behind me, cock sunk to the hilt inside. He's so deep I feel hung up on his length, pinned to the mattress where he's holding me.

My entire body trembles as I tighten my fingers in a death grip on the sheets and try to breathe. Between the moment he slid my maid of honor dress off and the second it hit the floor in a wisp of yellow fabric, he was on me. Mouth to tit. Hands to ass. In a flurry of activity, he'd removed his clothes and had my knees to the mattress, ass up in the air at the edge of the bed, and his dick impaling.

"Honey . . . I can't . . ." I hold off the desire to move, but he knows I want to circle my hips, thrust myself on and off his length until we're both screaming out. He *knows*, but he's keeping it from me, the bastard!

"What did I tell you was gonna happen if you played with fire . . . huh, baby?"

I open my eyes but see nothing but blurry night shadows while my vision adjusts to the room. The moon casts slices of light through the massive french doors of our master bedroom.

Parker runs his hands down the skin of my ass. "I said, you'd get burned. You played your hand, Peaches, snuck touches of my dick, my ass, my chest *all night*, and I warned you. Promised if you kept up your game I'd play . . . Well, baby, now I'm playing, and you are about to get *fucked.*"

He eases his hips back and slams home with a jolting thrust that has me crying out, "Yes!"

He hums deep in the back of his throat. "You like that . . ."

Again, my guy slowly releases until just the flared tip of his wide cock head is pressed to the lips of my sex before he plows home in a brutal lunge.

"Oh my!" My eyes roll in the back of my head, and I push up onto my forearms, no longer capable of breathing with my cheek against the mattress. "Honey . . . ," I mewl.

"I'll give you honey, Sky." He caresses both sides of my ass until his thumbs are where we're connected. He pets the swollen and plump skin edging around where his dick is piercing me, and I start to pant, every neuron focused on the slight touch of his fingers in that sensitive space.

"Like this honey seeping from between your legs, Sky. Mmm . . . love the way my girl weeps for my dick." He uses his thumbs to part me farther and grind the base of his cock deeper.

"Fuck yeah," he groans, pushing as far inside as he can get. We've never been closer.

I swear I can feel his length in my navel. "Baaaybee." I gulp air through my lungs and hold my position.

Parker rolls his hips in a circle, working every last nerve he can find inside me. Chills run up my spine, and I arch into it, wanting more, needing so much more. "Please . . . ," I murmur through the haze of lust that's controlling me.

"Please what, Peaches?"

I sigh and drop my head until my forehead rests on the cool sheets, giving me a moment's respite from the pleasure and agony of him not taking me there immediately.

"Please . . . fuck me," I beg, not caring in the least if I sound wanton, because I absolutely am.

Parker's hands glide back over my ass to my waist. "Your wish . . . my command, baby" is the last thing he says before he goes to town on me, thrusting wildly, pounding hard and long.

An intense fire builds between my thighs as he works me up until one of his hands comes around, and with an absolute precision built on months of very intimate knowledge of my body, he zeros in on my clit and doubles my pleasure.

"Jesus, honey, I'm *there*. I'm right there!" I cry out.

"Fuck yeah, you are. You take me while you go off. Squeeze my fucking dick!" He grinds out through his teeth. His finger is relentless on my bundle of nerves, but his powerful thrusts are more so.

Just when I think I'm about to shoot off into the stars again, he changes the plan by curling over my body, jacking an arm up the center of my torso, and lifting my upper half up so I'm practically hung up on his dick, my back to his chest. One of his hands wraps around my breast, fingers plucking away at my nipple, his other hand at my waist, jacking me on and off his cock. The mattress is bouncing with his efforts, aiding in the wild ride he's giving.

I glance across the room and see our reflections in the vanity mirror above our dresser. His body is misted with sweat and glistening in the moonlight as he fucks me. The light bounces off his powerful torso, thighs and arm muscles showing how they flex and move with his body in a beautiful symmetry I can't take my eyes off of. My guy's face is hard, teeth bared, nostrils flared like an animal, his entire focus on giving me the fuck of my life.

I lean back, arching my own body. My knees are spread wide, balancing on the bed as I lift my calves and feet, pointing my toes. As desired, the stiletto points of the gold heels he was drooling over earlier make perfect contact with his body.

He howls and jolts us both when the two spikes prod his muscular ass.

"Hell yes!" He smiles, running his hand down my body and cupping me between my legs. His face takes on a mask of complete confidence and concentration as he presses two fingers to my slit, where he's already stretched me with the girth of his cock. "You're gonna take more of me, Peaches."

"I'll take you any way I can get you . . ," I gasp, and moan.

He brings down both of his hands, and one goes straight to my clit and rubs circles until I'm mindlessly fucking myself on his length. With his other hand, he rubs his index and middle finger into the new wetness before he eases his cock out a few inches, making a little bit more room for what he plans to do. He takes long moments to bathe my neck, ear, and shoulder with kisses and love bites that have me shaking with need. Before I know it, he's tipping my body forward and working those two digits alongside his cock, so he's not only impaled me on his length, he's hooked my cunt with two of his fingers.

On a lion's type roar, he stretches the full length of his body, those two fingers piercing right alongside his cock as deep as they'll go.

"Now ride that, Peaches," he groans, but I'm so gone, overwhelmed with sensation and so full between my thighs I'm ready to burst. I'll do anything right now to get my fix.

I bring my hands to his bulging forearms, lay my shins back down to the mattress, and use the rebound of my weight to bounce my form up and down.

"Beautiful. My dream girl. Takes her man any way he gives it," Parker whispers in my ear. "You're filled up, Peaches. I've got my dick and my fingers so far up your cunt you won't be able to walk tomorrow."

His filthy words are my undoing. He takes over, thrusting and using the hand he has cupping me to fuck me stupid. I lose all rational thought besides every pleasure point that's being manipulated.

I come hard around his pounding cock and tugging fingers.

He doesn't stop.

I come again, right on the heels of the last one, only bigger, brighter, and louder as I scream.

This time, my entire body locks down around his, and his body responds, his hips offering one more powerful thrust, grinding home as his essence warms me from the inside out. He holds me still, his body wrapped around me, his forehead pressed to my nape, where I can feel the puffs of air leaving his mouth against my fevered skin.

My body is a lifeless doll in his arms. Completely wrung out.

For long moments, the two of us stay mostly still, him panting against the back of my neck, my chest powering up and down as I gasp for breath.

"I'll love you until the day I die, Skyler. You have my word on that." His words are guttural, blanketed in emotion.

"Honey . . . ," I mumble, hardly able to focus as he dips me forward enough that he can slip his fingers out of me. It burns for a moment when those large digits slip from my body, but it's worth it for the wild ride.

I blink heavily as I feel small presses of Parker's lips against every patch of skin he can reach on my neck and back.

"I mean it, Sky. I've never lost myself in another person so flawlessly I didn't know where I began and she ended."

"We're meant to be, honey." I wrap my arms around his holding me.

He sucks in a deep breath and lets it out. "No matter what has happened to us, or what we've had to face, it's made us stronger. Each time we've come out swinging, and Skyler, I'd do it all over again, every single thing we've been through, if it leads me right here to you."

I tip my head back and to the side so that I can look into his eyes. "You're it for me, you know that, right?"

He smiles and kisses me softly. "Yeah, baby, because you're it for me."

One more kiss, and then I feel him slip out of my body.

A groan I can't suppress leaves as my body wobbles until I fall forward, catching myself on my hands and knees. I slide to the side on my naked hip as Parker puts a knee on the bed and crawls up. He latches me under my waist and back and pushes me up the bed until my head is cradled on the pillows.

He dips down and kisses my lips, his mouth warm and moist in a way that, if I hadn't just had the holy heck fucked out of me, I would want more of, and more of his amazing cock. Alas, the man obliterated every muscle in my body with his iron man–style sexcapades.

"Be right back," he says, before walking his naked ass to the bathroom. I hear him turn on the water, open a cupboard, and then come back with a wet washcloth.

"Spread 'em," he says.

I crinkle my nose as heat rushes to my cheeks. "I can just get up and go to the bathroom myself." I yawn.

He shakes his head. "You think this is TMI. Peaches, baby, I just had my cock and fingers in your pussy at the same time. You just had the ends of your stilettos piercing my ass, and you think me wiping the mess between your legs is embarrassing?"

"Hmmm, you kind of have a point."

He grins and waggles his brows. "Always do; now do as I say."

Closing my eyes, I put on my brave face and open my thighs. Parker gently wipes the warm cloth between my thighs, cleaning me of our lovemaking.

When he's done, I watch his naked ass walk away again, though this time I scrutinize it. And right there on the edge of each cheek is a small, dime-sized purple mark. Holy smokes, I really did prod his ass with my stilettos.

Parker comes back, sits on the edge of the bed, and unbuckles one shoe and then the other before tossing them toward our walk-in closet.

"I can't believe you just threw a thousand-dollar pair of shoes like they were a pair of dirty socks!" I sit up on my forearms and stare at the pretties lying on their sides at the foot of the closet.

Parker crawls under the covers, nabs me until I'm curled against his chest. He proceeds to hook one of my knees and hike it up and over his hips so that my leg rests over his thighs. "You'll survive."

I frown and lift my head. "I most certainly will not," I grumble, and yawn against his chest. He runs one hand up and down my bare thigh, and the other he tunnels into my hair.

"I'll be nicer to your shoes from now on." He kisses my forehead.

"Thank you." I grin, feeling like I won a battle I didn't even have to start. If this is what married life is going to be like . . . sign me up.

"For the record, do you really need to spend a thousand dollars on a pair of shoes?"

On second thought . . .

"Ugh . . . you're so annoying."

Parker chuckles heartily and hugs me. "But you love me."

I groan under my breath. "Yeah, I love you."

"And you said I was it for you."

"Are you trying to piss me off?" I mumble, my eyelids becoming heavier and heavier.

He laughs, and I take pleasure in the fact that I can feel his laughter through my entire body since I'm draped over him.

"Love you more," he whispers, and kisses the top of my head.

"Mmm, dream of me." I sigh as thoughts of his naked body, warm and under me, fill me with images of the fun we just had.

"Skyler, I always dream of you, baby. This time, you dream of me." He nuzzles my forehead and squeezes my thigh.

"Mm-hmm. 'K, honey. Already ahead of you . . ." is the last thing I remember saying before I do as promised. I dream of my guy wearing a similar tux to the one he was wearing tonight, only standing at the end of the aisle with his eyes on me, and I'm wearing my own white dress.

4

PARKER

"*Mon cher*, please tell me your life is utterly dull and boring. No more exploding houses. No more hurt family, and you and Skyler are living happily in your beautiful home? *Oui?*"

I chuckle and spin my chair around to look out the window at the Boston skyline. "*Oui.* Though I wouldn't say life is dull and boring. Wendy was married this past week, we're all back at work, my dogs are settled in the new house, and Skyler is constantly changing her mind on what color she wants a certain room. Right now, she's set on the kitchen being purple. Purple, SoSo."

Sophie hums through the line. "I do not think that color is appetizing for the senses. I shall hope she has a change of heart."

"Thanks. What's up?"

"Well, my darling, I have bitten a gun." She sighs.

I blink a few times, watching Zeus, my stealthy ginger office cat, attack and catch a fly that somehow made it into my office, while trying to figure out Sophie's latest colloquial blunder.

"SoSo, I think you mean you've bitten *the bullet*. Did you make a decision about something, or did you literally purchase a gun and put it into your mouth?" I chuckle heartily. I love hearing my friend's voice.

"*Mon Dieu.* I can never get it right. Alas, I have made a decision."

"Well, that sounds rather vague. Care to explain that one for me?"

"I have agreed to marry Gabriel." Her voice is direct and matter-of-fact.

My heart starts to pound, and I stand up to pace, a smile slipping over my lips. "Really?"

"*Oui.* You were right. In the past few months that he has been back home, I have thought of nothing else. It has positively plagued me, the fact that I so easily tossed him away out of fear. The other night, I sat him down to a romantic candlelit dinner for two and asked him if he could have one thing in all the world, what would it be. And you know what he said?"

I grin wide. "I'll bet I can guess," I say with a teasing tone.

She continues without allowing me the benefit of guessing or playing with her any further.

"He said he would like nothing more in the world than to make me his wife and the woman who becomes the mother to his children one day."

"Go, Gabe!" I woot, and chuckle, mentally fist-bumping the guy.

"Hmm, yes. Well, I looked right into his eyes, and . . ."

"And . . ." I swallow, my mouth suddenly dry, dying to know what she said. Sophie can be a wild card sometimes. "Don't leave me hanging."

"I am not hanging you. Why would I do that?"

"SoSo . . . ," I growl. "What did you say to Gabe?"

"I asked him if he had an engagement ring," she says, as serious as a heart attack.

Not being able to help it, I tip back my head and laugh until my gut hurts. "And what did he say?"

"It is not what he said, *mon cher.* It is what he did. He promptly got up from the middle of our dinner, disappeared into the room that he uses as his study, came back with a velvet box, and got down on one knee."

"Smooth moves, Gabe. I'm proud of the guy. Taking charge and advantage of the situation to get what he wants."

"Mmm," she hums noncommittally.

"Did he score?"

"This is not a game, darling. This is my future."

"Sophie!" I roll my eyes, exasperated with her. "Did you or did you not accept his proposal?"

"*Mon cher*, that is the very reason for my call."

"I swear to God . . ." I groan loudly, wanting her to hear my exasperation all the way to France.

She laughs in my ear. "I accepted. We have received a date for September. I will expect you and Skyler in attendance."

"Fuck yeah. We'll be there with bells on, baby!"

"Bells? Why would you wear bells? That makes no sense. I want you to wear a bespoke suit that I will have my stylist design for you, as you will be standing as my sole official witness."

Punch.

Straight. To. The. Gut.

I clear my throat. "Sophie, are you asking me to be your maid of honor or man of honor?"

"The Americans have weird sayings for this. We do not have that same thing here, and Gabriel and I will not be doing a religious ceremony. We will have the marriage at the town hall, where you and Gabriel's brother will be the official witnesses to our commitment. Though Skyler may sit in if she chooses. Later that evening we will have a small but lavish affair in the Buddha-Bar."

The Buddha-Bar. Where Sophie got her head out of her ass and took a chance on the love of a good man. Excellent.

"That sounds perfect. You shoot me the details, and I will be there. Sky will be filming, but if she can get a break at all, she'll be there too.

I'll make sure the guys have the time set aside in their calendars for the reception."

"*Magnifique!* Now, tell me about you. I have been troubled by the hardships you and your mate have undergone. Has everything settled down now that there are no further threats and the people are exposed?"

I nod even though she can't see it. "Yeah, we're all trying to find our new normal. Bo's still working the pub for Pops full-time. Royce does their books and finances. I trade off weekends with Bo so he can have some time off, but he does the bulk of the work there. Though Baylee is a huge help."

"Baylee?"

"Our waitress slash bartender slash jack-of-all-trades. She's been a godsend to all of us. Works hard. Is never late. Stays out of trouble. I know for a fact when Pops eventually makes it back after he's through with physical therapy, he'll keep her on."

"That's lovely. And Bogart? How is the scoundrel?"

I grin knowing what she's really asking. "Same ol', same ol'. Chasing skirt and always on the go."

"One day his frivolity is going to catch up to him," she warns.

"Don't I know it! I've warned him myself, but he's dead set on getting the most out of life and *everyone* in it."

The memory of Bo telling Sky and me that he slept with Baylee flashes through my mind. I cringe. For the love of all things holy, I hope he didn't fuck that situation up. She could be a really great addition to my Pops's staff if he doesn't screw it up. Still, it's my job to trust him even when his judgment is jaded.

"Especially those of the female variety." Sophie clucks her tongue.

I chuckle. "Exactly."

"And Royce?"

"Doing well. Still, there's that push-pull between him and Kendra and the past they share, but mostly I'm just waiting to see what happens.

I truly believe those two are meant to be together. It's just a matter of time."

"And you and your Skyler?"

"What about me and Sky?"

"Are you going to settle down?"

"SoSo, I'm living with the woman. Bought a house with her. Share a bed every night with her. Not sure I could be more settled."

"Does your dear one feel the same as you?"

I narrow my gaze and focus on the view again. "What are you talking about?"

"*Mon cher*, a woman like her does not buy a house with a man, rescue dogs, move to his state, and take a job in her field that's in the area unless she has an ulterior motive."

The idea that Sky has some type of nefarious plan or motive of any kind when it comes to us burns me up inside. "Sky's not like that, Sophie. She'd never fuck me over."

Sophie tuts. "You are missing my point. Have you not talked about marriage and children? The future and what that looks like for the two of you?"

Oh. I see. She's getting married, so now she wants to know when I am.

What is it with engaged people?

I swear, the second Wendy got engaged she was all over us guys to settle down too. Hell, my mom started in on me the second I told her Sky and I were buying a home together. She thought that was absolutely insane to do without having a marriage certificate to back up such a large commitment.

I inhale full and deep and let it out slowly. "We've talked a little about the future. We both want to get married and have children. It's just . . . with everything that happened this year, I need to know she's mentally ready to take on the rest of our lives together, not just physically or as a default to the bad shit we've survived. Marrying her will be one of the best decisions of my life. It needs to be right."

"Does that mean you want to marry her?" Sophie pushes.

"Yeah, of course. I can't imagine my life without her. I just need to know she's okay in every way that matters. I can't be selfish in this decision or take advantage of her. I want my girl to be of sound mind and free of any negativity from the shit brought upon us before we go down that road."

"Maybe in order for her to be free, she needs something even more beautiful to hang on to?" Sophie suggests.

Her words run through my head. Could that be an option? Would asking for her hand be the final thing that heals the wounds my girl has sustained?

I shake my head and rake my fingers through my hair. "I don't know, Sophie; I'll think about it. Thank you for bringing it up, and I am honored to be your witness when you marry Gabe. He's a good guy, and he worships the ground you walk on."

"I know, *mon cher*. It is going to be wonderful. I shall have my assistant email you the details. It was good speaking with you. Take care of yourself and your mate."

"You know I will."

"*Oui*. Send my love to the guys."

"I can do that too."

"*Je t'aime. Au revoir.*"

"Love you too. Bye, Sophie."

I press the "End" button on my cell phone, put it in my pocket, and place my hands on my hips.

Sophie is taking the plunge.

Why the hell am I waiting on the sidelines?

***

My mind is still going over the call I had with Sophie yesterday as I flip through the contract Kendra approved for the next client. I've been avoiding travel the last couple of months, wanting to be home for Skyler, my father, and Nate as the lot of them healed physically and/or mentally. Nate's recovery was miraculous. The dude is a goddamned stud and proves it daily. He completed his physical therapy in record time and is already watching Skyler's back when she visits the studio people and has her sessions with Rick to run through lines. And with Rachel on the lookout, even if Nate isn't in peak condition, I know they have my girl covered.

Unfortunately my father hasn't fared as well. Therapy has been tedious and painful. Being in your fifties and getting both of your legs and hips crushed by a car is not an easy injury to heal from. The docs think he'll be in therapy for a good year. He's already in the beginning of month three, and he's just now in a wheelchair able to put pressure on his hip replacements. The legs haven't gotten much work, but the casts are off. Now it's all about learning to stand again. Then one foot in front of the other. It will be a while before he's behind the bar again.

I glance across the desk at Bo as he flips through the information Annie gave us once Kendra approved it as a solid contract.

Kendra lays out the deal. "Nothing to write home about on this one, guys. It's pretty straightforward. You have been requested for the TV show *Mix and Match*. You will help the couples get ready for the show and work with the production team to make everything run smoothly. You will also sit in the judging booth on the first episode to help the contestant choose her best match. They are paying through the nose for us, and I hate to say why, but it's because of the scandal involving Skyler and Tracey, plus Parker's involvement. Hell, the whole team's involvement."

I shake my head, and Royce's lips twist into a snarl. "Fuck this. We don't need the money if it's going to get us more questionable press."

"Technically no, but the projections the team made for the next two years will be severely affected if we don't take it. We took a lot of hits to the budget the last few months by not working much while things settled down," Kendra counters.

Bo shrugs. "We'll find another way to make it up."

"It's a million dollars out the door," Kendra adds softly.

Royce's gaze flicks to hers, and his snarl turns into a scowl.

"Holy shit, that's a lot of cash, but at what price?" Bo adds.

She holds her hands up. "Hey, hey, I get it. I don't want any more press either."

"I'm assuming you already ran this by Skyler's new publicist?" I purse my lips and focus on Annie, who's sitting primly in a chair off to the side taking notes. Her blonde hair, parted in the center, is hanging down in front of her face. One thing I noticed after she returned to the office is that she doesn't often look me in the eye. She's also not dressing much like Skyler anymore. It seems Annie's personal style is actually really plain, simple dresses or sweater-and-slacks combos. I can't say I appreciate her style the way I look forward to seeing what Wendy is wearing each day, but it's nice to see that she's finding herself.

"Yes, Parker. Ms. Black is the one who brought the contract to us. She personally suggested the job for us. Apparently, the producer is a friend of hers." She licks her lips as her eyes meet mine for a scant moment before she looks away and focuses on the wall.

"Thank you, Annie." I turn my chair so I'm facing Bo and Kendra, who are sitting in front of my desk, and Royce, who's leaning against the wall near the window. "Are we game for this project?"

Royce rubs at his bottom lip with his thumb. "The question is, are you prepared to leave, brother? You've been leery, and if you need more time, we could turn down the job. Family first. We always agreed on that."

I sigh and place my elbows to my desk, my fingers steepled. "I need to break the chain. Sky needs to be able to be alone again. Traveling is part of what we do in this role."

Royce nods. "I'm with you all the way. Whatever we gotta do."

"I can't go, guys. The bar," Bo says.

I suck against the back of my front teeth. "I can't ask you to stay. You go. I can work the bar—"

"Um, excuse me, guys," Annie interjects. "The contract said no deal if Parker is not on the project in person."

"Fuck me!" I sneer.

"Dude, it's cool. I got the bar covered. Kendra, you've got IG with Annie, right, ladies?" Bo glances at Annie, who nods, and then at Kendra.

"Absolutely."

"They said it should be really quick. A week at most," Annie adds, her voice only two steps up from a whisper.

"I gotta talk to Sky about this. Make sure she really is good, but she does need to get back to normal. The studio visits and running lines is helping. Her therapy is going awesome. She seems really happy and back to my life-loving girlfriend. This would be good for the two of us. Still, I want to run it past her. If she's okay with it, Roy, go ahead and sign the contract. I'll let you know in a few minutes, yeah?"

Roy nods, pushes off the wall, and moves to my door. Bo eases out of the chair beside Kendra.

"Gotta get the restaurant ready and open the doors for Baylee."

"Give her a key," I suggest.

"You think Pops would be cool with that?" Bo queries.

"Hell if I know, but what I do know is that you're gonna have to be able to come and go from here to there, and you need to be able to trust someone. The cook has a key already. Give Baylee one and test it out. If she was gonna steal or do damage, she'd have done it already, and Roy says the books are tight. Neither of you has had an off register yet."

Bo grins. "I always like it tight, man." He waggles his eyebrows.

"You're a pig," Kendra fires off.

"Fuckin' hell. Get outta here." I laugh and point at the door the ladies are headed for.

As Bo is walking to the door, I call out, "Hey, Bo . . ."

He turns around and holds on to the handle that he just pulled open for Kendra and Annie.

"I just wanna say thanks, man. For holding down the fort at the bar, being here for me, for all of us. You're rock steady. I appreciate you. I've got nothing but gratitude, brother."

He smiles wide. "I'll remember that for when I fuck up huge and you have to bail my ass out."

"No questions asked. You need me. I'm always gonna be there."

"Word," he says with a chin lift, and walks his motorcycle-booted feet out the door, a hand up in the air with two fingers in a peace symbol.

I take a deep breath and pick up my phone.

It rings a second before the most beautiful voice in the world answers, "Hey, honey . . ."

"Hi, Peaches, got a minute?"

"For you, always."

I grin and turn around in my chair, opening my lap and snapping my fingers.

Zeus looks at me from his perch on the arm of the couch. He slowly licks a paw and stares at me with that bored-to-tears look cats have mastered. I snap again and pat my leg. He lifts his head and tilts it to the side, assessing if he wants to move from the arm to my lap or not.

"This LA job coming up . . . Annie says your publicist referred us."

Her voice dips to a cautionary tone. "Yeah, is that a problem?"

"No, I was just wondering if she really thinks me being a part of a dating TV show is good press for you. I don't want to see the tabloids suggesting that I'm trying to replace you or something stupid." I rub at the back of my neck, trying to ease the tension formed by the idea.

She laughs heartily. "I think since the press now knows what we've been through, they've actually been really kind lately. A lot of the news has been related to hero worship over you and what you're willing to do to keep me safe."

I smile but know there was a lot more to it and a lot of other more-qualified people involved in figuring out what Tracey was up to, not to mention the stalker issue with Benny.

"The last thing I want to do is make anything uncomfortable for you, Sky. And this job, it's going to take me and Roy to LA for at least a week. That means it's the first time you'll be alone since it all went down. I need to know that you're okay with that and feel safe."

"In our home with Rach and Nate living in the side house? Our giant overprotective dogs? I'll be fine. You have nothing to worry about. I'm good, I swear! I want you to do this. I'm actually doing a two-minute interview promo spot for the producer to use in advertising the show. I'll be saying something about my boyfriend being part of the team and involved, but viewers will have to watch in order to find out how." She giggles, and the sound seeps straight through my chest, easing the nervousness I had at the suggestion of having to leave her.

Finally Zeus leaps off the arm of the couch, extends his entire body in this awesome stretch that would feel so good to me right now, and then comes over. He meanders through my legs, rubbing his fur against my shins until he's done, and jumps up into my lap, spins in a circle, and settles down across both of my thighs. Once he's situated, I finagle my fingers into the soft tufts of his fur. Instantly my cat purrs loudly. His presence eases me the same way Sky's happy voice does.

"So, you're totally cool with this job? No concerns whatsoever," I reiterate, just to be certain.

"Absolutely. Honey, I know I've been really needy when it comes to you and your attention, but it's only because I lost a lot. You, your family, our friends are my whole world now, and Parker, you're at the tippy-top of that list. I'm good, and frankly, I think it's time. We need a little space to miss each other."

"Peaches . . . I miss you the second I kiss you goodbye in the morning. I don't ever need to miss you."

"That's sweet, but I have a feeling this is going to be really good for us. You getting back to what you do best, me spending uninterrupted hours prepping for my role in the *A-Lister* series . . . everything is as it should be. At the very least, we're on our way."

"This is true. We're definitely on our way." I sigh, letting out a relieved breath.

"To a happily ever after?" She laughs.

"Every day with you, Skyler, is my happily ever after."

5

SKYLER

"Remember the plan," I remind Nate for the third time. "He can't know what I'm doing or where I am."

"First of all, you've already told me this. Second, I do not like lying to your man. I don't like to lie to *anybody* but especially not to Parker. He's family," Nate grumbles, and looks away.

I roll my eyes and settle in my seat on my private charter, waiting for the captain to announce we're taking off. Rachel is sitting next to him, and I watch while she places her hand to his forearm.

"Babe, do this one thing. It's not that hard. When Parker calls, and you *know* he will since he checks on Skyler through you as well as her *every day*, just go with it. She's happy. She's healthy. We're chilling at home. No big deal."

Nate scowls. "I don't like this plan."

I narrow my gaze at Nate while my new publicist, Elliott Black, maneuvers her tall, thin shape into the open captain's chair next to me. Ellie is my new right-hand woman. We clicked the second Geneva James and Amy Tannenbaum, her literary agent, introduced us to Geneva's personal publicist. Elliott Black is a down-home girl, from Nixa, Missouri, originally. She's young for a publicist and a full-on shark in the industry, but she's got a sweet side to her I think comes from being raised in the Midwest. Her chestnut-colored hair is cut in a short, chin-length bob. Her red tortoiseshell glasses match her crimson lips. She says the lipstick is her nod to fashion since she wears nothing but perfectly tailored suits every day. Though I wouldn't call her unfashionable. I haven't actually seen the woman in anything but the finest and most current designer suits in every color imaginable.

At this point, I'm just thrilled that Geneva is willing to share Ellie with me. Not to mention her involvement in my plan has been crucial. I wouldn't have known where to begin without her assistance.

"You don't have to like it, Nathan," Elliott states in a stern tone, always calling Nate by his full name. She does the same with me. She never calls me Sky. Always Skyler. Even after two months of working nonstop together after the Tracey and stalker debacle.

I've come to find the woman is beyond intelligent. She spun the entire horrible experience to the media in a way that ended up making Parker the hero to my damsel in distress, which worked huge on the public. Probably because it was closer to the truth than anything else.

Still, a pang pierces my heart thinking about my ex-best friend, knowing she's going to live out her days in a ten-by-ten-foot room in a high-security psych ward. Even with what she did, I can't help but feel sorry for her. Parker, however, is the complete opposite. The loss of her hand, which ended up being unsalvageable, and life in a penitentiary-style psych ward were not enough for my man. If the courts had allowed a firing squad, he would have been the first to sign up as a shooter, right alongside Bo, Royce, Randy Ellis, *and* Wendy. He loathes the woman to the point that even the mention of her name in any way makes him wince and snarl.

"Yeah, babe, you just have to go along with it for now." Rachel's words bust into my head, banishing all thoughts of Tracey as I watch Rach run her hand up and down Nate's arm in a soothing gesture.

345

"All will be revealed soon." Ellie grins a cat-that-ate-the-canary smile. Her part in my plan so far has been executed to perfection.

I lean over and pat Nate's hand, so happy to have him alive and well and sitting beside me on a plane headed to the City of Angels, Los Angeles, California.

"Nate, I promise, it will be worth a little bit of deception."

Nate frowns but nods, lifting his chin in assent. For him, my promise is enough.

I squeeze his fingers briefly. "Thank you."

Elliott leans over and digs into her briefcase, pulls out a folder, and rummages through the pages. "These are the contestants the IG team is working with now." She points to a handful of men's and women's names. When she turns to the last page, I gasp, seeing a woman who could almost be my twin.

"Holy shit. Who's that?" I ask, not capable of looking away from the woman.

Ellie grins and taps the face of the blonde-haired, brown-eyed woman in the picture. "That's Tara Darling, a budding actress and stuntwoman."

"No way! She looks just like me!"

"I know. I made sure she dyed her hair to your golden tone and put in brown contacts. She's actually a strawberry blonde with blue eyes normally."

I open and close my mouth, staring at the uncanny resemblance to myself.

"Unfortunately, she's much taller than you. About five eleven, but I've warned her to only wear flats on the set."

"You hired her? Why?" I stare at my doppelgänger.

"Of course I did. When you came to me with your plan and we formulated this idea, I started searching for prospective contestants to ensure the pool of people would suit the end result, but also make for some damn good TV. The producer, Louise Gonzalez, is one of my best friends. She actually knew of Tara and suggested her. It will play out so well on television to have someone who looks like you when the guys are having to judge the contestants. And hopefully, it also makes your man think of you when he's trying to tell her what to do or say, and makes him lovesick with missing the real deal." She winks and grins again.

I chuckle, grab the photo, and lift it up to show Rachel. "Look at this chick!"

Rachel's ice-blue eyes widen, and her mouth opens as she reaches across her husband's seat to grab the paper. "No way! I'm so pumped! This is going to be a blast, watching Parker squirm!" She chuckles and hands the image back to me.

I bite into my bottom lip and trace the woman's face in the picture. Her eyes are a little farther apart than mine, her chin pointier, but she really does look similar to me. It will be interesting to see how Parker responds to my doppelgänger in real life.

Butterflies take flight in my belly as I think about my man and what is on the horizon. I've never felt more confident in our love and future than I do right now. He may freak out, but once the shock wears off, I know his romantic heart will be filled with joy.

I sigh and hand the picture back to Ellie. "This is going to be so much fun!" I smile at her and slap my hands against my thighs in a mini drumroll gesture.

"It's definitely leaps and bounds away from my normal system for image promotion, but it has a fairy-tale quality to it I love getting behind. Your man and the media are going to explode when this goes down."

"As long as we stick to the plan and I stay out of Parker's sight in LA, we'll be golden."

She winks and closes the file, placing it back in her briefcase. "Leave that all up to me and you'll be just fine."

The captain's voice over the intercom tells us we've been cleared for takeoff and to buckle up.

The four of us clip our seat belts as directed, and I close my eyes, imagining it all playing out perfectly in my head.

The stage is set.

The pieces all perfectly placed.

All I need is my victim.

Victim being my tall, muscular, well-dressed, chisel-jawed, blue-eyed guy, who I love more than my own life, playing into each move I've laid out.

All will work out as intended. I just know it!

***

When we arrive at the studio in Los Angeles, Ellie sneaks me down the hall and into a viewing room above the stage.

"Hey, Louise!" Ellie holds out her arms and embraces a Hispanic woman with long, dark hair that's pulled back into a low ponytail at her nape. She's petite in size and stature, but her welcoming smile is big and bold.

"Good to see you, girl. As you can see down below, everything is going as planned. Between Royce and Parker working with the contestants the last three days, we are ready to rock and roll. Not to mention, that Roy is smokin' hot." She fans her face. "Parker is nothing to sneeze at either, but I already know he's taken." She smiles at me. "Been keeping up on the celebrity ins and outs the past year, and your girl and he have been on them . . . a lot. This is going to be excellent for the ratings."

"Glad we could help each other out," Ellie says, and turns around, holding her arm out to me. "This is the woman of the hour, Skyler Paige. Skyler, this is my good friend, Louise Gonzalez."

I take her hand and shake it. "Pleasure to meet you. Thank you so much for helping me out with my little project."

Louise jolts back a step. "Are you kidding me? You and your guy coming on my new show is a huge boon for us. The entire network is going crazy over it."

"Well, you realize it's just this first episode."

She shrugs. "Doesn't matter. We just need the one, and we'll hook the viewers right off the bat. I plan on making television history with this pilot, thanks to you and your guys down there. Check them out." She gestures to a glass panel about ten feet from where we stand.

"Can they see us?" I look below where I can see the camera team—a bunch of people running around with headphones on, others standing at the sidelines behind the equipment—and it's as if the clouds part and the sunrays shine through as my guy comes into sight, walking in from stage left.

Damn, he looks handsome.

Parker is wearing a stylish getup: a pair of navy slacks, a white dress shirt, sans a tie, and a beige jacket complete with tan suede patches at the elbows. On his feet are a new pair of camel-colored Ferragamos I bought him and added to his wardrobe. Even though there was considerable smoke damage to the furniture in my penthouse Tracey tried to burn down, the closet survived mostly unscathed, aside from the clothes smelling sooty, which a high-quality dry cleaning service was able to take care of without a problem.

Parker is moving his hands and shaking his head as if he's exasperated.

Louise interrupts my thoughts. "No, we have the tint on right now. We've found that when the contestants are on the stage, they get really nervous if they feel like Big Brother is watching them, so we black out the screens but can still watch and manage the team below."

"How come we can't hear anything?" I watch as Parker walks over to one of the production people who's holding a clipboard and points down at it then at one of the chairs. He then proceeds to move over to the side of the stage and walk with a little swagger to one of the chairs, turn, smile at the team, and sit down. He props one ankle on the opposite knee, leans back, and runs his index finger along his sexy, kissable lips.

Jesus, is it hot in here?

He stands, makes a hand gesture again at the chair, and points to the side of the stage. One of the male contestants proceeds to mimic Parker's movements exactly.

"Here you go." Louise presses a button, and the sounds from down below are audible in our control booth.

"Excellent, Josh, just like that, man." Parker claps his hands, and the blond guy in the chair smiles brilliantly.

"Next up? Lamar Williams." Royce points to a large black man wearing a pair of jeans and a red polo. His chest is broad with shoulders to match. Standing next to Roy, who's a very large man, the guy looks like he could be a solid contender on a football field. "Show us your swagger, bro."

The guy takes long strides over to the side of the stage, lifting his chin as if he's flirting with the camera right out of the gate. He moves like a panther, all sleek, dark-skinned yumminess in a big, muscular body. He gets to his chair next to Josh and takes a seat. Only he spreads his legs out wide.

Royce shakes his head. "Naw, man, what you can't forget is you're on stage. That camera"—he points to the one about a dozen steps in front of them—"is capturing your entire body. The viewers want to see how good you look from the top of your cropped 'fro to the tips of your Pumas. Ya feel me?"

"Yes, sir."

I snort as that hits Royce's ears, and he drops his head and runs a hand over his shiny bald head. "Just don't get too comfortable. Millions of people will be watching you. They do not want to get a shot of your crotch."

The younger man frowns, brings both of his feet to the footrest on his tall chair, and clasps his hands between his thighs where his legs are now opened an appropriate amount. "This work?"

Royce nods. "Yeah, man. Cool."

"Next up. Jimmy Jones." Parker scans the papers he's holding. "Jimmy Jones? Is that your real name?" he asks as a ginger-haired guy with a full red beard moves to the side of the stage. He's rocking a circular-brimmed hat similar to a folk-style fedora and paired with a plaid shirt, gray slacks, and a navy blazer. I'm not even sure what you'd call that look. Celtic-gnome chic, perhaps?

"Yeah. Born and raised."

Parker tips his head. "It's a roll of the tongue for sure. Not exactly going to sound too great on TV. You in the business?"

"Sure am!" He preens under Parker's attention.

"Suggestion. And you know this comes from someone who works with a lot of wealthy and famous people, including the fact that I'm living with a celebrity myself . . ."

My heart stops when I hear him mention me in a conversation my man doesn't know I'm eavesdropping on. I hold my breath to hear.

The guy swallows slowly and nods. "Anything, man. Any help would be awesome."

"Change your name. One or the other. Jimmy Jones sounds like a sausage, not a ginger-haired, good-looking guy in his twenties with his own unique style. Yeah?"

The guy licks his lips and nods.

"And that's no disrespect to you or your parents. It's just in my experience, even the best of them have pseudonyms working in this business. It helps make their name flow in the papers and fit the role they want to play in the industry. If you want to do commercials for egg-and-sausage biscuits, Jimmy Jones might be the way to go. If you want more serious roles, I'd dig a little deeper before we go live with the pilot."

Jimmy nods his head several times. "Cool, yeah. Thanks for the tip, man."

"All right, then. Show me what you got." He points to the last chair in the lineup.

I touch my fingers to the glass and watch my guy do his thing. In this particular instance, it's teaching men to be more confident, look the part, and play the game for the TV cameras. He works seamlessly with Royce; where one is better in one area, they switch off taking the lead easily with no break in the flow.

As I'm watching, one of the cameramen waves a hand to the glass screen; then a guy in the booth hits something, and the glass goes from blacked out and tinted to see-through.

"Shit!" I look around, trying to find someplace to hide.

I swear it happens in slow motion while I watch Parker and Royce turn around. Royce lifts his head to the booth, his ebony gaze zeroing in on mine. It takes only a moment for him to notice me.

"Baby girl . . . ," I hear come through the speaker in a very familiar, rumbly deep voice.

No, no, no, no, no!

Parker looks to Royce, his brow furrowed, and then he starts to lift his head up. At the same time, one of the booth guys stands up, towering in front of me, his back to the window, blocking me out completely.

"What's going on?" Louise says as though I'm not hiding behind a wall of man.

The guy in front of me is rotund. He's at least six feet and then some, with a large Santa-like belly protruding out, nestled against my form. He has both of his big hands on my biceps, but he's not digging in or touching me inappropriately. More like he's simply keeping me still, hidden behind his girth.

"Got you, girl," he whispers through his lips, which are encircled with a mustache and craggy beard. I look up into his kind green eyes and smile wide.

"Thanks!" I whisper back.

"Camera two is flickering. Need maintenance on this one. We might need to switch it out before we go live in a couple of days," one of the guys below says up to the booth, but I can't see him behind the wall of man guarding me.

I breathe as slowly as I can, trying to make my heart calm down from the little freak-out I had going regarding being caught. Still, I know Royce saw me.

"How about you guys take a thirty-minute break, everyone get a snack, and we'll get back to it after we diagnose the problem," Louise says, and presses the button blacking out the glass behind my human wall.

"That was close." Ellie lets out a labored breath and leans against the table.

"Pretty sure Royce got a good look at me. He's going to tell Parker I was here."

Ellie shrugs. "Then we'll tell him he saw Tara, your look-alike. Problem solved."

"Oh yeah! Perfect. Have they met her yet?"

She shakes her head. "Nope."

Louise cuts in. "The female contestants come later today. We have several so that we can see which two will work best for the first few episodes. Can't wait to watch that go down, now that I see just how much Tara and you look alike. This is going to be epic TV. Totally epic!"

I let out my breath and rub my hand over my heart. "I hope so. I have a lot riding on how all of this plays out."

"Very true. How about we go to my office and talk about the specifics of what you've concocted, and I'll see how much of it we can make happen, if not all of it. Sound good?"

"Great!" I smile wide and follow Louise and Ellie out the door.

Just outside of the box is my dream team, Rach and Nate. They pull up the rear, following us down the corridors, up a flight of stairs, and into a pretty room filled with flowers and TV posters. I scan each one and note how old some of these must be.

There's a *Remington Steele* poster. A *Moonlighting* poster. *Love Connection*. Though my personal favorite is the *X-Files* image of Mulder and Scully. As a kid, I watched a lot of that redheaded Gillian Anderson running down streets in heels and beating down bad guys. It was a show my mother and I loved watching together, even if some of the episodes were pretty scary. That show and the time I spent watching with my mom are part of what made me fall in love with acting.

As Louise offers the chairs in front of her desk to us, my cell phone rings.

"Shit. It's Parker!" My heart instantly starts pounding wildly as if I've already been caught.

Ellie pats my shoulder. "It's all good. Just breathe and take the call. Pretend like nothing is amiss, or your plan is going down the toilet fast."

I take a deep breath and let it out before hitting the green button and pressing my cell to my ear.

"Hey, honey."

"Hiya, Peaches."

"What are you up to? It's pretty early there, right?" I do my best to leave any jitters behind, focusing on steadying my voice.

"Late afternoon. We're taking a break. Cameraman is having some type of functionality problem with his camera." His voice is smooth and reminds me of how much I miss him, even though it's only been a few short days.

I nod. "Ah. That does happen. They'll get it up and running, I'm sure."

"Yeah. How about you? What are you up to?"

The lie ripples up my throat and out my mouth, tasting foul. "Oh, you know, a little of this, a little of that. Have you met all the contestants yet?" I change the subject back to him.

"Nope. The females are supposed to show up anytime. Roy and I have been working the fellas, and although it's a rough bunch, I think they'll make for good TV."

"Mm-hmm. That sounds good." I pace the office and try to keep up my ruse.

"You'll never believe this . . ." His tone changes to one that sounds painted in humor.

Fuck.

"Uh, what's that, honey?"

"A little bit ago, we were working, and Royce swears he saw you in the production booth. Crazy, right?" He chuckles. "I told the brother he needs to get his eyes checked, because my girl's pretty face was three thousand miles away pining for her man."

"I'm not pining!" I snort-laugh.

His corresponding laughter fills me with happiness. We've had such a hard road, every time we can laugh is a moment to be cherished.

"Just wanted to be sure you were paying attention. Though I swear, baby, even the mention of your name got me hopeful to see you." His voice dips low when he adds, "I miss you."

Now I'm grinning like a lunatic. I finger a lock of my hair and twirl it around and around, butterflies once again filling my belly with excitement. "I miss you too. When are you coming home?" I pose a standard question I would normally ask if he were really away and I didn't know all the details.

"Probably in a few days. We do the pilot filming in two or three days, depending on how the female contestants do."

"Makes sense to me. I hope you're having fun even if it's without me." I pout, imagining him all alone in his hotel room at night, no one to keep him company. These images lead me right to the thought of me crawling beneath the sheets, lips pressing to warm flesh until I reach his hard, long cock. I close my eyes and imagine my lips pressing a simple, adoring kiss to the bulbous tip before licking in a swirling motion that always makes him groan and thrust his hips, seeking my mouth and a deeper connection.

"I wouldn't say I'm having the time of my life, but I am enjoying this. It's nice to know that, when the job is done, I'll be coming home to you and our dogs and our life back in Boston, with no crazy stalker or whacked-out lunatic trying to harm either of us. Baby, I just like the idea of being normal with you. Plain, old, boring, day-to-day family life."

"I like the idea of being boring with you too, honey."

I glance at Ellie and Louise and find them both blatantly staring and listening to every word of my conversation, not that I'm being inconspicuous or speaking at a lower volume. It's hard when I get Parker's voice in my ear, and I haven't seen him for a few days. It's like being served a hot-fudge sundae. You don't think of or worry about the calories; you just indulge with *fervor*. That's how I feel when I'm talking to my man. *Indulgent*.

"Um, Parker, I need to go. Elliott is trying to get ahold of me on the other line. She has an opportunity she needs to discuss with me. We'll talk tomorrow?"

"Yeah, baby. Sleep well tonight."

"I will. Love you."

"Love you more."

I press the "End" button and slip the phone into my back pocket. "He loves me." I shrug.

Ellie's gaze is on me, eyebrow cocked, and a saucy smirk is on her lips. "That, Skyler, is obvious."

"I hate lying to him." I frown, the dishonesty clutching at my conscience. "Takes some of the goodness out of what we're planning."

Louise nods and leans against the arm of her chair. "Think of it this way: the end result will be worth the means."

I straighten my spine and firm my shoulders. "It better be."

Elliott tilts her head to the side. "It will. Have a little faith." Her tone is soft and compassionate.

"When it comes to Parker, I have all the faith in the world."

6

PARKER

A warm, paw-like hand grips my shoulder. "You good, brother?" Royce asks, his tone low and private.

I nod. "Yeah, yeah. I didn't think it would be this hard being away from her, you know?"

Royce sucks in his bottom lip and holds it in his mouth, a thoughtful expression on his face. "It's been a long time since I felt that way about a woman, but I get you. Can't say that I don't envy what you've got. I know what's happening in my own situation right now, and it's rocky as fuck, but I'm hoping to get through to the other side unscathed. Definitely don't want to have to go through what you and Sky did to find your happy." He licks his lips, squeezes my shoulder again, and dips his head. "Though I will say, what you got is special. The fact that you survived all the odds and came out on top means it's meant to be. You can't live life afraid every time you gotta take a trip for work. Have faith that no merciful God is gonna put you through any more of that shit. Believe it, bro. Sky's and your time is now. Dig deep, and it will be all right."

I close my eyes and let his words sink in. It's normal to travel, normal to be apart, for *any* couple. We have to get back to living our lives day to day in the knowledge that the worst is behind us.

With my brother at my side, supporting me in my every move, I inhale full and deep before clasping both of his shoulders. "Thanks for the pep talk."

Royce gives me an all-white, giant grin. "Anytime. I got your back. Always."

"Same." I grip him on the bicep and look beyond us as a line of females walk in from the back of the room. Six in total. I shake my head and squint, zeroing in on one in particular.

Golden hair.

Dark eyes.

Tall.

Smokin' hot body.

"What the fuck?" I narrow my gaze and squint to get a better look. Royce turns around. "Shee-it. Is that . . . ?"

I don't hear the rest of what he has to say because I'm storming over to the line of women approaching the stage. "Hold up, ladies," I say, one step down from yelling.

The six of them stop where they are.

I move right over to the last woman in the line. When I get closer, my eyes adjust to the light, and I realize it's not her. But holy fuck, she looks like my woman. "Who are you?"

The blonde blinks dumbly, raises her hand to her chest, and looks from side to side before she settles her gaze back on me. "Um, me?"

"Yeah, you." I can feel my entire body tighten.

"I, uh, I'm Tara Darling. Contestant for the show."

I frown and take her in from her hair to her ballet flats. She's taller than my Sky, but if I didn't look close-up, she'd be a dead ringer for her. Eyes a little wider apart, chin pointier, but the entire package together is uncanny.

"Who brought you here?" I ask, while Royce walks up and stands beside me, crossing his arms over his massive chest and staring down the blonde.

"Uh, Louise Gonzalez picked me out of a casting call. Is there a problem?" She grabs a lock of her hair and twirls it around her finger in a move that's so much like Skyler I have to grind my teeth not to rip her head off.

"You look a lot like Skyler Paige," Royce rumbles, laying the issue flat out.

She pouts and tilts her head. "Yes, I've heard that before. Is it a problem?"

"Did someone put you up to this?" My heart constricts as I think that maybe the shit storm hasn't passed. Maybe this is another person trying to fuck with me and my girl. Get my mind off the real Skyler while focusing on her carbon copy. My skin starts to tingle and itch as the need to call Sky becomes almost unbearable.

"N-no. I'm not sure what's going on or why I'm being singled out. I came to the casting call, got a call back, and here I am."

"Why did you choose to come to this show?" I ask, my temperature rising with every second I'm in this woman's presence.

"Because I need more airtime on the screen, it's a paying gig, and I get a free attempt at a love connection. Wouldn't any woman want that?" She blinks prettily, and I want to point my finger at the door and kick her out. Unfortunately that's not what we're here to do. Royce and I have to get these women ready to woo the audience and the men they can't see sitting behind a wall in order to get the show off the ground and high on the rating board.

Royce places his hand on my elbow and urges me to walk with him about ten feet away. He leans close. "I know you're thinking this is some type of setup, but even if it is, I don't think it's for nefarious purposes."

Just as I'm about to speak, Louise, the production director, enters from the back of the room where the ladies came from.

"Do we have a problem here, gentlemen?" She walks up, her dark ponytail swinging as she goes.

"Louise, my friend and I are taken aback by one of your candidates as a contestant on the show." Royce points to the women.

Louise's dark gaze lasers in on me, then Royce, before scanning the contestants. "Am I to assume this has to do with Tara?"

Interesting how she knew exactly who we were referring to.

Can you say . . . setup?

"Yeah." I cross my arms over my chest in a defensive move. Her dark gaze glances at my arms, and her lips twitch.

"Would it have anything to do with the fact that she's Skyler Paige's doppelgänger?" She announces the exact concern we have without making us give it up. Strange tactic.

"I think that's obvious, Ms. Gonzalez. Care to tell us why you'd have a look-alike on the show when everyone in the world knows that my man here"—Royce hooks a thumb over his shoulder toward me—"has been in a relationship with the actress for a year?"

Her lips press together before she tips her head back and laughs. "Uh, you just answered your own question. Skyler Paige is hot stuff. Tara Darling looks just like her. With you two in the judging panel, the audience is going to eat that shit up with a shovel! It's pretty genius, if I do say so myself, and since I chose her, and your contract is with me, she stays. Do you have a problem working with someone who looks like your girlfriend, Mr. Ellis?"

Holy shit. Louise turned the situation around on me so fast I didn't even feel my head spin around on my neck.

Before I can speak, she continues.

"Honestly, I think your issue with her says a lot more about you and your inability to see beyond your personal life than it does about me and my show. Are we going to have a problem?"

I open and close my mouth, feeling like I just got bitch-slapped. I shake it off and put my hands in my pockets while taking in Tara

Darling. She looks so much like my Sky it's almost hard to look at her . . . but, she's *not* my woman. I just have to remember that and do what I came here to do.

"No. Though I assume you're up to date on the things that have plagued me and my girlfriend over the past year and have been spread all over the newspapers and celebrity rags."

She nods.

"Please excuse me if I jumped to conclusions about Ms. Darling's involvement in the show."

"Straight up, Mr. Ellis, she's here because she looks like your woman and will bring more viewers based on that alone."

I inhale, giving myself precious moments to calm down. She's not here to hurt me, or mess with me; she's here to up the ratings. Now that is something I can deal with. Heck, Skyler will think it's a hoot.

"Fine. We'll continue on as planned."

"Excellent. Do your thing. We need to have the women ready in forty-eight hours. Then we'll mix and match up the contestants and the women for some practice rounds, making sure they don't see each other. We'll choose the final pairings for the live show at that time."

Royce's head shoots to the side. "Live show? I thought you were taping this."

"Yeah, we were going to, but once upper management realized we could do it live and have you and Parker sitting in the judging booth, we could pan to the two of you and the live audience reactions more often and hopefully score more viewers."

I close my eyes and grind my teeth.

I have to remind myself that they're paying through the nose for this contract, and people use Skyler's celebrity status all the time to get ahead. The happier the client, the more likely they'll refer us additional business contacts in the future. Win-win. I just need to focus on ending this job with a happy client so that I can go back home to my girl as soon as possible. They want to change the plan and go live with the pilot, that's on them.

Royce holds his hand out to Louise. "Thanks for the discussion. We'll get back to work."

She shakes his hand and reaches around to me. I shake hers.

"This is going to be fun, Mr. Ellis." She grins wide and saunters off toward the production booth stairs.

Fun. Yeah right.

Hmm. Something deep inside my gut is telling me there's more going on here that Royce and I are not part of. Tingles prickle at the back of my neck as I watch her walk up the stairs.

I turn around and take in the six females standing patiently under the bright lights, waiting for direction.

Royce looks at me and nods toward the ladies.

I clap my hands. "All right, ladies, let's have a quick introduction and find out what your goals are for being on *Mix and Match*."

***

"Let me get this straight, Crista. You signed up for *Mix and Match* because you want to get married and have a baby in the next two years?"

The pretty, redheaded woman with a lush, curvy body and big, bouncy curls hanging down her shoulders nods emphatically. "Exactly! You know me so well!" she practically squeaks.

I look down at her detail card. "Nope. Sweetheart, you put it down under the section marked *interests*."

She pouts, and I'm not gonna lie, with the woman's puffy, plump lips, she looks cute doing it. I can't imagine, based on her looks and mannerisms, that she would be unable to get a date or hook a man to her star. Though I have an idea why she's striking out.

"Do you tell men on your first few dates that you're looking to get married and have a baby?"

She smiles wide and nods. "Oh yes. I believe in complete honesty, always. I tell them on the very first date."

Sweet Jesus. "And uh, how many second dates have you had recently?" I soften my tone.

She frowns and purses her lips. "Hmmm, not many . . . Actually, come to think of it, I haven't had a second date in a while."

"See a pattern there?"

Crista scrunches up her face in a manner that makes me believe she's attempting to connect the dots but coming up blank.

"Let me lay out something you need to know about men. We don't often want to think about marriage and children even on the *fifth* date, let alone the first. Maybe after six months of a committed relationship when we've had a chance to really get to know a woman, spend time with her family, see how we pair up in the other areas of the relationship . . ." I let my words dangle in the hopes that she'll pick up on what I'm getting at.

She frowns and fiddles with the hem of her too-short skirt. Don't get me wrong, I'm a man who loves a lot of skin and a lotta leg on display, but when you're first trying to score a man who's going to last long-term, the last thing you want to do is lead with your physical attributes. This woman is going to need to turn on a man's mind as well as his body if she's going to have any staying power with him.

"Meaning . . ."

"In the bedroom."

She grins wide and lifts her chest in a move akin to being prideful. "Oh, I sleep with them on the first date if I'm attracted to them, so there's no worry there."

I groan and rub my temples with thumb and forefinger. "Crista, right off the bat, I'm going to warn you against sleeping with a man you're interested in on the very first date. It can give the impression that you're easy even if you're not."

Her eyes widen. "But then how are they going to know what I give in the bedroom is so good they're going to want to keep it in their bed for the rest of their lives?"

"Sweetheart, what goes down in the bedroom is a definite plus for a man, especially if his woman has skills in that arena. However, it's not the only thing that matters. Regardless of popular opinion, not all men think with just their dick. I know when it comes to my girl, I fell in love with her smile and laughter, her giving heart, the way she makes me feel, not just how good we are together in the sack."

Crista taps at her chin. "What you're saying is I'm giving up the goods too quick, and freaking men out by talking about what I really want, which is marriage and children."

I reach for her hand and take hold, putting my other one on the top. "Let a man fall in love with *you*, not with what you can do for him in the future and vice versa. You need to really think about what *you* want in a man who you plan to spend the rest of your life with. Date. Have fun. Relax a little, and stop worrying about what the future will bring."

"You're not married, and you've been with that awesome actress for, like, forever!" She pouts. "I don't want to wait a long time to have my family."

I shake my head and sigh. "You don't have to wait forever. Though it's not unusual for a couple to date for a year or *several* before taking that ultimate step."

"So you don't want to get married and have babies with the world's hottest woman?" Her voice rises. "If *she* can't get *you* to commit forever, I don't stand a chance in hell." Her voice wobbles, and I can hear the emotion pouring through, which usually is a precursor to tears. And I hate to see a woman cry.

"Crista, you misunderstand. I absolutely plan on marrying my woman, when the time is right for the both of us. Every couple is different. There's not an exact amount of time that has to pass, but the ideal scenario is you getting to know one another for a while before you make that life commitment. Understand now?"

She sniffs, and I can see her chin wobble, but she holds it together. "I just . . . I just want to find the right man so bad. I'm not getting any younger, and I just know I'm meant to be a wife and mother. That's all I've ever wanted to be, and the older I get, the less likely it is I'm going to find a man who wants me."

"Sweetheart, that's not true. You can't be more than what, twenty-five?"

"Twenty-six actually."

"Well, I'm thirty. My woman is your age. We've been together a year, and we're working on our forever and what that happy ending looks like for us. I promise you will find the right man for you; just don't play all your cards on the first go. Make him work for the beauty that is you. Get me?"

She tips her head from side to side as if she's thinking about it. "Yeah, I guess I could try your way for a while, see how it goes."

"And as for the show, just pick the guy who seems the most fun to go out on a date with. No crazy questions about marriage and babies or you'll scare the three of them off right away."

She giggles, and it sounds musical. "I can do that."

"All right. Head over to Royce now so he can go over your TV persona."

Crista stands up and tugs down her skirt.

"And make sure when you do the show that you wear a skirt just a tad longer." I grin and waggle my eyebrows. "Give the man something to look forward to uncovering on a future date. Hopefully somewhere around the fifth!"

She laughs and waves her hand as she struts off in high-heeled sandals.

Before the next one is done with Royce, I pull out my phone and note that my brother called and didn't leave a message.

I go to the favorites and press his name.

Paul answers in his standard bark-like manner. "Yo, P-Drive."

"You called me, dude. What's up? How's Dad?"

Paul sighs, and I can hear him moving around, a door opening and then slapping against wood. That noise is the distinct sound of my parents' back screen door slamming shut. I've heard that sound a million times in my life and can recognize it anywhere.

"Bastard's cagey as hell. Tired of being locked up in his house. He's in his fifties and doesn't like to be told what to do, how to do it, and how hard to push his own body. He's mad as hell, and the rest of us get the brunt of his anger. Mostly, he wants his body to bounce back as if he's still twenty years old, but it's not that simple."

"And therapy?" I ask, knowing my dad. He's a terrible patient when he has a cold. I can only imagine what he's like having to go to therapy two or three times a week.

"Aw, brother, Pops hates going to physical therapy, but he's actually improving. Was able to put a little bit of weight on his feet when the therapist and I held him up today."

The image of my father standing between two metal bars, spaced apart enough to fit his body, burns my mind like a blowtorch to the chest.

"And Mom?"

Paulie chuckles. "Ordering him around like normal. Only this time she does it when he's stuck in his lounger and can't run off. The thing is, in the end, what she nags him about, he listens to. He may bicker back, grumble, but he's not giving up. He's a fighter, always has been, always will be."

"It's what he taught us. Never give up if you want something bad enough." I rub at my forehead and sigh. "What you're doing, Paulie, stepping up for Dad and Mom . . ." I run my hand through my hair and stand up to pace the room. Anxiety and negative energy pump off me so intensely I have to move in order to calm them.

"Wouldn't be anywhere else. 'Sides, you and the brothers have got Lucky's, and I've been living here, so no reason not to pony up, yeah?"

"Yeah. Still, I know it's got to be a lot on you when you and Denny are going through the start-up of Ellis Imports. Still can't believe he named it after you."

He chuckles full and deep. "Yeah, well, I think that was a subtle hint that my man wants us both to carry the Ellis name."

I grin. "Denny is definitely slick and goes after what he wants, which is you, my man!" I laugh, enjoying Paul's romantic ups and downs.

"Speaking of . . . I've got good news!"

I smile, needing a dose of some happy family news right about now. "Lay it on me, brother."

"Not only did Denny and I start the interior design on the business, we found a little house, bro."

"No shit?"

"Straight up. We finally found a pad of our own. Denny is over the moon. I thought he was excited when he bought the warehouse on the pier for our company. Not even close. My guy is ecstatic about the house."

"Tell me about it. Where is it? Close to me and Sky?"

Paulie laughs again. "Too rich for my blood. It's a two-bed, two-bath with a yard big enough for me to have a dog, and the kitchen and living room are open plan so Denny can entertain to his heart's desire. He says he can't wait to have you all over for dinner." His voice dips into a command rather than a suggestion. "We'll be setting that up soon, so I can make my guy even happier he made the move from his country to ours. You good for that?"

"Definitely. Sky and I are in all the way. Stoked for you, man. Layin' down roots with your mate, buying a home, building a business . . ."

"It's what it's all about. The American dream. The nice thing about that is everyone's dream is different, but it all settles on being free to live life how you want to."

"It's why you fought so hard, brother. This is your time. You've served your country with honor and commitment; now it's time to give that same attention to your guy. Give yourself and your man the life you've always wanted."

"Fuck yeah."

"Fuck yeah."

"When can I tell Denny you'll be back, so we can show you the house? He also wants to get with Skyler about the interior. He said he likes your home so much he wants to soak up your girl's talent for making a house a home."

I smile wide. My girl has done a damn fine job making our home perfect for us. Even though some of her choices seemed wild and wacky at the time, I've chosen to just trust her judgment. There's nothing you can't paint over or replace except for the woman who put it there. I prefer to let her go wild and sit back and watch the show. It's always a good one and ends with both of us being happy.

Paul continues. "Figure Denny and Sky can knock some ideas around, and while they do that, you and me can toss some meat on the grill. Maybe get Mom and Dad outta the fuckin' house for once in the past three months."

"Grilling with my brother, my mate and yours shootin' the shit about interior design while we leave 'em to it? Bring Pops and Ma outta their shell for some food and easy laughter? Sounds perfect to me. When I get home, we can set it up. In the meantime, happy for you, Paulie. It's all coming together for you. After what you've done for our country, you deserve this. All of it. Everything good the world has to offer."

"Man, I don't need or want for much. Just my man, my family being around me and healthy, a cold beer, and a place to put my feet up and lay my head at night. Everything else is just aces."

And he's right. The bare necessities are what truly make a person content.

"We'll set it up. Happy for you," I say again.

"Thanks, Park. Call when you're back, yeah?"

"Will do. My love. You know you got it," I say, my voice thick with emotion.

"You know you got it right back, little bro."

I chuckle and end the call. When I turn around, Tara Darling is sitting in the hot seat waiting for my instruction.

"Are you going to grill me like Royce did?" she says as I approach the empty seat in front of her and maneuver my body into it.

"Absolutely."

7

SKYLER

"Calm down, Skyler. You're making me nervous, and I never get nervous." Ellie walks over to the bar in our hotel room, pours a glass of red wine, and brings it over to me. "Here. Drink this and relax. She'll be here any minute."

I nod, grab the full glass, and take a sip. The cherry and currant notes of the wine flutter against my taste buds in a welcoming flavor I can appreciate. I lean back into the cushy leather chair and let the anxiety of the day flow out of me with each sip.

"You know, we've worked every angle of this plan from top to bottom. Worst-case scenario is he finds out what you're up to and that you've been fibbing recently."

"No, the worst case is him finding out and breaking up with me because I lied to him. We promised we wouldn't ever lie to one another again." I worry the bottom of my lip with my thumb and index finger.

"Skyler, are you having second thoughts?"

I frown and drink more wine. "Not exactly. It's just the longer it goes on before the big reveal, the more scared I get of doing something that will make me lose him. He's my life now, Ellie. Without him, Tracey might as well have taken me out that day."

Ellie makes a slashing move with her hand. "Cut that thought off right there. I do not want to hear any more negativity. You're deep in this now. There is no going back. The pieces are in place, and a lot of people are in on this. It's time to go with the flow and let the plan work its magic." She places her hand on her hip and taps her foot. "Honestly, Skyler, if I thought Parker was going to be unhappy about what you're going to do, I wouldn't have agreed to help. That man dotes on you. He's a hundred percent in love with you. You share a home. Animals. Friends. There's nothing to worry about. Okay?"

I suck in a huge breath and let it out slowly. "Okay. I just needed a little pep talk, I think. I'm good. Back in the game."

She chuckles as the bell to our penthouse suite rings. We chose to stay in a different hotel than the guys to be extra careful that we wouldn't accidently bump into them.

I gulp down a good deal of wine as I wait while Rachel and Ellie go to the door. Nothing like liquid courage to soothe all that ails you.

Elliott enters from the hall with a tall blonde trailing behind her, and Rachel behind them.

"She's clear. Patted her down, checked her purse." Rach lifts her chin and goes back to her crossword puzzle where she was sitting at the bar-top kitchen area across the suite. She sits in a way that's still facing us so she can assess the group and keep an eye on the door and balcony at all times. Nate is in his room getting a much-needed nap. He hates to admit it, but even though he's back, he still has to take it easy and build up his strength.

"Oh my God," I whisper, my mouth dropping open in shock when Tara Darling shuffles toward me with her hand out in greeting, a wide smile on her face. It's not every day that you meet your doppelgänger.

"Ms. Paige, it's such an honor to meetcha! I'm a huge, huge fan of yours." She squeezes my hand brutally and yanks it up and down. "I can't believe this!" the woman practically squeals as excitement gets the best of her.

I yank my hand out from hers and shake it. "Wow. You've got quite the grip."

"Oh shoot, I'm so sorry. My daddy always said I had the handshake of a wrestler." Her voice dips into a bit of a southern accent.

"Yes, well, thank you for coming, Ms. Darling," Ellie says. "Would you like something to drink?"

"A Coke will do just fine if you have one. And you can call me Tara."

"Sure." Ellie opens a cabinet in the bar until she finds a can of Coke, grabs a crystal tumbler, adds ice, and pours the drink before bringing it over to Tara. She then picks up her own glass of wine and proceeds to sit on the couch next to the woman, turning her body toward her.

"We appreciate you coming to speak with us," she says to start the conversation.

Tara pushes a lock of her hair behind her ear, licks her lips, and swallows. "Oh, surely it is all my pleasure, Ms. Black." Tara's gaze moves to meet mine. "I'm just so thrilled to be working on a project with you, Ms. Paige. I can't even express my gratitude."

"You're welcome. And you may call me Skyler or Sky. Everyone does."

"*Sky* . . . ," the woman says with a hint of wonder in her tone.

I smile and set my wine on the glass coffee table before bringing my hands together in front of me, my elbows resting on my knees in a casual position. "Let's talk about how it went today, shall we?"

Tara nods several times while twisting her fingers in her lap as though she's an eager puppy looking for attention. "I played it so cool. At first, I was worried he was going to throw me off the stage. He did not like seeing a look-alike of you appear in the lineup of contestants. Definitely made him uncomfortable," she gushes.

A niggle of worry taps at my subconscious. The last thing I want to do is make him uncomfortable. I know leaving me was hard on him in the first place after all we've been through recently.

Maybe I'm going about this the wrong way?

The scary thought is a seed in my gut, growing bigger with each word that Tara says.

"And then when Louise came in and laid it out that she *intended* to hire a look-alike, he seemed to feel a little bit better about that, though I don't know why."

"Shit, he was probably worried more drama was happening." I look at Ellie, my heart pounding and my stomach twisting into knots.

She shakes her head. "Skyler, it's not a big deal." She gestures to the woman sitting next to her. "Did it seem like a big deal in the end, Tara?"

Tara shakes her head. "No. Though his partner, Royce, that really hot African American guy . . ." Her voice deepens. "You ever see a man wear a suit better than him?" Her eyes bug out as she fans herself with one hand.

"Yeah, I have. *Parker*," I state flatly, my mind flashing on a variety of images where my man was suited up and looking fine as hell.

Tara beams. "Well, he wasn't wearing a full matching designer suit, so I guess I'll just have to wait until I get the pleasure of seeing that to base my decision on."

I clench my jaw. "You were saying about Royce . . ." I lead her back to the point of the conversation, the part that I'm interested in hearing.

"Oh yes. He grilled me. Wanted to know where I came from, who my parents were, what school I went to, and why I wanted to be an actress, as well as why I wanted to be on the show."

"And what did you tell him?" I ask, my heart thumping against my rib cage in a beat so loud I can almost hear it outside of my body.

"The basics. Answered everything truthfully except why I was on the show. Told them I was looking for airtime—which isn't untrue, I totally am—but also that I wanted a love connection."

"And do you think they bought it?" Elliott interrupts.

"Definitely. I'm a good actress. I've won awards and everything back home in Tennessee." Tara lifts her chin and stretches her spine, making her seem taller.

I grab my wine and sit back, tapping the edge of the glass with my nail. "They're going to have her story checked. They'll find out that she doesn't usually look so much like me and will wonder why."

"Didn't you say that Wendy was on her honeymoon? Who are they going to have drop everything and look her up?" Ellie asks.

My publicist . . . on point and so freakin' smart.

"That is true! Mick will not let Wendy anywhere near her phone or laptop. They'd have to call him and only if it were an emergency. If they called about a random actress who happens to look like me, he'd hang up on their asses so fast." I giggle and lift my hand to Ellie, who high-fives it. I turn to Tara, and she smacks my hand in the air too, following along, not really knowing who we're talking about or why we're excited but doing it anyway.

"Rach!" I lift my hand in the air, and without her even looking up from her crossword, she air-fives me.

My badass guard. So cool!

Rachel's always paying attention, even when I don't think so. It's a little creepy and a whole lot awesome.

"Okay, I feel a little better. What did Parker ask you?"

Tara maneuvers her body so she's sitting exactly like I am. Her gaze flickers from my hand movements to my body, and she matches me exactly. Not too shabby. In our business, every actress loves having the object of her role available to her so she can pick up on subtle nuances, gestures they make, their body language, how their voice rises and falls in cadence in order to make the character we're portraying more realistic.

"He asked me what type of man I was looking to connect with and why."

"And what did you tell him?"

She chuckles. "Basically, I told him everything I saw in him. Tall, brunette, light eyes, great physique, talented in business, knows a good woman when he sees her, and makes those moves to secure his position in her life."

"And what did he say in return?"

"He laughed rather brilliantly and said in a joking manner, 'Have you been talking to my woman?' I waved it off as if it wasn't anything, but I knew what I'd said hit the mark."

I can't help but enjoy this, even if Parker's a little uncomfortable. Tara doesn't have any ulterior motive other than to move her career forward, and she's not being too pushy. It's all going to make for really great TV when it's all said and done . . . provided it goes my way in the end.

"Skyler, it seems as though Tara is doing as requested of her. Do you have any concerns?" Ellie asks.

"Besides the risk of my man being pissed that I concocted this entire thing? No." I toss back the rest of my wine and stand up. "You're doing a fine job, Tara. Actually, really great."

"Anything you need, I'm your gal!" Tara pours on the charm.

"Thank you so much, Tara. We appreciate your work so far. We'll let you be on your way then." Ellie stands, gesturing quite specifically that it's time for the woman to get a move on.

I reach out my hand. "Thanks again."

This time she doesn't strangle it.

"Like I said. Anything you guys need, I'm your go-to gal. Thanks, y'all." She waves, heading toward the door. Rachel is already there, prepared to walk her out.

When Rach returns from the entryway, I take my glass and head over to the bar to refill my wine. "I want pizza, with extra cheese and extra pepperoni," I grumble, wanting to consume my feelings. The same could be said when I pour a much-larger-than-standard "four" ounces of wine, almost draining the bottle before I take the remainder over and top off Ellie's glass.

"You think Nate is going to let you get away with *pizza*? You're outta your mind." Rachel shakes her head. "And I'm not even going to tell him you're knocking back three-quarters of a bottle when you are supposed to be training for the first day of shooting, which I will remind you starts in two weeks." Rachel turns the page of her game book, moving to another puzzle. I'm not sure if she finished the first or is just moving ahead because she's stuck.

"I can have pizza," I state snottily.

"You *can*. You can also have three times the number of burpees to do, miles you have to run in the morning, pull-ups, and the row machine for partaking." She shrugs in a bored manner. "Up to you."

I suck in a sharp breath, wincing. "Not if you don't tell him."

Finally, Rach lifts her head up and nails me with an ice-blue stare. "Really?" The way she says *really* is sarcastic, but it also carries a hint of a challenge.

I smile around my glass and stare her down. "I'm positive my girl can get her husband's mind off my diet and onto other things . . . oh, let's say, whatever else pops up."

Rachel grins. "Are you suggesting I seduce my man with some mind-altering monkey sex so he'll forget about your diet?"

I lift one shoulder and take a big sip of yummy wine that's getting even yummier the more I drink down. "If you think you've got the skills." I sigh dramatically.

"Oh, I've got the moves." She stands with her hands on her small hips. "Don't ever doubt my man is well satisfied in the sack."

Smirking, I glance at Ellie. "Guess you'll have to prove that while Elliott and I hammer back a large pizza, my friend."

"*Large!* For real? You can't even get a personal size for yourself? One that has tons of veggies on it?"

I shake my head and wait out the storm brewing behind that icy gaze.

Rachel groans and looks up at the sky. "I'm going to have to bust out the big guns for this. We're talking bedroom calisthenics, maybe a little yoga thrown in for flair. Don't expect us to arrive early tomorrow. My man is going to need to sleep in after the smackdown I have planned."

I laugh hard, covering my mouth.

Rachel points at me and narrows her gaze. "Don't you dare say I didn't do you any favors. Freakin' large pizza," she gripes. "You better follow up tomorrow morning with a serious dose of protein. I'm talking egg white omelet filled with spinach and a touch of asiago, no cheddar!" She continues to grouse, then firms her chin and puts on her game face, which makes her look even more fierce than usual. "Fine. Challenge accepted. Order your freakin' pizza already. I'm getting antsy to attack my man now that you've got me all riled up." She moves from her space in the kitchen to the open area in front where she can lean against the couch and do some push-ups.

Both Ellie and I watch her stretch as if she's preparing for a full marathon.

"Pizza!" She snaps her fingers. "Now. Or I'm going to change my mind." She shakes her head. "The crap I take for the sisterhood."

"Oh please, like you're not going to be getting yours." I roll my eyes for dramatic effect.

She grins wickedly. "For every one I give, I get two to three in return. It's Nate's own personal man scale of orgasms. He thinks if a woman's not getting it on a one-to-two or one-to-three ratio, a man is no man at all."

Damn. Go, Nate. And yay for Rach. I want to applaud, but I rein it in so I don't get clobbered or get my pizza taken away.

"Did you say whether or not Nathan has brothers?" Ellie queries, holding up the phone to her ear without missing a single beat in the conversation.

I look at Rach, who stops mid–side stretch and stares at me, and then we both move our gaze to Elliott and crack up laughing.

***

"Baby, it was the weirdest thing. You have no idea. This chick looks so much like you, I did a double take. Then I got pissed and was convinced our shit luck had come back." Parker's voice is in my ear lulling me to a relaxed state while I rub my very full and totally protruding belly from the pizza baby I just ate.

"Yeah, that's strange. It was all good after you grilled her and spoke to the director, right? Just designed to up the ratings since the public knows you're working the project and I did that promo piece for the show?"

He sighs, and the sound has me imagining him lying cuddled up with me in our bed, my leg slung over his thighs, his hand on my ass, and his breath moving me with every exhalation. I can almost hear a phantom echo of his heartbeat in my ear, the same one that usually knocks me out within minutes each night. We can't even get through one TV program before we're both conked out, especially after a round of Parker-style lovemaking, which is usually pretty adventurous and physically draining.

"It felt odd seeing this woman who looked like you, had some of your mannerisms, but wasn't you. Like I was being pranked," he grumbles, clearly put out by the experience.

A knife prods at my heart. "Honey . . . ," I whisper, wanting him to know I'm there for him. His tone makes me want to call the entire surprise off, but I've put too much into it to go back now. Elliott was right earlier. There are a lot of people counting on the success of my harebrained idea.

"I know what you're going to say . . . ," he groans. "Don't read too much into it. Not everyone is trying to screw us over all the time."

"Only some of the time," I say with a hint of humor.

He chuckles and lets out a long breath once again. "Being away from you is harder than I thought it would be."

"For me too. It's like a piece of me is gone and I'm waiting patiently to get it back."

"Yeah." He clears his throat. "Tell me something good about your day."

I smile, enjoying the fact that he's trying to put us both at ease prior to bed, talking about something positive in our lives.

"Well, Ellie and I halved a large pizza that had extra pepperoni and extra cheese! We also drank a bottle and a half of wine to wash it down."

He laughs. "Bet that didn't go over well with the big guy. How'd you manage it?"

I grin wide and snuggle deeper into my blankets. "I challenged Rach to seduce him into submission so that he would be busy giving her the *business* while Ellie and I gobbled down two nights' worth of calories and fat in one go."

"Shee-it." He uses Royce's coined curse word. "Nate's going to be pissed if he finds out." He laughs hard.

"Part of the secret of the sisterhood. I promised her I wouldn't expect them to work early if she made sure he forgot to ask me about dinner."

"Nice. You think it will work, or do you gather you'll be paying in blood in the gym tomorrow?"

"Mmm, it's a risk I was willing to take. Now me and my pizza baby are going to sleep like a rock." I rub my gut, which is finally starting to feel less stuffed.

He snickers. "Your pizza baby?"

"Yep, I'm naming him Gordo."

"Gordo is *fat* in Spanish, baby."

I lower my voice. "Shhh, he doesn't know." I add to the ruse. "He'll have hurt feelings if he knows his momma called him fat."

He cracks up laughing, and it fills my heart with such joy. "Ah, Peaches, I miss your brand of crazy. It suits me just right."

"And I miss your dick." Oh shit, did I say that out loud? Looks like the wine is still in effect. I can't stop the train of my thoughts while my mouth keeps talking, spilling all. "Yeppers. Your cock, honey, suits me just right. Literally fills me up so I don't feel so empty when I try to sleep without you. I don't have to drink and eat myself into a food coma in order to catch some z's."

"Damn, Peaches. If you could see me, you'd see that the object of your current obsession is standing up waving its flag of surrender. It's hard on me too. Physically and emotionally, but I know what might help."

I grin. "What?" I say in what I hope sounds like a sexy timbre.

"First I want you to put your thumbs into the sides of your panties and shimmy them down those sexy-as-fuck thighs and kick them off. Then push the tank you're wearing up and over your perfect tits. I can't get over how beautiful your tits are. Perfect handfuls, just right for my hands. Enough that they spill over in a way that makes me fuckin' crazy to put my mouth on them. Then I want you to hang up the phone and play with your nipples the way I would."

"Hang up?" I say with a strained tone. "But . . ."

"No *but*s, baby. We'll get to your ass another time. Right now, I need you to hang up the phone and play with your tits. And don't you dare think about touching your pussy. Do you understand me?"

"And what are you going to do?"

"I'm going to get settled in bed and call you back with your surprise. All right? Take direction from your man and play with your titties for a few minutes and wait for me. Can you do what I say?"

"Honey, I can do anything for you."

"Prove it, Peaches. Prove it now."

8

PARKER

My dick is painfully hard and weeping at the tip when I kick off my boxer briefs before wrapping my hand around the base to stave off the need to rush through what I have planned.

Pressing up into a sitting position with my back against the headboard, I widen my knees and let them drop to the sides as my cock stands at attention.

Taking my phone in my other hand, I rest my forearm against one of my knees and point the screen down, then press "Record."

I close my eyes and wrap my left hand around my length, imagining it's Skyler's small warm hand. Pleasure ripples up from my groin to my abdomen, making me clench those muscles as I work my hand up slowly, swirling my thumb at the tip to spread the wetness there and bring it back down again. I gasp at the need curling inside me and thrust my hips as I work my length up and down to a beautiful rhythm.

More precum drips from the slit as I imagine Skyler working my cock, her tongue circling around the tip. She'd sop that mess up with her mouth and moan while tasting me. My girl loves to suck my cock. Loves the control it gives her over me.

I bite back a groan and move my hand faster, until I can feel nothing but nirvana, every inch of my cock buzzing and tingling, ready to blow.

"Fuck yeah," I whisper under my breath, watching my hand move up and down, keeping my other as steady as possible so that she'll get the perfect fucking view. I want her to watch what she does to me, how thoughts of her mouth on my cock, her hand on me, her heat wrapped around me set me off.

Only her.

I've never been so taken with a woman in all my life. Never been able to just imagine the same woman every time I jack off, but she does it for me.

Every. Fucking. Time.

I grit my teeth as I run my hand down to my balls, then cup and squeeze them until the need to come is moments away. I wrap my fingers once again around the base and grip hard, harder than I normally would; it's as if I'm physically pulling my seed out of my cock for her benefit.

Stars light behind my eyes, and my abdominals tighten and flex with each thrust and grip until there's nothing but bliss. The need roars through my body, balls lifting high, dick straining as jet after jet of my release pumps out of the tip, coating my hand and belly in a messy display of my desire.

Puffs of air burst out of my lungs with every aftershock until there's nothing left to give. I've given it all up . . . for her.

I hit the button on my phone to stop the recording. Put the phone down and grab for the tissues by the bed to clean myself up. Once I'm done, I hit the head, wash my hands, and go back to my bed naked.

I pull up the messages section of my phone and find our text string at the top, then attach the video I just took and click "Send."

Once I see that the entire thing has gone, I call her back.

"Honey . . . ," she sighs, her voice sounding needy and sexy as hell.

"You've done what I asked. Played with your pretty titties until now."

"Bay . . . bee, they're on fire. I need . . ."

"I know what you need, Sky. I'll always know when and how to give you pleasure."

She moans, and I know she's being naughty, touching her slit before being told.

"Are you touching yourself?"

"Mm-hmm."

"Does my voice turn you on?"

"So much . . . ," she gasps.

"Put your phone on speaker, then go to the messages on your phone. Click on the video I just sent but leave the phone on speaker. I want to hear you."

"Uh, okay." She sounds breathless as I listen to her moving the phone. I know the second the video starts because she sucks in a sharp breath.

"You see my cock, baby." I lower my voice to the sexy, deep timbre that gets her going.

"Oh yeah . . ."

"Watch me pleasure myself for you. While you're watching I want one of your hands playing with the sweetest cunt I've ever tasted." I bite down on my lip, thinking about being between her thighs right now, her scent in my nostrils, her taste on my tongue. I have to fight back the urge to grind my teeth at the carnal images flooding my mind.

"God, Parker . . . ," she moans, her breath so loud I can hear it coming in labored gusts through the speaker.

"See my hand all over my dick and balls . . ." I taunt her with my voice as much as the image on the video.

"I-I want it." She stutters in her desire.

"I know you do . . . Shove your fingers deep inside like I would. Right now, fuck yourself with two fingers, baby."

She cries out, and my dick perks back up to attention. Jesus, the bastard is hard up for her. Literally.

"It's so good. Watching your beautiful hand stroke your length. Oh God . . . ," she whimpers.

"Now bring those fingers out of your pussy, baby, and press them to your clit. I want you to spin them around and around while I jack off to you in the video." Though technically, I could take my dick in hand again just from hearing her get off on my gift.

"Parker, baby, I . . ." Her voice is strangled, lost to the sensations overcoming her.

"Mmm, you gonna come, Peaches?"

"Yeah . . . ," she whispers.

"Go ahead and come. Let me hear it."

A tortured groan and whimper tease through the line, and I can't help but wrap my hand back around my cock, giving it a few tugs while she comes.

"Don't stop, Peaches."

"Wha-what? But I . . ." Her voice is strained, so I know she's still got her fingers on her clit.

"Another. Have I come in the video?"

"N-no, but I . . ." She loses her ability to speak clearly.

"Keep watching. See what you do to me? How hot and hard you make me? Put three fingers inside your cunt."

"Honey . . . ," she gasps.

"Do it," I growl, and know the second she does because the tortured moan coming from my girl is so long and deep.

"Are you pretending it's my cock or my fingers?" Either makes me hard as stone in my palm.

"Your fingers. Your cock is way too big to pretend."

I grin. "Good. Now watch me stroke my length, how hard I thrust into my tight grip. Mimic my thrusts." I follow my own instructions, fucking my hand for the second time tonight.

"Now use your thumb on your clit the same way I would."

"Oh my God, Parker!" she calls out in ecstasy.

"Fuck yourself harder. I want to hear how juicy you are watching me fuck my hand. I'm so hot for you, Sky, I'm jacking off again. Right now." I groan. "Am I moving faster in the video? Tell me what you see, baby."

"Yeah, yeah, I think, oh, I want to put my mouth on you, swallow you down and suck it so hard. I'd suck you so good, honey," she promises.

"Jesus!" I growl into the phone, my mind spinning with visions of her doing that very thing.

I listen closely to her ragged breaths, knowing exactly when to push her further with more instruction.

"Hook those fingers high, baby. Take hold of your pussy the same way I would, and fucking come when I do." I close my eyes and listen to her moans and cries.

"Oh God, you're coming on the video. It's so sexy, I'm going to . . . ahhhh . . ." She whimpers and moans. The sound is so high pitched it's as though she's being fucked into next week.

"Jesus, fuck me!" I groan as my dick goes off for the second time tonight, covering my hand in my own release.

For at least two to three minutes we both lie there just listening to one another breathe.

"Peaches?" I call out.

"Mmm."

"You good, baby?"

"Mmm," she sighs. "So good. I love you," she whispers, and her voice seems to be fading away.

"Sleep good, Sky."

"Mm-hmm. Dream of me," she mumbles sleepily, and I smile.

"Always, baby. Good night."

I can hear her soft puffs of air signaling that my girl is knocked out. She's fallen asleep while listening to my voice, probably with the phone right next to her head.

I leave my phone on and put the volume way up so I can hear her breathing and sleepy little sighs as I clean myself up. Once done, I get back in bed, flick off the table lamp, and turn on my side with the extra pillow in my arms held tight to my chest as if it's my girl instead. I set the phone on the bed right next to my head.

"I love you, Skyler. I love you so much."

She hums and mumbles, "Love you, Park."

I grin, close my eyes, and fall asleep to the sound of my woman breathing, the same way I do every night back home.

It's the best night's sleep I've gotten all week.

***

"All right, ladies and gents, stand on your marks. We're going to run through this group first, then the second round. Tomorrow is showtime, and we do not want any of you to look unprepared," Louise calls out in a stern tone that demands attention. Royce and I sit to the right of the stage in the voting booth on the guys' half.

"Okay, action."

The male host lifts the mic to his lips as one of the cameras zooms in on him. "Today is the day you've all been waiting for. The next generation of love connections making television history on . . . *Mix and Match!*" His voice rises on the name of the show as he nods and smiles wide into the camera. He looks out to a pretend audience; his hair is perfectly coiffed, his trendy designer suit fitting his frame like a glove.

"Thank you to our live audience for being here, and all of you at home. I'm Rod Gentry, your host, and this is *Mix and Match!* Let's meet our first three male contestants. First up, Lamar Williams . . ." Rod's voice rises and dips excitedly.

Lamar approaches the stage just as we taught him. He stops in front of his chair, looks at the camera, and offers a sexy smirk and a chin lift before sitting down. Thankfully he sits with one leg on the rung and the other on the floor. He's wearing shorts and a polo, but on the day of the show he will be dressed to the nines. The outfit Royce and I chose with the show's stylist should make him look his best.

"Welcome, Lamar!" Rod waits an appropriate amount of time as the stagehand plays the sound of an audience clapping in the background. It fades away, and Rod addresses the camera again. "Next up, Joshua Tipton."

Josh enters the stage, his blond hair swept back, his blue eyes dazzled with excitement. He struts over to his chair, lifts a hand, and offers a jaunty wave before easing down and putting his ankle up to his opposite knee like we practiced. He rests his hands on the crossed leg at the knee and ankle in a casual yet still attractive pose.

"Thanks for coming, Joshua," Rod announces. "And last but definitely not least, we've got Jimmy Handle."

Jimmy Handle? What the hell was the kid thinking? He went from Jimmy Jones, sounding like a sausage or a pizza place, to a name that makes people think of grabbing their dicks?

I shake my head and sigh.

Royce grunts under his breath and covers his mouth while he laughs silently. Fucker. He knows I'm going to have to have yet another uncomfortable conversation with the guy.

Jimmy walks across stage, his ever-present folk-inspired hat on, ginger beard trimmed to perfection. He smiles so wide when he sits down he looks like a loon. Switch out his rounded fedora, place a dunce cap on his head, and you've got a life-size garden gnome. I roll my eyes and press my finger and thumb to my temples to work out the tension.

"Shee-it, brother looks like a creepy leprechaun in his plaid shirt, hat, and crazy-as-hell smile. He needs to tone that back."

"Yeah, I'll talk to him. When I'm telling him about his name . . . again."

Royce grins and dips his head.

"Next up is a beautiful lady some of you may recognize from her screen time and Broadway appearances, Ms. Tara Darling!" Rod watches Tara strut out of a special side of the stage blocked off so the guys can't see her. She's working the camera, swaying her hips from side to side. Rod licks his lips as if he's interested in far more than just her attendance on the show. His eyes are glued to her body and travel up and down her form so fast I swear he has X-ray vision and can see through her clothes or is trying damn hard to.

Tara stands in front of the camera that focuses in on her. She winks saucily and smiles before spinning around, her golden locks flying behind her as she goes to her chair.

"Men, if you'd seen this girl, you'd be beyond excited to meet her." Rod rubs at his bottom lip with his thumb, his eyes on Tara a moment too long.

The guys make different gestures to this, like clapping their hands and fist-bumping, and Lamar does the super over-the-top kissing of two fingers and directing them out toward the audience as if he's LL Cool J himself. Hell, he probably doesn't even know who that is.

The show does a great job of keeping the male and female contestants out of sight from one another, except for the questions. For now, we're practicing with questions the writers put together, but when the show goes live tomorrow, we're allowing the two females we've chosen to decide what to ask their potential suitors. The showrunner and producer will have viewed the questions to make sure they're not inappropriate, eliminating stuff like "Have you ever had anal sex?" or "What type of veggie would you compare the size of your dick to?"

You know. The obvious no-no's.

"Thank you so much for having me here, Rod." Tara pours on the charm.

"Oh, the pleasure is all mine," Rod says instantly; then his eyes widen as though he just realized what he revealed. He plays it off. "I mean, the pleasure is all of ours, right, gentlemen?"

This time I chuckle under my breath.

"Speaking of gentlemen, we have two very special guest judges. One you may recognize since his face has been plastered all over the media lately." I narrow my gaze at the comment but force a fake smile to keep with the plan. "We've got Royce Sterling and Parker Ellis from International Guy Inc. They have been instructing our male and female contestants on how to best be ready and open for love. How are you doing, guys?"

Royce leans forward and smiles. "Just fine. Ready to hear how our boys do tonight."

I smile at Tara and then glance across all of the eager men waiting to be asked their questions. "Looking forward to seeing who Tara chooses. All I have to say to you men is, one of you is going to be very lucky indeed."

The men clap, hoot, and holler jovially, adding to the fun of the practice round.

"Well, all right, I'd say it's time to get right to business." Rod instructs the candidates on how the show will work, making comments to the pretend audience, which will be a full house tomorrow.

"All right, Tara, why don't you ask a lucky gentleman a question so we can get this party started?"

She smiles into the camera and lifts a blue card. "Contestant number one, what do you think makes a woman beautiful to you?"

Lamar rubs at his chin as if he's thinking about it. "Well, sweetheart, she'd have to be confident and sassy. Nuthin' prettier than that."

Tara giggles. "Contestant number two, same question."

"Well, Tara, I can already tell by your voice that you're beautiful. So, for me, her voice being sultry like yours goes a long way," Joshua says.

"Okay . . ." She smiles and looks down at her card. "Contestant number three, if I choose you, what would be a perfect date?"

Jimmy sits up taller in his chair. "For you, Tara, I'd take you to a music festival. Bring along my banjo, a blanket, some great food I'd make myself, and we could sit under the stars, watching the people, hearing great music, where I'd then break out my own little ditties for you."

Tara makes a face of surprise. "Wow, that sounds like a blast."

"Pick me, darlin', and I'll make it your reality."

The questions continue for another half hour, the director stopping and starting them again, giving feedback on things she likes and dislikes.

The first group finishes, and the men are ushered off to a separate section of the stage to keep Tara hidden. The second group goes through the process next. There are even fewer problems with this group. They seem to fit right into the program and have taken our feedback to heart and put it into action. Louise is thrilled and decides that they'll be first up, with Tara in the second group.

Once the rehearsal is finished, Tara hustles over to where Royce and I are sitting at the edge of the stage, coffee in our hands.

"Hey, um, guys, I just wanted to get your thoughts, see if there were any pointers you had for me. I'm pretty nervous about tomorrow."

"Don't be. You did well out there," I offer.

Her corresponding smile is wide and enthusiastic. "Thank you."

"Have you given any thought to who you're going to pick for your date?" Royce asks.

She shrugs. "Based on their answers, I'm leaning toward Jimmy," she says, surprising me.

I glance at Royce and see that he's surprised too, especially since we know what he looks like. Now I really need to make sure he's on his A game tomorrow.

"He seems really funny and nice. He'll be so focused on making me happy, I might actually have a fun date. Lamar and Josh seem a little too full of themselves. And besides"—her eyes lift to mine—"it's not like you're on the stage, Parker. If that were the case, those other guys would have to watch out, because I'd be gunning straight for you."

A niggle of trepidation pricks at the back of my neck and runs down my spine. "Uh, Tara, that's really sweet of you to say. Though you know I'm completely off the market."

She moves a couple of steps closer and puts her hand on my knee.

Royce lets out a breath. "Aw damn." He looks the other way, trying to give me a little privacy but still be there in support.

"We could, you know, have fun together and maybe, um, not tell anyone." She whispers low, but I can tell Royce heard because he grunts loudly.

I grab Tara's hand on my knee and remove it. "Like I said, Tara. That was a nice compliment, but I'm gone for Sky. There is no other woman on this planet for me."

She takes a couple of steps back, giving me space while pushing her hair off her neck. She presses her lips together. "Does she know that? In my experience, all men are dogs, and they never tell a woman what they really think. Usually the woman finds out the guy's not as committed as she is when she hears about her man in bed with another woman."

Damn, this woman has some issues hiding under the surface, some demons the next guy she finds is going to have to unearth and get to the heart of in order for them to find happiness together.

"I'm glad you're a good guy and didn't take what I was offering. Not a lot of guys turn me down, even when they're in a relationship. I sure hope your Skyler knows you're so committed, since you haven't put a ring on her finger or anything."

Spear. Right to the heart.

I frown. *Do women expect that?*

I mean, I get that women want their men to be so into them they take that ultimate step, but we've already got a house together, dogs, share just about everything. Sky and I have talked about our future. She seems ready to take that leap, maybe even a little eager to, but I've been worried that she's doing it to substitute for something she's missing, like her ex-best friend and her parents. Now that things are settling in, I want her to be happy and confident in the fact that I'm not going anywhere. I guess an engagement ring might go a long way toward showing her that in action instead of my just telling her that I'm committed.

"Shouldn't you be getting back?" Royce gestures with a chin lift to where the other female contestant is being chatted up by the producers, getting her orders for the next day.

She hops and then claps her hands, twirling around. The move is exactly like something my Sky would do. My heart clenches at the thought of Skyler back home, all by herself, waiting on me. At least I hope she's waiting. Not pining, but at least thinking about me too.

I groan and rake my fingers through my hair, leaning back and looking up into the dark abyss of the studio ceiling. Pipes, walkways, and a variety of other equipment, all painted black, crisscross paths like a spider's web above our heads.

Royce puts his hand on my shoulder. "That woman don't know shit about you or Sky. Don't take anything she said to heart, hear?"

I frown. "Yeah, but doesn't mean it doesn't make me think."

"Thinkin' is good. What you did, pushing her off without being a dick, was kind. You took the compliment and told her like it is. You're into your woman. You're all about her, and she's got no in. Period. No harm done on either part. She made her play; you thwarted it. That's done."

"Still, she had a point. Sky and I have been talking about the future, about marriage and kids. The whole enchilada."

"Did you come to a conclusion?"

"Not really. She seems ready to move forward, but—"

Royce interrupts. "What, you're not ready? Puh-leeeze. Brother, you've been ready since the two of you fell all over yourselves in London working the James case."

"Yeah, and then all hell broke loose in our world, but most especially in hers. I don't want to rush into something when her head isn't clear. Sky needs to want to be my wife because she wants nothing more in life than to build a life with me, not because it's an answer to all the loss she's sustained recently."

Royce sucks in his bottom lip so it disappears before he lets it go to speak. "I think you need to give your woman a little more credit. She's smart. Not the type of woman who doesn't say it like it is. If she says she's ready, brother . . . she's ready. A woman doesn't fuck around when it comes to putting on that white dress if she's got her man willin' to give it to her." He purses his lips. "I say you roll with it and buy your girl a big rock to prove you're all in."

"Is that what you would do?"

"Damn straight. That's what I did do a long fuckin' time ago when I thought I had it all. Wish like fuck I'd sealed the deal before shit went haywire."

I reach out and grab Royce's shoulder and give it a squeeze. "Things happen for a reason. Back then, it wasn't meant to be. Maybe that time is still coming, maybe not. Only time will tell, but I do know one thing for certain."

"Yeah . . . What's that?" His dark gaze meets mine.

I grin wide. "I'm going to enjoy the hell outta watching you two figure it out."

Royce narrows his gaze and pushes me away. "Fuck you."

I laugh heartily and catch up to where his long strides are eating up the concrete floor heading to the back door.

"As a matter of fact, I take it all back," he says. "I hope she leaves your punk ass for a rock star. A girlie-man type with long-ass hair, a belly ring, and a tattoo that says 'Mother' across his heart." He points a long dark finger at me. "That would serve you right."

I can barely contain the wheezing that comes with the uncontrollable laughter spilling out of me. "I'm sorry. I didn't mean it. Well, I did, but in a good way!" I try to catch up to him, but I'm still laughing hard, which hinders my ability to move quickly.

As he walks away he lifts his hand above his head and flips me off.

9

SKYLER

It's showtime. My palms are sweaty, and my knees are shaking. I clench my teeth and watch as the live audience screams when Parker and Royce are introduced and walked to their special seats in the judging booth. The plan is in place, and today is the day. There's no going back from here.

Royce and Parker sit, and the host announces the first set of three men, then moves on to the woman. She's a brunette, pretty, very girl-next-door looks that will connect easily with the viewers. It's ideal for a show to have individuals who viewers can swap places with in their minds. She's not exactly thin or thick. She's average sized, with a simple beauty about her.

The host introduces each man and then the woman. While Parker and Royce are watching I wait for it to happen as planned.

Louise rushes over to Parker and Royce when the cameras are off them, leans down, and whispers something frantically in their ears. She has another man standing behind her. Royce and Parker both stand up, but Louise shakes her head. Parker ends up coming with her while Royce stays behind and the other man sits next to him, taking Parker's place in the booth.

I know for a fact that Louise just shared that Jimmy Jones Handle, whatever his name is, had a family emergency and had to leave. There was no emergency, but Parker and Royce don't know that.

Louise will be freaking out behind the scenes, telling Parker the entire show is a bust and that she's screwed. Parker will offer to help in any way he can.

While I wait, it feels like a hundred years have gone by and, as planned, Parker and Louise do not return. The contestants go through the first half hour of the show, the woman picks her guy, and the audience roars with glee, clapping loudly for the new match.

"You ready to rock and roll?" Elliott's hand curls around my bicep and nudges me toward the side of the stage.

I follow behind her, hoping that Louise was able to pull magic out of her ass and set the next part of the plan in place.

When we get to the curtain where Tara is standing, she gives us a cheesy smile and a thumbs-up. I sneak a peek through the black curtain and hold my breath.

Lamar walks onto the stage as Rod introduces him. He looks polished in a fine black suit that plays against the bright color of his dress shirt and his dark skin.

The crowd whistles at his entrance. He does this weird move where he kisses two fingers and makes a peace sign to the audience, which I don't get. Is it supposed to mean peace and love? I don't know.

Next up is a young blond guy who looks like he strutted right off the pages of Abercrombie & Fitch, complete with a white cable-knit sweater tied around his shoulders, a rich-boy smirk, and a golden tan that sets off his pretty blue eyes.

And then it happens: the audience goes quiet as the third guy doesn't come out yet. I cross my fingers and my legs in a gotta-pee dance move, hoping against all hope that Louise made it happen. Then I see a pair of arms push my man out onto the stage. He stops and looks at the camera, shakes his pristine navy suit jacket, and casually buttons it while walking up the steps and onto the platform.

"And here we have Jimmy Handle," Rod says without looking, until he sees another stage person shake his head and wave a hand to Parker. Rod looks his way. "Oh wow, we have quite the treat for the audience and the show. It looks like the third contestant is actually International Guy's very own CEO, Parker Ellis. Looks like he's left the judging booth to participate in tonight's *Mix and Match*!"

The crowd goes absolutely bonkers.

My man gives a sexy smile he's perfected and that *always* hits the mark, making my panties wet from it. Especially when it's blazing down on me when he's hovering above my body, naked. Parker gives the audience a little wave, and the ladies lose their ever-loving minds, screaming so loud I want to cover my ears to save my eardrums the pain.

He makes the universal hand gesture for the audience to settle; then he puts his finger in front of his lips in a shushing gesture.

"Okay, well, after that little surprise, let's have you meet our female contestant. One who I'm sure has no idea who's sitting on this stage right at this moment. Let's play along with it, shall we, friends?" Rod asks the audience, and they nod, pump their fists, and clap.

"All right, and your prospective match tonight is . . . Ms. Tara Darling."

Two and two get put together as Tara walks out, and the entire crowd gasps. I can't help but have a very recognizable look after so many blockbusters, and Parker and I have had a rather public relationship. Their seeing Tara and how much she resembles me is a surprise. After the initial shock wears off, the crowd once again goes berserk, screaming, yelling, laughing, clapping, and stomping their feet.

Rod makes a gesture for the audience to simmer down so the game can begin. That's my cue to move around to the side of the stage. Ellie follows me, her hand on my back in a supportive manner.

Tara asks the guys her first question, ones that I've already written for her.

"Contestant number one, if you could fall in love anywhere in the world, where would it be?"

Lamar licks his lips and nods. "Excellent question. I'd have to say Paris, because it's known to be the most romantic city in all the world."

Tara shimmies in her chair. "Oooh . . . I like. How about you, contestant number three?" she asks Parker.

He cocks an eyebrow and looks right at the camera. "Anywhere. New York. London. Rio. The only thing that matters is I'm standing in front of the right woman for me."

"Awww." Tara touches her heart. "So sweet."

While Tara asks number two a question, I start walking on the stage from where Tara entered. The audience goes dead silent. One of the stagehands rolls up a television on Tara's side of the wall, showing the three guys so that the two of us, as well as the audience, can see them respond. We want the audience in on it so they realize that this is all a setup and don't yell out my name.

I put my fingers up to my lips the same way Parker did and make a point to show the screen, and tiptoe to stand next to Tara. When I get there, she grins. I stand by her side and hand her another card. A special one.

"Contestant number two. If you could have your dream girl—I'm talking celebrities—who would yours be and why?" Tara says.

Josh grins wickedly at the camera. "Dakota Johnson. Any man who sees her in *Fifty Shades of Grey* . . ." He shakes his hand and whistles. "Whoo weeee, absolutely stunning woman."

I make a point to shrug my shoulders and nod, then shake my head while pointing a thumb at my chest without saying anything so I don't ruin the surprise. The audience chuckles.

"Contestant number three, same question," Tara says.

Parker grins and shakes his head. The audience laughs even louder, all smiles on their faces and shimmering eyes centered on the stage, their necks twisting from one side of the stage to the other where Tara and I are.

"Hands down, my dream girl is Skyler Paige. There is no substitution for her beauty, intelligence, that smokin' hot body, and how big her heart is." He looks straight into the camera, and the audience this time makes a collective *aw* sound at his statement.

Tears prick my eyes, but I hold them back and patter my hands against my heart so the audience here and at home gets the real experience of what's happening.

I hand Tara another card.

"A follow-up to that question then, since you seem so smitten. If Skyler Paige were here right now, professing her love, faith, and commitment by getting down on one knee and asking *you* to marry *her*, would you?"

The camera zooms over to Parker and gets close-up. I watch the screen in front of Tara, and the entire room fades around me. There's nothing in this moment but the man I love on the screen in front of me. I barely refrain from reaching out and tracing his beautiful face.

Parker licks his lips, closes his eyes, takes a breath, and opens his eyes again.

Love. Honesty. Determination. All flash across his face as I wait with bated breath.

"Absolutely, yes."

I smile wide, take my cue, and grab the little black velvet box I had set on the table next to Tara.

I step down the few steps and move around the wall.

Parker sees me and stands up. He looks left and right as if something is happening, but he doesn't know what it is.

"Baby, what are you doing here?" He points to Louise. "I got thrown into this show! You can ask the producer. There was no way

I was going on a date with someone else. I swear!" He makes a "safe" gesture with his arms and hands the same way an umpire would call a play in a baseball game.

I smile wide and stretch my arm out for him. He takes my hand and steps right up to me. No delay whatsoever and no distance. Just the way I like it.

"What's going on?" He smiles but looks completely confused.

The cameras zoom in closer to both of us, but I ignore them. In this industry you have to.

With my heart in my throat, I take a breath and look right into his smiling face. "Parker James Ellis. You came into my life during a time when I thought I'd lost it all. With your smile, your support, and eventually, your love, I came out of that strange place better than I'd ever been."

Parker cups my face and caresses my cheek with his thumb. His other hand is holding mine against his chest, right above his heart. I continue, needing him to know how I feel.

"We had the hardest year of our lives. People we loved got hurt. Still, you were my rock. The one calm spot in a sea of crashing waves. Always there for me. By my side through it all, taking away my pain and filling me with hope and love. I want that forever." My voice shakes, and a tear slips down my cheek. "I want *you* forever."

I take a deep breath and let it out, looking intently into his beautiful blue eyes. "So today, in front of millions of viewers and this live audience, I'm making the ultimate leap of faith, and I'm going to ask you to take it right by my side."

I step back, keeping hold of his hand, and get down on one knee.

His eyes widen to the size of saucers, and he tugs at my hand. "Peaches . . . ," he whispers.

I shake my head and clear my throat so the words I'm saying are loud and clear to him, and to everyone viewing this moment.

"No. I kneel before the man I love, showing you and the *entire world* that there will never be another man for me. I'm ready to make it official. You and me, against it all. Forever." I close my eyes as tears gather and my voice wobbles. "Parker James Ellis . . . will you marry me?" I open the black velvet box to show him the simple, thin, handsome platinum wedding band I picked just for him. Its beauty is in its simplicity and lack of frills, just like the man I love.

Parker swallows and looks up at the sky. "My woman is always outdoing me."

"Well . . ." Fear ripples down my chest as I wait with my hand out, my heart balancing at the tippy-top of my fingers for him to take. Begging him to.

"Come here!" He grips me under my armpits and hauls me up and into his arms. I wrap my legs around his waist, thanking God himself I had the foresight to rock a sexy jumpsuit that allows for the gesture. With one hand wrapped around my ass and the other around the back of my head, he smashes his lips over mine. He delves his tongue deep, instantly taking the kiss to a heated one thousand degrees and then some, before he eventually lets me go and rests his forehead against mine.

"Skyler, I'll marry you today. I'll marry you tomorrow, and every day after until we take our last breath, if that's what you want. I give everything I am, all that I have, to you."

I smile wide. "I love you."

He kisses me softly and then makes a funny face. "Always a dramatic event with you, Peaches." He kisses my nose, dips his head into the crook of my neck and shoulder, and inhales deeply. When he leans his head back, he smirks. "Now gimmie my ring," he announces, and a burst of laughter and clapping rings throughout the room.

I slide down Parker's body and pull out the ring, dropping the box to the ground. I take his hand and slide it on his left ring finger. "There."

"Your ownership mark? Right where it's supposed to be." He tunnels his hand into the back of my hair, cupping my neck. "Woman, you are *crazy*. Crazy beautiful. Crazy mine."

"Crazy in love with you." I smile and accept his kiss. Eventually he lets me go, and the audience goes wild as ever, chanting, "SkyPark, SkyPark, SkyPark," at the tops of their lungs.

Parker puts his lips to my temple and whispers, "You know now I'm going to get a ration of shit from Ma and Pops because you did the asking."

I lift a shoulder and drop it. "I think they'll be happy with the end result."

He grins wide. "I think you're right."

I cuddle into his arms as confetti bursts out from the ceiling and drops in sparkling pieces over all of us. Music blares, and the host starts his spiel about the end of the episode and joining the show next time when they have another set of couples wishing for a mix and match.

"You happy, honey?" I hook my arms around his neck and stare up into the only eyes that have ever looked at me with love shining from every inch of their depths.

"More than happy. I'm elated, and to tell you the truth . . . kind of relieved. Proposing to Skyler freakin' Paige in front of the world would have been a shit show!" he jokes, smiling.

Laughter bubbles up my throat and out my mouth. "This is true."

"Thanks for saving me the trauma, baby."

I frown. "Oh, you're not off the hook."

He dips his chin and pouts. "What do you mean?"

"You still have to ask me back. I did the hard part. And besides . . ." I smile and pat his ass. "I want my own ring to show off!"

He shakes his head, lifts me up, and spins me in a circle, confetti floating like snow all around us, creating the most magical moment of my life.

Until later that evening . . .

***

"Jesus. Christ. Fuck. Me. Woman!" Parker pounds me against the headboard. He's up on his knees, one arm locked around my back and up, cupping my head, the other at my waist. I have my arms spread out wide against the headboard, fingers curled around the wooden edge, legs wrapped around his waist, ankles locked at his lower back as Parker fucks me raw.

We've been going at it nonstop since we tumbled into the hotel room hours ago. The first time was on the floor in the entryway.

Let's just put it this way: the badass jumpsuit didn't survive. It's a pile of shredded fabric lost somewhere between the tile floor in the entry and the kitchen area.

"Honey, please . . . no more. No. More!" I moan in ecstasy at the same time I beg, my head shaking back and forth as if I can will myself not to fall apart *again*.

Parker won't hear it.

He's relentless.

Sweat drips off his brow, and his face twists into a snarl as he rocks his hips. The muscles of his shoulders, arms, and chest are straining, veins protruding with his effort to sink so far into me he makes a Skyler imprint on the headboard behind me.

"Need. More," he growls, before sinking his face into my neck and sucking the skin there.

Chills race out my arms, gooseflesh rising as another intense wave of pleasure shreds me from the inside out.

"Want you to come again. Squeeze the goddamned life right out of my cock. One last time, baby. Come on. You can do it. Give. It. To. Me." He groans an animalistic sound against my skin that reverberates down my spine and straight to my clit. A pulsing throb starts there and spreads out as he continues to hammer his length deep inside.

I move my hands from the death grip I have on the headboard to tunnel my fingers into his hair. With all I have, I lift my chest, then rock my hips with every plunge, wanting to take every centimeter of him inside me. Parker hisses with pleasure or pain. I don't know anymore. The line is so fine between the two that I can't tell the difference. All I know is they are both brilliant and life altering at the same time.

Parker uses his chin to nuzzle his way between my breasts, pressing me firmly against the headboard until he's got my nipple in his mouth. He sucks so hard I cry out, splintering apart with every pull of his lips. My eyes water, and I enter this space of nothing but dead air and silky bliss. I can feel that my skin is soaked in sweat and saliva from his endless kisses, my limbs locked so firmly around his body that I no longer feel the pain of the overused and abused muscles. My mind swims on this plane of bliss until he crushes my clit with his pelvic bone, and I'm gone. My pussy locks down around the base of his cock, and I scream, and scream, and scream . . . letting it all go in that one final moment of eternal ecstasy.

Parker makes a choking sound and buries his mouth at my neck. Heavy bursts of air rocket against my heated skin as his body jolts and jerks.

One thrust.

Two.

Three . . .

He bites down, so hard he might actually break the skin, adding another bruise to the wasteland that he's made of my body. His own form shakes as his release heats me up from the inside for what feels like the millionth time tonight before he grips me fully. My guy loses his strong hold once we fall to the bed and are against the sheets, him shifting immediately to his side, taking me with him, still connected. One of his hands lands on my ass and stays there, keeping me close. His other is under my head and around my back. I'm locked in his embrace, a happy prisoner.

After our breathing calms down, I can barely open my eyes long enough to see his baby blues rolling up, and he's out. I follow him a moment later.

10

PARKER

I wake to the incessant ringing of a cell phone. It stops for a couple of minutes, then starts back up again.

Hers. Mine. Hers. Mine. An endless, devilish loop of annoyance.

For a minute I take stock of my body. I'm warm. Crazy warm. My entire body is hot, with a heavy weight pressing my bicep into the mattress to the point it's now numb. I open my eyes slowly and find I'm face-to-face with the prettiest woman alive. My Skyler, sound asleep, her body half-glued to mine. I wiggle around, and my dick slips wetly out of her.

Jesus! I groan as copious amounts of our combined lovemaking trickle out of her, sliding down one toned thigh, then trailing onto mine. I glance down and watch the proof of our passion with a twisted fascination. It may be sticky as hell, but I sure as fuck love watching my seed drain out of her. I scan what I can see of her body and wince as bluish fingerprints appear on her thighs and hips where I gripped too hard, got carried away. At the tantalizing curve of her neck and shoulder I can see a series of teeth marks and a whopper of a hickey.

Shit. When was the last time I got so lost in the moment I gave a woman a hickey?

Skyler does that to me, and after her asking to tie herself to me for life, I couldn't keep my hands off her. I literally fucked her until we both passed out. We've had some serious sexathons in the past, especially when we first hooked up, but nothing like last night. I lift my hand that now carries an unfamiliar weight and inspect the ring she put on my finger. It's thin with a simple twist of metal running down the center looking like two lines that have merged. The same way Skyler and I have merged. Two people on our own paths, now tangled up seamlessly with one another.

I grin wide until the damn phone starts to blare again.

Skyler mumbles in her sleep and swats at me. "You fuck too much." She sighs, and her mouth lands in a sultry bow-shaped pout, her lips swollen as fuck from my nonstop kisses.

I chuckle under my breath at her cuteness and watch the little puffs of air leave her beautiful lips. God, I'm one lucky son of a bitch. And last night, I simply could not get enough.

She rocked my world when she proposed to me on live television, and I couldn't get the image of her on her knee, professing her love to me in front of the world, out of my mind. Every time I thought about it or caught a glimpse of my ring I lost it. My dick got hard, and I had to have her.

She didn't turn me away. Not once, even though she repeatedly begged me to stop giving her orgasms. A request I straight-up ignored, making her sing as many times as I could. I'm pretty sure we hit a record last night.

The phone starts to ring again, and this time, my sleepyhead beauty finally hears it. Sky opens one eye, and her golden-brown gaze meets mine. "Honey . . . why is someone blowing up our phones?" She lets her face fall back onto my bicep, where she nuzzles and then kisses me a few times.

I lock my arm around her, lifting her limp body and dragging her on top of me. Her wet slit makes contact with my once-again hardening cock.

She moans but also groans. "Honey, you broke my lady parts," she says, playfully miffed, and yet . . . her hips start to move, picking up a scintillating rhythm. Up and down my cock, spreading the moisture that's between us.

I cup her ass cheeks and grind her back and forth, allowing her body to lazily move against me. It feels so good I don't care that I'm not inside her.

She continues to shift her weight, rubbing her clit along my cock. "God, honey, you feel like heaven . . . I just can't stop!" She catches the opening of her cleft at the wide knob of my tip and gasps. I grip her ass more fully and grind hard.

I help her rock her hips, dragging along my length, but especially making sure the tip grates along her sensitive bud over and over until her body moves faster and her breath picks up a laborious pace. "Park . . ." She sets her lips over mine, not exactly kissing, just letting them touch, sharing our breath as our bodies rock and roll. "Honey, you're gonna make me come."

"Fuck, I hope so, or I'm going to look like a horny goddamned teenager when I come all over you." I slam my lips over hers and delve my tongue deep. She sucks hard on the bit of flesh as her body arches and she loses her hold.

Sky cries out, and her body tightens with her release. I grip her hips, keeping her body sliding up and down my cock, the tips of her breasts rubbing along my chest until I follow her over the edge.

We both breathe against one another, enjoying the sated feeling of being together like this once more, this time during the light of day, until the damn phone starts ringing again. She lifts her head and looks at me with her dazzling, sex-hazed gaze. "That was, um . . . different."

"Different good?" I cock an eyebrow and wait for her thoughts.

"Oh yeah, different good. Made me feel young again," she teases, as if she's old. The woman's only twenty-five, but she is about to get another year older.

"Well, since your birthday is next week, I'm glad I could be of service." I smack her ass, and she howls, sliding off.

"We need a serious shower . . . and, um, probably some new sheets." She picks up the rumpled mess of our linens and makes a sour face as though what she's touching is smelly as well as dirty.

"First, we need to find out who the fuck is on our ass with these calls . . . ," I growl, getting out of bed and storming over to the pile of discarded clothes.

She giggles and stretches her sexy-as-fuck body along the mattress, her hands out above her head, her toes pointed toward the headboard. Jeez, we didn't even sleep the right way. Just conked out where we dropped after that last bout of sex. Though I can't say that shit wasn't inspired.

A shiver races down my spine with the memory of taking her up against the headboard and wall.

"I thought I was the one who was on your tip . . . ," she teases.

I filter through our clothes and pick up the phone. It says "Mom and Dad" on the display. I point at my girl, still holding the phone. "Quiet, before I fuck you again." Any mention of her and my tip will make "the beast" rise again.

She grins and makes a motion of zipping her lips.

Fucking cute.

I hit the answer button and put the phone to my ear. "Yeah?" I growl into the phone, not wanting to talk to anyone right now, least of all my parents.

"You're getting married! It's all over the news! Oh my God!" Ma screeches into the phone. I hold it away from me and toss the phone to Skyler, who heard the scream and is smiling like a loon.

"Baby, it's for you," I say, before walking my naked, filthy ass to the bathroom for a much-needed piss and a shower.

I turn around and see Skyler sitting up on her knees holding the phone to her ear, a big smile on her face. "Hi, Cathy, you got me, Sky," I hear her say. "I know. He said yes. Isn't it awesome! I can't wait to be part of your family."

My family.

Me. Skyler. Mom and Dad. Paul and Dennis. And the rest of our wild clan.

Skyler Ellis. It has a nice ring to it. Now all I have to do is get her a ring and pop the question in reverse. And then it dawns on me. What Skyler did, she made public, which I think she did because she wanted everyone to know I was it for her. It was a beautiful statement not only to me, but to the rest of the world. Except Skyler is the kind of girl who craves belonging, and she wants to belong to me. To a family. Be a crucial part of something real and everlasting.

I grin wide as the idea comes to me. I've got the perfect fucking place and plan for when and how to pop the question right back.

Opening the shower door, I flip on the hot water while I do my business at the toilet, then step into the steamy shower.

I'm going to need some reinforcements.

***

"It's all ready to go, man. Trust me. I got this on lock," Bo says jovially in my ear as I pace the entryway of our house waiting for Skyler to finish getting ready and make an appearance.

It's been a week since we've been back from LA, and it's my woman's birthday. Everything needs to go smooth or I'll lose it.

"Today is the day, man; it has to be perfect. Make sure every single fucking person is there," I warn.

"You've got Nate and Rach, right?"

I glance up and look at Nate, who's standing on the porch, survey-ing the front of our house, waiting for us to exit and get in the car.

Rachel is sitting on the bench in the entryway rebraiding a chunk of long platinum hair that's part of her ponytail.

"Yeah, they're here. You got Ma and Pops? The Sterlings? Mick and Wendy. Annie. Kendra. Paul and Dennis. Baylee. Elliott. Geneva. Rick the Prick."

"Aw, man, that's not right. Rick's a cool cat." Bo's tone is chastising, but I don't give a rat's ass.

"Bogey, the guy has seen Skyler naked, had his mouth and hands on her body, and pretends regularly that he's in love with her," I grate through clenched teeth.

"Yeaaaah." He drags out the word. "Good point. I'm sure you hate that shit."

"I've learned to live with it." I let out a strangled breath, pushing any thoughts of my woman and her costar out of my head. No good thoughts come of that. "Still, he's her friend. What about Sophie? She and Gabriel were cutting it close as I recall . . ."

"Brother. Re-fucking-lax. You gave me the list. Annie made sure every flight was booked and arrived with plenty of time. Sophie is chat-ting up and charming the pants off Ms. Sterling and Roy's sisters. All that we're missing is you, the birthday girl, and He-Man and She-Ra."

I chuckle. "Don't let Nate hear you say that or you might be in some trouble."

Bo lets out a hiss. "He's not the one I'm afraid of. That chick could make Wonder Woman shake in her red boots, and she's got a Lasso of Truth that I imagine hurts like hell when Superman takes a lashing."

I shake my head and press my fingers into my temples. Leave it to Bo to bring sex and superheroes into regular, everyday conversation.

"You're trying my patience. Is the food ready?"

"Yep. Cook's got the roast for the pulled pork cooking low and slow, all the fixings, that special potato salad that Sky loves, and everything.

We've even got champagne chilling for the toasts. Just get your asses here already. Got shit to do," he clips, before hanging up abruptly.

I drop the phone to my side and keep up my pacing.

"Park, you're making me dizzy, and you're wearing a circle in the rug," Rachel says. "It's all going to go perfectly. Stop worrying."

"It's an important moment. I want it to be just right. For her."

Rachel smiles a wide grin, her ice-blue eyes sparkling. She stands up and puts her hand to my forearm and gives it a squeeze. "It's not like you don't already know the answer. Remember that. You're wearing her ring already. Take it easy, or you're going to ruin the surprise."

I nod and place my hand in my pocket, making sure that the ring is still there. Yep.

I hear a noise from the other room, and then my girl is here, pretty as a picture.

Skyler spins in a circle, showing off her tanned, long legs. The outfit she's wearing is a black chiffon bohemian minidress that's tied at the waist, but the front is a wide V straight down past her boobs. If she weren't wearing an electric-blue lace bralette-type job, her tits would be falling out of the thing. The blue of the lacy bra matches the teal and aqua flowers running down the front of the dress. The fabric hits midthigh and is flowy and flirty. On her feet are a pair of coral wedges that zip up the front.

"You're enchanting. What's this look? Rocker chick?" I tease, and flirt with the edges of her short dress even though my heart is pumping a wild beat in my chest and I'd like nothing more than to ravage her where she stands.

She wiggles her body away from me. "I call it boho chic. Do you like it?" She looks up, and her gaze meets mine. Those beautiful brown eyes swirl and sparkle with pure joy. Her golden hair is in beachy waves, parted down the center, except she has something bright clipped in the mess of waves.

I lift my hand and reach for the colorful item and find it's a series of multicolored feathers. My Sky, always a bird in flight, but she always comes back home, back to me.

"You are gorgeous. Now let me take my best girl out for dinner on her birthday."

She skip hops to the door. Rachel holds out a tan purse that has a leather fringe dangling off the base.

"Thanks, Rach. I always forget my purse."

Rachel grins. "Job security, babe. You'd forget your head if I weren't there to remind you to take it with you when you left somewhere."

Skyler winks. "Too true."

I open the door for the ladies and let them through before setting the alarm and locking the door. Nate is already at the SUV holding the back door open for Sky and me.

After we get in, we're off.

***

It doesn't take long for us to make it to Lucky's on a late Sunday afternoon. When we roll up, Sky turns to look out the window, her nose scrunched up.

"You're taking me to Lucky's?" A hint of sarcasm in her tone. "We go there all the time." She pouts. "I figured we'd go somewhere new, maybe a place we haven't been a bazillion times?"

I run my fingers through her hair and cup her nape. "Just a happy-birthday drink with the folks. Now that Pops is in better spirits, they wanted to wish you a happy birthday too."

She grins wide. "Well, why didn't you say so? Come on, let's not keep them waiting." She opens the door, and Rachel is right there, ready for anything.

Nate walks around the back of the SUV before I can maneuver out. Even though the paps aren't staking out the place every second, I'm a little surprised to not see any creeping out of the bushes since they must know it's her birthday.

Not wanting to push our good fortune, I rush forward to the front door and pull it open for Skyler. The second she walks in everyone in our private party screams, "Surprise!"

Skyler stops in her tracks and puts her hands up to her face, covering her mouth. She spins on her high shoes and loses her balance but I'm right there to catch her.

"You did this? A surprise party? For me?"

I tip my head down and look at her teary eyes. Not at all what I expected for a happy occasion. "Baby, what's the matter?"

She sucks her bottom lip between her teeth as another couple of tears slip down her pretty cheeks. I hook her around the neck and bring her face into my chest. She cries there silently, and I let her as our friends look on, concerned.

"Sky, what's wrong?"

She presses her nose into my chest harder and moves her head back and forth before eventually pulling it out. I keep her tucked close but far enough away I can look into her eyes.

"I haven't had a birthday party since I was five and my parents were alive. We never had the time when I was working, and I didn't have any real friends, and then they were . . . you know . . . gone."

"Are you uncomfortable?" I whisper. "I'll turn us both around and tell them I'm not feeling well, and we'll get the hell out and have a private date, just you and me."

She shakes her head and pats my chest. "No, I'm okay. Happy. Really happy. Just taken aback by all the love."

I grin wide and loop my hand around her waist, turning her toward everyone. "My girl just got a little choked up at how amazing you all are for coming. Now who in this place can hook us up with a drink? Get that music going; it's time to celebrate!"

Our friends and family clap and cheer while Baylee hits the remote for the jukebox to start playing. The first song up is Maroon 5's "Girls Like You."

I grab Skyler's hand and push her out, twist her around and back against my chest, before dipping her in front of everyone and giving her a sloppy kiss.

She kisses me through her laughter but enjoys it nonetheless. I swing her back up, and she's grinning wildly.

"Love you, honey."

I nuzzle her nose and kiss it. "Love you more, Peaches." I run my hand down to her ass and give it a playful smack. "Go say hi to our friends and family."

She hops out of my arms and claps, then screeches when she sees Wendy and Mick across the room. "Oh my God, I can't believe you're here! You're supposed to be on your honeymoon!"

Wendy opens her arms and runs toward Sky. "Can't miss my best friend's surprise birthday party. Parker got ahold of Mick, and he fired up the jet. Said we needed to make a pit stop in our travels for a couple of days, and here we are!"

"I'm so happy you're here." Skyler looks around at everyone, awe filling her expression. "I'm so happy you all are here. This is the best birthday ever!"

Knew with my girl simple was better. I just hope the next surprise is just as exciting, but I'll hold out for a bit to let her get loose, have some fun, eat, and hang out with our friends.

While Skyler greets everyone, I see a pair of chocolate-brown eyes I adore waiting for me across the bar. I make my way over to Sophie and Gabriel. I hold my arms out, and she comes into them easily. Her sugar-and-spice scent fills my nose, and I breathe it in.

"SoSo," I say softly. "Glad you're here. I missed you."

She hugs me tight, eases back, and double kisses my cheeks. "You are quite dashing this evening, *mon cher*. Love looks good on you." She smiles sweetly and cups my cheek.

I smile and take in her long, dark hair, familiar face, and rosy cheeks. "As it does on you, my sweet."

Sophie hums and turns toward her fiancé, who's standing a few feet behind us, watchful yet respectful, as I have come to expect from him.

"Must have something to do with your fella." I keep one hand locked around my friend as I hold out my other hand to Gabriel. "Gabe, always a pleasure."

He takes my hand and shakes it. "Any occasion we can spend with Sophie's extended family is a good one."

Extended family.

I look around the room and realize, yes, we are an extended, big family, one that has come together over time and circumstance, but our bonds are solid, unbreakable. We've chosen to be together, and I believe we're better as a group than any one person apart.

"Congratulations on securing our girl here." I jiggle Sophie in my arms a little for emphasis.

Sophie pats my chest playfully.

"The same for you, I hear. It's all over France." Gabriel lifts his chin, clearly proud that he's following American celebrity gossip. After our dinner together in Paris, Sophie introduced Gabe to American block-buster movies. He felt a little embarrassed he hadn't heard of Skyler, so they now subscribe to several American celebrity rags and read through the bits about Skyler and me. And Sophie is constantly calling to verify whether or not something is true. It seems she hasn't exactly picked up on the fact that most of what she reads is bullshit. Since I like hearing from her, I play along.

Eventually I take my leave of Sophie and Gabe while they chat it up with Bo. I catch Baylee at her usual station.

"Hey, Baylee, shouldn't you be enjoying the party, not behind the bar working? You do that most days, right?"

Baylee licks her lips and nods. She's a very beautiful woman with wide sky-blue eyes and incredible waves of honey-brown-colored hair that are hanging down to her lower back. I usually don't see her hair down, and it's a damn shame. It's gorgeous.

I glance down her body and note she's back to wearing the simple jeans and shapeless male Lucky's T-shirt. "You know, we can swing for some Lucky's shirts in a female cut if you'd like."

She glances behind me, her gaze going to where Bo and Sophie are before she looks away again. "Let me, uh, get you a drink. Gin and tonic?"

"That would be great. Thanks."

She nods and goes to get the gin, but the bottle is superhigh, which has her reaching her long body up to get the bottle. I'm about to look away when I notice something weird about her jeans. At the front they're unclasped but still held together with a rubber band looped through the hole and around the button as if it's to give her an extra inch or two at the waist.

Weird.

Baylee gets the drink made and passes it to me alongside a glass of champagne for the birthday girl.

"What about you?" I gesture to the glasses.

"I can't drink. Um . . . I mean, I'm not drinking tonight."

"Okay, well, thank you."

Before I leave, Baylee reaches for my arm and stops me. "Um, quick question. Is Bo in a relationship with Geneva or, um, that other brunette?"

Fuck. And this is why you don't sleep with your coworkers.

I shake my head. "Bo doesn't do relationships. He has fun with, uh, friends. Geneva is a friend, and Sophie is marrying Gabriel, the man who's standing off to the side."

Baylee plucks at her shirt, pulling it down over her waist. "Ah, okay. Thanks. Um, have fun tonight, Parker."

Everything about the encounter is disconcerting and something I need to talk to Sky or Bo about. Maybe both. I don't want to get involved in Baylee's personal life, but why would she wear jeans that don't fit and make a point to try and hide it? And second, she's asking after Bo like a girl who's interested in more than the one-night stand they had. This does not bode well for any of our futures if she gets hung up on Bo. He is not the relationship type. Far from it.

I walk over to my girl and hand her the glass of champagne.

"Ohhh yummy! Thank you, honey." She takes the glass and clinks it with mine. We both look in one another's eyes as we take a sip.

"Happy birthday, baby."

"Best. Birthday. Ever," she responds excitedly.

I shake my head and kiss her cheek. "You're too easy to please. My father's bar, our family, friends, and you act like I just hung the moon."

My girl wraps her arms around my neck, her glass in one of her hands as she kisses me. "Maybe to me, Parker, you did hang the moon. I can't think of anything better than this moment."

"Oh yeah?"

She smiles. "Yeah."

I shrug and purse my lips together. "I think I can top it."

Skyler giggles. "I doubt it. My man, friends, family, booze. And I can smell the roasting pork. What more could a girl like me want on her birthday?"

"You'll see . . ." I smirk and turn sideways. "Everyone, may I have your attention? Baylee, the music, please."

The music cuts out, and everyone turns toward where I'm holding Skyler. "First of all, I want to thank you all for coming. Second, I couldn't think of a better way to show the woman of my dreams how much I love and adore her."

I set my drink down on the table in front of me, grab both of Skyler's hands, and drop down to one knee.

11

SKYLER

"Oh my goodness! You're going to . . ." I look at all of the people watching Parker down on one knee in front of me. "Yep, you're doing it now." I stomp my foot. "I thought I'd be prepared!" The tears prick my eyes for the second time tonight.

"Relax, baby, and go with it." He grins.

"I love you so much!" I blurt, and our friends laugh.

"Sky, baby, you gotta let your man do this right. Be quiet and listen to me!" Parker aims that heart-melting smile my way, and I swoon all over again.

My hands feel heavy in his, but my body is light as air. If he weren't holding me to earth, I'd float away on a cloud of bliss.

"Skyler, you shocked the hell out of me when you asked me to marry you on national television. As you know, I was worried you weren't ready, that you might want to get married in order to replace the hurts you suffered recently. I know now that was stupid."

"Yeah it was!" Bo shouts alongside a couple of catcalls.

"Anyway, I realized with my time away from you that, for one, I hate being away from you. I want to spend every day of my life waking up to you. Every night falling asleep with you by my side. And I want to do those things not as your man but as your husband. The man who's meant to protect and love you for as long as we both are breathing."

"Honey . . ." I want to share in the gift of his words. "I want those things too."

"Good, because you're gonna be mine. I'm not asking you to marry me; I'm telling you, baby, you have no choice. You're it for me, and I'm it for you. Fate, destiny, whatever you want to call it, decided the minute you opened the door in your underwear." He grins wide. "Kidding."

Embarrassment floods my cheeks with heat as everyone chuckles. "It was a misunderstanding!" I say to everyone else, but feel my fingers being squeezed so that my attention goes back to my guy, on his knees at my feet.

"Skyler Paige Lumpkin, you've always been my dream girl. You will always be my dream girl. I will do my best to give you an incredible life. In front of all the people we love the most, I'd be humbled and honored if you'd agree to be my wife. Will you marry me?"

He pulls out an aqua box with a white ribbon on the top. I'd recognize that Tiffany brand anywhere.

My throat clogs up as he opens the top, and inside is the thinnest band of diamonds meeting in the center where an emerald-cut diamond sits delicately. The stone seems huge to me, with no real experience to compare it to, and it sparkles like a full moon on a dark night.

I gasp and reach out my finger to touch the stone but pull back at the last second, almost afraid to get burned it's shining so bright.

"Yes. As long as you always remember that I asked you first!"

Parker laughs while pulling out the ring and placing it on my left hand. He leans forward and kisses the stone. "No going back. It's you and me against the world. From here on out."

I smile so wide my cheeks hurt. "It's the only way I would have it."

"Kiss the girl already, you fool!" Randy Ellis hollers out.

Parker stands and glares over his shoulder. "I'm getting there!"

Then my man wraps his arms around me and kisses me so fully I forget where we are, and I lift my leg, wrapping it around his thigh in order to get my lower half closer to every dreamy part of him.

"That's enough!" Cathy calls out. "Hoo-boy. If they keep going at this rate, I'm going to be getting grandbabies before the wedding takes place. Praise the good Lord above!"

Parker snort-laughs against my mouth and pulls back enough to speak against my lips. "She's already talking about grandkids."

I shrug. "You know I'm game."

He kisses me hard once more. "I'm thinking when the *A-Lister* movies finish up, it's something we can talk about." Parker dips his lips to my neck and inhales deeply. "I want you all to myself for a little while if that's okay."

He's not saying no. He's saying a couple of years from now. "That I can handle. Though I plan to talk about it . . . a lot, mister!" I poke his chest playfully.

"Speaking of having babies, when you due, pumpkin?" Momma Sterling gestures across the room.

I turn around and realize she's got her eyes locked on Baylee, who's behind the bar, wide eyed, fingers kneading a bar towel as though it's a pound of dough.

"Um . . ."

"Oh please, no hidin' from me." Momma Sterling keeps going. "You've looked green since we got here. You keep running off to the bathroom, and every time someone mentions the pork, you make a gagging sound. Mm-hmm. That will pass, pumpkin. I know morning sickness. It don't last forever, child."

Baylee's mouth drops open, and she grabs for the bar, maybe to hold herself up.

Momma Sterling is relentless as she lifts her hand and points a perfectly painted red acrylic nail in Baylee's direction and swirls her finger in a circle. "And that little trick you're using on your pants, to widen them at the waist because your stomach's gettin' too big but you're not quite ready for maternity clothes. Sho' been there. Done that. What, you about ten to twelve weeks?"

Bo's chair scratches across the wood floor, sounding unusually loud. He stomps up to the bar and stares Baylee down. "Is this true? Are you pregnant?"

A tear slips down Baylee's cheek, and it is not one of happiness.

Ho-lee shit!

"Is it mine? We fucked on Christmas Eve." He waves his hand. "Someone tell me how long ago that was."

"Twelve weeks! I know because I got pregnant on New Year's Eve. So I'm eleven weeks. Yay, we can be prego sisters!" Wendy claps.

Bo lifts up a hand behind him to shut Wendy up without even looking at her.

"I asked you a question. Are you pregnant?"

Cathy gasps and holds her hands over her mouth.

Baylee's eyes grow wide as she glances around the room, looking at everyone but Bo. He slams his hand down against the bar, and she jumps back, covering her stomach and her face at the same time.

Shit. She's scared.

I move out of Parker's arms, but he tries to hold me back. "Sky, no. This is none of our business."

I shove his arms down. "She's scared out of her mind!" I strut on my wedges over to the side of the bar, lift the latch, and go to Baylee. I loop my arm around her waist. "Sweetheart, we're all family here. You don't have anything to fear."

"Are. You. Pregnant. With. My. Fucking. Child!" Bo grates, his tone rising with every word. "I don't give a shit if you're scared. I have a goddamned right to know!"

Momma Sterling stands up. "Bogart, you better stop right there, or I'm gonna knock some sense into you, boy. You're frightening the poor thing. Calm down and let her speak, son."

Baylee's body shakes uncontrollably in my arms, but she nods her head up and down. "I'm sorry. I didn't mean to. D-don't h-hurt me," she stutters, and the tears flow down her cheeks in buckets.

Hurt her?

"Oh Lord, dear child." Momma Sterling's voice dips in understanding as she shakes her head.

Bo backs up one step at a time until he runs right into Parker, who puts a hand to his neck. Next to him Royce curls a hand around his shoulder.

"Brother, it will be okay. We'll hash this out. All is well," Royce reassures him, his tone steady and calming.

Bo's mouth twists into a snarl. "All is not well. I'm going to be a father. A goddamned piece-of-shit *father* I never wanted to be." He lifts a hand up toward Baylee. "This shouldn't have happened. It never should have happened."

"I'm, I'm so sorry!" Baylee sobs as she pulls out of my arms, then rushes through the opening at the end of the bar and out the front door.

Kendra gets up and takes off after her.

Bo drops his head to stare at his boots. His shoulders slump, and his hands hang in fists at his sides. He looks destroyed.

"Come on, man, let's get you a shot . . . or four." Parker leads Bo over to the bar, and I spin around and pick a bottle of Patrón, grabbing a glass and setting him up with a double. Before I can even cap the bottle he's already slammed it back.

"Another," he rumbles. I fill that up, and he repeats it. "Again."

"I don't think—" I start to warn him off. He's already had two doubles.

"Don't think. Just pour." I glance up to Parker, who nods his assent, so I fill that glass again. This time Bo sips it.

"We'll figure this out," Parker assures Bo, speaking low enough so only the four of us can hear.

Bo shakes his head. "Nuthin' to figure out, man. I knew it was coming. One day the curse would hit. It's my legacy. Happened to my father, his father, and his father before him. No matter how many times I wrapped it, there was always a chance I'd end up right *here*." He taps the top of the bar with his index finger. "Should have gotten a vasectomy. Tried once, but the doctor said I was too young. Wanted me to wait until I was thirty. Well, fuck you very much! I'm turning thirty this year, and wha' d'ya know, I'm going to be a father."

"It will be okay, brother," Royce rumbles in that deep baritone all women love.

"Naw, man, it won't. It will never be okay again." Bo scoots off the stool and heads for the door. Mick stops him with a hand to his chest when Bo reaches the door of the bar, preventing any exit.

"You're not driving. We'll take you wherever you need to go." Mick's voice is a command, not a request.

"Not driving. Just gonna take a walk. A long fuckin' walk." He pats Mick's chest and pushes past him and out the door.

As he leaves, Kendra comes in and shakes her head. I guess she couldn't catch up to Baylee.

Cathy Ellis bustles around our friends and then claps her hands. "Okay, now I know that was a bit uncomfortable, mostly for Bo and Baylee, but let's move on. This is a party, for crying out loud, and we're celebrating Skyler's birthday, and my baby is getting married! I think it's time for some pulled pork!" She raises her hands in the air like a cheerleader.

I love that woman, and more so, my mother would love her. And she'd love Parker, but she'd love Parker for me above all.

Parker sits at the stool, and Royce takes the seat next to him. Since I'm standing behind the bar, I grab another three shot glasses and pour us all a shot of tequila.

"Thanks," Parker says.

"Baby girl." Royce dips his chin.

425

The three of us shoot the fiery liquid back.

"So what do you think?" Royce asks Parker.

"I think we're going to have another interesting year," Parker responds flatly, not sounding very excited that more drama is on the horizon.

Royce smiles wide and glances over his shoulder at Kendra, whose hazel eyes are lasered on the three of us. "Brother, I heard that."

"At least we have each other's backs." Parker pats Royce's. "Looks like we're going to need it."

I wait until there's silence between the two guys and pour us all another drink.

"So . . . I'm guessing it's too soon to be excited that two of our extended family are having babies?" I clap just my fingers together.

Parker chuckles and Royce groans.

"You hooked your star to a handful." Royce laughs for Parker's benefit and winks at me.

Parker's gaze lifts to mine, his blue eyes dark and intense as love seeps out of them and straight at me.

"I definitely hooked myself to a star. To my dream girl. My future wife." Parker nods his head to me and spins on his stool. Royce follows his lead. I come around the bar and curl into Parker's side. He squeezes my hip, and we take in the room.

Our friends and family are laughing and carrying on. Cathy and Wendy are dishing out plates piled high with food. Momma Sterling is cackling away with her daughters and Paul and Denny. Rachel and Nate are canoodling in the corner when they think no one is looking. Gabriel kisses Sophie sweetly while always keeping her close. Mick watches his woman like a hawk, seemingly unhappy about her carrying plates, which I can only imagine he thinks she shouldn't do in her condition. My buddy Rick and his girlfriend are shooting the breeze with Geneva and Elliott.

There's one woman who doesn't look as happy as everyone else—Kendra. She's sitting next to Annie, but her gaze shifts to Royce every couple of minutes. Parker told me that Royce confessed he'd been sleeping with her on and off but that their relationship seemed more explosive and combative than anything else. According to Parker, I am definitely not supposed to ask Kendra or Royce about it, nor am I allowed to get involved. I figure I'll wait this out until Wendy gets back from her honeymoon, and we'll put our heads together and come up with our approach, regardless of what Parker said. We're family, and when one or two of us is hurting, it's our job to pitch in, help lighten the load.

First up, however, has to be Bo and Baylee. Neither of them seems pleased that she's having his baby. Besides, what do we really know about Baylee? Her name. That she's a sweet, beautiful woman who hides behind boxy shirts and ill-fitting jeans. She's hardworking, has been instrumental in keeping Lucky's afloat alongside Bo, but what else? I don't even know where she lives. Never met any of her family. She doesn't have any friends come in the bar to visit, which, when I think about it, seems really strange.

I tap my finger against the shot of tequila I'm sipping. More than ever before I feel the need to wade into another person's life. Another *few* persons. I smile and catch Wendy's gaze as she comes up with two plates of food.

"Here, take these before Mick kills me. He thinks they're too heavy for a pregnant woman." She rolls her eyes. "I told him he could suck it."

Parker chuckles. "How'd that work for you?"

She grins coquettishly. "Very well. I'll be blowing him in the limo on the way home as punishment." She smacks her lips and dips a shoulder before sauntering away in impossibly tall, knee-high leather stilettos paired with a cotton T-shirt dress that stylishly accentuates her thin body.

I snicker and kiss my guy on the temple.

Parker nudges my side and lifts his chin. "You happy?"

"Happiness is a choice. And I choose all of this. Everyone here." I run my hand down his face and cup his cheek. "Most of all, I choose you, because you're what makes me happiest."

"We're going to have a beautiful life together, Peaches." He says it low and deep, a promise I'll cherish forever.

I lift my arm, showing him my leather bracelet. He does the same so that our wrists are next to one another, our bracelets touching, engagement rings gleaming.

"We trusted our hearts and lived our truths," I whisper against his lips.

"Yes, we did, and it brought us to this very moment." He cups my cheek and locks his gaze with mine. "You're my truth. You're my heart."

"And you're mine."

EPILOGUE

Three years in the future . . .

I've never seen a more beautiful sight in my life, and I've been enormously blessed in my thirty-three years on this planet. Not even the moment my dream girl walked down the aisle toward me in her white dress tops this one.

Skyler looks up as I stand in the hospital doorway holding a desperately needed cup of coffee. A tired but glamorous smile slips across my wife's lips before she looks back down. I shut the door softly and walk over to sit at the end of her bed, not wanting to disturb her. She's cradling our world to her chest, softly stroking his rosy-pink cheek as he suckles from his mother's breast.

A tear slips down Skyler's cheek, and her voice is but a whisper when she says, "I never thought I could love another human being as much as I love you, Parker. Until now. How is it possible that I've known him an hour and have so much love for him bursting inside of me I don't know how to contain it?" She glances at me, tears running down her face unchecked.

I set the coffee cup down on the nightstand and shift my body so I can wrap her and our son in my arms as he feeds. She sighs against me when I press my lips to her temple.

"I think that's the way the big guy intended it. When you're given such a precious gift, you cherish it. He's a product of you and me, the best thing we'll ever do until we give him a brother or sister down the road." My voice cracks as I reach my hand out and cradle my son's head to my wife's breast. After a minute or two, his puckered lips falter while his breathing relaxes.

"No, my love bug, the nurse says you need to stay awake to eat," Skyler admonishes lightly, so I tickle his cheek, and he picks up the suckling once more.

He's amazing. Just like his mother.

Together we watch our son feed for the first time until keeping him awake is impossible. Skyler slips him off her breast and hands him to me so that she can adjust and get up to use the bathroom.

I take my boy for a little walk around the small hospital room and pat his back until a small burp leaves his mouth, but he doesn't wake.

While she does her business, I share a moment with my son, taking in his dark hair and long lashes. I dip my face to his neck and chest area and inhale deeply. I close my eyes as his baby scent imprints on my soul for eternity. I'll never, ever forget the scent of my son. Sweet, a little powdery, with a hint of his mother's peaches and cream wafting at the edges like a protective coating.

My son.

Montgomery Sterling Ellis.

Named after the two extraordinary men we've chosen to share our lives with as family.

"You are loved, son. More than I can ever say, but I will spend my entire life showing you just how much."

***

Five years in the future . . .

"Monty, your mother and I have someone we want you to meet!" I hold on to the small bundle in my arms and watch as my ma stands from where she was playing blocks with our son. My father is holding down the fort at the couch, looking on at his wife and grandson playing. He too gets to his feet when we enter.

"Momma! Da-Da!" Monty dashes his little toddler legs over to where Skyler crouches.

"Mommy missed you, love bug. So, so, much . . ." Skyler kisses our son's face anywhere she can reach. He tries to cling to her so that she'll pick him up, but after having just had a baby, it's impossible for her to lift his weight right now. "Let's go over to the couch. We want to introduce you to someone, sweetheart," Sky instructs.

My mother helps Skyler up and ushers her over to the couch. My father leans on his cane, resting some of his weight on it but otherwise standing strong. "You look happy, son," he says with pride in his tone.

I grin wide. "Every time I think it can't get any better, life hands us another blessing."

"Absolutely. Felt the same when your mom and I brought you and Paul home. Though I gotta say, there's nothing like seeing my son bring home his own children, my grandchildren. Proud of you. So damn proud." My father wipes at his eyes quickly, dashing away the flood of emotion as fast as he shared it.

"Da-Da!" Monty squeals, sitting next to his mother.

"Okay, little man, you ready to meet your baby sister?" I bring my precious load over to Skyler and hand off my sweet girl.

Skyler takes our daughter and lifts her own chin. I dip down and kiss her softly. Monty leans over and kisses us both messily on our cheeks and pats our faces. He never misses an opportunity to share in the love.

I cup the back of my son's neck. "Now be careful, Monty. She's delicate. Remember how Mommy taught you with your baby?"

Monty's eyes widen, and he scrambles off the couch and rushes over to his toy area, where there's a baby doll in a basket. He grabs the doll's hand and brings it over. "Baby!" He shows me the doll and then hugs it to his chest.

Maybe the doll wasn't a great idea. He's not supergentle with it now, and I don't want him thinking he can pick up his newborn sister that way.

"Cuddle baby," Skyler urges.

Montgomery gets up on the couch next to his mother and cuddles the doll in his arms as softly as a two-year-old can manage.

"Good, love bug. Now look . . ." She maneuvers our daughter so he can see her face.

His little lips open wide, and he claps his hands together. "Sissy!"

Skyler beams. "Yes, it's your sissy, my love. Your baby sister, Jillian Catherine."

Behind us my ma makes a choking, sobbing sound. It's the first time she heard the middle name. We wanted it to be a surprise for when she could meet her granddaughter. We had my folks stay home with Monty since he's so small, and we thought introducing him at home where he's comfortable would be better than amid the busy nature and strange antiseptic smells of a hospital.

My mom is just barely holding back from barging in with grabby hands for her newest grandchild, but so far, my father's arm is around her waist, and they're enjoying watching the show.

I glance up at them and smile at my mother. "We named her after your grandmas, little man. Jillian, after your grandma Jill in heaven, and your grandma Cathy."

Monty looks at his grandmother and points. "Memaw Cay!"

"That's right, little man. Memaw Cay."

"Sissy!" he squeals, and leans down and kisses his sister on the top of her head. "Wuv sissy." He kisses her again.

I clear the emotion in my throat and wipe at the tears building in my eyes. "Yeah, bud, we love your sissy. And we love you."

Monty reaches out his arms toward me, and I pull him off the couch and rest his precious weight against my chest. He squeezes my cheeks. "Wuv Da-Da."

"I love you, son. So much."

He kisses me sloppily on the mouth and then kicks his feet to get down.

I look over at Skyler, and the joy on her face is unmistakable.

"You've done well, Peaches. One of each. We've finally got it all." I inhale full and deep, feeling completely relaxed now that my entire family is home.

She grins and looks up at me. "Oh no, we're not stopping at two."

The floor falls away from beneath my feet, and I have to catch the arm of the chair to sit my ass down. "Uh, I thought . . ."

She shakes her head. "No way. I want more." She purses her lips. "I'm thinking two more."

My mother raises her arms in the air and looks at the ceiling. "Praise the Lord!"

"Peaches . . . ," I attempt, but she leans her face down toward our daughter and kisses her cheeks.

Her chocolate gaze lifts away from our girl and meets mine, stealing my heart all over again with just a glance. "We'll talk about this again in six weeks." She winks.

"Fuck me," I groan.

She's going to use sex to get what she wants. The beast stirs in my pants just thinking about how it's going to be a stellar reunion. In the meantime, I'll become familiar with Lefty over the coming weeks.

"Tuck me, tuck me, tuck me." Monty stomps around, cursing in baby speak.

Skyler's head shoots up. "Honey . . . ," she says in warning, her brown eyes now blazing with frustration.

I move over to my little man and scoop him up. "How's about we go play with Midnight and Sunny? Wanna go throw the ball?"

"Ball, ball, ball, ball!" He pounds on my back as I hold him on my hip.

I point at Skyler. "We planned on two," I remind her with a stern tone, not that my woman ever listens to my serious voice.

She shrugs and lifts our daughter, pressing her nose to her little forehead. "Jilly Bean and Monty need another playmate or two." She kisses our girl again, and my heart implodes.

"You're lucky I love you, woman," I say while Monty tries to grab my face.

Skyler smiles wide. "I know. I'm the luckiest woman in the world."

***

Ten years in the future . . .

The sun is high and warm as I watch the horde of children play in our large pool, their uncles and grandparents making sure everyone is safe. Monty is long and lean at seven years old, diving into the pool like a mini-Olympian in the making. His dark hair is curly on top like mine was as a kid. My sweet baby girl, Jillian, is on her uncle Paul's shoulders hitting the ball back and forth with her cousin, Paul and Denny's daughter, Paula, who's just a year older. The two are inseparable when together.

After we had Monty, Denny got the baby bug, and bad. He would not leave Paul alone about having a child. And as the Ellis men are prone to do, Paul set about giving his man what his heart desired.

Paul found a woman who was widowed and needed the money in order to take care of the three young children she already had. Denny wanted a child with his husband's characteristics, so they determined that Paul would be the biological father. She got pregnant through in vitro and gave them a little girl they named Paula. The situation worked so well with the birth mother that she agreed to have another child for them two years later, using Dennis as the biological father this time, giving them their son, Luca. Since the children are related by blood to Paul and Dennis, as well as to their birth mother's three children, they have added Sheila and her three kids into their lives. They share birthdays and holidays together, and Paul takes care of the handyman duties in her home while Dennis is her best friend, but as a job, she runs a day care center and watches Paula and Luca. The three adults make it work smashingly, and in the Ellis clan, the more, the merrier.

Off to the side, Rachel and Skyler sit on a sun lounger playing a game with our three-year-old twins. We named Randi Lynn after my father, Randall, and Wendy's middle name, Lynn, then our son Pritchard Steven after Mick, and Skyler's father.

Man, the twins were a whopper of a surprise. When the doctor told us we were having fraternal twins, I laid down the law with my wife. No more. Four children were more than enough. Twins with a four-year-old and a two-year-old in tow had me seeing stars, as in I got dizzy in the doctor's office and almost passed out. Skyler has taken it all like a champ. She exudes motherhood from every ounce of her being. Me, I got a vasectomy after the twins turned one to ensure my wife's charms couldn't win me over again. Don't get me wrong, my kids are my life, but four are more than enough for anyone.

Once Monty was born, Skyler quit the big-screen jobs and focused her attention on building an activity center in Boston for the less fortunate. She's since hired a program director and some staff to run the place so she can focus on her four children. She says she might go back to acting one day, but for now, her life is with her family.

I still run the day-to-day operations at International Guy, but we have a new team of men and women running the jobs while Royce handles the finances and Bo trains the travel teams.

Off to the side I see Nate manning the grill, cooking up burgers and dogs, his sons by his side. They are exact duplicates of Rachel and Nate.

Nine-year-old Theodore, who we all call "Thor," is a towheaded mini–macho man with a kind voice and his mother's easy smile. Their seven-year-old rascal, Jack, who they call "Joker," is just like his namesake from the Batman movies. He's wild, charismatic, and a true charmer.

Standing at the deck of our veranda, watching my family, makes me wonder where the guys are. Royce and Bo and their families should be here soon. As I think that, off in the distance I can see Wendy and Mick making it over the hill down the path we built between our two properties. They're carrying their swim gear and holding the hands of their two children.

I head inside to grab a few extra towels, a fresh bottle of IPA, and a chick beer for my wife. She's been into the Angry Orchard apple ciders lately. On my way to the linen closet I pass through our master bedroom and glance at the red lipstick streaked across Skyler's vanity mirror. It's a message we wrote together the night I asked her to marry me, ten years ago. She refuses to wash it off even ten years later. Thinks it will bring bad luck if she does.

Today and every day, I wake up and see that message we wrote to one another, and it still fills me to the brim with peace and serenity. The words mean as much today as they did the day we wrote them, and they remind me to never take my beautiful life for granted.

To my Dream Girl . . .
To my Dream Maker . . .
HAPPINESS IS A CHOICE . . .
Love,
US

The real end.

Though this is the end of this particular International Guy's adventure, stay tuned for more sometime in the future. Bo, Royce, and Wendy have their own stories that need to be told, and I don't imagine their voices will let my muse rest for long.

Until next time in the International Guy universe, I hope Parker and Skyler's love story ended the way you needed it to. Thank you for following along as they found their happily ever after.

In love and friendship,
Audrey

ACKNOWLEDGMENTS

I saved this part for the very end. Why? I don't know. Maybe because there are so many people who helped me get to this point. So many editors, betas, friends, family . . . even places that moved me to finish. I never dreamed how this world would take over my life.

First, I want to thank you, the **reader**, for sharing in this experience. Parker and Skyler's adventure has been with me a full year, and leaving them is so hard, but knowing that you've fallen in love with them, their story, and their clan lifts me up with such extreme joy it makes it easier to leave them in your capable hands. I can't promise this is the end for Park and Sky. I'm sure I'll revisit them when the muse moves me to, and of course you'll hear more about them in the spin-offs for Bo, Royce, and Wendy that I intend to write in the future. For now, I think we can all just be happy that they are happy and finally got their beautiful ending.

This wouldn't be an acknowledgment if I didn't thank my husband, **Eric**, and his commitment to letting me do my thing even when I hole myself up in my office, forgoing family time, events, paying bills on time *(grin)*, and everything in between. You are my rock, babe. Always and forever. Thank you.

Huge, ginormous thanks to **Jeananna Goodall**, my extremely patient and compassionate personal assistant and friend. I dedicated this installment to you because *we* did it. We made it to the end, lady.

An entire year of ups, downs, plot issues, and character drama, not to mention unending travel and events in between all the rounds of editing, marketing, and freak-out sessions where I didn't believe I could figure out the end. You were there for it all, and I'm so grateful. I love you, lady. Tell Jasen I'll try not to be so needy for your time in the future . . . but I make no promises.

Amy Tannenbaum, my badass agent. You waited a full year to work with me on this series. Providing me feedback, guidance, and support when you didn't have to. You found my babies a beautiful home in Montlake Romance, making sure that the publisher and author fit one another beyond anything else. You understand that it's not about money, it's not about status—it's about the story. About people. About living our truths and creating beautiful things with those we care about. Thank you for being you. I think you're beautiful in every way and am very happy to have you on my team. Also, thank you to your partner in crime, **Danielle Sickles**, and entire team at the Jane Rotrosen Agency for sharing the International Guy love all over the world. Every day I feel as though I'm living a dream come true.

Ekatarina Sayanova, my longtime editor and friend. Can you believe we just finished another twelve-installment serial? This is the thirty-fifth title of mine you've edited out of thirty-nine. It's almost like we're married now with thirty-five children between us. *(Wink.)* How we made it this far is a miracle. Every story is unique and special in its own way, and you've become so instrumental in my process that I can't imagine it any other way. So I think it's best if we just don't ever stop working together, and you *never* retire. How do you feel about making another baby? Thirty-six sounds like an awfully good number! LOL. Looking forward to many more stories (babies) in the future.

Lauren Plude, my publishing editor and crazy new girlie BFF. You are a one-in-a-million-type personality to work with. Your mind is acute, brilliant, and startlingly accurate in how you evaluate an overarching storyline and multiple character developments. You've taught me so much, I feel blessed to be able to take those gifts with me throughout my writing career. Not everyone gets assigned an incredible editor by their publisher. I'm so thrilled you were mine. I have never in my career had an easier process than working with you and Montlake on this twelve-book serial. Thank you for everything.

Irene Billings, the most incredibly accurate copyeditor in the business, you blow me away. Your attention to detail is quite magical. I'm in awe of your talent. Thank you for your commitment and contribution to making this series the best it can be!

Ceej Chargualaf and **Tracey Wilson-Vuolo**, my superfans, my superbetas extraordinaire. You keep me honest. You love the characters as if they were your best friends. You show me what it's like from the reader's perspective. There aren't words to express the feeling I get every time I send a chapter and get feedback within mere hours of sending it. I adore the way you both play off the characters' adventures and have your own intriguing take on what happens moment by moment. This process helped me to move the story forward during times when I felt overwhelmed and under too much pressure. Because of you, I was able to keep moving forward. I counted on you ladies, and you never failed to deliver. *Thanks* isn't enough. Mad love.

Thank you to the real **Wendy Bannerman**, **Rachel and Nate Van Dyken**, **Dennis Romoaldo**, **Amy Tannenbaum**, and **Christina Kaarsberg** for allowing me to use your full names, and for some, your likenesses in this serial. It made the story far more special to me, the readers, and hopefully to you as well. I love you all.

I have to give an unbelievably huge, massive, whopper of a thanks to the entire team at **Montlake Romance**. The team there, from the editing, to the graphic design, to the marketing, is the best I've ever worked with. My experience with this publishing house is one I'll cherish for the rest of my life. I hope that we can share many great stories in the future. Your company changed my entire opinion on the process. I learned, I laughed, I participated in everything, and I was pleasantly surprised at the author-publisher involvement process. I never felt pushed to the side, or left out. You gave me the largest voice because you believe in telling the story the author wants to tell. That is rare and so special. Thank you for choosing me to be a part of the Montlake Romance family. I'm honored.

Incredible thanks to my amazing model, **Forest Harrison**, who plays the role of Parker Ellis perfectly. I loved working with you on this series and at events. You are a bright light and a true star. There are big things to come in your future. Keep dreaming.

I couldn't ever leave out the fantastic photographer who captured my guy exactly as we'd hoped. **Wander Aguiar**, you have a keen eye and a stunning talent. Between you, Forest, and **Andrey Bahia**, you helped bring my story to life. Thank you.

Jena Brignola, you are a rock-star graphic designer. The teasers, banners, and IG swag you've created for this series are absolutely stunning. I love how you've helped make the IG team a household name!

I must, must, must thank my readers group, **Audrey Carlan's Wicked Hot Readers**. You guys lift me up when I'm down, cheer me on when I'm afraid no one cares, and keep me laughing every day. If you're a reader and want to join my Hotties, just look up the group name on Facebook. Together, we Hotties are living life . . . one book at a time.

ABOUT THE AUTHOR

Photo © Melissa McKinley Photography

Audrey Carlan is a #1 *New York Times* bestselling author, and her titles have appeared on the bestseller lists of *USA Today* and the *Wall Street Journal*. Audrey writes wicked-hot love stories that have been translated into more than thirty different languages across the globe. She is best known for the worldwide-bestselling series Calendar Girl and Trinity.

She lives in the California Valley, where she enjoys her two children and the love of her life. When she's not writing, you can find her teaching yoga, sipping wine with her "soul sisters," or with her nose stuck in a steamy romance novel.

Any and all feedback is greatly appreciated and feeds the soul. You can contact Audrey through her website, www.audreycarlan.com.